A DANGEROUS INHERITANCE

ALAN WILKS

BALBOA.
PRESS

A DIVISION OF HAY HOUSE

Balboa Press books may be ordered through booksellers or by contacting:

Balboa Press
A Division of Hay House
1663 Liberty Drive
Bloomington, IN 47403
www.balboapress.com.au
1 (877) 407-4847

Print information available on the last page.

ISBN: 978-1-5043-1857-0 (sc)
ISBN: 978-1-5043-1858-7 (e)

Balboa Press rev. date: 07/24/2019

THE MAIN CHARACTERS

John Naxos.................................Naxos Restaurant.

Jean White.................................... Johns wife

Stephen Naxos............................. Johns brother

Robert Naxos................................. Johns son

Barbara Naxos............................. Roberts wife

Colin Naxos.................................. Roberts son

Sev Cockini ....Johns friend

Elizabeth Spalding............................ Sevs first wife

Gloria Brown................................. Sevs second wife

Paul Cockini.................................... Sevs first son

James Cockini................................. Sevs second son

Maria Cockini................................ James daughter

Frank Bennett................................. Business partner

Gladys McMurray........................... Sevs landlady

Charlie Thornton........................... John Naxos friend

Hester Thornton.............................. Charlie's wife

Trevor Donaldson............................Collins friend

Joan Stirling.................................. ... Police officer

Sergio Capaldi................................. Italian friend

Mario Leotta..................................... Italian adversary

CONTENTS

PROLOGUE

John and Charlie were regulars down on the riverbank, meeting most afternoons to fish or maybe just chat over a beer and enjoy the environment. These scruffy old codgers jealously guarded their spot, and anybody who dared to encroach on their territory would get short shrift and be told to go find somewhere else to fish. Charlie was short and rotund with a full and happy face. In contrast John was tall and slim with a down turned mouth and a permanent frown from years of stressful living.

Home to them was The Entrance, a small holiday village on the central coast of New South Wales, so called for being where the great Tuggerah Lakes run out to sea with the changing tide. For John it was a place where he could remain anonymous.

Old Charlie Thornton came to The Entrance from Sydney suburban Bankstown after a life of working on the Railways. Due to a problem with the grog his wife kicked him out, which led him to drink even more. He would often start the day with a beer and a fag for breakfast. In the end, his questionable sobriety at work cost him his job. Despite union intervention on his behalf, and the fact that he was not about to give up his beer, he sadly left his mates at work and the local pub, took his retirement pension, and resettled in The Entrance.

John's was a different story. He lived in a modest apartment and apparently did not have any friends or family. The only clue to his past was that he still drove his old Mercedes which he had kept from his previous life.

Sitting on the riverbank fishing with Charlie, he said very little unless asked.

To Charlie, John spoke in a cultured voice and obviously had been a man of some substance.

As time went by, they became closer as friends and looked forward to each other's company.

Sometimes they would get a slab of beer and just talk. At first Charlie did most of the talking, regaling John with stories of his life on the Railways.

As time went by John started to open-up and speak of his other life. The stories that unfolded were, to Charlie, of another world where he had never been, one of business, high finance with graft and corruption.

Charlie was to become worried about carrying some of this information, most of which he did not understand, and in his own simple way wondered if it would someday become a problem for him. On the other hand, in some of his infrequent times of sobriety, he felt that John had a need to unburden himself of some of his past life.

One evening they were down at the river drinking a cold beer from the esky and watching the sun go down over the water.

Sometimes during the early summer months, before the tourists arrived, they would take their light rods and fish the channel. This was where the water from the lakes rushed out to sea with the tide change and brought with it an abundance of whiting.

To be successful it was necessary to stand in the shallows and cast out to the deeper water where the fish were. It was not comfortable, and one could certainly not hold a can of beer in one hand while fishing; however, they were always certain of a feed.

In the summer months when the tourists arrived, it was like wall-to-wall fishermen on the sandy banks, which was a good enough reason for John and Charlie to go back to the river bank near the car park.

The locals took little notice of them. They looked just like a couple of old bums drinking beer and trying to catch a fish. Charlie did not care what he looked like and, mostly, was quite grubby and in need of a bath. John was always clean but untidy. Charlie reasoned that John had another agenda in being there. "Who cares." he thought, "It's not my concern."

Tonight, John was tired and unusually grumpy, they had run out of beer, and the fish were somewhere else. Without speaking, he packed up his gear and wandered off across the park in the gathering twilight.

"See you later, You grumpy old bugger," Charlie called from behind him, and with a chuckle began to collect his own gear.

"Fuck him!" John thought, as he stumbled across the park,

"I will see him tomorrow."

Then a blinding flash in his head, next another even worse. He was barely conscious when he felt a terrible thud and pain in his chest. "You bastards," he thought through the haze; 'I will get you for this,' and then he realised that he could not, in any way, defend himself from his attacker. More terrible pain as his attacker continued to kick him in the chest and groin.

The only words he heard were, "So, John, we found you at last. Now you will learn to keep your fucking mouth shut."

The pain continued, and he could feel his heart racing, then erratically slowing down, missing a beat. He felt dizzy, then hot and clammy. John then became aware that he was not going to survive this.

Memories flooded back, as he knew his life was slipping away, "What a bloody waste," he thought. Then a realisation came to him that family and business secrets would die with him.

Then he heard, "John! John! What have they done to you?" "Hang in there you old bastard, while I call an ambulance."

"No Charlie, before I go, just listen to me!"

As John's life drifted away, he said "Go to my flat, the key is under the geranium pot, and in the bottom of the coffee jar you will find a key. Take it and hide it carefully. Next you will find a number scratched under the lid of a biscuit tin, do not write it down, just remember it. After all this settles down, take the key and the number to the Bank of New South Wales in George Street. The key and number will give you access to a safety deposit box. To open it you will have to complete the code by adding my flat and street numbers."

John's last words were, "My friend, I hope I have not passed on a huge problem to you, Good luck."

With tears flowing from his eyes Charlie listened and made a promise. "John, I will follow your wishes."

This was in the year of 2005 and John was just 72.

Over the following week, the police interviewed Charlie several times, trying to establish if he had had anything to do with the attack. In the end they were happy to put it down to a random act of violence by persons unknown.

Only then did he feel safe enough to go to Johns flat.

Charlie waited for two months before going to the bank.

He cleaned himself up, had a haircut, shaved, and put on his best clothes. At the last moment before leaving to catch The Entrance bus for Gosford to link up with the Sydney train, he picked up his old Gladstone bag, sensing that he may need it.

The train trip to Sydney brought back many memories of his old days on the railways, and he wondered what might have been if he had not been such a piss pot.

He justified his drinking then, and still did today, as a way of escaping his memories of his days on the railways and his complaining wife.

"The old bitch", he thought, "I am better off without her."

Charlie left the train at Wynyard Station and walked the short distance along George Street to the Westpac Bank, formerly the Bank of NSW.

Nervously he walked through the huge entry door into the foyer, which was more like a theatre than a bank. This made him feel even more nervous. He was thinking, "This is a bit out of my league," when a uniformed attendant approached and said, "Can I help you sir?"

"Well, I'm looking for where I go to find the safety deposit boxes."

"No problem, sir, go to the inquiry desk over there, and they will take your details and assist you."

"Hell, I will end up in slammer over this," he thought.

At the desk, a Grey-suited man about his age asked how he could be of help.

"I have this safety deposit box that I would like to access please."

"No problem just fill out this card, and then Mary here will take you to the vault. Do you have your key and security number?" John just nodded.

"You are required to enter your number on this card and it must match our records."

He then spent some agonising minutes poring through a large indexed leather- bound book with gold letters on the front N to Q I-100.

"All appears in order sir, please follow Mary."

On shaky legs, Charlie followed the girl down the marble stairs, through Several security doors into a huge room that was lined floor to ceiling, with metal drawers.

The girl said, "I suppose you know the routine, I have the master key and you have yours. We need both keys to open the box, and then I will leave you. You can use the table and chair over there if you wish. When you are finished, ring the bell and I will come and get you."

Gingerly, Charlie opened the box and he nearly fell over when he found that there were bundles and bundles of high denomination notes. Underneath was a large envelope with a smaller one stapled to the corner. Charlie opened the large one first to find dozens of Commonwealth of Australia Bond Certificates that were issued in the sixties through to the mid-eighties.

There was also a bundle of BHP share certificates and others that meant little to Charlie. On the bottom of the pile was the most important one, what looked like a very legal document to transfer all the shares into Charlie's name.

"If this for real, then I could sell the whole lot and disappear." "Jesus Christ" he thought, 'There is a bloody fortune here."

Finally, in the smaller envelope, was a letter from John, which read:

> *Dear Charlie,*
>
> *Whatever is here is yours; I have no one to give it to so you may as well have it all. However, I must warn you that there are some old business associates who have been trying to find me for some time. So, beware!*
>
> *I suggest that you take it all and leave, go to Queensland, anywhere but Sydney, and don't tell anybody where you are going, just disappear. Many thanks for your friendship, and best of luck for a happy retirement. You may now buy that fishing boat you always dreamed about.*
>
> *Greatest regards and affection,*
> *John.*

Charlie packed the whole lot in his Gladstone, rang the bell and was ready to leave.

The girl appeared and asked if he would need the box any more, Charlie replied, "Err, no thanks."

They walked back up the stairs into the foyer and Charlie headed straight for the door. He was in a near state of panic waiting for somebody to call out, or to feel a hand on his shoulder. Suddenly he was out in the street, heading back to Wynyard station. His legs were shaking, and his stomach felt as if he was going to be sick as he negotiated his way along the footpath through the crowd of shoppers.

He held tightly onto his bag, forever fearful that someone might grab it and run, but it never happened.

When he finally walked into his flat back at The Entrance, he let out a big sigh and blurted out loud, 'Christ I need a drink!"

He grabbed a bottle of whisky, which he rarely ever touched, and took a long slurp straight from the bottle. As it hit his throat and then his stomach, he lost his breath, his eyes watered, and his head spun.

"Boy, that was good" he said to himself, "I really needed that!"

Then he thought, "*This is not the time to get pissed, I have some planning to do. Plenty of time for a booze-up later.*"

In the following days he paid any outstanding bills, brought the rent up to date and prepared to leave.

Old Charlie was not as dumb as some may have thought. He worked out a strategy that would enable him to cover his tracks so that it would be nearly impossible for anyone to find him.

Paying cash, he flew to Adelaide and using a non-existent number in a suburban street he set up a bank account using his own name. Next, he took a Post Office box, using his name and the new address, to be used for all mail from the bank and share dividends. To avoid mail from the post office for the box rental, he paid two years in advance.

Charlie's next move was to fill out a form at the Post Office to have the contents of the mail box forwarded to another undisclosed address should he need to. His final move was to go back to the bank, deposit the cash and rent a safety deposit box in which to keep the bonds and share scripts. Later he planned to sell all the bonds and shares and deposit the cash in another bank.

He was careful not leave any forwarding address, or even his new post office box number in Adelaide. Nor did he tell anyone he was leaving; he was just going to disappear.

The only exception was that he rang his estranged wife and just told her he was moving on, probably interstate where the fishing was better; perhaps some quiet spot like Port Augusta. Without any further conversation and despite her protests he just hung up. This was done deliberately to throw any lookers off the track.

Returning to The Entrance, he packed a few possessions in a small suitcase, went down to The Entrance Road, caught the bus to Gosford, then a train to Sydney for a connection to Melbourne for a flight to Brisbane.

Charlie Thornton just disappeared. His only parting comment, to himself, was, "Goodbye nobody, I wonder what I will have to pay for a marina up on the Gold Coast?"

INTRODUCTION

THE IMMIGRANTS

Following victory in Greece by Allied forces in 1944 over the Nazis, Greece experienced serious economic and political problems. A civil war broke out in 1946. The war meant that the Greeks continued to experience terror and hardship as they had done during World War 11. In a little over 3 years of civil war, approximately 100,000 Greeks were killed. In 1967 a military dictatorship took over the government of Greece.

During this period many Greeks fled their homeland looking for peace. At the end of the civil war the new government encouraged citizens to migrate as there were food shortages and large numbers of unemployed.

This coincided with an agreement between the Greek and Australian governments to provide migrants with assisted passages to Australia. Thousands of Greeks accepted this offer if only to escape poverty and poor living conditions at home.

From 1952 to 1974 nearly one million Greeks migrated to other countries, nearly 200.000 of those chose Australia.

In addition, thousands more migrated from the Eastern Bloc or Baltic countries.

Many of the migrants settled in Melbourne where to this day there is the highest number of Greeks outside Greece in the world.

It was in this environment that the Naxos family made a huge decision to migrate. To add to the challenge the family of 4 had only a rudimentary grasp of English, very little money and virtually no possessions when they stepped off the boat in Sydney.

There was Father Andreas, Mother Amilios, sons John and Stephen, although their Greek names were changed on the way out to sound more English.

The surname was Naxos taken from an island off Greece.

During the weeks spent on the boat they met another couple with one son who in years to come would play a big part in their lives. Their surname was also very Greek- 'Cockini'.

The sons name was Sev.

Both Andreas and Sev senior started work as labourers with a construction company, it was hard work, but they were both fit and strong, so they adapted quickly. They worked hard while trying to ignore the continual racist remarks which most times they did not even understand.

Most Australians had never been exposed to foreigners, so they had little understanding of other cultures, and they treated them badly. Immigrant workers were called, Refos, Balts or Wogs. In a sometimes-warped sense of humour local workers would trick them into using inappropriate words in public, like when shopping for their lunch they were told to say- *Two fucking pies please- and sometimes much worse.*

Inevitably, a lot of poor English filtered into their homes. The boys started school early and soon developed a firm grasp on the local language which over a period was passed on to their parents.

Andreas and John worked hard, took all the overtime they were offered and earnt more money than they could have ever dreamed of back in Greece. The war and later years had taught them to be frugal and they both quickly accumulated significant savings.

Gradually café food in Australia began to change from the Aussie chops and vegies to more European type food. The different foods from all over Europe began to influence home cooking but more notably menus in restaurants.

Andreas was quick to see the change and upon finding an empty shop, with a two bedroom flat above, in King Street Newtown he decided to go into the restaurant business.

Andreas (now John) had never cooked in his life but Amilios had been taught by her parents to cook their home meals and was more than competent around the kitchen. Few people would want old style Greek food, so they opened with a mixed menu of Aussie grills and some traditional Greek. Over the years the menu evolved and as the public's tastes changed so did the menu.

There was always a racist attitude by some extreme locals and it was not unusual to get up in the mornings to find

"*fuck off Greeks* "painted across the restaurant window. However, they persevered and over the years the clientele increased, and their efforts were rewarded. John carefully managed the money and many years later was able to buy the building.

He continued to correspond with old friends back in Greece and hit upon an idea to have them send out parcels of herbs and spices. Soon he had more than he needed so he started a little business selling his excess to other restaurants around Sydney.

Many years later son John was to comment

"Growing up in a Greek- owned café wasn't easy. Before school I had to scrub the floors, and after school I served on the tables.

JOHN NAXOS

CHAPTER ONE

The Naxos Greek restaurant in King Street Newtown was not in any way special, it certainly would never make the Sydney Morning Herald Good Food Guide. In fact, it was not even Greek, but a mixture of Aussie, Greek, Italian or whatever took the chef's fancy at the time. It was a real mum and dad show with mum doing most of the cooking and dad doing as little as possible.

Their elder son John was the general hand, and after school he was called in to do all the odd jobs and cleaning up. The second son Steven, being several years younger, escaped most of the chores, much to John's irritation.

However, the food was generally good and cheap, which attracted all types from around the district, including students from the nearby Sydney University.

The family lived above the restaurant, and rarely ventured far from home. As John moved into his teens and began to discover a world outside, he grew to hate being there and yearned for freedom.

His Dad extolled the virtues of education and instilled in him, the belief that this was his only ticket to freedom and independence. Although he worked hard at school and was in the top level of students, he still dreamed of finding an easy way to future wealth.

John's best mate, Sev Cockini, fuelled these dreams with tales of his own imagination of fast cars, easy girls, mansions on the water overlooking Sydney Harbour, and overseas travel.

1

Now, at 18, John was restless and looking for something, he was not sure what, but girls and sex were never far from his mind. One night, as was his usual habit, he was sitting on the footpath in front of the restaurant when his friend arrived. "G'day mate, how's things? Bit dull round here, where's the action?"

"I've finished my jobs so why don't we check out the pub. They let me in now that I'm over 18."

"Okay by me," said Sev, "Let's go."

Their "pub" was an old hotel in King Street Newtown, not far from the Naxos restaurant. Built in the thirties, and despite some attempts to update it was still small and dingy. The public bar smelled of stale beer with cigarette smoke and was packed with drinkers. The customers were a mixture of locals and young people from the university.

"Order me a schooner, mate, while I go to the loo."

John took the schooners across to the wall shelf where he could check out any girls in the crowd. Sev returned quickly and said, "There's some action out in the loo. Some guy's selling pep pills, guaranteed to put you on cloud nine."

"Don't worry about that; just check out that bird over there, she's a real looker!"

"Go and chat her up, she's got a girlfriend."

"No, you go, you have all the bullshit."

Sev swaggered across, "Hi girls, why don't you come and join us?"

They both looked and thought, "He looks a bit of a jerk but his mate's Okay."

"Are you offering to buy us a drink?"

"Yeah, why not?" replied Sev.

They followed him across to where John had secured a corner seat and introduced themselves as Betty and Jean.

John, always the gentleman, asked what they'd like to drink. "Pimm's thanks." replied Betty, who was more outgoing than Jean.

After they were settled, the game began of trying to impress the girls as to how smart and worldly wise they were. The girls probably guessed that they were a couple of boys out for a pick-up, which was true.

John was decidedly nervous and didn't quite know what to do or say next. However, he didn't have to say much as Sev did most of the talking; telling the girls how good he was on the football field, when in fact, he was hopeless. John was the one with all the skills and could equip himself very well at all sports.

Several drinks later, when they were all feeling jolly, Sev decided it was time to make the big move.

"Okay girls it's time to get out of this hole. Let's go for a walk in the park." Neither had a car.

Surprisingly, Betty and Jean agreed, and off they went.

John was tall and gangly, at the end of his teenage growth spurt. Jean was more mature with a well-developed figure but tending to be a bit on the chubby side. With it, she had a pretty face and flawless complexion. John found it hard to keep his hands off her. He would have loved to just touch her.

Out the front of the hotel they paired off, Sev with Betty and John with Jean. John found that Jean was, like him, quiet and did not have a lot to say.

First step, he thought was to hold her hand. This was Okay, and although feeling a bit nervous, he tentatively took the next step and put his arm around her waist. Their bus stop was opposite the park, and that was where they were heading.

Nervously John stammered, "How about a walk in the park?"

Very sweetly Jean replied, "No that would not be sensible." and turned offering herself for a kiss.

After a fumbled start, kissing Jean up against the bus shelter was pure heaven. Any further action was out of the question, so John was more than happy to wrap himself in Jean's warm embraces.

Regretfully, her bus arrived, and the best John could do was to get her home phone number for later contact.

Sev was nowhere in sight, so he walked off down the street with a bulge in his pants and a spring in his step. He was feeling good.

The next day was the last day of the school year, and his last day with his schoolmates before university. Dad had hammered him through his last year at school and he easily managed a mark high enough for university entrance.

John chose Business and Commerce, a choice that would help significantly in the years to come. His mate, Sev, also qualified for university and chose law.

The weekend following their outing at the pub, Sev called around regaling John with stories of his adventures with Betty. John was impressed, but thought to himself, "Bullshit Sev!"

Then Sev came up with a staggeringly imaginative idea on how they would get rich quick.

'Now listen John, remember that guy I told you about in the pub who was selling pills, well I met up with him in the pub again and he suggested that we could act as his agent to distribute the happy pills. John, we could make a fortune!"

"No way", declared John. "Firstly, I'm not into that scene, and secondly, I would be crazy to jeopardise my place at uni, as you would too."

"Okay, maybe you're right." was Sev's reply, "but it's an idea for the future."

John's insight into life outside Newtown and the Naxos Restaurant came during their end-of-school holiday to Surfers Paradise. He recalled the huge arguments he'd had with Mum and Dad just to be able to go. Finally, he wore them down and, using his own money saved from the restaurant work, he took off with Sev in tow, promising not to do anything silly.

The first days were just great, staying in an apartment close to the beach where they had to look after themselves. John and Sev spent their first days on the beach strutting about like prize peacocks, trying to impress the girls. The only downside was the occasional call from the local boys "Hey wog boy." But they were used to that stuff, so they just ignored it.

Looking along the beach at what must be thousands of bikini-clad girls, Sev gushed, "John this is a virtual smorgasbord. We must be able to score somehow before we go home."

"You find the girls Sev, and I'm ready, I've got my rubbers."

John's problem was that he was easily influenced by Sev and tended to go along with his sometimes-crazy ideas. However, underneath, he followed his strict upbringing and had a strong sense of decency. This did not stop his youthful exuberance wanting to get out and experience life.

Mum was always warm and loving, doting on him and caring about everything he did. John had great communication with his mother and felt comfortable confiding in her. With Dad it was a different story. Although outwardly gruff and demanding, John knew he would always be there for him. He was the one who made the demands on him for work at the restaurant, always with the over-rider, "This will all be yours one day!"

John would privately think, "Hell, who wants it!"

It was understandable therefore that John, with a little prompting from Sev, was quite capable of kicking his heels up when given the chance.

On their third night at the Gold Coast Sev said, "Let's go to that Nightclub joint in Orchid Avenue. That's where the action is."

"I don't know Sev; I hear there is a lot of heavy stuff goes on there."

"We can look after ourselves, it's only a dance. Come on let's go."

As usual John caved in, and after fortifying themselves with a few beers, they headed off to Orchid Avenue.

The Surfers Paradise central area was all glitter, with the tourist shops touting their wares, and a seemingly endless supply of places to eat. The hub of Surfers Paradise was Cavilll Avenue, which ran from the Gold Coast Highway down to the beach. The beach, with its huge expanse of golden sand, was famous and attracted tourists not only from all over Australia, but from all over the world.

It was a little after dark when John and Sev got to Cavilll Avenue to find a mass of teenagers all hell bent on a good time. With the crowd and the world's brightest neon lights flashing their messages the atmosphere was electric.

The dance hall was in a small street, Orchid Avenue, running off Cavilll Avenue.

After the customary check-over by the doorman, they entered the hall to an explosion of sound and light that shook the senses.

"You get the drinks John, two whiskies. Make them doubles."

"Okay, but you behave while I'm gone." replied John.

The place was packed with young people and it seemed to John like wall-to-wall scantily clad girls.

Another drink gave them the courage, and they managed to find girls to dance with. Talking over the loudest music they had ever heard was out of the question, and they really felt in the groove. On the dance floor John gyrated and threw himself around with the packed mass of bodies.

He lost contact with Sev but wasn't concerned as he was having too much fun, and his girl was looking better every minute. She had a pretty face, full lips and long hair pulled back in a ponytail. Her full breasts seemed ready to tumble out of her dress as she danced.

During each dance break John managed to hold onto his girl and quickly swallow another whisky before the band started up again. For the next dance, the band began with a slow, modern waltz, which allowed him to hold his girl close, and even steal a quick brush of lips. Holding his partner close, rocking slowly to the music with his leg moving between hers, he became increasingly sexually excited.

Feeling brave, John sighed, "Let's get out of here and go down to the beach!"

"Why not?" Kathy replied.

They were both a little unsteady but feeling really good as they left the nightclub and headed down to the beach via Cavilll Avenue.

There were young people everywhere, all bent on having a good time.

"God, Kathy you look good. Why didn't I find you in Sydney?"

"We move in different circles. I'm from Lindfield, where do you come from?"

"Newtown, do you know where that is?"

"Sure, everybody knows that, how old are you anyway?"

Exaggerating a little, "Twenty" John lied.

"Who cares anyway?"

Down on the beach leaning against the sea wall they quickly dispersed with conversation in favour of some heavy petting. She was warm and sensuous, and John could feel the contours of her body pressed against his. The effect was electric, and Colin trembled as he gently caressed her neck and shoulders as they continued kissing. Tentatively he brushed his hand across her breast felling erect nipples through her flimsy shirt. As there was no reaction Colin became more adventurous and slipped his hand under her shirt and removed her brassier allowing him to actually hold her breasts in his trembling hands.

Dizzy with excitement John mumbled, "Kathy why don't we lay down on the sand?"

"Okay." Kathy whispered. As she lay down on her back John was thinking, "this is 'it' and moved to undo his jeans, suddenly he felt nauseous and light-headed.

"You're not going to be sick, are you?"

"No, no I'm okay."

But he was not okay, and his head started to spin, along with an urge to throw up.

A blackness, over which he had no control, engulfed him.

His only sense was of sheer terror.

"Are you all right mate?"

John opened one eye to broad daylight seeing a boy leaning over him with, "God Squad" printed on the pocket of his shirt. He could not answer and found himself lapsing into unconsciousness again as he heard a voice saying, "We need an ambulance for this one, down on the beach at the end of Cavill Avenue."

In his next wakening moment, he found himself in a bed with crisp white sheets. After a moment he realised that he was in a hospital with a nurse and doctor standing over him.

"Have you any idea what you were drinking?"

"Only beer and whiskey," John mumbled with a thick tongue and nasty taste in his mouth.

"Well when you embark on any crazy ideas like that, we suggest that you stop and think, because next time you may not be so lucky as to have someone pick you up before it's too late."

"How long will I be here?" John asked, "my friend will be looking for me."

"Well you should have thought of that last night, you can go home this afternoon as long as you stay in bed and rest."

Apart from feeling terrible, John was mortified by his actions. "Hell, what if mum and dad found out." Underneath a sometimes-confident appearance, John was an emotional and quiet young man lacking exposure to the world outside their Newton home above the restaurant. His parents had a very strict Greek upbringing and did not offer much direction for their eldest son, most notably, in the area of alcohol and sex. So, his experience at the nightclub and with the girl on the beach left him shattered and confused.

He took a taxi back to the flat and fell on his bed and slept for what seemed like minutes, but was in fact, two hours.

"Where in the hell have you been?"

It was Sev. "I've been looking all over town for you."

"I have been in hospital mate, being treated for an overdose of whisky, if you must know," John replied.

"What? You're kidding me! I don't believe it."

"Sev, it's true."

Sitting on the side of the bed, John made a promise to himself that he would never again do anything that would leave him not in control of his actions again. Sev agreed and he too made the same declaration, but not with the same degree of conviction as John.

They spent the rest of their holiday resting, enjoying the beach and surfing. John never saw Kathy again (was that her name?) and was thankful that he did not bump into her on the beach! Although he did often ponder on what might have been if he had not blacked out at that crucial moment.

The time came to head for home and they were both quite keen to return to their families and home environment. They arrived home looking fresh, tanned and healthy; Even Mum was impressed with how well they looked after a week at the beach and resting under the Queensland sun.

Christmas came, and with it the hectically busy times at the Naxos Restaurant keeping the whole family occupied. Strangely now he did not mind the work and enjoyed talking to the customers and feeling part of their celebrations. He was a good-looking young man with a bright personality, and he quickly endeared himself to the regulars.

Time came for John to start the university year and he was eagerly looking forward to the challenge and social interaction with fellow students.

He hadn't seen Sev for a while and wanted to catch up before they started. They met down at their local pub again and just sat and chatted quietly over a couple of beers. Although they spoke at length about their trip to Surfers Paradise, John's disastrous night out was not mentioned.

While John was out trying to discard his youth and get on with the challenge of being an adult, his younger brother, Steven, was plodding away preparing himself for his last two years at secondary school. He was generally quiet, to the point of being withdrawn, and was not a good mixer. Academically, he was very much middle-of-the pack and showed little hope of keeping up with his elder brother. At the restaurant he contributed little, doing only what was forced upon him by Dad.

He seemed to have a special affinity with his mother and looked to her for direction and comfort in troubled times.

He fought with John regularly over kitchen duties and would go to great lengths to avoid work.

During the busy Christmas period, while on wash up duties, John came out to the kitchen in between waiting on tables to find an ever-increasing pile of pots and utensils waiting to be washed.

"Steven, what the hell are you doing? How about contributing something, or are you going to leave mum and me to do it all!"

"Piss off John, why should I cop this while you're swanking around bull-shitting the customers, particularly the girls?"

"don't you think I've done my share when you were still running around in short pants? So, shut your mouth and get on with it, or I might just shut it for you"!

"Yea, have a go if you like!"

John stalked off in exasperation back to look after a couple of late customers.

Mum arrived on the scene after hearing the altercation saying, "Don't be too hard on him, John he is only a boy."

"That's okay, but he's got to learn to pull his weight, because I may not always be here, and you and Dad are not getting any younger. In fact, I would not be surprised if he took off altogether after he finishes school and finds a job for himself. That is, if any one will have the little jerk."

"John! That will be enough, or I will get your Dad."

"Okay, okay. Let's just forget it. I just want to get finished for the night. It's now Sunday, and I have a lot to do before I start Uni next week."

Later, John went up to bed thinking that his younger brother was becoming a bigger and bigger pain in the arse, feeling that in the long term he would not stay and support the family. Then another thought, "he does look quite effeminate."

On Monday evening Sev called to suggest they go down to the local for a quiet drink and to talk over their plans for university. With the restaurant was closed on Monday, he readily agreed.

"How are you going John? Your old man not working you to death, is he?"

"Close to it, but I will survive."

"You know John; there must be a way to earn a dollar without killing ourselves doing it."

"If you can find it Sev, let me know first, as I don't intend to work the restaurant for the rest of my life and end up like mum and dad. After all these years, they still don't even own a decent car."

"But the restaurant must be worth a packet by now."

"Maybe so", replied John, "But that's not much good if you don't have the cash to have a good standard of living."

"They do own the building. I think they should sell and retire and enjoy what's left of their lives."

"Well maybe we'll learn the secrets of the world at university", replied Sev.

"Don't kid yourself Sev, maybe the only way to get there is to work your butt off or find something illegal without getting caught."

"Well John, you might just have all the right answers."

"Time to go Sev, what day do you start at uni?"

"Wednesday, you start on Tuesday, don't you?"

"Yes" replied John, "Anyway, give me a ring and let me know how it went."

With that he turned to go, and to his shock he saw his younger brother Steven down in the corner with a schooner of beer in his hand. Quietly he walked over, and firmly took the beer out of his hand and said, "Steven you are only sixteen, now get your arse out of here fast before I call the publican." Steven could see the anger in his eyes and decided he had best take off, fast!

Later that night, lying in bed, John thought again that his little brother could become a problem. Mum and dad certainly wouldn't like to learn what their favourite son was up to. And- to John he looked like a poofter.

John had a lot on his mind, how would he cope with university? What would he do when he finished? How would he extract himself from the restaurant without letting his parents down?

Why don't they just sell the bloody place? They have never made more than a decent wage out of it. The only way they managed to pay for the building was by living an extremely frugal life, for what? Where is their enjoyment of life? The only excitement for them is when they go back to Greece for one week every year. "But the old bugger is smart", thought John.

John reminded himself that years before his Dad had set up a network to import his own condiments, and from this, he now also supplied quite a few other restaurants around the district with herbs and spices. Maybe one day we may be able to turn this into a real business, he pondered. A wholesale operation like that would have to be easier than the grind of running a restaurant.

Before dropping off to sleep, John thought of Jean and those kisses at the bus shelter. "I must try my luck and give her a call." he mused.

Walking through the gates of Sydney University for his first day, John had a sense of both excitement and uncertainty; he was in fact in awe of his surroundings.

This was March 1955.

After registration, he made his way to another point where he collected his lecture time sheets.

What unnerved John was the sheer number of people, all rushing from one place to another, presumably trying to do the same as him; however, he gained some comfort from the huge diversity of ethnic backgrounds, particularly people who, like him, were obviously southern European. There was also a sprinkling of Asians.

After all his formal enrolment was done, John walked back to the main gate for the short walk home. Lost in his thoughts about what he would face in the ensuing days he nearly collided with a girl who was also lost in her own thoughts.

"Jean! What are you doing here?"

"Enrolling for my courses, what about you?"

"The same," John replied. She was so much prettier than he remembered. Her hair was cut in the short style of the times and her skirt and blouse accentuated her full figure. He became quite nervous and lost for words. "What courses are you doing?" he asked,

"Commerce," Jean replied.

"Hey, that's great, so am I. We might swat together."

"I would like that", replied Jean.

"Jean, I still have your number, can I give you a ring tomorrow? I have to get home now to give a hand in the restaurant."

"That's a pity but give me a ring."

John walked off feeling very good about seeing Jean again and considering the chance of an ongoing relationship.

"Hope she likes Greeks, particularly the old folks." He thought

Back at the restaurant Steven was home from school and lying on the couch. John tried to hold back his annoyance, "Okay Steven, aren't you supposed to be helping mum in the kitchen?"

"Stuff that, what are you doing anyway? Where have you been?"

"I have been to uni for enrolment day if it's any interest to you."

"I suppose you reckon you're a big shot now?" said Steven.

John held back his anger and headed to his room to get changed before he carried out the urge to hit him right in his smart-arse mouth.

Later, after cleaning up, he rang Sev to tell him how he got on at uni. With Sev doing Law, their paths would not cross much, as their timetables would be different; so they agreed to keep in touch for updates and nights out. John could not resist boasting about his soon to blossom romance with Jean.

The relationship did develop over the next months, and they became very comfortable with each other enjoying regular outings as well as swatting together. Jean was boarding with a family in Glebe, which was within walking distance of the university. Her parents were still in East Ryde but were quite happy for Jean to board closer to the university. Dad even paid her rent.

On many of these nights, their studies would be cast aside in favour of some heavy petting, and John was sure that one night they would "go all the way", but Jean was just as determined not to.

"I want to get through uni, not get pregnant," she always vowed, "and besides, I want to keep it for later." She was so good looking, and just to hold her and feel her softness would send John into spasms of excitement. He did not take Jean home, as he felt some concern about her reaction to his very Greek parents and the Naxos Restaurant.

When he finally did get around to it, he was quite nervous escorting her up the back stairs of the restaurant to their modest dwelling above.

Then he thought, *"What the hell, I have nothing to be ashamed or embarrassed about. She can take my family and me the way we are, or not at all."*

After the formal introductions, he was knocked out by how warmly she embraced his parents. She was interested in their background and life in Greece, and just as importantly, they adored her. "Well," thought John, "that's a big plus."

John enjoyed his uni times, with the mix of cultures, and the diverse background of his friends. There was always a party to go to, and it could be with the Aussies one week and the next could be Greek, Italian or even Asian. It enriched their lives and broadened their outlook.

Mum and Dad still struggled along with the restaurant, flatly refusing to even think of selling. Surprisingly, the part that was holding the finances together was not the restaurant, but the importing and wholesaling of condiments. Although he was not giving it a lot of thought it crossed John's mind again that maybe this was the future direction to take rather than fooling yourself that there was real money to be made in the restaurant business. One thing John was determined about was that he was going to accumulate enough wealth to make sure that he had a much more affluent life style than his parents.

His mate Sev continued to come up with wild schemes to get rich.

John often thought that his mate could end up the best dodgy lawyer in town; however, they were good mates and understood one another.

GROWING UP

CHAPTER TWO

The next couple of years slipped by with Mum and Dad Naxos still struggling along at the restaurant with lots of help from John, and very little from Steven. As well as his hands-on in the restaurant, working in the kitchen, waiting on tables, and cleaning up, John also began looking after the restaurant accounts.

Steven finished school and went to Greece to live with relatives for a year. It was felt that this would round off his education and broaden his outlook on life. His school results were only mediocre and not good enough for university entrance. Although Steven was his brother, there was something about him that irritated John. He felt that underneath Steven was devious and could not be trusted. No way would he get his hands on the business while John was still breathing.

When Steven returned from Greece, he and a friend rented a flat and he took a job as a sales representative selling imported foodstuffs.

On the odd occasions when he called into the restaurant to see their parents, he did not have much to say. There was never any mention of girls; in fact, John had never known him to go out with a girl.

"My God, maybe he's a poofter?"

Particularly, since his return from overseas Steven had, to Johns eye, taken an even more an effeminate or softer appearance. Anyway, that's his problem thought John, as long as he doesn't bring any off-beat attitude home.

Towards the end of his time at university, John and Jean had a couple of serious disagreements, and the relationship took a big tumble. John then hit the party scene, mostly with Sev in tow, and soon found himself waking up too often in the morning with a king-size hangover, all of which started to affect his studies and work at the restaurant. Dad was quick to spot that something was wrong.

One night after hurriedly cleaning up the kitchen, finishing at about ten thirty, he was about to go out to meet Sev at the pub when he found his Dad waiting at the door.

"Now John, just where in hell do you think you are going at this hour?" he snapped.

"Just out", was John's reply.

"Not good enough son I want to know what you're up to these days. There's too much at stake for the family to have you going off the rails at this stage. We are relying on you to take over the business. If we fail now, it means that I have wasted my life for you. You are drinking too much, that much is obvious. Come on, your old man is not silly you know."

John was feeling very uncomfortable about Dad's barrage at him and did not quite know how to respond. His first thought was to admit to nothing. Then he noticed that his Dad was getting more and more agitated and appeared to be short of breath and quite pale. To Johns horror he then slid slowly down the wall with his hands clutching at his chest and fell into a crumpled heap on the floor.

"Christ, he's having a heart attack", thought John.

Calling for his mother, he ran to the phone to call an ambulance.

As the station was just down the road from the restaurant the ambulance arrived within a couple of minutes. Old John was still breathing when they arrived but was obviously close to death. After stabilising him the ambulance officers took him to The Royal Prince Alfred Hospital, which fortunately was also close to the restaurant. As John was to find out later, it was the promptness of the treatment that saved his Dad's life. In part, he blamed himself for his Dad's sudden heart attack.

After talking with the doctor, he was assured that it would have been coming on for a long time; however, the tension at the time could have finally triggered the attack.

Early next morning he rang Steven with the news and was surprised by Steven's depth of his concern for his Dad.

He had not seen Jean for several weeks but because of her affection for his parents, he felt that he should let her know.

Next morning, Jean arrived at the hospital full of concern and had an emotional reunion with Dad. She quickly took control of his mother, giving her comfort and support.

They only had six months to complete their uni courses, and she further surprised John by offering to step in and help in the restaurant until things could be sorted out.

John suddenly felt quite emotionally moved by this girl and noticed again how wonderful she looked. He also noticed a new maturity about her that had not been there before.

"Hell," he thought, *"How did I nearly let her get away?"*

Gratefully he said, "Thanks, Jean, I hope that one day I may be able to show you how much I appreciate your help and just being here with us."

Apart from the typical Greek emotional outbursts, Mother was holding up well, and made the point very clear that there was no way she would let the restaurant suffer or be neglected.

'John,' she said, "You will have to stop home more and give up your parties or whatever you do. Think yourself lucky that Jean is here to help as well. Even Steven has offered to help at the weekends."

John was bewildered by all this show of support, and made a commitment to himself that, for him, party time was over. With the use of the family car he took Jean home, but she did not ask him inside. In their time apart, he had played the field a bit, but hadn't met anyone who interested him enough to form an ongoing relationship.

During one of these dalliances, he had lost his virginity, but sadly, it was in a fog of alcohol, so everything went by in a haze. He had never found the same thrill elsewhere as being with Jean. Next day at uni he sought her out and asked her to have coffee with him in the canteen. Without any outward enthusiasm, she agreed, and they met after lectures.

John was not always good at putting his feelings into words, but this time it all tumbled out.

"Jean, I know I have acted like a fool and have probably upset you but the last couple of days have made me realise just how much I miss you. Can you forgive and forget?"

Jean replied, "Yes, of course. I have been waiting for you to settle down and come back to me." He gave her a quick kiss on the cheek, and partly to hide his emotions he stood up and said, "Thanks Jean, I will give you a ring tonight after I finish at the restaurant."

John also contacted Sev who was quite shocked to hear the news and offered his help if needed. Later that day before the evening diners started to arrive John took a moment to walk out the front and wander down King Street, which in effect, had been his front yard all his life.

He had not thought about it for a long time, just taking it for granted that this was home. King Street was the end of the great Princes Highway, which followed the Australian coastline all the way from Adelaide to Brisbane. But here it was no highway, just a two-lane suburban road flanked by shops and restaurants of all descriptions. The never-ending traffic, with the subsequent noise, was part of his life.

Directly behind King Street was the University of Sydney and next to the university was the Royal Prince Alfred Hospital. All of which was just one and a half kilometre from the Sydney CBD.

The area had its own charm and history with a huge mix of people from all over the world as well as the local Aussies. For cheap restaurants with good food from around the world, it was, for people across Sydney the best place to go for an evening out.

John walked Several blocks down the street seeing the shops, restaurants and hotels in a new light; it was as if he had never noticed the cosmopolitan society before. He started to feel good about it and for the first time, felt comfortable with his Greek background and his future. What was behind all these feelings he then admitted to himself was that he was in love with Jean. Up to this time, he had never seriously thought about falling in love and wanting to spend his life with one woman.

"Well, I can thank Dad for all this!" he thought.

That night, Jean came over to wait on the tables while John and Mum ran the kitchen. Later, even Sev came to lend a hand waiting on the tables. John's only instruction to Sev was, "Keep away from my girl!"

After closing, he offered to drive Jean home. "I have my own car now", she declared; "Dad bought me a second-hand Ford Prefect."

"That's great" John replied, but he wanted to see her alone.

Jean added, "Why don't you come over to my place tomorrow night?"

Eagerly, John replied, "Great, but it's not too late for you is it? I won't get away till about ten."

"Look, I will come over and help on the tables again, and we can get cleaned up early." Jean suggested.

Dad was improving, and the doctors thought that he would be okay to come home in another week. One concerning thing was that he would never again be able to work, at least not in the same capacity as he did previously.

John thought that there now had to be some serious family decisions made about where they would go from here. One thing for certain was that it would be very difficult to get mother to move. Overriding these looming problems was his desire to complete his reunion with Jean and have a good talk with her. He was excited about his arrangement for the night.

Jean arrived early to help on the tables and John could not help but notice how chirpy she was, as well as looking good enough to eat!

Finally, the doors were shut, the kitchen cleaned, mum sent off to bed, and they were ready to go. John took his dad's car, and with Jean in her own car, they drove to her flat in nearby Glebe. As her landlords were away on holidays, they had the house to themselves.

With good intentions of sitting down with a cup of coffee for a chat they met in the hallway, and immediately fell into an embrace.

There was no need now for words, and the urgency for them both to be close was overwhelming. Without any further thought or discussion, they both knew that tonight they would make love and cement their relationship.

In the lounge room John slowly removed Jeans shirt and then her bra, marvelling at her beauty. Neither felt any embarrassment or shyness; everything seemed natural for them. Jean then stepped out her slacks, and proudly stood naked before him. Without any haste John gently touched her breasts, and then trembling with excitement gently caressed her body.

Jean gasped, "Oh John, keep going."

With a croak in his voice John breathed, "Jean you are so beautiful, I love you, and want to spend the rest of my life with you."

"I know", replied Jean; "I have been waiting so long for you to say that."

John quickly removed his own clothes, and they held each other close before lying on the couch. His lips met hers again, this time with greater urgency; he then kissed her neck, ears, shoulders, and breasts and without any rush most of her beautiful body. Feeling her touch him he prepared himself for the moment that they would be totally together.

"John, John, please," she whispered in his ear.

He controlled himself enough not to rush, wanting to savour this moment as long as possible.

Slowly they came together and in unison slowly rocking until they simultaneously exploded in orgasms.

For quite some time they just lay there in each other's arms, marvelling at the experience they had shared.

"Before we move." John whispered, "You will marry me, won't you?"

"I can't wait", replied Jean.

"As soon as we finish uni and I get the situation at home sorted out, we'll make plans for the middle of next year."

Jean replied, "As long as I see you nearly every night, then I can wait that long."

"Unfortunately for now I had best go home and get ready for tomorrow, it's a pity that I can't stay all night."

"We'll have plenty of time for that later", said Jean.

John drove home feeling totally euphoric, the only cloud that crossed his mind was, "I hope I didn't get her pregnant. I should have taken some rubbers, but then if I planned something like that it would not have been the same."

The spontaneous nature of the experience helped, in many ways, to make it very special for them both. In his own way, he also realised that sex was one thing, but sex with someone you love, made it something special.

Another thought, "I will have to go and meet her parents, I hope they are not racist towards Greeks!"

During the following week Jean and John drove over to East Ryde to meet Jean's mum and dad, Heather and Bruce King. John was nervous in the extreme and was petrified that they'd say; "No daughter of ours will marry a bloody Greek."

To his absolute delight and relief, they welcomed him warmly, and were genuinely interested in his background and family. They had a typical Aussie barbecue out the back with John gladly taking over the role of cooking the steaks and a huge pile of onions, while Jean and her mother prepared the salad.

With a cold beer in his hand it was not long before John felt totally relaxed with his future in-laws

They left late in the afternoon, with a promise from Heather and Bruce that they would come to the restaurant one-night next week to have a meal and meet John's parents.

They arrived unannounced in the restaurant the following Friday night.

John, with a little help from Jean, prepared and served the meal. She was full of fun with jokes about John's cooking, which was all taken in good spirit.

Having lived in the restaurant all his life, John had unintentionally become quite a good cook. He felt that it was appropriate that he prepare this meal himself.

For starters he served Tzatziki, a yoghurt and cucumber dish, followed by Moussaka with Eggplants and traditional Greek salad as his main. Halvas, a sort of pudding with walnuts and syrup, finished off the meal.

Bruce and Heather thoroughly enjoyed the meal and were suitably impressed with John's culinary skills, staying until all the other diners had left. John then brought out a bottle of Greek port to celebrate the occasion.

They all had a great time and enjoyed each other's company. Both Jean and John were ecstatic that both sets of parents fitted in so well with each other.

John Naxos senior became increasingly less mobile, and it soon became obvious to the family that his health was deteriorating. He always blustered about it and put on a brave face; he was never going to admit that his health was failing.

One evening he sat down with John and explained to him all the details of the business.

"John, all my records are in that blue box in the safe. Whenever you are ready, take the box and familiarise yourself with all our history and details of the business.

This is not the stuff that used to go to the accountants for tax.

You will also find details of my overseas contacts, which will help if you decide to continue with the herbs and spice business. Keep in mind that there is money to be made if you put in the time and effort. It is now nearly Christmas John, and as my eldest son I want you to accept your family responsibility and take over the business completely in the New Year."

This was not what John envisaged as his business career after spending all that time at university obtaining a degree in commerce.

After a disturbed night, next day he was determined to explain to his Dad that this was not what he wanted to do with his life.

However, when he saw his frail, aging father sitting in his

favourite chair, his determination evaporated, and his strong sense of family loyalty took over.

He accepted his situation.

Christmas 1958 came, bringing much joy to the now expanding family. John arranged a typical Australian Christmas dinner of roast turkey and ham followed by Christmas pudding for dessert. He was so happy that Jean's parents joined them making a large extended family.

Steven also arrived and displayed none of the anti-social behaviour he seemed to usually carry with him.

Jean had decorated the restaurant and it really looked a picture.

Streamers, paper lanterns, fairy lights and the traditional tinsel covered tree with presents underneath set the mood.

It was Dad's role to give out the presents with oohs and arrs from the recipients. Jean had given John a leather brief case and was secretly disappointed when there was nothing from John for her.

The only cloud over the celebration was the obvious deterioration in John senior's health.

Mum was her usual loud robust self, although everybody noticed her concerned glances at Dad. After they had cleaned up, John took Jean by the arm and said, come on I want to take you home. Jean felt a familiar flutter in her stomach, which she recognised as the beginning of sexual arousal. They took a taxi for the short trip to Jean's flat sitting quietly in back seat holding hands.

John said, "You're quiet, is anything the matter?"

"No, not at all, I was just thinking what a lovely day it was and I am so pleased that our parents get on so well."

When they arrived, John switched on the lights and sat Jean on the couch. Jean knew they would make love but there was something different going on which she did not understand. John then gave her a quiet kiss on the cheek and pressed a small red box into her hand. "Happy Christmas and forever my love", he said. With trembling hands Jean opened the box to find the most beautiful diamond ring she had ever seen.

As her eyes flooded with tears Jean sobbed, "Thank you. I love you so much", I know it's only small, but one day I will buy you the biggest diamond you have ever seen."

In the warm evening, they then lay on the floor and made love with a passion taken to new heights by the occasion.

The restaurant was very busy over the December-January period and under John's care, keeping a tight rein on costs and wastage, they made a substantial profit.

"If I am going to be stuck with this place, at least for the immediate years, I will make it the best restaurant on the strip."

When trade slowed off in February, John made the decision that they had to update the dining area, as it had not been touched for years.

With Jean's help they cleaned and painted the interior, replaced the old tables, and bought all new cutlery and linen. A new polished timber floor completed the refurbishment. The one thing that was retained was the Greek theme. Not that they would ever get away with anything different while Dad was still hovering about.

Late February 1959 John opened the mail to find two job offers, one from a leading and international accounting firm, Price Waterhouse, and another from The National Australia Bank.

"Shit! Just my luck", thought John.

They had obviously targeted the high achievers from university, and John being in the top ten percent of students, was sought out for a future career. In frustration, he stepped out the front of the restaurant into King Street and took a quiet walk along the strip. Without being totally aware of his surroundings, he kept walking until he found himself at the gates to his university.

"What could have been", he pondered, thinking of the corporate career he had planned and had now lost.

Walking slowly back home he found an acceptance of his fate, but in so doing he resolved to make as much as he could from the opportunity that life offered. Most importantly he felt some sorrow in that he could not offer Jean the life-style he had planned.

They were married in a simple ceremony the following March. Mother Naxos fought hard for a traditional Greek wedding. Jean's parents were happy with whatever they wanted. In the end, John and Jean were married by a celebrant with a small gathering of friends at the restaurant. They both felt that their relationship was something very special.

Because of commitments to the restaurant the honeymoon was a short but a delightful weekend at the Hydro Majestic Resort in the Blue Mountains.

They travelled up from Sydney by train, marvelling at the mountain villages they passed through on the way. The weather was cold and misty adding to their sense of being right away from home in Sydney. Their hotel was opposite the station at Medlow Bath, and they made a mad dash across the road to get inside out of the freezing wind.

Jean ran as fast as her legs would take her, leaving John behind struggling with their cases. They both burst into the foyer with Jean giggling like a schoolgirl at John's antics in crossing the road.

Their room had a large picture window overlooking the Megalong valley, which ran as far as the eye could see. After a couple of relaxing drinks in front of the huge log fire in the lounge John and Jean walked arm in arm to the dining room. In the warm intimate setting they gorged their way through a typical Australian menu of soup, then roast lamb, followed by custard tart with fresh cream.

John kept saying, "Jean, don't you think it's time we went up to our room and that big warm double bed?"

The weekend went all too quickly, and they would have loved to stay a little longer, but John said, "Business calls. One day we'll return and finish our holiday."

In the following June of 1956, Dad finally gave up his battle for life and passed away quietly in his sleep.

In the coming months, John's mother grew noticeably older and lost a lot of the spark that she had carried all her life.

Jean gave up any ideas of working outside the family and, happily worked in the business full time. She had a great rapport with the customers, and sometimes John thought that some of them came just to see her. He would often look across the dining room, thinking, "I love this woman."

She had a habit of cocking her head to one side when talking, and her hair would fall across her soft round face covering one eye. This and other mannerisms, like holding her finger to her cheek when thinking, captivated John.

With the restaurant now running well, John started to spend more time with the wholesale condiment business and was surprised at the demand for the herbs and spices they imported. To expand the business, he realised that he would need to spend a lot of time out on the road, visiting restaurants and food retailers to get the products on the market.

Without a lot of confidence, but with a sense of loyalty, he rang his brother, Steven, and asked if he would join the family business and take the salesman's role to get the products out in the market.

Steven's blunt reply was, "Sorry John, but I was coming to see you tomorrow as I'm going overseas to live for a couple of years."

Without sounding too pleased, John remarked, "What about your share of the business?"

Steven replied, "You work out my share at this time and pay me out when you are in a position to do so."

He came around the following day, to say his goodbyes.

It would be several years before he was to return.

Feeling free of any restraints or responsibilities, John and Jean set about building up their business. Jean took complete control of the restaurant and John concentrated on the wholesale condiment business.

Taking a punt, he doubled the next overseas order with the intention of expanding the number of restaurant customers and slowly start supplying retailers.

He also started to see another market to complement the existing business in importing speciality foods for restaurants and food stores. As his knowledge of the industry grew, the scope of the opportunities became apparent. Not only were there herbs for cooking and spices for flavouring, another emerging market was for alternate medicines. Health food shops were opening at a rapid rate, and a part of their product range was herbs for medicinal purposes.

John knew that the most notable use of herbs and spices in very early times was in medicine, in the making of holy oils and unguents, and as aphrodisiacs.

Hippocrates, the Greek "Father of Medicine" employed them in his everyday practice. Herbs and spices were for the first time used in food by the Prehistoric Greeks.

In the following year John travelled to Greece to establish contacts with his Dad's suppliers and any new sources he could find. This was to be a significant move, which would be the basis of the business for years to come.

The rest of the year went by in a flurry of activity with the now expanding business. The one thing hampering growth was the lack of money to fund the new ventures. Without an injection of serious money, they would be stalled.

Busily working in the restaurant one-night John's old friend Sev Cockini appeared with a glamorous girl on his arm. "Hello John, meet my friend, Elizabeth." After introductions all round were completed, they sat down for a meal, (waited on exclusively by Jean) then stayed behind after closing for a drink and catch up.

Sev had completed his law degree and was now working with one of the large city law firms specialising in commercial law.

He appeared to be very affluent and surprised John by telling him that he had just purchased a flat in Rose Bay. John could not but comment that there must be big money in law practices.

"Not quite." replied Sev, "I will tell you about it one day."

Hearing about Sev and Elizabeth's lifestyle made John feel quite inadequate, particularly that they were still living in the flat above the restaurant.

One comfort for him was when he looked at Jean he thought "How lucky am I?"

As the night wore on, John told Sev of his plans to build the condiment business.

The only thing holding them back was lack of capital.

The next evening at home with Jean he was to find out why she was looking so radiant. Laying in bed feeling relaxed and content after making love, Jean softly purred, "John, I have some news for you."

Dreamily he replied, "Okay what is it?"

"Well, err, well, we are going to have a baby."

"What!' John exploded, "You're kidding me."

"No, I'm not", Jean replied, "The doctor confirmed it today."

After a moments silence to absorb what she had said he turned to her,

"Jean, that is absolutely terrific. When does it happen, the birth I mean?'

"June next year, winter of 1961", replied Jean.

John then added, "By the way, what happened to that pill you were taking?"

"It didn't work for me, perhaps it's because you are such a horny bugger", Jean giggled.

After they both had time to digest the news and talk about it, they were both excited and happy.

They lay awake well into the night, talking about what life would be like with a child; how they would bring him or her up, and where they would be living, (certainly not above the shop).

With good news, sad news sometimes follows, and within a week they were to learn that Mum had been diagnosed with cancer. At best, she only had three to four months to live.

She passed away the following March.

With a modest living now coming from the herbs and spice business, and only a pregnant wife to run the restaurant, John had some decisions to make. Their accommodation above the shop was also going to be a problem, as there was no way Jean would get up and down the stairway with a pram. Also, the only entrance was through the restaurant.

Sev and Elizabeth started visiting the restaurant on a regular basis; they were both fun companies. It was good to have them around, particularly as they had so few friends, which was a product of their work commitments and lifestyle.

Late one-night Sev inquired, "John, how are you going to run the restaurant without Jean?"

"Frankly, Sev I don't know how we are going to handle it. We certainly couldn't afford to employ extra people to do the work. We may have to consider selling and concentrate on the wholesale spice business."

"Well, why don't you?" Sev replied.

In the following days John agonised over deciding on the restaurant. He knew that the best decision would be to sell and use the sale money to buy a house to accommodate his wife and child. He was acutely aware that his parents would be disappointed if they were still here. But, time moves on.

After talking it over with Jean, he finally made the decision to sell and use the money to buy their home. John was also aware that, technically, half the money belonged to his brother, Steven, and he could reappear any time and ask for his share. Well, he would worry about that later.

The restaurant and the flat above was the only life John knew, having lived there all has life. The smell of cooking permeated the whole building and was always there; it was even in his clothes, although he'd never noticed it until now.

King Street Newtown, with its cosmopolitan mix of people and seediness, was his back yard. Walking along the street now, he was full of mixed feelings, part of release and part of apprehension of the future, and if he could support his wife and soon to be born child. As well as purchasing a home, he also had to find suitable premises from which to run the spice business.

He listed the restaurant for sale with the local relator,
L. J. Hooker, and indications were that proceeds from the sale would be nowhere near enough to purchase a property and fund the new business, as well as a new home.

If it were not for his Dads foresight and frugal ways to purchase the freehold of the restaurant, he would have nothing, and be out looking for a job.

So, it was with a lot of emotion and nostalgia that he walked along the familiar street waving to his neighbours in other shops as he went. There was the local newsagent, greengrocer, butcher, gift shops, clothing and haberdashery stores, and of course various restaurants, including the local Chinese. He knew all the shopkeepers and considered them his friends. The local pub was also handy and continued to be a favourite meeting place for the local community.

On that night, Sev rang and suggested that they go down to the pub for a beer and catch up. He arrived, smartly attired as usual, an impressive figure in both stature and looks. Sev stood out in the crowd of local knockabout's and shopkeepers.

John felt that Sev really enjoyed being noticed and tended to thrive on attention. He could not help but notice how prosperous Sev had become in the short space of time since their uni days and wondered how he did it.

"Well Sev, you're looking good" John said, "Being a lawyer must be good to you."

"Law is only a part of my life, John. One day I will tell you how to really make a buck, but first things first. Have you sold the restaurant yet?"

"The agents told me only today that they have an offer in the pipeline, so hopefully I will find out tomorrow. We now have a degree of urgency, as we only have another three months before the baby is due."

"Crikey,' replied Sev, "The baby due in June then?"

"Yes", drawled John, "I wish we had a bit more time to get out of the restaurant and set up the Herb and Spice business. Apart from that, we're going to be really pushed for cash to do it."

"Let me get you another beer John, I have a proposition to talk over with you", When Sev came back, and they were settled on their stools with a schooner of beer each, Sev asked, "How would you like to take me in as a partner, 50/50, and I will match in cash whatever you have to put up?"

John nearly choked on his beer at this unexpected turn of events, and after gathering himself, he said, "Okay, this is certainly worth talking about. My first reaction is we must be sure that the business can be developed far enough to generate enough profit to split two ways. Secondly, with equal cash input, we would have to recognise the goodwill value of the business as it is, which should then make the partnership at least 60/40 my way."

John then added, (lightly) 'I would need to have my own lawyer to do the contracts."

"All of that's fine with me", replied Sev.

"My shout", said John. "I need another beer to help me absorb all this."

A couple of hours, and Several beers later, they had worked out the basis of a partnership.

When John arrived home, Jean's first reaction was "Where have you been all this time? Leaving me home on my own not knowing where you are."

"Hang on, hang on", replied John, "I have some great news."

"Well it had better be good, because I am not about to start looking after the restaurant on my own while you are down the pub with Sev, while being six months pregnant as well."

"I'm sorry love", replied John. "If we're finished here, let's go upstairs and I'll tell you all about it."

After settling at the table with a cup of coffee John then broke the news.

"Sev has offered a partnership in the new business and will match whatever money we put up. Jean, this will give us the start we wanted. We can buy our home as well as getting the right premises for the business. We can then really expand our distribution base and who knows how far we can take it."

"John that's great and I'm pleased for you, but I have never said this before, do you really trust Sev?"

"Well, this is a surprise Jean; we've been mates since we were kids."

"That's not the point", replied Jean. "He is such a wheeler dealer, you would never know what he was up to, and where does he get all this money from anyway?"

John took a big sigh, and said, "He is a practising solicitor for a start and who knows, he may have got money from Elizabeth as well."

"I doubt it; I think Elizabeth just goes along for the life-style."

"John, I trust you and your judgement, but if we enter into this deal then we must always retain control and be vigilant. Somewhere underneath I see ruthlessness, if not violence, in Sev that worries me. I am sure it's there, but he keeps those emotions well hidden."

In the absence of any workable alternative, and concern about the soon to arrive baby, John and Jean decided to go with Sev's offer of cash for a partnership.

John had no doubt that the little sideline to the restaurant his Dad started had big potential. He sensed that there were real opportunities in importing foodstuffs, many of which could initially be sourced through existing suppliers.

Restaurant and catering equipment were also hard to find in Sydney.

During his last trip overseas, he saw that after their recovery from the war the Italians were producing excellent equipment and utensils. Currently little was reaching Australia. With the influx of migrants from around the world, eating habits in Australia and patronage of restaurants would change dramatically. John could see the opportunities but was conservative by nature. Sev was more flamboyant and a risk-taker, but John could see that with his confidence and drive they might make a good team.

By April the restaurant and freehold property was sold, and after a short hand-over period it was time to move. The new owners were Greek and intended to continue with the restaurant as it had been for the last twenty years under the Naxos family.

It was a very emotional time for John, as the restaurant was the only home he had ever known and was the connection with his now departed parents.

As the Naxos name was to continue with the condiment business, the restaurant was renamed.

Finding a home within their price range, without going out too far from the city, proved to be difficult. Day after day they explored the inner western suburbs and came home tired and frustrated. They argued over every house they saw. Jean, in the late stages of pregnancy, was easily upset, and John worried about the huge amount of money they would be committing.

At the end of one arduous day of disagreements, John in exasperation, flashed, "I have had enough, let's just go and rent somewhere."

Jean, thinking that this was not what she wanted replied, "Look John, we are both tired, let's have an early night and try again tomorrow. There is still that house in Croydon that we haven't seen yet and If there's nothing by the end of the week then we will have to consider renting for a while, as the baby is due in six weeks."

Early next morning they went to the realtor's office and asked to see the house advertised in Croydon. As soon as they pulled up out the front, they both got the same feeling.

The solid red brick home, Californian bungalow style, was as pretty as a picture.

It had been freshly painted and had a nice front lawn and neat garden. Annuals were in bloom in the garden beds, and rose bushes lined the fence and pathways.

Inside there were three bedrooms, one bathroom, lounge, separate dining room and a big eat-in kitchen. The laundry was at one end of a veranda, which covered the whole back of the house. The rear yard was spacious with enough room for kids to play. They did not need much discussion before agreeing to buy it. That night, in contrast to some previous nights, they went home happy and excited.

They moved into Hammond Avenue Croydon during the second week of May. 1961.

Having spent all his life in the concrete jungle of Newtown John was excited about moving and started planning all the things he could grow.

First step was to buy a lawn mower and some gardening tools. He was like a kid with new toys. He cut the lawn, pulled the weeds out of the gardens and set about building a vegetable plot down the back. Not having a clue how to go about all this, he bought a book that told him everything he needed to know. The Yates Garden Manual.

Jean would watch him out the kitchen window, seeing how he was enjoying himself, and thinking, "I have never seen him so happy."

Their first child, Robert, was born the week after they moved into their new home.

SEV COCKINI

CHAPTER THREE

Sev Cockini arrived home at his Eastern Suburbs apartment feeling excited about getting John's agreement for a partnership, a move he had been planning for months.

This euphoria excited him sexually, and finding Elizabeth standing at the kitchen table in her nightie inflamed his feelings further.

Her body and full breasts were clearly visible through her sheer slip. With anger flashing in her eyes she said, 'If you think you are going to use this place as your casual boarding house you are very wrong. Where have you been?'

"Never mind I'll tell you later; but first I want you", he exhorted, dropping his pants to the floor.

"No way", said Elizabeth turning away, "I will think about it when we get to bed."

Sev put his arms around her waist and gently pushed her against the kitchen table saying, "No waiting, I am going to have you now, right here."

Lifting her nightie, he sat her on the table and almost brutally entered her. The table slid across the floor until it was hard up against the cupboards with Sev frantically continuing his thrusting. Very quickly a medieval wail escaped his lips as he climaxed. Withdrawing, he slumped onto a chair still breathing heavily.

Elizabeth quipped, 'That was obviously great for you, but it didn't do much for me. It was like you raped me. Don't ever treat me like that again."

"Never mind", said Sev, "We'll do it again when we get to bed. Let's go."

"What's all the excitement about anyway?'

"I have convinced John to take us as partners in the business. This will open a lot of doors for us."

In the bedroom Sev completed undressing and fell onto the bed. Elizabeth quietly got in next to him expecting not only to hear the full story, but also to continue with the sex they started in the kitchen.

She slowly ran her hand across his stomach expecting some reaction, there was none! It was then that she realised that he was asleep.

Lying in the dark, Elizabeth thought, "Why is it that I sometimes feel frightened of Sev? There seems to be an under-current of violence that could, if fuelled get out, but then, he has never been overly rough with me. On the other hand, I can recall only a couple of occasions when his lovemaking has been soft and gentle.

Is this indicative of his underlying personality?"

Everything Sev did, he did with urgency and determination, and he wanted everything now, even sex, as was demonstrated tonight.

Driving it all was his never-ending pursuit of money. Although Elizabeth was happy to enjoy the lifestyle, she was beginning to see that with Sev money was an obsession. She had never been to his office and sometimes wondered what type of people he had for clients.

As a teenager Sev supported himself and worked his own way through university. His Greek parents had too many problems of their own and never settled into life in Australia. When Sev was sixteen, they returned to Greece, giving Sev the option of going with them or looking after himself in Australia. He chose the latter.

He worked part time wherever he could get a job, sponged off his mates, and many times just went hungry. In later times, he became a pimp for some of the local brothels. In university he built up a network of customers for 'pick-up pills,' the so-called recreational drugs.

These were his secrets.

His best friend John Naxos was very different to Sev, and he sometimes felt an intense jealousy of John and his relationship with Jean.

Although he loved Elizabeth in his own way, Sev knew that basically their love did not have the same depth. He also felt a strong sexual pull towards Jean and often wondered why he hadn't chosen her when they first met down at the pub all that time ago. In much later years, his attraction to Jean deepened.

However, he had a strong attachment to John, probably because he was the one stabilising influence in his rather sordid and sometimes lonely life.

He went to great lengths to see that John never ever knew of his other life.

Sev took comfort in his belief that John was the one person who would never let him down.

The morning after his meeting with John, he had a talk to Elizabeth and told her as much as he thought she needed to know. He glossed over the finer details and told her nothing of his grander plans.

"Well I am impressed", sighed Elizabeth, "but where is all this money coming from, last week you told me we couldn't afford a holiday?"

"This is different money and we'll borrow most of it through the solicitor's office. Believe me, this move will work."

"Okay, but don't think you are getting my little nest egg that Dad left for me." said Elizabeth.

That night after Elizabeth had gone to visit her mother Sev sat in his home office planning his next moves. Firstly, I will resign from my position with the firm and open my own office, this will give me the flexibility to choose my own clients and what direction I take. Next, I will take whatever time is needed to help to get the new business with John set up and operating.

For all outward purposes, I will not get involved in the day to day running of the business. That could come later.

All my plans are going to hinge around increasing our imports, even to the point of diversifying into other goods for the restaurant and food trade.

Sitting at his makeshift desk, he began to think about his early life.

Sev's early memories were of the beatings he took from his father. Now, years later, he realised what lonely lost souls his parents were in Australia. His father's constant ribbing at work, being called a wog, and of his inability to learn English meant that he was never able to understand the Australian psyche.

The beatings handed out to Sev were for trivial reasons, like getting home late from school or not doing his homework. He recalled one beating that kept him from school for a week.

All the other kids seemed to have pocket money for sweets or ice blocks; he was denied any such treats.

Their local corner store was a mixture of groceries, drinks, fruit and vegetables, sweets and ice cream. The groceries were down one end and the rest of the goods partly hidden down the back.

Sev noticed that when the owner was busy down the front with groceries, the back of the store was unattended.

He quickly worked out that if he picked the right moment, he could duck behind the counter and open the cash drawer and help himself to some coins, being smart enough not to take too much that would be missed immediately.

For several weeks Sev collected pocket money in this way. He even went back to the shop with the other boys to buy sweets and ice blocks.

On one of these regular visits just when he had his hand in the drawer, "Got you, you little bastard."

The shopkeeper stood over him and gave him one vicious smack across the ear. With his head ringing from the blow, Sev fell to the floor. Looking up, the shopkeeper appeared to be about ten-foot tall.

"Right", he directed, "Down to the police station with you."

Sev was mortified, thinking of the belting he would get from his Dad.

Following a lengthy lecture, the constable and shopkeeper decided that he would have to work at the shop every night after school until he made enough money to pay back all he had stolen. His job was weighing up and bagging potatoes. The constable then took him home and explained to his father what he had been doing.

After the Constable left his father roughly pushed Sev into the bedroom and with a raged look in his eyes took off his heavy leather belt. He was short and stocky and well-muscled from years of labouring.

Sev had prepared himself mentally for the coming punishment and was ready for the pain, which would not last long, and he knew he would survive it.

His father asked, "What sort of boy are you? You have disgraced yourself and your family. Have you anything to say?"

"No", replied Sev, "Just give me my own pocket money."

This only inflamed his father's anger, and he flayed into him with all his considerable strength.

When he had spent his anger, to Sev's surprise he stood there and cried. Before he left, he declared, "I only hope that you have learned your lesson and will never disgrace yourself or your family again."

Later when Sev took off his shirt he was not surprised to see that it was covered in blood.

When his wounds had healed Sev's resolve was that one-day he would have enough money to control his own life. The question of honesty never came into it; rather, whatever you do don't get caught.

It was to be only four years later that his parents returned to Greece and left him to fend for himself at the tender age of sixteen. Before they left, his father gave him one hundred pounds and said, "This should keep you going for a while, it is all I can spare. "The only advice I can give is to finish school, get into university and break the mould we are in now of being working people struggling to survive."

From now on, you will have to make your own decisions, but remember, never do anything that would disgrace yourself and family, although only God knows what will become of us."

He gave Sev a quick embrace and walked away.

Sev found his mother crying uncontrollably in the kitchen,

"I am sorry son, but I must do as your Dad says."

Inwardly, Sev was distraught. He could not believe that it was necessary for the family to break-up. However, there was no way he would consider leaving Sydney to live in the old country. Even at his young age he saw Australia as a land of opportunity.

His problems at home with his parents about to return to Greece soon became common knowledge around the school.

One day his mathematics teacher approached him and asked if he had found anywhere to live. Sev replied that he was still looking, but if he did not find anywhere soon, he may have to ask his friend, John Naxos, if he could live with them until he found his own place.

The following day the teacher came to him and suggested he go and have a talk to a lady who used to help in the school canteen. She lived on her own in Glebe and had a spare room to let.

Sev found the two-story terrace home in Ferry Road, which was in easy walking distance to the school and public transport. The home was typical of the area, with a kitchen, dining, lounge room, plus one-bedroom downstairs, as well as a bathroom and toilet next to the laundry. There were three bedrooms upstairs, and another bathroom.

The front veranda and first floor balcony were decorated with lace patterned wrought iron, typical of the district and era.

In response to his tentative knock, a plump elderly lady with a smiling happy face opened the door.

Her name was Gladys McMurray.

Sev began, "Hello, my name is Sev Cockini and I am inquiring about your vacancy for a boarder."

She had a big welcoming smile that put Sev at ease.

"Hello Sev, come inside and we will have a chat."

Sev followed her down the passageway with a red-carpet runner over polished pine board floor boards.

Sitting at the kitchen table Gladys explained. "I can offer you full board with all meals and laundry for twenty-five shillings a week. Would that suit you?"

Seeing Sev's hesitancy she continued. "Perhaps you would like to see your room first?"

Chatting all the way, she led Sev up the carpeted stairway to a first-floor landing.

"There are two rooms, this one on the left is the larger and can be your bedroom and the smaller next to it you could use as your study. Well what do you think?"

Sev needed no further encouragement and was happy to accept her offer.

Gladys was a kindly soul who took a liking to Sev with his cavalier ways, treating him like the son she never had. As time went by Sev developed a strong affection for Gladys, seeing in her a replacement for his mother. The difference was that he felt comfortable confiding in her as he could never do with his parents.

Sitting in his room studying, it always made him feel good to hear her call at 5.30 sharp every night,

"Sev, your tea is on the table."

"Coming Nanna, what have we got tonight?" he would call as he bounded down the stairs.

"Your favourite, roast lamb and veggies, none of that funny Greek stuff you used to eat." Gladys replied.

The banter went back and forth every night, right through to sweets, usually bread and butter pudding or rice custard.

Then Nanna would talk to him about his studies, taking a genuine interest in what he was doing.

"I never went past sixth grade, can't understand all that stuff." she would say.

Sometimes they would sit at the table after tea, and Nanna would love to tell Sev stories of her school days, teenage years, and the parties she would go to. Sev was a good listener.

In the ensuing years Nanna became his surrogate mother and the rock that held him together to get through university. It did not take long for his money to run out, and there was no way he would rely on charity from Nanna, believing that she had to manage on her meagre Government pension.

When asked about his money he would say, "Now look Nanna, you don't have to worry about me. I will always pay my board. Dad still puts an allowance into my bank account." The fact was, he had never heard from his parents, and did not even know their address in Greece.

"Are you sure?" Nanna would reply.

"Of course, I'm sure, but it will only last until I finish University."

Nanna remarked, "That's good Sev. We don't want you worried about those things; you must concentrate on your studies."

Sev was a good student applying himself with a zeal that surprised his teachers. He knew that as he had no support, he would have to make it on his own; this was his motivation. Ignoring other interests and sport over the weekends, he devoted all his time and energies to his studies.

Towards the end of his high school year, he was down to his last five pounds.

Over tea one night, he said, "Well Nanna I've done it!'

"You have done what?" exploded Nanna.

"Got myself a job."

"Well don't make me drag it out of you, what is this all about?"

"I have got a job selling papers after school for the local newsagent, and I start next week. They have given me a good corner to sell from, opposite Central Station in Broadway. With a bit of luck, I might make a pound a week", said Sev.

Nanna was trying to show some excitement for him and said, "That's wonderful, but will it affect your school studies?"

"No way", I will be home by six and can still put in an hour before bed. You will keep my tea for me, won't you?"

"Of course, I will. We will just have to have tea an hour later, that's all."

At the end of his first week as a paper-boy he collected his pay of fourteen shillings. He was enjoying the experience, standing in the bustling crowds cradling his papers under his arm calling, "paper, paper, get all the news here."

He soon had a band of regulars whom he greeted with a smile and, "G'day mate."

On his way home one night, after a particularly good day, he called into the florist at Central Station and bought Nanna a big bunch of flowers. It was the first time he had ever bought anything for anybody.

He was embarrassed travelling home on the bus and tried to hide them under his coat in case he ran into any of his school friends.

Nanna was overwhelmed and started to cry.

Sev spluttered, "Hey, don't cry, the flowers were to make you happy."

"But I am happy that's why I am crying. Come and give me a big hug."

In their embrace, Sev felt an emotion he had not felt before, even with his parents.

After putting the flowers in a vase on the hall table and taking off her apron, she said, "Come on let's eat, and you can tell all about your day."

In his second week selling papers, another boy appeared on his corner selling papers. Sev quickly approached him and said, "Listen mate, this is my territory, so piss off!"

He gave no thought to the fact that the boy was considerably taller and heavier.

"No fucking way", he replied. "Who said you own it, anyway?"

"I did, so move now, go somewhere else."

"Are you going to make me, wog boy"!

Dropping his papers to the footpath, without giving the boy any time to see what was coming, Sev hit him full in the face with a huge looping right cross.

He fell to the footpath with blood streaming from his nose.

As he tried to get up, Sev hit him again, and then continued to belt into him. Don't ever call me wog boy he yelled. It was as if all his life's frustration was going to be exonerated in one frenzied attack on this boy. Before he could hit him yet again, a man grabbed him from behind and said, "Okay that's enough; you have made your point, now leave him alone."

Shaking with anger, Sev picked up his papers and moved a little further down the footpath, watching to see that the boy left.

When he arrived home, Nanna noticed his badly bruised and swollen hand.

"Sev, what have you done to your hand?"

He was tempted to make up a story, but then thought, what the hell!

"Nanna, a boy tried to muscle in on my territory and if I didn't stop him, by the end of the week I would have six other kids to compete with, and he called me a wog."

"Why didn't you just go to the newsagent and get him to settle it and save the violence."

"He wouldn't care as long as the papers get sold."

"There is enough violence in the world now Sev without you adding to it; besides, what if he comes back tomorrow with some of his friends."

"I don't think he would be game", replied Sev, thinking of the damage he must have done to his face.

Later that night lying in bed, Sev wondered about his own violence, and the fact that he enjoyed punching that boy.

Word soon got about of Sev's fight protecting his paper corner, and nobody ever came near the area again.

The rest of the year went by uneventfully, with Sev feeling a contentment he had not experienced before with his family. Nanna fussed over him, seeing him as the child she was denied herself. They both needed one and other, and over time, built up a unique relationship.

Sev even helped with jobs around the house and with Nanna's small vegetable garden.

He sailed through his final years exams and was rewarded by being named as one of the top ten students. At the end of the school year, with his mate John in tow, they took a break and went to Surfers Paradise on the Gold Coast to celebrate the end of Secondary School.

Sev had never been out of Sydney before, and it was an education for him to see another very different part of the country.

During their holiday, he learned some valuable lessons in how not to drink, and how to use his good looks to pick up girls.

Christmas came with Sev and Nanna having a quiet, if not lonely, dinner together. Neither of them had any family or friends to share it with. They made the most of it, with Sev erecting some fancy decorations and Nanna cooking a Christmas dinner big enough to feed the whole street.

With balloons and decorations hanging from wherever Sev could find somewhere to tie them, the house looked quite festive.

However, there was something missing in that there was only the two of them. Sev, and no doubt Nanna, felt sad that there was no family for either of them. How different it would be to have a big family gathering such as the Naxos.

"One day I am going to correct all this", thought Sev.

"Sev, I think you're old enough to celebrate Christmas with a drink," said Nanna, as she produced a bottle or Reschs Dinner Ale from the fridge.

He and his mate, John Naxos, were already experienced in the wonders of drinking beer, so the taste was not new to him.

Sitting there with the cold bottle between them, Sev felt at peace for the first time in years. He also felt a deep affection for Nanna, who had virtually rescued him, and given him a home with the love and affection he missed so much from not having a family of his own.

After the first bottle, Nanna said," That was good, let's have another; this is the first drink I 've had for years."

After finishing the lavish dinner, washed down with three bottles of Reschs, Nanna said "Sev I think I'll go and lie down for a while and have a rest."

"That's fine, you have a rest and I'll clean up."

Sev thought, *"I think old Nanna is a bit tipsy."*

The New Year started full of promise and hope for Sev, he was happy living with Gladys and had gained top marks in his year-end exam, qualifying him for university entrance. A further bonus was that his level was in the top ten percent of students. This gave him a choice of courses.

He chose Law.

His one concern was a serious one, how was he going to pay his fees, as well as support himself.

Around this time, Sev had secretly started to frequent the nightclub district of Sydney known as Kings Cross. The area later gained prominence and became known as Sin City. Sex shops, sleazy nightclubs, prostitutes and drugs were there for all. The bright lights, people of all types (particularly the girls who had their defined areas for pick-ups), fascinated him.

Sev liked to talk to the girls and would have bought some action for himself if he were able to afford the price. He soon got to know the girls and what the business was all about.

One girl befriended him; her name was Gloria Brown. While she claimed to be 20, she was, in fact, closer to 25; but in the dark, who cared!

In her trade-mark long blond hair, low cut blouse showing plenty of bosom, short skirt and high heels, she looked good.

One quiet night, he found her wandering down Darlinghurst Road. "Sev, how would you like a free one, like on the house?"

That was an offer he could not refuse!

Gloria's "office" was in a terraced cottage in Darlinghurst. It had a narrow frontage with a wrought iron gate and laced verandas, typical architecture of the early nineteen hundreds.

Nervously, he followed Gloria through the front door, down a narrow passage-way, and up a long flight of stairs. All he could see was Gloria's shapely bottom swaying from side to side, with glimpses of her thighs in front of him. By the time he reached the top of the stairs he had a huge erection, which Gloria quickly noticed.

"My, you are a strong boy", she said leading him into a small bedroom with a huge double bed.

Sev often masturbated, thinking of a moment just like this, and he was quickly getting himself in a frenzy of excitement. He'd had a few quick kisses before, but had never touched a girl intimately, let alone had sex.

It was here with Gloria that he experienced his first serious sexual activity.

Initially it was a bit of a fumble, and he was so anxious he nearly ejaculated before he even started. Gloria was wise and experienced in the ways of boys, and she quietly coached him along. "You can undress me if you like."

Needing no encouragement, with shaking hands he fumbled with her skirt and panties. With great difficulty, he then tackled the hooks on her bra.

When her breasts tumbled out, it was almost too much to bear.

Gloria whispered, "Now slow up, we have plenty of time. Here, let me help you get your pants off."

For a moment he felt embarrassed, standing there without his pants and his penis sticking straight out in front of him. He soon forgot that when Gloria took it in her hand and drew him close.

She encouraged him to touch her naked body and kiss her breasts. He then tentatively put his hand between her legs and felt the silky warm wetness of her. His whole body tingled and trembled in excitement.

"Gloria I can't wait any longer."

She then lay back on the bed and gently guided him slowly to her. The sensation was nothing like anything he had experienced before. Gloria took him to dizzy heights he never knew existed, and he quickly exploded.

Lightly kissing him she said, "Now would you like to do it again, only slowly this time?" He had no trouble with that.

After he lay spent on her bed she asked, "Sev, would you like to earn some pocket money?"

"You bet I would. What do I have to do?"

"All you have to do is scout for customers and bring them to me, and I will pay you a pound for each one. You could sort of act as my agent."

"Do I get any side benefits?"

"Any time I'm free," she replied.

His relationship with Gloria started to give him some serious cash to pay his university fees and live without sponging off Nanna.

Not only did he recruit customers from the bars of Kings Cross, he soon found willing customers from the party scene around the university.

Such was the demand for discreet sex, that he soon had several of Gloria's friends for referrals as well.

He was smart enough in the way he handled his referrals that nobody suspected that he was in it for the money. He became in effect, a successful pimp.

In quieter times, he would have long conversations with Gloria, and learned of how she had been deserted by her family when she was only fifteen. To support herself she had found the streets of Kings Cross. They had a common bondage, and soon became friends.

Sev looked forward to her company, apart from the sex he enjoyed.

As time went by and he felt himself drawn closer to her, he became increasingly concerned about how she had to earn her living. He began to dream and plan of the day when he would rescue her from the life she led.

He was always concerned that somehow Nanna might find out about his relationship with Gloria, and how this would disappoint her. However, he considered this to be a chance in a million.

Sev's next step into the shady side of inner Sydney was easy. He soon found that the same people who were using his girls were also looking for recreational drugs. It wasn't hard to find a source through Gloria, and he was soon supplying pep pills to party goers around the Cross, and later to his fellow university students. These were in the form of Benzedrine or Excedrin and used as uppers or downers. When taken in large doses, instead of inducing sleep, they had the opposite effect and gave a euphoric state of mind.

Nanna could not fail to notice that Sev was never short of money nowadays. When she quizzed him on it, he covered himself by repeating his early story that he still received the allowance from his parents in Greece.

Time over this period went quickly for Sev, and even with his night-time activities he never neglected his university studies. He had great affection for John and Jean Naxos and visited them regularly. They had no knowledge of his other activities, although John had heard whispers around the university that if you wanted drugs or sex, Sev was the man to see.

Towards the end of his studies Sev fostered his party-boy image and was always available for a party. He was tall dark and handsome, dressed well and a popular figure with the opposite sex. At one such party, held in a fellow student's parents' home in Strathfield, (they were away on holidays) he was to meet the girl that would change his life.

The home was a huge impressive federation-style building, set in expansive grounds with manicured gardens. Sev had never been inside a house as opulent as this and he could only marvel at it and wonder how he could make enough money to live like that. Lost in his thoughts, looking across the spacious back patio he noticed a tall, strikingly beautiful girl standing next to the barbecue on her own.

The girl looked every bit an expensive package and a designer's dream: beautiful, chic, petite, blond-haired and twenty at the most. She was wearing a black silk dress with high-heeled sandals, all of which accentuated her flawless complexion and slim figure.

"Wow!" he thought. *"I must check this one out."*

Not being backward, he strode across to her and said, "Hello, my name's is Sev, what's yours?"

Sizing him up she saw a tall extremely attractive man with the swarthy features of a southern European. He was impeccably dressed in grey slacks, open-neck shirt and dark blue reefer jacket. With some hesitation she replied, "Elizabeth."

"Elizabeth who?"

"Elizabeth Spalding." She felt both attracted and intimidated by this tall attractive man; however, she was not about to fall over in a swoon.

Looking directly into her eyes he said, 'Are you on your own?"

Returning his gaze, "I'm with a girlfriend."

"Good." he replied, "let me get you a drink."

Elizabeth was not used to being controlled and was not about to be swept away by this stranger with a cock-sure swagger, or so she thought.

Her aloofness and outward disinterest made Sev even more attracted to her and determined to win her over. While the rest of the crowd partied, danced and drank, he wisely took the quiet approach and just talked.

After a while they danced, and the feel of her body through the silk dress inflamed his passion, and he soon felt the beginning of an arousal. *Cripes*, he thought, *this could be embarrassing, so he carefully backed away.*

What further attracted him was that she was certainly of good breeding and intelligence, she was no street floozy. He could already see her at his side as a successful solicitor's wife. Before the night was over, he had a dinner date for the following week.

Wisely, he did not push the relationship on the first night.

She played hard to get, outwardly remaining aloof to his charm and good looks. After a while he felt comfortable with Elizabeth, and within limits, confided in her about his background and life with his parents as a young boy.

His big test was to play the Jekyll and Hyde act, and never let her get any smell of his other covert activities.

Elizabeth was a Sydney North Shore girl, a product of affluent parents and an education in the exclusive private school system. Her father was a doctor with a practice on the lower North Shore, an opinionated arrogant man, one that would surely clash with the likes of Sev Cockini. Only someone with his idea of breeding and education would be good enough for his daughter Elizabeth.

Elizabeth had steadfastly refused to follow him into medicine and, apart from the fact that her final exam marks were not good enough, it did not interest her.

To appease her father Elizabeth took an arts course at NSW University but did not take it any further.

At least he could say that his daughter went to university.

At the time of meeting Sev, she spent her time helping as a receptionist in the surgery.

Much to Sev's frustration, Elizabeth strongly resisted his advances for sex. Long sessions of passionate kissing and touching, using all the tricks he had learned from Gloria failed to make any impression on her. This made her even more desirable, and he was determined to totally capture this girl.

Playing the successful solicitor role, he took her to the best restaurants and the theatre. Although it was not his scene, he also escorted her to her Saturday netball matches. Watching the girls run around the court in their short skirts did have its appeal and he found it quite easy to let his imagination run wild.

For their part, the girls could not help but notice this tall handsome man and feel some envy of Elizabeth.

One girl was quick to say, "Hey Elizabeth, when you've finished with him, send him over to me. He can sleep in my bed any time."

It was on one of these days that he went to collect Elizabeth from home and by chance had to confront her parents.

The Spalding residence was in the up-market suburb of Pymble, known for its trees, bush-setting, large homes and wide streets. It certainly was not a place for the working battlers.

Walking down the long circular driveway, Sev thought, "*Wow, this will do me; it's certainly a long way from Nana's terrace in Glebe.*"

As there was no answer to his knock on the front door, he took a punt and wandered around the back. He was amazed at the scale of the property. There was a 50-metre swimming pool, a grass tennis court, and a lush green lawn sloping down to bush at the rear. Distracted as he was by the splendour of the place, he failed to notice Elizabeth's parents sitting by the pool.

He was jolted back to reality when a loud voice called out, "Hello, can I help you?"

Collecting himself he replied with a stutter, "W-well, Y-yes, I have come to pick up Elizabeth."

With more confidence than he felt, he marched over with his hand outstretched. "Hello, my name is Sev Cockini, you must be Elizabeth's parents."

Dad replied sarcastically, 'Well we live here, so I suppose that's reasonable. Did you try the front door?"

He was small in stature, and Sev was thinking that his opinion of himself was far greater than his size.

To save any embarrassment Elizabeth's mother quickly came to the rescue "Hello, I'm Elizabeth's mother, Beryl, this is her father Ronald." She was a mature woman, with greying hair framing a pleasant open face.

Sev quickly thought, "*She looks too good for that little prick.*"

Composing himself, Sev replied, "Nice to meet you both, I have been looking forward to it."

At that moment, Elizabeth came out of the back door and was surprised to see Sev standing there talking to her parents.

"Well hi; I see that you have all met?" She gave Sev a quick kiss on the cheek and said, "Sorry Mum, we haven't got time to chat or I will be late for netball, we'll catch up later. Come on Sev, let's go."

Sev was relieved to be able to extract himself from the meeting which he felt would have turned into a full-on interview.

Out the front he said, "Boy that was tough, I'm glad you arrived when you did. I think your Dad was ready to give me the third degree."

"Serves you right for wandering around the house unannounced. You're lucky the dog didn't get you."

Sev replied, "What, have you got a man-eating dog as well?"

"Okay, that's enough. They are really a couple of softies looking after their little girl; both are great if you get to know them, that's if you get the chance. So, behave yourself and get me to netball or I will be late."

Any irritation Sev felt quickly disappeared, as he glanced at her long brown legs and shapely body squeezed into her sports uniform.

Her full lips and soft skin stirred his manhood, and it was all he could do not to stop the car and make love to her there and then. Driving along, he hoped that Elizabeth was not aware of his excitement.

With that thought, he had a quick flash of picturing himself on one of his now regular visits to Gloria. I will have to marry this girl he thought.

At the Netball Centre, Sev paced up and down the sidelines cheering and yelling like an over-excited schoolboy. This was a most un-Sev like behaviour and not the image of an Eastern Suburbs solicitor that he liked to portray.

Later Sev dropped Elizabeth home after deciding to pick her up that night for dinner at his friend John's restaurant in Newtown.

This time Sev had the foresight to make sure Elizabeth was out the front waiting for him so he didn't have to face her father twice in one day.

Travelling down the express-way with Sev towards the Harbour Bridge, (although she had done it countless times) Elizabeth could not help but marvel at the vista of the Harbour surrounded by the city lights. It would be accurate to say that Elizabeth's view of the world was filtered through her life in the exclusive North Shore suburbs of Sydney. She never understood, nor had been exposed to, the fact that most of the four million Sydney- siders lived west of the North shore in less affluent areas.

Travelling past the city and on to the old district of Newtown Elizabeth was seeing a significant change in the landscape and environment. This was the old Sydney, home to the settlers and workers in the early part of the century. Little had changed since the nineteen twenties and thirties.

Along the shopping strip of King Street, with its old shops and distinctive round ball streetlights hanging under the awnings, Elizabeth started to feel quite lost.

"Sev, where on earth are you taking me?" she exploded.

The restaurant in the heart of the King Street shopping district was called The Naxos, taken from the family name of John's parents.

Luckily Sev found a parking spot in a rear lane not far from the restaurant, so they didn't have far to walk. Elizabeth felt quite uncomfortable in this strange environment, sharing the footpath with a mixture of people of all types and races.

Being strikingly beautiful she stood out in the crowd and could feel people staring at her.

Feeling more nervous by the minute, and holding firmly onto Sev's arm she appealed, "How much further, can't we get a taxi?"

"Don't worry we are here now", Sev replied as they stopped in front of a featureless shop with a sign in both Greek and English saying, "The Naxos Restaurant."

To Elizabeth, the interior was all dark and mysterious, and she was starting to wonder what she had let herself into by agreeing to come. Once inside, it appeared much better with a polished timber floor and tables covered in bright check tablecloths. The back wall was covered with a mural of a Greek countryside. Elizabeth conceded to herself, but not to Sev, that it did sort of have a warm family feel.

A good-looking bloke about Sev's age, burst across the room and warmly embraced him. "Welcome Sev, it's great to see you." Turning his attention to Elizabeth he gushed, "And you must be Elizabeth. It's nice to meet you at last, but you're too good looking for him."

A little embarrassed, but charmed anyway, Elizabeth replied, "Well thanks, John, I think you're right too," which brought a laugh from Sev.

"Now come and meet Jean" he said, as an attractive, fresh-faced girl, with a big smile, appeared from out the back.

Elizabeth quickly noticed that while she was not strikingly beautiful in the classic sense, she did carry certain vitality and underlying sexual appeal that would attract most men. "Hello, it's so nice to finally meet you. John has told me so much about you, now come and sit down. I'm sorry that I won't be able to sit with you all night, but you will have John all to yourselves. One of the waitresses rang in sick, so I'll have to help out on the tables."

Sitting down at their table, Elizabeth thought, *"I think I will like these two."*

Spread out over the next two hours, they had a fabulous Greek meal, which was all very new to Elizabeth. The meal was washed down with copious amounts of Greek and Australian wine, which put them in a very happy and relaxed mood.

In between rushing about looking after the other diners, Jean managed to spend a part of the evening with them, as well as serving their meal.

They stayed behind after the restaurant closed, drinking Greek port with coffee and catching up on their respective lives. Sev was keenly interested in John's plans to develop the condiment business.

Later, Sev drove Elizabeth home, and during the usual sexual battle in the back seat he managed to get her skirt up and his hand between her legs; but when he tugged at her pants, she stiffened and sat up.

"No way Sev, I have told you before."

Frustrated, he conceded defeat and headed for home.

Crossing over the bridge, with the Harbour below, he was still feeling a little miffed at Elizabeth for resisting his sexual advances yet again. On impulse, he turned left onto the Cahill Expressway and headed for Kings Cross to see if could find Gloria to help relieve his frustration.

She was there at the "Office," and made herself available.

Sev attacked her sexually, with urgency bordering on violence that Gloria had not seen before.

"Hey, slow up a bit" she said, "you're hurting me."

"Just shut up," he snapped, "You are mine and always will be."

After he had finished, and his sexual urge subsided, he again became soft and tender towards her. As many times before, he was overwhelmed by his feeling for her. "Gloria I'm sorry if I got a bit carried away then, I wouldn't hurt you for anything."

Gloria suddenly realised that her boy had grown up and changed with it; or was he always like this but she had never seen it?

Sev arrived home in the early hours of the morning, and as he put his key in the front door, he felt that something was wrong.

Opening the door, he found the house was in darkness, which was strange, as Nanna always left a light on for him. Waiting for her welcoming call of, "Is that you, Sev?" he became aware of a strange odour, and a silence that was uncomfortably strange to him.

Suddenly a fear overtook him, and he bounded down the passage to Nana's room.

He found her lying across her bed as if she had tried to get in but never quite got there. He instinctively knew that she was dead.

Then he could not help but notice a sickly smell that came from her vomit across the bed. At that moment, he also became aware of another mess where her bladder had let go.

With his head swimming, he ran to the phone, only to throw up in reaction to the scene. "*Christ, what a mess*", he thought.

The ambulance arrived a short time later.

The officers just said, "We'll get her to hospital."

Sev sat up in the front parlour for what was left of the night feeling devastated. He had lost the one person who had really loved him; and he, in his own way, loved in return. For the first time since his Dad had given him that belting years ago, he cried and with tears streaming down his face, he realised with a sinking feeling, that he was on his own again. But he was not thinking of himself, but of his adopted mother.

Next morning, he thought, *"I had better clean up the house, there's no one else to do it."* His foray into housework, up to his elbows in the left-over dishes, cleaning the bathrooms and using the mop and bucket to clean up the bedroom, was not something he enjoyed.

His final job was to vacuum the rest of house. His one good thought was, *"I think Nanna would be really pleased with me if she was here."*

For a moment he sat at the kitchen table, and even surprised himself with his emotion, as tears again started to roll down his cheeks.

"Enough of that", he sobbed out loud, "I must now get on with my life."

Another thought suddenly came to him, *"Who gets this house?"*

As far as he knew, there was no family or living relatives to advise of her death.

Feeling the need to put some food in his stomach, Sev drove over to Glebe Point Road where he knew several restaurants that served breakfast. Over an omelette with toast and plenty of black coffee, he started to formulate a plan. My first job is to decide for her funeral.

She would like something nice with lots of flowers, and I will see that she gets it.

The only people Sev knew, who may go to her funeral, were the elderly couple from next door who occasionally came in for a cup of tea and John and Jean Naxos.

"Next I must start going through her things to see if she left any sort of a will. He recalled seeing envelopes in her mail from the Commonwealth Bank at Glebe so that would be a starting point.

Back at the house, it was a strange feeling for Sev, walking through the rooms without Nanna there. He felt that the house had a strange sort of emptiness, and it felt cold.

Then thinking of Nanna, his surrogate mother, and all those happy times they spent together, his feeling changed. Her spirit and natural happiness is in this house, I can feel it and I should be positive and embrace it.

Where he had intended to start sorting through her personal things, he decided, no, there's plenty of time for that.

With a comfort he had not felt before, Sev walked up the familiar staircase to his room, where he had spent so much time in recent years. He had an eerie feeling that Nanna was still there watching over him and offering him her encouragement and counsel. He remembered her saying to him, "Go for it Sev, do the best you can. Take life's challenges head-on and you will win. You don't have to end up a lonely old person like me."

He fell into his unmade bed and was reminded again that Nanna always came up and made his bed.

With clearer thoughts, he soon fell into a deep sleep.

The funeral was a quiet sombre affair, with only a handful of people to witness the passing of an unrecognised, but remarkable person, whose great asset was her love for other people. Yet, at the end, there were few there to witness her final departure.

The next day, Sev started to go through Nana's drawers.

He was not surprised to find that all her personal papers were neatly filed, obviously to ensure that she didn't leave any problems behind should anything happen to her. That was her nature.

Her Commonwealth Bank statements were all together with the last one showing a balance of nearly thirty thousand pounds, which she must have painstakingly saved from her meagre pension. In the same folder Sev found a small buff coloured manila envelope.

With shaking hands Sev opened it to find what appeared to be a relatively new document, headed:

The Last Will and Testament of
Gladys Ann McMurray.

I Gladys McMurray being of sound mind, leave all my assets to my friend and adopted son in name, Sev Cockini. This includes cash held in the Commonwealth Bank of Australia Glebe, and my house at 85 Ferry Road, Glebe, with all furniture and fittings. To Sev I say, "Thank you for the affection, love and comfort you gave me when I had no one.'

Signed
Gladys McMurray

"Wow! The old bugger." he thought affectionately. "The house must be worth fifty thousand, plus the thirty in the bank, gives me enough to set myself up nicely."

Going through the rest of her drawers, he found some old photos of a stern looking man holding the hand of a young boy. Written on the back was, Bill and Trevor 1946.

Sev thought, "Now who could that be? She never ever said she was married or had any family. In fact, she always led me to believe that she was a single lady without any family. What ghosts are there in her past?"

Next Sev tackled her wardrobe, putting all her clothes in a heap on the floor, thinking that he would send them off to The Salvation Army. When it was all empty, he found a large red gift box with a "Prouds the Jeweller" gold label on the lid. "Hello, another surprise." he thought

Inside was a bundle of yellowing papers tied together with a piece of pink ribbon.

Spreading them out on the dresser, he found her birth certificate, a birth certificate of a W E McMurray, and a marriage certificate between William Edward McMurray and Gladys Ann Beaumont. There was also another, not so old, a birth certificate for a Trevor John McMurray.

"So, there was family. I wonder what happened?"

The answer was found in a death certificate pinned to an old newspaper clipping.

"MAN AND SON DROWNED IN BOATING TRAGEDY."

Early this morning the bodies of a man and his son were recovered from the waters of Sydney Harbour off Glebe Point. It is believed their small fishing dingy overturned in gusty conditions late last night. Mrs. McMurray of Ferry Road Glebe was too distraught to be interviewed and is being comforted by officers from The Salvation Army.

It is believed that there are no other living relatives.

Out aloud Sev thought, "Well this explains a lot, but why didn't she tell me. Perhaps the memories were too painful for her to talk about. I wonder if I should contact the Salvo's to see if they have any records of other relatives. Hold on, if they found some long-lost relatives, they may claim a share of the cash. No Way! Forget that idea."

Over the next weeks Sev visited the bank and claimed the money, which he withdrew and put into a new account in his own name. His next step was getting the house title transferred into his name. When this was completed, he listed it for sale with the local L J Hooker Real Estate office. An offer came up quickly, and although Sev felt it was below its value, he was happy to grab the cash and run.

Cashed up, he then purchased an apartment in an up-market area of the Eastern Suburbs, which he felt was more appropriate for a solicitor, and about to be, successful businessman.

The apartment was in Wentworth Road, Vaucluse with sweeping views of the Harbour. On the third floor of the unit block, and quite small with only two bedrooms, it did have a spacious living area and a usable balcony. Sitting on his balcony watching the boats darting across Sydney Harbour did a lot to repair the inner anger carried over from his childhood.

He never fraternised with the neighbours; and other than an occasional polite "Hello", kept to himself.

Sev's assumption was that in the future, it could become a very valuable property. About this he was correct.

Another aspect was that it was discreet, separated from nosy neighbours, and above all, the building was secure.

Partly to get the image right, and that he was genuinely fond of the girl, or more accurately, sexually attracted to her, he proposed to Elizabeth. She readily accepted, but he had a battle with her parents to get their approval. Her father disliked Sev and felt sure that he was not as he portrayed himself.

It was rare for marriages to take place without the approval of the girl's father, and without his consent it would be unlikely that the marriage would go ahead. Ronald Spalding or Doctor Ronald as he preferred to be called dragged Sev unmercifully through his and his family background. "Checking the bloodlines", thought Sev.

However, Sev was ready for him this time, and after some time massaging the doctor's vanity, he lied magnificently, portraying his parents as Greek aristocrats who were back in Greece attending to family business.

"What sort of business are they in", asked Doctor Ronald.

"They are mainly into exporting food products; their main business is with condiments like herbs and spices." Sev replied. "Our friends John and Jean Naxos, the restaurateurs, import products for distribution here, and I will be working with them as a silent partner helping to expand their business."

All through this he was thinking, "Hell, I hope Elizabeth does not turn out like her father."

There was enough truth in Sev's story to make it all sound impressive, at least enough to obtain the doctor's approval for the marriage. He had no serious grounds for objecting but underneath, he felt that Sev was just a bit too slick.

Later, voicing his concern to Beryl, he received a mild rebuff from her, saying, "Ron, you are a born worrier. I think he is quite nice, and so handsome"

"Looks don't matter, it's what is underneath that matters."

They were married six months later in the Presbyterian Church in Pymble.

Sev, being very much an atheist, had to swallow hard and control himself, listening to all the garbage about, "Before God and that God's wrath would be on him if he was not behaving according to God's Scripture."

He was not very comfortable with the whole service and the following reception, particularly that out of all the eighty-five guests, he was represented and supported only by John and Jean Naxos.

He had one moment of sheer terror when he came out of the church with his new bride.

Standing under a tree on the fringe of the crowd, he saw Gloria. From a quick glance, he noticed that she was well-dressed, and in fact, looked very smart.

"What the fuck is she doing here?" he thought.

She raised one eyebrow in a familiar fashion, as if to say, "Well how's at my little boy now, but what about me?" She then nodded and walked away.

He was brought back to reality by someone calling, "Come on Sev give us a smile for the camera."

For the rest of the day, he played the role of the happy groom, but underneath he was thinking, "What the hell have I let myself in for?"

John Naxos, as best man, made a light but emotional speech at the reception, touching lightly on Sev's school and university days and his determination to do well with his studies. Sev's speech was short and to the point, only thanking those he had to thank.

They were to have a short honeymoon at the seaside village of Terrigal on the Central Coast.

After marvelling at her beauty for so long, and all his sexual battles, he was excited and eagerly anticipating their first night in bed. She was indeed a virgin and the whole experience of their first sex act together was a disaster, which left Sev frustrated and disappointed. The following nights improved, but to his shame Sev kept comparing her to Gloria. By the end of the honeymoon, Sev was beginning to think that his new wife was frigid.

Philosophically he thought, "I must gently train her to feel like I do about sex."

After a few days, he was anxious to return home, to the challenge of becoming a successful lawyer and the beginning of a new life.

NEW DIRECTIONS

CHAPTER FOUR

John and Jean shared a lot of grief and soul searching before committing to sell the restaurant and the accompanying freehold property. There were also some feelings of guilt thinking of all those years John's parents had worked so long and so hard with very little return.

In the end, John rationalised the decision by accepting that no matter how long they stopped there, or how hard they worked there were never going to be any riches at the end. The final encouragement was seeing Sev looking so prosperous and offering to put in cash to match John's goodwill value of the expanding Condiment business. This, with a small amount of borrowing would be enough to find larger more suitable premises and set up the new business.

With the restaurant sold, Jean had a chance to relax and start to catch up with her old friends from school and university. One of her best friends and confidante was Ann Croft. They were friends since secondary school days and later went through university together. Jean had not realised how much she missed her friends, just talking girls talk and having fun. She met Ann in the city and they did a tour of the stores, looking at all the clothes they could not afford. After trying on some outrageously expensive dresses, they bought a packet of sandwiches each and headed for Hyde Park.

Sitting on a bench with the sun filtering through the trees Jean told Ann of her life since university days. Talking of these times, good and bad, made her stop and think of how hard she had worked over the years, waiting on tables and helping in the kitchen seemed like a hell of a hard life.

No meeting would be complete without Jean's stories about the mystery man, Sev Cockini.

Ann said, "I know him. I met him at a party once, and he was the one that had drugs available for whoever wanted them. He was a shady operator. Our entire crowd knew about Sev Cockini. Apparently, he would find girls for the boys as well."

Jean was aghast. "You're joking"!

"No way" said Ann. "Anybody on the party scene knew about Sev Cockini. The story was that that was how he financed his way through uni after his parents left him and returned to Greece.

Later, Jean was very troubled by this and thought she should discuss it with John, but rightly or wrongly, she decided to keep it to herself. Jean and Ann made a commitment to continue to keep in touch and have their special girl's day out.

A lot happened over the next six months, the restaurant was sold, John and Jean purchased a nice bungalow in Croydon, and Sev officially became a partner in the new company trading as "Naxos Condiments."

The plan was to kick off expanding the core herb and spice business followed by establishing a market for kitchen utensils and catering equipment sourced from overseas, particularly Italy. Supplying restaurants with equipment and bulk foodstuffs was also high on their agenda.

John leased a small brick warehouse conveniently located in Kent Road Mascot, (not far from the airport) which was central for customers and transport.

As well as a large open area which could be partitioned off for storage and functional areas, there was a mezzanine floor with accommodation. It boasted two bedrooms, a living area and a passable kitchen. This was to prove very handy in times to come.

Opening day came and it was a good reason for a party. Business wise, it was important to start with a big splash, mindful that most of the existing customers started with John's father.

Clients were invited as well as all the Greek restaurant owners and anybody with whom they had had previous contact. Elizabeth even helped with the invitations and spent hours going through the phone book listings of restaurants. Jean was a natural to arrange the food menu, taking care to get a good mixture of Greek, Italian and local Aussie.

Sev was the one to arrange the drinks, taking care to cater for all tastes. Imported wines and spirits were very much part of the menu. The last thing they wanted was to turn the show into an Aussie beer party. Hiring a Greek band and decorating the warehouse was John's job. He was in a near state of panic as how much this party was going to cost.

Sev kept reminding him that it was all good advertising and tax deductible.

They were all excited and surprised at how many turned up for the party. Jean was at the door recording and welcoming their guests and giving everybody a name badge. Elizabeth was backing up, by pinning a small flower on the ladies' dresses.

John and Sev greeted the guests and told of the new range of condiments and utensils they were offering.

John made an excellent welcoming speech, referring to their heritage and restaurant background. He paid tribute to his parents and his Dad's foresight in establishing, in a small way the Herb and Spice business.

Recognising that Sev might come over as a bit brash, he suggested that one speech was enough.

After his speech, John stood with Jean holding her hand, and looking at her he felt a wave of emotion. How lovely she was, this mother of my child. "How lucky am I?" he thought. "I hope I don't let her down?" He felt so proud of her as she continued to mingle in the crowd; everyone wanted to talk to her.

John knew a lot of the people, whereas Sev knew very few, but with his natural confidence, he worked his way around the crowd like a veteran politician.

Looking across the crowd, he saw a couple standing alone next to the sample table. The woman with her back to him was shapely and dressed like a model out of the Vogue magazine. Her partner, appropriately dressed in a dark blue suit and with swept back greying hair, looked a business type very much.

"Here we go again." thought Sev.

"Hello, my name is Sev Cockini, welcome to our show."

The man acknowledged and received Sev's offered handshake. The lady turned around and Sev nearly fell over!

"Sev it's nice to see you again," she teased. "Meet my friend Frank Bennett."

"Hello Gloria, what brings you here?"

"Frank is in the restaurant business, in fact he owns, how many was it Frank?"

"Eight not counting the night club."

"Well we must get together soon; there must be areas where we can do some business." said Sev.

"We have already done some business", Frank replied, "but you may not have been aware of that."

Sev's stomach started to churn, thinking of where his pep-pill supply came from.

Frank was a little amused by Sev's apparent discomfort and said, "Sev, here's my business card. Give me a ring next week."

"Sure," he stammered as he watched him walk away with Gloria holding his arm.

"Christ, what was that about", he thought. *'What's the deal with Gloria? She looks like a million quid, not the Gloria he knew."*

At that time, the band started up with John announcing that the special floor show was about to begin. From behind the screen came a group of girls in national costume to entertain them with traditional Greek dancing.

Sev thought, "What I want more than anything now is another drink." He quickly downed a full scotch and refilled his glass.

After the second one, while everyone was watching the dancers, he reached for another top-up. "I feel better now", he thought to himself. Over to his left he noticed Jean, "My god she looks good."

It was only a month since the baby, Robert John, had arrived and she had quickly regained her figure. Rather than showing the strains of parenthood, she was radiant.

Her figure was full and rounded rather than heavy, and there was a strong sexual aura about her. He wandered over to her and said, "Hi Jean, how's it going?"

Before she could answer he continued, "You look absolutely wonderful, and sexy too. Motherhood is good to you."

Jean quickly replied, "Thanks for the compliment but forget the sexy bit."

"How could I, I have felt it for years."

"Sev, you are drunk, and I suggest that you do not have any more. This is a business function, in case you have forgotten. It is best that we finish and forget this conversation, and you go and look after Elizabeth."

Sev took the rebuff and moved off to mingle with the guests.

As the night progressed John was more than happy with the response. The feeling he was picking up was that, apart from the ongoing condiment market, there was a big opportunity with small kitchen utensils and restaurant equipment.

After all the guests had left, John, Jean, Sev and Elizabeth cleaned up then stopped for a celebratory drink before heading for home. John was in high spirits and was already talking of plans they must now make to expand the business. The girls shared his enthusiasm, but Sev appeared more subdued.

What with seeing that Frank bloke with Gloria, then getting a stern message from Jean, he was in a foul mood when he arrived home.

Elizabeth, noticing this said, "What's the matter with you? I thought you might be happy for a change after a successful night, I think you've have had too much to drink."

"Just shut up, I'm going to bed."

"Well keep over on your own side" replied Elizabeth.

Elizabeth then thought of other times when he frightened her.

About an hour later he got out of bed and dressed in a tracksuit. Elizabeth woke and mumbled, "Where are you going?"

"I am restless and am going for a drive." he replied and walked out.

Even to himself, he could not reason why the hell he had got out of his wife's bed and was now driving across the city with a tracksuit over his pyjamas. The one thing he knew was that he had to see Gloria.

She would explain why she was there with this Frank Bennett and settle his inner turmoil, or was it jealousy?

Surprisingly, he found her sitting at the front reception desk looking well-groomed and smartly dressed. He was a bit stunned at first, thinking, "Hell she looks good."

"Hello Sir", she mocked, "Do you have a booking?"

"Gloria don't play the smart arse with me, what's going on?"

"Not that it's any of your business, but Frank Bennett owns the business and he has made me the head girl. You sent him an invitation to your opening and he asked me to go with him. It always looks better for a man like him to have a partner."

Sev interrupted, "Where's his wife?"

Gloria replied, 'Look Sev, I don't know, nor do I care. The rumour is that she died some years ago."

"Bullshit to all that, let's go out the back", he said, taking her by the hand.

"Sev, if he walks in here and finds you with me you'll be dead meat." Calling for another girl to take over the desk she reluctantly followed.

He quickly, almost forcibly, took off her clothes and sat her on the bed while he removed his tracksuit. Much to her surprise he then gently held her in his arms for a moment and whispered, "Gloria, stay with me." She had never seen him so emotional before.

Then he kissed her passionately, while softly touching her breasts, which aroused her more than she had felt for some time.

When the moment came for them to be totally together, they started moving slowly, building up to an urgency that neither could deny. Somehow, she felt special in his arms, and that he really wanted her. They were together.

They climaxed together, a feeling which Gloria had not achieved for some time.

He dressed slowly, and after softly kissing her said, "Gloria it is you and me. Remember you are, and always will be, my girl. Don't get involved with that Bennett fellow; soon I will be in a position to look after you."

He then quickly left, leaving Gloria sitting on the bed feeling very confused. One thing she admitted to herself was that she never wanted to lose him.

Driving home he felt good. *"Why is it that I feel so strongly about Gloria, why is it that I keep returning to her?"* A little guilt crept into his mind about Elizabeth, but he quickly dismissed it. Arriving back home he quickly took a shower, climbed into bed, and was soon asleep.

Elizabeth was awake and wondering what that was all about.

The following week with some apprehensiveness he rang Frank Bennett.

A girl answered with, "Hello, Bennett Hospitality, how can I help you?'

A little taken aback, Sev replied, "Thank you. My name is Sev Cockini, Could I speak to Mr. Bennett please?"

"Sorry, how do you spell that please?"

A little miffed, Sev snapped, "S-e-v C-o-c-k-i-n-i, I am a solicitor and he is expecting my call."

"Thank you, Mr. Cockini, I will see if Mr. Bennett is available."

"Shit,' thought Sev, "do I have to go through all this?"

Then the voice was back, "Mr. Bennett has someone with him. Would you give me your number and he will call you back shortly?'

Okay, he thought. 'I think he is playing games.'

"My office number is 2223 3609, I will be there for another hour, and then I'm due in court, Thank you."

An hour and ten minutes later the phone rang, and as pre-arranged, Elizabeth answered and crooned, "Good morning, Cockini Legal."

"Frank Bennett, Elizabeth, tell Sev to cut the bullshit and get his arse over to the phone."

Sev picked up the phone and said, "Hello Frank, thanks for ringing back. How are you? I hope you enjoyed our evening last week, and thanks for coming and supporting our new venture."

Frank replied, "Yes, I did enjoy the evening. I found your enterprise very interesting, I'm sure that with John Naxos at the helm the business will do well. I think you have hit a gap in the market."

'Thank you," replied Sev. "How about we get together for lunch one day this week, which day would suit you?"

The reply was clipped, "Friday, at my Oxford Street restaurant, The Oasis. By the way, I happen to know that you finished with your employers and have not even opened your office yet. Say another hello to Elizabeth for me and I'll see you at 12.30 on Friday." Without further words he hung up.

"Christ again", thought Sev. "What am I in for with this guy?"

Sev spent the rest of the week finalising a lease for an office in the city. The premises were in an up-market building in Elizabeth Street overlooking Hyde Park and tenanted mostly by other solicitors. Image was important to Sev. Furnishing was easy as the previous tenant had left behind a lot of furniture and fittings.

His biggest outlay was the reception area where he needed a new desk console, office chairs and typewriters. After new carpet, a couple of pictures for the wall, two couches for waiting clients completed the office. Next Sev hired a mature woman, Vivian Edwards, as his legal secretary to handle the front desk.

"Cockini Legal Service" was open for business.

In later years Vivien became his confidant and most loyal employee.

Friday came around, and dressed in his best suit, Sev left for his lunch meeting with Frank Bennett. He decided to walk taking the short cut across Hyde Park.

Lost in his thoughts he was wondering, "*What am I actually doing with this bloke anyway. Was it for the Naxos business, Cockini Legal, or something more personal?*"

The restaurant was more, "silver service" than he was used to, with an expensive decor, starched white tablecloths, polished silver and uniformed waitresses.

The maitre'd was quickly there to meet him, "Good afternoon sir, you must be Mr. Cockini. Mr. Bennett is expecting you, please come this way"

She led him to a large table towards the rear of the restaurant where

Frank was sitting. He rose offering his hand. Sev was surprised how tall he was and noticing that he was certainly younger than he originally thought.

"Hello Sev, here take a seat. Would you like a drink, Scotch perhaps?"

"No thanks Frank, I try not to drink in the middle of the day, perhaps a glass of wine with my lunch. I would like a glass of water to start though, I have just walked from Elizabeth Street across the park to Oxford Street."

Frank nodded to a hovering waitress and she quickly brought him a large crystal jug of iced water. He was surprised at how affable Frank was compared to the reception he had received on the phone.

"Well Sev, how are you going? Have you opened your office yet? Gloria has been saying that I must look after you.

Is there anything I can help you with? I have many contacts in Sydney so don't hesitate to ask."

As the waitress brought the menu Sev thought, "*This bloke would not tolerate any bullshit.*"

He also quickly decided that Frank Bennett would wear any hat that suited him at the time.

"I'm looking for business, both legal and for our restaurant supply business, anything you could direct our way would be appreciated."

"No problem" replied Frank. "We need to look at our condiment supply for the restaurants, and to replace some of our kitchen utensils. Can you handle the scale we operate on?"

Without even knowing how they stood, Sev said, "Sure, just give us the business, and we will make sure you get looked after."

"Well ask John to contact our supply manager and they can work out what is required."

He then wrote a name and phone number on the back of one of his cards and said, "Okay, ask John to give this fellow a ring. Enough of business let us order our meal. "I'm having the grilled whiting with a side salad, I recommend it if you like fish. I know it's fresh and great for a light meal in the middle of the day."

"You've convinced me, I'll have the whiting as well."

"Good, I will order one of our best white wines to go with it."

The rest of the meal went pleasantly with social talk and Sev was surprised to hear that Frank's parents, who had died Several years ago, were also Greek. He had lost his wife in tragic circumstances two years ago, but he did not elaborate any further. He travelled overseas regularly, and never missed an opportunity to visit his native country.

Over coffee Sev was feeling relaxed and comfortable, when suddenly Frank said, "What about that other business you were in, Sev?"

Sev suspected that this was coming, so he was partly ready for it and replied, "Yes, I did a little dealing to earn enough money to get me through university. Why do you ask?"

"The stuff you were peddling came through my people, did you know that?"

"No, I didn't," Sev replied.

"Are you interested in continuing with some distribution?"

"No way, now that I'm out of university I've lost my contacts anyway. If I ever went back into the business, it would be further up the supply chain. Besides I wouldn't risk jeopardising my legal practice."

He was not going to reveal to Frank that he did have a long-term plan that may involve Naxos.

Frank replied, "Well that's interesting. Let's keep in touch; we may be able to work together in the future. There is some serious money to be made. In the meantime, make sure that John looks after my restaurants, and when the opportunity arises, I will put a bit of legal work your way."

With their coffees finished, Sev felt it was time to go, so he stood up and said, "That's great Frank, I appreciate your help, and thanks for the lunch. Your restaurant is very good, and the food was excellent. Certainly, better than the Naxos."

"Thank you Sev. I've been to the Naxos many times and always found the food and service to be very good. That girl, Jean, was it? She was certainly an asset to the place. Is she John's wife now? I never met her at the function."

With a chuckle Sev said, "Yes she is. Between you and me Frank, I wish I had married her myself."

Smiling at Sev's confession, Frank said, "Too close to home for you now Sev, but there are still plenty of good-looking girls out there. By the way, how is Elizabeth? Is she looking after you all right? You had better not let her find out about Gloria."

Sev was sure that this was said to embarrass him and keep him on the back foot, so he chose to ignore the comment.

Walking to the door they said their goodbyes, with Frank assuring Sev that he would be in touch and they would have lunch again soon.

The next months were hectic. Sev was starting to get established in his practice, with quite a few of his client referrals coming from Frank Bennett. Some for simple conveyancing, others were criminal cases which were becoming a significant part of his practice. He was quickly building up a reputation as a top criminal lawyer. Soon he hired two more secretaries to assist in his now expanding practice.

Sev had lunch with Frank about once a month, and came to enjoy his company, however he was always aware that, given the opportunity, Frank would manipulate him to the point where he controlled him. He made a point of taking in as much work as he could that was not referred by Frank Bennett. Up to this time, he had never again mentioned anything about Sev's early involvement in drugs.

His relationship with Elizabeth was running along smoothly, albeit without much excitement. She didn't harass him about the hours he was away from home and appeared quite content to spend a lot of time with her parents.

Sometimes, after a scotch or two, he would think deeply, and admit that apart from her beauty, it was her unavailability that had attracted him to her. Perhaps it was just feeding his ego. There was a quiet coldness about her that stopped him from getting too close.

Why did he continue to feel such a pull to Gloria? Was it because she was the only one that really knew him, warts and all? Their affinity with each other was also because they both were deserted as children and left to fend for themselves. Maybe she was the replacement parent, or for Nanna. He needed her; she listened to him and made him feel good about himself.

With his practice now going well, and money in the bank Sev put a deposit on a small unit in Rosebery. While it was not over luxurious or large, the single bedroom with a small lounge/dining area was more than adequate for a single person. A coat of paint and new carpet and it was quite a comfortable unit. Sev was uncharacteristically excited about this project, thinking that he would let Gloria choose her own furniture.

Then on one of his regular visits to Gloria's "office," he took her off the front desk, sat her down in the back room and looked her straight in the eye.

Since working in a secretarial role rather than looking after "client's needs" Gloria had blossomed, her complexion had cleared, her hair was neatly cut, and her dress and grooming was impeccable.

She thought, "Hello, Sev's a bit randy tonight."

To her surprise Sev said, "Now Gloria, I don't want any argument on what I'm about to tell you. I have purchased a unit for you over in Rosebery and I want you to leave here and move in.' Gloria was shocked, "But Sev, what will I do? I need a job to live."

"Don't worry, until you get on your feet and find a real job, I'll look after you. So just resign, but don't tell Frank Bennett where you're going, or my involvement. Here's five hundred dollars to help you get settled. We can have a look at the unit together tomorrow, and then you can go out and buy what furniture you need. Just let me know where you buy it, and I'll go and pay the account.'

At Sev's bidding, Gloria resigned; left her "office" and moved into the unit. New curtains, mats for the floor plus a smattering of femininity gave the unit a totally new look. With minimum expense Gloria managed to transform what was a cold characterless place into a comfortable warm home.

Sev of course became a regular visitor.

Gloria was so thankful to be out of the "Business" and have a friend, even if he was only part time. They had regular meals together and acted out a husband and wife routine. Sev poured out all his problems to her, and she loved listening to him. With help from Sev, Gloria found an office job with a local Real Estate agency and happily settled into her new life.

Elizabeth believed that Sev was always working, taking on extra briefs to establish his practice. Secretly she did not care too much and was happy for him to be away. She was becoming increasingly tired of his moodiness around the house. His sexual demands on her had slowed up, for which she was thankful. All she asked for was for him to let her know if he would be home for dinner.

Despite trying to avoid it, half way through the following year, much to her initial horror, Elizabeth found that she was pregnant. She was not ready for that sort of commitment and wondered how she could possibly cope with a child, knowing that Sev was not the homely, family type. Facing up to the fact that she had to tell him, she picked a night when he said he could be home early and prepared a special dinner. Setting the table with the best linen and cutlery, even putting candles on the table, she set the scene for the announcement.

Elizabeth prepared his favourite meal, rack of lamb with roast vegetables, and extravagantly purchased two bottles of very good red wine to compliment it. She was just about ready. Next, she showered, carefully applied her makeup and dressed in one of her best and most provocative dresses. Elizabeth then felt ready and more confident for the ordeal in front of her.

Feeling ridiculously nervous, when he walked in the front door, she gave him a lingering kiss, and sat him down with a scotch. Noticing the table all set up and the aroma of roast lamb wafting from the kitchen Sev sensed that there was something going on.

He quipped, "Hey you look great. What's the occasion, have I missed a birthday or something?"

"Sev, you just relax and finish your scotch then we can eat."

Halfway through the meal Sev took another gulp of his wine and said," Elizabeth this is great, why don't you do this every night. It might even get me home from work early."

Elizabeth replied, "Is it that good?"

After sweets, apple pie and cream, Elizabeth poured coffee for them both and as they sat in the dimmed lights she thought, *"Well this it, I can't delay any longer now.'*

Making it easier for her to get started Sev said, "Can you now tell me what's on your mind?"

Without any preamble Elizabeth blurted out, "You're going to be a father."

Sev sat without a murmur for what seemed an eternity, then suddenly he stood up and with an enraged look on his face, ripped the tablecloth off the table and all the dishes with it.

Glasses and plates crashed to the floor, coffee went all over Elizabeth and the carpet. The candles went flying across the room, and Sev just stood there amongst the mess staring at her.

Then he erupted, "You stupid fucking bitch, how did you let that happen, don't you realise what this means?"

Elizabeth was mortified by his outburst but quickly recovered.

"Are you forgetting something, I didn't do it on my own, it takes two you know."

Composing himself Sev asked, "How far are you?"

"Nearly four months."

"Well, why didn't you tell me before this?"

"I didn't know that's why. I found out for sure yesterday."

Holding his head in his hands, totally distraught, Sev roared, "This is a bloody disaster. I have too many work commitments to worry about a baby for God's sake. How will we cope with a baby in this poky little flat on the third floor and no lift? Have you thought how you will get a pram up and down all those stairs?"

"We will have to rent a house somewhere." she retorted.

"And how can I afford to pay for two houses, and a baby", he screamed. You will just have to go home to your mother."

"Great idea Sev! I can just imagine you getting on with dad every night."

"Well you go, and I'll stop here."

"No way. You have a responsibility for the baby the same as I have."

Sev softened, and just sat there amongst the mess not saying any more. He stood up, stepped over to the buffet, picked up a bottle of scotch and poured himself a large drink.

Elizabeth got up and said, "Well that's not going to change anything or make it go away, and we are not going to resolve anything tonight. Help me clean up this mess and we can go to bed."

Sev quietly commanded, "You clean it up and go to bed, I'll be in soon."

Later in bed as Elizabeth lay quietly crying Sev put his arm around her and said. "I'm sorry for that outburst; but it's just that I am not ready for parenthood, I have too much to do and achieve. I am not going to let us end up like my parents." He tried to say. "I love you,' but those special words would not come out.

She sensed that Sev was crying as well. She had never seen him emotional and didn't think he was capable of those feelings.

What scars lay there from those early years when his parents abandoned him?

Elizabeth put her arms around him and said, "We can work it out. We have five months before the baby is due, we can do it together. But for now, we need to get some sleep."

When Elizabeth awoke early the next morning, she found that Sev had already left for the office. She got up and rang the office to say "Hello" and 'are you all right?"

There was no answer to his phone. That night he did not get home until after eleven, so there was no further communication.

In another part of town, Gloria lay in bed thinking of how distraught Sev had been as he poured out to her all his problems and concern about becoming a father.

She had comforted and listened to him, like a loving parent. Gloria knew and understood him.

She was like a "mother confessor" and Sev always felt cleansed when he left.

What concerned Gloria was how this new development would affect their relationship. She was very happy with her life now, even if Sev was only a part-time husband. All the other girls and sales people at the office believed that Sev was her husband. Another spin-off for Sev was that he picked up quite a lot of conveyancing work from the office.

About a month before Elizabeth was due to have her baby, Gloria found that she too was pregnant.

"This will test the relationship." she thought.

In contrast to the antics with Elizabeth, as soon Gloria was sure she rang Sev at his office.

"Hello Sev, are you free to talk for a moment?"

"For you my dear, any time. Why do you call in the middle of the day?"

Not one to hold back Gloria said, "Well I hope you are sitting down, because this will rock you."

"Come on Gloria spit it out, what have you done, burnt the house down?"

"No, worse than that, I'm pregnant."

"Christ Gloria, why didn't you tell me before, that's wonderful. Are you pleased?"

"I am actually, I was only a little worried about how you would feel."

"Well you don't have to be, I am thrilled. But I must go now; I'll call around as soon as I can get away from the office."

Gloria put the phone down, and then just sat there and cried as she had never cried before, with total happiness.

On his way home to Vaucluse Sev called in to see Gloria. When he opened the front door, she was standing in the hall with the biggest smile he had ever seen.

After a moment of just staring at one another without saying anything, she coyly said, "Well daddy, are you coming in, or are you going to stand there all night?'
"

Sev took her in his arms and just hugged her. They both had tears in their eyes, and at that moment, Sev felt closer to Gloria than anyone in his entire life.

Over a celebratory drink they discussed their future, and Sev promised that he would always look after her, and she need not be concerned about the future.

Because of his commitments to Elizabeth they would have to keep going with the current arrangement.

Sev explained that, morally, he could never just desert Elizabeth in her time of need.

Arriving home at the Vaucluse apartment to a very pregnant Elizabeth, Sev had a moment of guilt, which he quickly brushed aside. She was in the kitchen and ready to serve their meal. "Hello darling, I thought you were going to be early tonight, I rang the office and they told me you had left early."

"Yes, I did, but I had to call and see a client on the way home. I was lucky to get away from him as early as I did."

"Sev please let me know where you are from now on, as our baby is due any time."

'Do you think it would be better if you stayed with your mother for the last two weeks?"

"No Sev, I do not want to stay with Mum. We are going to go through this together. Maybe after I come home from hospital, I could stop with Mum for the first couple of weeks. Anyway, what are we going to do about the unit?"

"Well, I looked at a couple of units to rent this morning, and there's a nice ground floor one over at Woollahra, perhaps you might like to have a look at it tomorrow.

If its" Okay, I can move in while you're in hospital. At least we won't have any trouble to rent this one, which will mostly pay for the rent in the other unit."

The following week Sev was late home as usual, only to find a neighbour waiting at the door to tell him that his wife had gone to hospital. He said that they had tried to ring him at his office but there was no one answering the phone.

After thanking the neighbour, he got back in the car and drove over to the Crown Street Women's Hospital.

Rushing into the foyer, he asked the receptionist where his wife, Mrs. Cockini, was. After studying her list, she said, "Second floor sir, but you had better hurry."

Rather than wait for the lift, Sev bounded up the stairs with a terrible feeling that something was wrong.

At the nurses' desk he bellowed, "My name is Cockini, where is my wife?"

"Congratulations Mr. Cockini you have of a healthy six-pound boy."

"And how is my wife, can I see her?"

The nurse replied, "I am sorry sir, but your wife had a really difficult birth, and she is very ill. She is sedated now, perhaps you can see her for a while later on. If you wish the nurse could take you to see your son, what are you going to call him?"

Without even considering the issue, remembering some vague conversation he had with Elizabeth he said, "The boy's name shall be Paul."

Sev was in a state of total confusion with a roller coaster wave of emotions. His understanding of childbirth was minimal at the best, and he had no idea what was going on.

The nurse handed him this tiny bundle all wrapped up in a cotton blanket. Sev gingerly held the bundle for a moment before handing it back to where it belonged. It was all too much for him to absorb; all he wanted was to get out of the place as quickly as possible.

As he was about to retreat, a doctor came over to him and asked, "Are you Mr. Cockini?"

"Yes, I am", he stuttered.

"Well come over here and sit down, I need to talk to you about your wife. She has had a massive haemorrhage and we are very concerned about her."

All Sev could say was, "Well, can you fix it?"

"Well it's not as simple as that; but we are doing everything we can to help her."

At that moment Elizabeth's parents arrived and "Doctor Ronald" was ready to take over, much to Sev's relief.

Ignoring Sev he spoke to the resident doctor in a quiet tone, making sure nobody else could hear him. He obviously liked to be in control.

Sev moved into the background, thankful that he did not have to deal with any of it. He sat on a bench down the corridor and waited for them to tell him what to do. At that time, he suddenly thought, "Christ, I wish Gloria was here, she would know what to do."

Pushing those thoughts aside, he sat and waited until someone told him what to do next. He did not think much about the baby, his son.

This entry into parenthood was just all too much for him to cope with.

Sometime later, his in-laws, Beryl and Ronald came across and explained to him that Elizabeth was gravely ill but they wouldn't know anything for quite some time.

They suggested to Sev that he should go home and get some rest; they would ring him in the morning. He agreed and was thankful to get out of the place.

Instead of going home, Sev went straight to Gloria and poured out the long sorry story.

She understood these things, and after giving him a meal, suggested that he go home and gets some sleep. As Sev left she asked, "Please Sev, give me a call as soon as you hear how Elizabeth and the baby are getting on."

Elizabeth died two days later of Puerperal Fever.

In his own way Sev was distraught, not only for Elizabeth, but his own conscience that he was not the husband he should have been.

He thought of his relationship, not only with Elizabeth, but also with his own parents, his time with Nanna, and then his involvement with Gloria.

The funeral service was held in the chapel at the Northern Suburbs Crematorium. Elizabeth's parents offered to pick him up and ride with them, but he declined and accepted an offer to go with John and Jean.

Walking across the lawns, past the gardens, with the sun filtering through the trees, Sev felt an overwhelming sense of sadness. Elizabeth did not deserve this he thought, nor did she deserve my infidelity. The only good thing was that she never knew.

The funeral went by in a blur. In respect for Elizabeth Sev did not ask

Gloria to go, nor did he see her for several weeks. John and Jean came to offer their condolences and support.

Sev's biggest concern was what to do about his son.

He was not able to, or capable of raising him on his own. What was equally concerning was that he had no great feeling for the child.

The problem was overcome when Ronald and Beryl suggested that they should raise the child. Several days later he went to visit Gloria and brought her up to date on what had happened. Mutually they agreed that it would be in poor taste to change their existing arrangement and would continue, at least for the present, as they were.

The important thing for Sev was to get back to work and look after his practice and the growing number of clients. He visited Ronald and Beryl regularly but was never made to feel welcome. Sev made an offer to contribute to the expenses which was rejected, and he never connected to his son or Elizabeth's parents.

To himself he kept excusing his lack of support and interest by claiming that one day, when Paul is older; I will look after him and do things with him. I might even take him fishing or to the football, whatever Dads do with their sons.

Although he would never admit it, he knew in his heart that it would never happen.

Much later, Gloria offered to take the baby and raise him as hers.

Sev went to Ronald and told him that he was now able to look after his son. The doctor's reply was less than enthusiastic, and he suggested that he call back in a week's time to talk it over.

A week later Sev drove up the Pacific Highway, through the leafy North Shore suburbs to see his in-laws.

He was acutely aware that the outcome of this meeting could materially change his life-style over the coming years. As he drove down their tree-lined driveway, as always, he felt uncomfortable with their affluence and the grandeur of the property. It sort of put him on the back foot before he even began to talk to them.

This time, for some unknown reason, he had a gut feeling that something was wrong. There was no welcoming party to greet him and he had to ring the front door bell like a visitor.

Doctor Ronald came to the door and without any preamble said, "Let's go into the office."

Sev duly followed and with more confidence than he felt, sat down and said, "Well Ron where do we go from here?"

"I will tell you now where YOU go, as soon as you listen to what I have to say. You will then walk out of here and we never want to see you again. I have done some checking on you and let me tell you right now, you will never, I repeat never get custody of Paul. He will remain here and be raised by this family.

Did you really think we would allow our grandson, Elizabeth's child, to be raised by a prostitute?

How low can you get! You were not only seeing this "street girl" during your marriage to Elizabeth, you got her pregnant as well. And you have the hide, the audacity, to think that we would not find out and allow you to have this immoral creature raise our daughter's child. May you experience perdition forever. We only hope and pray that the child does not inherit your morals. So, there's the door, now get out of our house and our lives.'

Sev was absolutely livid. He jumped to his feet and for a moment he was close to physically attacking Ron as he had done to that boy at Central Station many years ago. Partly controlling himself he raged, "How dare you, you pompous old ass. You know nothing of the world out there. You know nothing about me, or the lady you referred to as a prostitute. That lady has more morals, class and compassion for her fellow human beings than ten of you. You have grown up cloistered in your North Shore environment and you know nothing of the real people of the world. She is a beautiful human being and I have found that it is a privilege to know her. You are such a self-centred arsehole you would never understand.

In return I only hope that my son has not inherited any of your genes. I will consider my legal situation and be in touch, so good night."

Sev stalked out, got into his car and took off at a furious pace down the highway. "Whoa!" he thought. "This won't help, just slow down, calm down, I can sort this out.

How dare that arsehole talk to me like that, one day I will eat him up and spit him out!"

Driving over the Harbour Bridge, left onto the Cahill Expressway, keeping within the speed limit, he kept telling himself to breathe easy and just relax. His first reaction was to go straight to Gloria, and then he thought; "No, I will just go straight to the Vaucluse apartment, collect my thoughts and hopefully get a good night's sleep. I have a full day tomorrow."

Wearily, as he climbed into bed, one of his last thoughts was of how he smashed that boy all those years ago, who tried to muscle in on his paper corner at Central Railway. Now, that's what I'd like to do to that arrogant, pretentious prick

Sev had no idea how he would handle the situation as to the fact that Paul was his son, and at that time did not care.

Over the next week, he looked at where he stood legally and morally with Paul. He concluded that if the matter ever got to court, which was most likely, the only way he would win would be to totally break his relationship with Gloria. He was not prepared to do this. For the moment he formulated a strategy to accept the situation provided he had reasonable access to the boy. Using his office stationery, he forwarded a letter setting out grounds for regular access to his son.

In turn they realised that, if this request was denied and the matter went to court, the outcome could be in Sev's favour.

They accepted without further comment,

However, Sev knew it would always be a battle and it was. The very first time he requested access he was told that the time was not convenient. The second time, they would be away on business.

This was the pattern over the next months and Sev just gave up. He justified this in his own mind by thinking that the boy would most likely be better off without him.

In the December of 1962, Gloria gave birth to a healthy seven-pound boy.

This time there were no dramas. The birth was uncomplicated, and both mother and child were well. Sev was the epitome of the happy father, walking around the hospital corridors with his chest puffed out like he was the only one to achieve parenthood. Looking at his red-faced, tiny son so comfortable in his mother's arms Sev could not but wonder how his life would be.

Using his surname, they named him James Alan Cockini.

Allowing a respectful time since Elizabeth's death, Sev moved out of his Vaucluse apartment to live with Gloria in Rosebery. It was a semi-detached villa close to the street, with a small front veranda. Inside, there was a passageway running all the way down to the rear kitchen and porch.

Off the passage were a formal lounge, two bedrooms and a dining room. Although not as big, it reminded Sev of Nana's old place over in Glebe.

Sev felt that the short tree-lined dead-end street offered some quietness and security which was hard to find in the Rosebery area. Coming home from work it gave him a real buzz to turn into the street, park out the front, open the front door and be greeted enthusiastically by Gloria.

Sometimes he would think to himself, "How good is this?"

Since leaving Frank Bennett's enterprise Gloria had blossomed into a very attractive woman. Gone was the scruffy poorly groomed young girl that Sev first met.

They married in June of that year in a simple private ceremony. Their only guests were, John and Jean, Jean's friend Ann Croft, Sev's Secretary Vivien Edwards and Frank Bennett.

Frank had long been aware of Sev's involvement with Gloria and her reason for leaving his "establishment." As soon as he heard of the planned marriage, he insisted that they be his guests at one of his restaurants for the reception and celebration dinner.

Sev's relationship with Gloria deepened, and for the first time since Nana's death he found an inner peace and happiness. He could not get home from the office quick enough to see his wife and son.

Business was booming, partly with referrals from Frank Bennett, and he was becoming very well known in legal circles around the city.

He continued with his monthly luncheons with Frank, sometimes inviting clients and business associates to join them. As time slipped by, he arranged his schedule, so he could spend at least half a day with John out at their warehouse.

DIFFICULT TIMES

CHAPTER FIVE

John sat on the Qantas Lockheed prop-jet waiting for take-off for the long haul to Athens. He was thinking, "This is going to be absolute torture, some twenty hours locked up in this oversized cigar. Thank God we have a few stops. That's why they call it the Kangaroo Hop to Europe."

He had an emotional parting with Jean and baby Robert at the airport, with Jean assuring him that she was quite capable of looking after the business while he was away. Sev had a good grasp of the business now and he could certainly help if needed.

After the last hugs and kisses, in the late afternoon he walked through the barrier, past the customs zone, and that was it.

He thought, *'There is something strange about crossing that line. Once you're past it, you feel like you are in another world, cut off from the one you know.'*

He took the long walk down the passageway past the Duty Free and Souvenir shops looking for gate 12.

There was quite a crowd milling about, eagerly waiting for final instructions for ticket checks and boarding. Looking across the room he saw a tall aristocratic looking man standing alone with a small satchel under his arm and a ticket folder in the opposite hand.

"Hell", he thought, "I know him, that's Sev's mate Frank Bennett. I can't avoid him, so I may as well say hello now."

He strolled across and said, "Hello Frank, John Naxos." Frank looked a little surprised and taking John's offered hand said, "Of course, we met at your warehouse function, and have spoken on the phone a couple of times since. I must say we have been very pleased about the way you have been looking after our restaurants."

"Well I'm glad to hear that, we appreciate your business."

"Where are you off to Frank? Obviously your first stop is Athens, holidaying or business?"

"A little bit of both John, I will visit some relatives first and then I have business matters to attend to. What about you?"

"I am going to see some of our old suppliers and hopefully find some new suppliers as well, so we can broaden our range. After that I'm heading to Milan for the Catering Trade Fair, where I hope to pick up a new range of utensils. The other project is to look at equipment and machinery, so I will have my hands full, but it's an exciting challenge for me."

Frank replied, "I wish you well, but if you get into the heavy machinery and need financing give me a ring back in Sydney. I'll be home in two weeks."

"Thanks for the offer Frank; I don't envisage going that far, but who knows?'

They passed through the final ticket check then into the plane together, with John looking for his economy seat.

He was not surprised to see Frank going to first class.

A couple of hours out of Sydney the hostesses brought a meal, which John washed down with a couple of glasses of passable red wine. Inclining the seat back as far as it would go, it was time to try to get some sleep.

The noise and activity made it difficult, so he took a book out of his satchel and immersed himself in that. It was not long before he dozed off, only to be woken, in what seemed like minutes later, to be told that it was breakfast time and they were not far out of Singapore.

Well, that is a good start he thought, despite having a headache. His seat neighbour, an elderly Englishman said, "Well you had a good sleep, I wish I could sleep like that."

Not wanting to spend the journey communicating with anybody, John said, "I was tired before we left, so I was ready for a sleep. I hope I can sleep again on the next leg."

"Business or pleasure." he asked.

"Strictly business."

"What sort of business is an Aussie like you doing in Greece?"

"Catering supplies, but I'm not an Aussie as you refer to them, I am actually Greek."

"I would never have picked it, you speak so well." he said.

Just for the hell of it, John said, "I learnt it at Oxford."

This set him back a bit and he was saved from further conversation by the arrival of the hostesses with breakfast.

On the next legs, John managed to get a little sleep but mainly was happy to just sit and read. Frank came down from first class a couple of times, looking fresh and relaxed, to see how he was coping with the rigours of economy class. Feeling like the poor relative, John remarked, "Frank, this is the last time I will be sitting in economy."

With a smirk on his lips Frank replied, "You had better come into business with me then?" Without waiting for a reply, he sauntered back to the luxury of first class.

After a bumpy landing at Athens John negotiated customs, found a taxi, and headed for his hotel. Having a good grasp of Greek allowed him to extricate himself from the airport with a minimum of fuss and time.

Over the next day's John visited his old suppliers, all of whom were happy to see him and ask how he was getting on since his father had died.

John went into great detail about selling the restaurant and being full-time in wholesale condiments, and of his plans for also moving into kitchen utensils and catering equipment.

After placing some substantial orders, he then set out to find and visit as many other suppliers of herbs and spices and other food stuffs suitable for export and the Australian market.

Driving around the ancient towns and countryside in his rented Fiat, he felt a pull towards the old homeland and the birth land of his parents. And yet, he still felt very much an Australian himself. We lack the history of these countries, but that will come, at least we don't carry their cultural baggage either. However, he also gained some understanding as to why his parents, and millions of others, had migrated to other lands, particularly since the war.

He thought about Sev's parents and considered trying to track them down, and then, "I had best keep out of that one. If Sev had wanted me to see them he would have asked."

What niggled at his mind was, 'What sort of business opportunities does Frank Bennett keep alluding to?"

Feeling more than happy with the supply chains he had set up from both the old suppliers and new contacts, he allowed himself two days R&R in Athens before leaving for his big challenge in Milan.

John took a morning flight to Rome hoping that he could fit in some time to see at least some of the attractions in this ancient city. By the time he found his hotel and settled in it was evening, and as he was tired, he decided to eat in the hotel and have an early night.

Before going to the dining room, he rang home to see how Jean was getting on. She was thrilled to hear from him and anxious to hear how he was getting on.

John briefly filled her in on his progress and asked if everything was okay at the warehouse.

Jean replied, "Yes, everything is fine and going well. We have had some good orders as well as a big one from Frank Bennett. Sev has called in nearly every day and has been a big help, particularly keeping the accounts up to date."

"Jean, by the way, I met Frank Bennett at the airport, he was on the same plane for Athens. He is a real mystery man, I sometimes wonder what his real business is."

"I wouldn't not worry too much about that, as long as he keeps sending those orders in, he is still a big part of our business."

John continued, "Anyway it's great to hear that everything is okay, but I had better get off the phone. It is very expensive from here. I love you and miss you. I will ring again from Milan."

After hanging up, John thought that he really could not afford the time to wander around Rome doing the tourist thing and decided to catch the morning train to Milan.

He had forward booked at the Milan Hilton which was close to the station. When he arrived at the hotel he found that it was far too expensive and decided to look for an alternative. Searching his tourist map he found a cheaper hotel close by, called the De Este, which was only a block from the station, so he decided to walk and save the cab fare. Lugging his suitcase and satchel, his luck ran out and it started to rain. It quickly turned into a downpour and without an umbrella and very little shelter he was soon drenched.

Finally locating the Hotel, he quickly registered and found his room. He was not a happy fellow and was anxious to get into the shower and freshen up before going down to dinner.

Later, sitting in the dining room, his eyes swept the room and he found it to be surprisingly formal. "Even more Swiss than Italian", he thought, "This is a long way from the Naxos in Newtown."

The patrons were the sort of people you would expect to find at this sort of establishment in Milan, solid, professional, well-healed, and preoccupied with their own concerns. They were in couples or larger groups and none paid the slightest attention to an Aussie on his own feeling slightly out of place.

The menu was all in Italian, and although he tried to interpret this to Greek, he was not sure enough to be too adventurous in his choice. He ordered a pasta dish and washed it down with some of the local red wine. He had just finished and was feeling much better when he became aware of someone watching him.

Ignoring the feeling, he was deciding whether to have a port with his coffee when a middle-aged swarthy man approached his table and said in accented English, "Would you be Mr. Naxos?"

John was taken back and replied, "Yes I am."

"Do you mind if join you for coffee? I am sorry, I should introduce myself first. My name is Sergio. We have a mutual friend, Mr. Bennett, and he insisted that I look you up to see if I could be of any assistance to you in Milan."

Not knowing quite what to say, John answered, "Yes, please sit down."

"How did you know where I would be staying?"

Sergio replied, "I had a call from Frank and he asked me to look for you, that's all I know. He suggested that I put myself at your disposal.

I know the city very well and can take you wherever you need to go. In this city it is also much better if you have an interpreter to do business.

Do you want to visit the Exhibition Fair tomorrow?

Yes, then I will take you there and show you around."

"Well, thank you, that would be kind of you; but I'm not sure that I want any help."

"I'll tell you what we will do then. Tomorrow I will take you in my car to the Exhibition Centre and show you about so you will know where to go and get an understanding of where the exhibitors you wish to see are. After that, you can then decide if you need me. Is that okay? Besides, I would not like to report back to Mr. Bennett that I have not helped you."

John thought, "This is a good offer and it may save me heaps of time, why not!"

"Yes, thank you, I will accept your generous offer."

"Good, then I will pick you up at nine from the foyer."

Sergio then stood, bowed slightly, offered his hand and said, "Well, good night. Have a good sleep" and left.

Back in his room John quickly undressed ready for bed, thinking, "What is this Frank Bennett up to? I don't think that he's the type to do anything for nothing. I suppose it will come out one day, if it's a bit of, "you scratch my back and I'll scratch yours, what is it that he wants?"

The next day, John was escorted around the huge exhibition centre and had to admit that it was much easier having a local interpreter. He did not argue when Sergio offered to spend a few more days with him.

The next day, with Sergio's help, he found an excellent manufacturer of cooking utensils which were suitable for both the domestic and commercial market. Nervously he placed a large order, subject to confirmation from home. "This will make or break us", he thought.

Leaving the Exhibition grounds, after insisting to Sergio that he could find his own way and walk back to the hotel, he found himself in a narrow street packed with people heading towards the station. Suddenly he was struck from behind and his satchel was wrenched from his grasp.

He saw his assailant sprinting through the crowd. "Shit," he thought,

"My passport, travellers' cheques, plane tickets and room key are all in that bag." He took off in pursuit, barging his way through the crowd yelling, 'Stop thief." Nobody was taking any notice, and as he was quickly losing ground on his attacker he stopped, realising that he had no hope of catching him. "What the hell am I going to do now; I do not even have one Lira in my pocket."

Totally out of breath, he slumped to the pavement then sat on the gutter trying to breathe normally. He could not imagine what he was going to do. Sitting there as the crowds walked past not taking any notice of him, he felt totally dejected and pissed off.

His sheltered life had not prepared him for this, particularly in a foreign country; he had no idea what to do next.

Then out of the crowd stepped Sergio. "Hey, my friend, what are doing there, you have a problem?" John quickly explained that some arsehole had snatched his bag.

Sergio said, "Just stay where you are for a minute,' and ran off into the crowd.

He returned a few minutes later telling John that all was okay. He would get his satchel back for him.

"Here is money for a taxi back to your hotel. Wait there for me."

About one hour later, John was sitting in his room with a much-needed scotch and there was a knock on the door. Opening the door, he was surprised to see Sergio standing there with his satchel.

"Thanks very much, how did you get it back?"

"We know these bad boys that roam the streets, so my friends had no problem picking him up. It didn't take much persuasion to make this fellow hand it over before he sold everything. It was either give it back, or he would not walk again for a long time."

John was very relieved saying, "Sergio, how can I reward you, to show my appreciation?"

"You can't; Mr. Bennett will look after me."

Later, John was to ponder again as to how far the tentacles of Frank Bennett extended.

The next day, feeling a little subdued from the previous day's experience,

John visited the machinery section and was excited to see the range of equipment that was available.

His first order was for a packaging machine to handle the small packs of spices that he intended to put into the retail supermarkets. This machine had the ability to pack small or large quantities of spices into cellophane packets.

Commercial restaurant equipment, not previously seen in Australia; mixers, blenders, ovens and gas cookers were of great interest. John had a strong gut feeling that the market back home for this modern equipment was huge.

He thought, for a start we could sell a hundred of those thermostatically controlled pie ovens.

What he needed was money; capital to get going.

The flight home was just as tedious as the one going over, but this time he was swallowed up in his achievements and thoughts on his plans.

As the plane banked over Sydney on a bright sunny day, he had a wonderful view of the Harbour and the famous Bridge. He could not help but think that Sydney had to be one of the great cities of the world and he felt quite an emotional attachment to his home city.

There was much excitement at the Airport, with lots of hugs and tears from Jean. John found himself caught up in the excitement and emotion of the moment. Even Sev was there with Gloria.

John glanced furtively over at her and could not help to be impressed by how smart she looked. There was also an air of confidence and bearing about her that he had not noticed before. He unashamedly thought, "She is a very attractive woman."

Over the following days, John and Sev thrashed out their problems of financing the planned expansion into commercial kitchen and catering equipment.

John remarked, "I thought you may have been able to do something Sev. What about the money from the Glebe house?"

"That has all gone on the apartment at Double Bay and the one we live in at Rosebery. The rest you already have in the business. You mentioned that Frank Bennett was making some offers, what do you think about that?"

John thought for a moment and said, "I would take his money, but there is no way I would give him any access to, or a share in the business."

Sev said, "I have thought about this before, and I believe there might be a way. Why don't we take a loan, just to set up the commercial division? We could suggest that we pay him only basic bank interest rates, the same as home loans, and offer him some sort of profit share on the results on that component of the business. We could further stipulate that we have the right to pay him out any-time after the first year. What do you think John?"

"The idea sounds good, why don't you put it together on paper and we can then have another look at it."

After ironing out a few wrinkles in the proposal, Sev and John took it to Frank. He was most amenable to the proposition and said, "This looks good boys, I will let my lawyers look it over. If they give it the all clear, then I will help you. Sev, in case you're reading this wrongly, my lawyers do not include you!"

Sev replied, "Of course Frank, I never expected you to go down that path."

The following year was a flurry of activity with all the new stock arriving as well as the new packaging machinery. They were now able to handle all their orders efficiently and promptly and start seriously expanding their client base within the industry. The next step was the retail stores, particularly delicatessens. After they had the brand more strongly established, they would look at the big supermarket chains.

Towards the end of the year, although not totally unexpected, John's brother Steven returned from overseas.

Gone was the slightly effeminate youth. The new, mature Steven was tall and solidly built, but there was still a unpleasant air about him. With this there was also a shrewdness that was not apparent in his teenage years. What did surprise John was that he had a wife. Her name was Millie; he had met her in Israel. Millie came from America where her parents still lived in New York.

Within the first week of his sudden re-appearance, Steven approached John about his share of their parent's estate. John made it quite clear that there was no way at this stage he could afford to pay Steven out. He also reminded him that he walked out when the family needed him most.

John then expounded, "Furthermore, any entitlements you may be claiming would be for a share of the property, not the restaurant or the new company. Remember you contributed absolutely nothing to the restaurant."

While he held the initiative, he continued, "Look Steven I don't want to cheat you out of anything, so here is my offer, which I think is more than fair. If you don't accept it, then we could quite well end up fighting it out in court.

I only own sixty percent of Naxos Condiments, Sev has the other forty percent. I will, as your inheritance, give you thirty percent of my share, which in effect gives you an eighteen percent stake in Naxos. That leaves me with forty two percent and the balance of control.

I've already discussed this with Sev and he's drawn up the legal papers to formalise the arrangement. I suggest you go and see Sev at his Elizabeth Street office as soon as you can to sign the necessary documents."

Steven stood up to shake hands, "Thanks John, you have been more than fair."

By the end of the next week, all the legal aspects were settled, and Steven returned to see John at the warehouse.

They sat down in John's office, which was in a converted bedroom of the upstairs apartment. For some moments Steven stood at the window without speaking, looking at the expanse of industrial buildings stretching across Mascot towards the Airport.

He then turned to John and said, "John, I am most impressed by what you've achieved here, and I feel that I have something to contribute if you would give me the opportunity."

"What you are saying is that you want a job?"

"Well, yes I am."

"What do you see yourself doing, Steven?"

Gaining a bit of momentum, Steven replied, "As I see it, what the business needs now is some strong, full time representation out there, on the road, looking after existing clients and more importantly seeking new business, particularly, in the area of commercial restaurant and catering equipment. Your condiment range is the best in the country. We should have self-serve display stands in every delicatessen and supermarket.

Imagine the sales if we had a stand in every Coles and Woolworth's across the country. John, I made a point to study this across Europe and, believe me, I know what we can do.'

John was not surprised, at Steven's suggestions, and without being too committed, he said, "Okay Steven, you're pretty well spot-on in your assessment. Let me talk to Sev about it and we can meet again on, let's say, Friday."

John was very aware that with the four other employees working on packing and delivery, with Steven on board, his weekly salary commitments would be far too high for their current income. If he went down this path Steven would have to bring in additional business almost immediately. His university accounting training said, "No way!" His gut feeling went the other way and said, "go for it."

Sev was in accord with him and suggested that they put him on the lowest base salary with a monthly incentive bonus on results. The other issue Sev raised was to say that it was time for John to formalise his own position and to draw a regular salary as General Manager of Naxos Condiments. He also suggested that it was time to set a profit-share distribution scheme based on his share of the business. John agreed to this and was thankful to have a lawyer on his team. He was also becoming more and more aware as to how smart Sev was.

Steven started the following week, and over the following months John and Sev were impressed by the impact he was having on their orders. Not only did he bolster the sales of Herbs and Spices, orders were also coming in for kitchen and catering equipment.

Another big plus was that Sev himself stitched up a deal to introduce their range of kitchen utensils into a chain of Home Wares stores across

New South Wales, with a chance to go national if the sales results were strong enough.

They were now at the stage when they were accepting orders based on delivery from overseas, and orders in all areas were escalating faster than they could supply the products. The business grew at a rapid rate and it was more of how to control it than wondering where the next sale was coming from.

John continued travelling to Europe every year to source new products and to keep in touch with current suppliers. Sev went with him several times, to learn the ropes and meet their suppliers, whom he liked to refer to as their business partners.

Because of his intimate knowledge of the business, the client's needs and shifts in demand, John occasionally sent Steven on his own. He had a particularly good knowledge of foodstuffs and it was partly through Steven that they started importing pasta, canned goods and olive oil from Italy. Olives were also in demand and they imported those from Greece in five-gallon drums for repacking at home.

Most products were suitable for repacking, but with their increased quantities there were many smaller lines in herbs and spices that could be packaged and labelled to their specifications overseas.

It was not long before the warehouse became too small and, with a bit of help from their bank, they purchased the freehold on their existing building along with its duplicate next door. This was dictated by the need to separate the commercial catering equipment and utensils from the foodstuffs. There were several factors that changed the direction of the business.

The significant one was the huge number of immigrants arriving in Australia from Europe. The eating habits of these people, and their greater patronage of restaurants, created a huge impact on the way people cooked and ate out in Australia. The old Aussie steak, eggs and chips mentality was disappearing fast.

Naxos Condiments were in the right place at the right time and over the next decade the business boomed.

Inevitably, Frank Bennett came on board as a financial partner, helping to finance development of the business.

Because of his significant financial investments, he was given a ten-percent stake in the company, which also meant that there was some debt that did not have to be repaid.

They set up a management team to plot direction, operational issues, and marketing. This consisted of John, Sev, Frank, and Steven for his marketing contributions, plus a new-comer, Michael Green, from their recently appointed independent accounting firm.

John understood if the others banded together, they could out-vote him on any issue.

Sev continued with his law practice and by the late sixties had a staff of thirty including three partners.

Shortly after son James had arrived into the world, Gloria was happily pregnant again and, in 1958, daughter Vanessa was born. With two children, the Rosebery apartment was too small and by selling it, and the Vaucluse apartment they put together a sizeable purse to purchase a four-bedroom home in Woollahra.

After her rough start in life, Gloria was ecstatically happy and gave Sev the security and comfort he needed.

In the early times Sev had made a few attempts to keep in touch with the Spalding's and his son Paul but was effectively locked out. On the rare occasions that Sev did meet Paul, it was always in company of his adoptive father, and the atmosphere was so strained that, in the end, he just gave up.

At one stage he resorted to writing to him, letting him know what was happening with the rest of his family and particularly his step brother and sister.

After Several unanswered letters, Sev received a reply from Doctor Ronald suggesting that he desist from writing as it only unsettled and confused the boy.

Sev found that, while his law practice was pulling in some significant money, he enjoyed the hype and thrust of the commercial world with Naxos Condiments.

He tended to hassle or interrupt John's day more than necessary, and there were many occasions on which John would tell him to just go away for a few days and leave him to get on with his work.

In contrast to Sev, Frank Bennett was very much the silent partner and only appeared at their monthly management meetings.

Brother Steven, although he was now earning a substantial income, remained as an employee and never made any moves to try to get a greater share of the business.

Steven and Millie kept very much to themselves, and only visited John and Jean at home on special occasions. They never had any children.

John often suspected that he had a gambling problem but never raised the issue with him.

John and Jean lived happily in their Croydon home and, to their disappointment, never had any more children after Robert.

Jean soon had a wide circle of friends in the district, mostly gathered from contact with other parents at Robert's school.

John did little other than work and was content to spend the little spare time he had tending his vegetable garden. However, he was a born worrier and to Jean's annoyance brought too many of his work problems home. The business was an obsession with him and he became morose.

When Jean complained his stock answer was always, "Do you want us to end up like my parents, or worse still, like Sev's?"

Jean would reply, "Come on John, life is too short. The business is going well, you could sell out now and we could retire comfortably."

"What about Robert? One day he will take over."

"John, don't push him into the business. If you do, it could turn him away. He might want to be a doctor or lawyer, something totally different."

"In that case all my work could be for naught."

This sort of talk made Jean angry, and she would say "John that is absolute rubbish. It's like your Dad expecting you to cook in the restaurant for the rest of your life."

John had no answer for this, so he would take off outside and potter in his vegetable garden.

Jean still loved him, but sometimes felt the growing strain on their marriage. The exciting sex life they had started with had almost disappeared. In bed it was John who was always too tired, or he had drunk too much whisky. Many times, Jean fell asleep feeling sexually frustrated when she was in the prime of her life. She wished he was a bit more composed and attentive like Sev, a thought she would have never harboured in the early times.

Over the years, despite their increasing affluence, Jean never changed. She remained a pleasant, happy person. She retained her good looks, which to her annoyance, Sev kept reminding her about. Every time they met, he greeted her with an over enthusiastic hug and a comment, "Hello, my oldest and best girlfriend."

If anything, her small weight gain suited her more in her mature years, and in some ways, the older Jean was more attractive than the young Jean.

She did not encourage or welcome Sev's flattery, and always was ready with a quick retort, like, "Yes Sev, but how many girlfriends do you have?"

Jean had to admit to herself that Sev had a sexual magnetism on a level that few men had, and there were times that she enjoyed some private fantasies about him.

Begrudgingly, she also had to respect Sev for his contributions to the business and his unconditional love for Gloria and his children.

He did everything with the kids, took them to their sports days, or spent hours just playing Dad. He was also relentless in keeping track of their school work and seeing that they completed homework assignments.

This was a huge contrast to John who thought work was more important.

Robert was an average student and did not work particularly hard at improving his marks. Jean suspected that he had more capacity than he was using, and his efforts reflected a quiet revolt against John's demands.

Unlike his Dad and Greek heritage, he was fair-skinned with blond hair. He was softly spoken and undemonstrative.

He chose his friends carefully, and sometimes would be just as happy with his own company. By contrast to this, sometimes his mother could see in him a steely determination, which rarely surfaced. Rather than assist him, give advice or direction, John demanded.

Jean was always disappointed that John did not connect or communicate better with his son. She excused him believing that he had inherited old attitudes from his parents.

John arrived home early from work on one occasion to find Robert still down the street playing footy with his other teenage mates. He called, "Robert, why are you still outside? Have you completed your homework yet?"

"Coming Dad, I'm on my way."

When he got inside, John sat him down in the kitchen and said,

"Robert your school work is not good enough. You will never get into university with your marks. How will you take over the business without an education behind you?"

"Dad, I've said before, I don't want to go to university, and I do not want to take over the business. I hate it."

John exploded, "You are still a boy, you do not know what you want, and you have a responsibility to the family to take over the business when the time comes."

Robert thought, "I have had this lecture many times before. What's the point of arguing." Picking up his books he just said, "Okay Dad", and headed for his room.

Later, after John had gone back to the office for a meeting, Jean went to Robert's room, sat down with him and said, "You must understand dad's position with the business. He started with nothing from the restaurant and has built the business to where it is today. His father expected him to carry on where he left off and he expects the same from you."

"Mum, I hate the place; it is just not my scene. I could never see myself working there for the rest of my life. The Christmas vacation work time is bad enough."

"Robert, you've not said this before. Why did you wait till now?"

Robert replied, "Mum I just knew that it would cause a fight with Dad, that's why."

Jean coaxed, "Well, now that we've got that out, the big question is, what do you want to do? You are nearly fifteen now, and you must have some idea of what you do want?"

"I have been thinking about it for a long time and I really want to do something in the Arts. I could be a teacher and teach art at school or even become a graphic artist for commercial work. That would be great. One day I would even like to become an artist and do my own paintings. You may have noticed that this my best subject at school."

Jean was a little taken aback, and looking at Robert, saw that he had tears in his eyes. Suddenly she realised that he may have been carrying this burden for some time.

She went to him and put her arms around him and cried, "What matters most to both your father and me is to see you happy. So, let's have a plan. Firstly, you need to go to university for an Arts Degree, and at this time your marks are not good enough."

"Mum, I know I can do better at school, and if I could go for a Visual Art Degree, then I will work really hard."

Jean added, "if you can make that commitment, I can have a talk to dad and I am sure he will agree."

"Gee, Thanks mum, do I start now?"

"No time like the present", replied Jean wondering how she was going to convince John.

Robert looked at his mother seeing a pretty youthful face that projected her nature, thinking, where would I be without Mum?"

Robert sat at his study desk under the window looking out over the back yard. His room gave him a degree of comfort, and when he was unhappy, he could cocoon himself there away from the world. It was a boy's room with car and pop star posters on the walls next to his single bed, shelves laden with books above his desk and a general air of untidiness.

He very much felt a lack of direction in his life and was always uncomfortable with his father. His continual criticism and demands really became an issue with him. He often thought that if he was told the story of his grandparent's migration from Greece and their struggle to live and raise a family one more time, he would scream.

The other part was Dad's harping on how he had to give up his university education to run the restaurant; and Robert, on hearing the story yet again, would say, "But you did very well with the business after that."

At that, his Dad would puff out his chest, and remind Robert that he had achieved his success by using his university education and just plain hard work and commitment.

And he would not allow two generations of effort wasted because of a frivolous attitude.

Robert now saw that with his mum's help he could choose his own direction, and at least pacify Dad if he could get into university. In his room at that time, he decided to change his attitude to school and work to make university entrance. From then on, he applied himself with a vigour and commitment that surprised both his parents.

Dad insisted that he spend his vacation times working, and Robert did build up a very good working knowledge of the business. Working also gave him enough money to look after himself without going to dad for handouts.

Three years later, Robert went to university and excelled in his chosen fields as his father had done before him.

Also following in his dad's footsteps, he met a girl whom he would later marry, her name was Barbara White. They married in the University chapel in 1978.

Their first and only child, a son Colin, was born in 1980.

Although Robert had ideas for a much more creative working life, he began his career teaching. In his spare hours, he took up painting and soon became well known for his watercolour paintings of Sydney Harbour. It was not long before he had his first serious exhibition, held in a leading Sydney Gallery in Darlinghurst.

There was great excitement for the opening party with all the family there as well as the Cockini clan. Frank Bennett arrived, with a new glamour girl on his arm; she was no older than Robert's wife Barbara. Frank was the first to make a purchase selecting the most expensive picture.

Seeing that red sale dot spurred a flurry of buying and Several more were quickly sold.

Champagne was being splashed around, and it seemed to Robert that the more they drank the more they bought.

John had clearly got over his disappointment of Robert not going into the business and was immensely proud of him.

By the mid-eighties, the Naxos Empire was far too large to continue with the management structure and changes were needed to revitalise the business.

John had changed over the years, and Sev could not help but notice how he had aged and become withdrawn. He seemed to have lost his enthusiasm for life. He had put on weight, probably from lack of exercise. His face was lined and he was prematurely grey.

It worried Sev to see his old mate looking so worn out.

Following a Friday meeting Sev asked, "John why don't you stop behind for a drink with me?"

"Sure Sev, but I have to be home early tonight as I promised to take Jean out for dinner."

Sev went to the cupboard and took out a bottle of Johnnie Walker and a couple of glasses. "Do you want soda or just tap water?"

"Tap water will be fine thanks, but what's the occasion, is there something on your mind?"

"Well John, we have come a long way since those days at school and uni and our trips to the local pub in Newtown. I often think of how raw and innocent we were. Remember that crazy trip we had to Surfers Paradise, and you nearly lost your virginity on the beach. We really did have a lot of fun considering all our dramas at home with our parents or my lack of them. What concerns me now John is that the fun seems to have gone out of your life."

John did not immediately reply and slowly put his glass up to his lips. Sev could not help but notice the tremor in his hand.

After taking a good swallow of his whisky, John put the glass down and looking across at Sev he said, "I guess that the work and worry of the business has got to me a bit. Lately I've been thinking about how I could back off a bit and hand over the reins, but there is nobody to take over.

Robert is not interested, and even if he was, he would not work with his old man. His only interest is his art. Jean has had enough of me, with the hours I keep. Nowadays she leads her own life and goes out with her friends; even when I'm home she goes out alone. Even our sex life has become non-existent

I would not say this to anyone but you Sev, but sometimes I think that our marriage has fallen apart."

"Shit John, you cannot let that happen. Most of it is your fault, and it's time to do something about it before it's too late. Firstly, let's look at how we can restructure the business. How about we both give it a couple of days to think about it, and we'll sit down at the end of the week and work out where we're going. Do you want Frank in on this, or leave him out of it?"

John replied, "If we end up doing some sort of break up, then we should ask him to the meeting. How about you and I work out what we want, then we meet again with Frank included."

"Okay, I'll call around on Thursday for a quick chat, and then we'll arrange a meeting with Frank for Friday afternoon."

On Thursday, John uncharacteristically came into the office late. He walked in across the factory floor hesitating to watch the packing machines grinding away and the white-jacketed workers going about their chores.

He thought, "*What a contrast to the old days when we started with virtually nothing and did all the work ourselves. Jean, sometimes with the baby, worked all day packing orders. Maybe it's time to get out totally. I could sell my share to Sev and Frank.*"

With that he ambled across the packing floor and up the stairs to his office. Sitting down at his desk, he suddenly felt very tired of it all.

"Here I am with this huge business and I am not sure if I even know what's going on any more.

Steven does all the importing and the overseas trips, I look after the warehouse.

The accountants look after the books and Sev keeps an eye on everything."

I will see what Sev has say when he comes in this afternoon. He usually comes up with the right ideas."

At the meeting they agreed that John's day-by-day workload be reduced, and he be appointed Managing Director. To fill the gap, a General Manager recommended by Frank Bennett was appointed.

Steven Naxos's work in the sales field was recognised and he was appointed Sales and Marketing Manager.

Separate sales teams were appointed for the now two separate divisions; foodstuffs and catering equipment.

A new share split was done for tax purposes, bringing Robert Naxos in as a shareholder, and splitting John's holding with Jean. Sev also did a split giving his children a share. These and the generated income were to be held in trust until they reached the age of 25. Sev's estranged son, Paul Spalding, was left out of the distribution.

The Naxos business was in effect owned by- John 14%, Jean 13%, Robert 10%, Sev 25%, James 5%, Vanessa 5%, Steven 18%, and Frank 10%.

The apartment above the original warehouse was refurbished and it was agreed to let Steven have it rent-free.

John tried hard to readjust his life style, taking days off, getting home early and offering to take Jean out to the theatre or dinner. To his frustration he found that Jean was always busy with her friends and seemed to have little time for a reformed John.

She did offer to take him to her Bridge Club, to which John replied, "Never will I sit around on my arse playing cards in the middle of the day."

"Well I will continue to go on my own then."

She could see that John was getting increasingly agitated and tried another idea.

"There is a Bowling Club over in Croydon Park, so why don't we take up Bowls?"

Jean received the same response, "Sorry, but I am not about to stand out the sun all day dressed up like a fairy with all those old codgers."

"Well you think of something then, I have plenty to do with my life", said Jean.

"I will take up fishing. They catch lots down on the river."

"You can do that on your own", replied Jean.

The result was that little changed. Jean kept up her activities and

John continued to go to work, if only to fill in the day, as all his old responsibilities had been delegated to the new General Manager.

Sitting at his desk, he flipped through his diary and in bold letters, (written by Jean) was "Wedding anniversary next week"

Suddenly he had an inspiration. Jean has never been overseas. I'll take her away as an anniversary present.

"That's it", he thought. Jumping up he put on his coat and went straight down to his car and drove into the city.

After parking, John walked along Elizabeth Street to Sev's office.

In the opulent reception area, he asked at the reception desk for Mr. Cockini and after getting the usual run around of, "Who shall I say is calling?"

"Just tell him to hurry up, John is waiting."

Looking a little uncomfortable, she picked up her phone and said, "Mr. Cockini, sorry to disturb you, but there's man called John here asking to see you. He's in a hurry."

"Thanks Beverly, he's an old friend of mine. I'll be right out." Sev walked out into the foyer, "Hello John, this is a rare visit, what brings you here? Come in."

John followed him up the passage past Several offices with serious looking people bent over desks covered with stacks of paper and files in manila folders. When he was in Sev's office, looking around he said, "Hey, how do you pay all those monkeys out there?"

"There are a lot of people who need my protection from the law."

"Bullshit, Sev, you were always good at it, but I suppose that's what makes great lawyers. You have a very impressive office here; it makes mine look a bit dingy."

"Now John, would you go to a lawyer working out of a hole in the wall. Having the office is all part of the theatre."

Sev felt good about seeing his old mate away from the warehouse and acting so animated, and wondered what had brought this on?

"John, don't hold me in suspense any longer, what are you up to?"

"I am going to take your advice and get myself away from the business altogether for a while. I am going to take Jean on a world trip and I thought you might have some suggestions on where to go."

"That's the best idea you've had all year, but you don't need me, just ask Jean where she would like to go."

"No, I want to surprise her. We've not been getting on too well lately; in fact, things have been a bit shaky to say the least."

"John, sometimes you act like a dickhead. Jean has been absolutely wonderful all these years and you let things get to this stage, surely you can see that. It would be a real tragedy to let your relationship fall apart now, so just go around to Thomas Cook Travel in Pitt Street and book a tour, the company can pay for it."

"You are right yet again Sev, I just let myself get too immersed in the business and selfishly neglected home."

Sitting in his big leather office chair Sev looked across at John and felt a rush of emotion and sorrow for his old friend and wondered how he could end up in such a mess after starting out with such happiness and promise.

"It's not too late to fix it John, so go and get your tickets and take off as soon as you can. You don't have to worry about the business, and you know it's in good hands."

John looked at Sev and mumbled, 'You're right as usual Sev and I will go straight around to the Travel Agent and book an around-the-world tour."

John did not go back to the office, deciding to go straight home and tell Jean the good news. Walking in the front door with the tickets stuffed in his pocket, and feeling full of hope, he found Jean sitting quietly at the kitchen table with a cup of tea. Giving her a quick kiss on the cheek he gushed, "Jean I have some news for you."

Before he could say another word, Jean said. "John before you say anything, sit down I have something to say."

Without any preamble she said, "Robert is going overseas to Paris to further his art studies and he has asked me to go with them, and I have decided to go."

John felt as if he been kicked in the guts and said, "Jean don't do this to me, we have had our problems, but we can work it out, I love you."

"We have been down this road before and I have had enough. You have treated me like your hired help for too long and this is the end. It is not a quick decision, I have thought about it for months.

Maybe it's the Greek way, but it's not mine."

Without even trying to argue, feeling totally defeated and incapable of further discussion, he just stood up and walked out.

Walking down the street with tears, streaming down his face, he felt totally devastated. "What have I done to ruin what started out as a beautiful relationship?"

He thought of those days in the restaurant when they were so happy working side by side and planning their future, and later the joy of the arrival of their first child.

"I have lost all this in the pursuit of money, what good is it to me now?"

He soon found himself outside the local pub and he went straight into the public bar and ordered himself a schooner of beer.

He sat there on his own, wallowing in self-pity until they asked him to leave at 10 o'clock.

When he arrived home the house was in darkness and he let himself in and fell into a drunken sleep on the lounge room floor.

When he woke early next morning, without bothering to shower or shave he got in his car and drove to the office and showered in Steven's apartment.

Steven got him a cup of coffee and said, "Rough night?"

"Yes you could say that, looks like Jean is leaving me and going overseas with Robert."

Steven did not react and added, "Have you tried to talk her out of it."

"No, what's the point. You know Jean, when she makes up her mind about something, she is not likely to change it."

You knew about this didn't you, why didn't you tell me?"

"It's not my business John."

"You bastard! thanks for nothing." John retorted as he got up and walked out.

Two days later Sev had a rare call at his office from Jean.

"Sev, I will be leaving soon, and I would like to see you before I go.

Can I come to your office tonight? I would prefer it if you did not tell anyone of my visit."

Sev replied, "Certainly Jean, how about 8"o clock. We can be sure then that we won't be interrupted. I'll wait for you out the front as there won't be anybody to let you in."

That evening standing out at the front of the office block, Sev watched all the people scurrying past in a hurry to catch their train home, some heading the other way possibly on their way to a theatre. The last of the day's sun was filtering through the trees in Hyde Park when he saw Jean come out of the park and hesitate before crossing the road towards him.

When Jean reached him, she offered her hand and turned her cheek for a chaste kiss. Sev thought, *"Hell she looks better than ever."*

"Hello Jean, you look wonderful."

"Now Sev, you always say that."

"And I always mean it; anyway, let's go up to the office."

Sev led her into the foyer and was glad that there was no one there to see them. Standing close to her in the lift he was aware of a subtle whiff of expensive perfume and the sexual pull she still had over him. She exuded warmth that he never felt with anyone else other than Gloria and all those old desires came rushing back.

In his office he offered her a seat, and purposely sat behind his desk reducing the temptation to touch her.

"Now Jean, what is this all about, do you come as a friend or for legal services?"

Jean looked him straight in the eye and said, 'Both Sev.

As you know I've left John, and in a few days I'll be going overseas for an undetermined time. It is important that my affairs are in order before I go. I want you to revise my Will to see that my share of Naxos and our Croydon home go to Robert. I have already taken my half of our cash; any other incidentals John can have."

"That's easy Jean, we can just revise the existing Will now, you can sign the amendments and that's done."

Sev had anticipated this and had the papers ready in his drawer.

He had already typed up the amendments, and after Jean had signed, he attached them to the originals for filing.

With that all done he turned to Jean and asked, "Now that business is done would you like a drink."

"Most definitely, but first there is something else I must tell you. I am sure that someone is bringing drugs in from overseas and shipping them in through the business. This is serious stuff and I don't want any part of it. Before I leave for France, I'm going to compile a report and send it to the police. So be prepared for some fireworks."

"Jean are you sure of this? There could be enormous implications",

"I am sure, but it does not involve you or John. Somehow, I am not surprised. It is time for me to sell my share and get right out of the business. Either Frank or Steven would buy me out. I wonder if Frank is involved?"

"I cannot in any way risk having my legal practice associated with any of this."

Sev went to his concealed bar and poured a Gin and Tonic for Jean and a Scotch for himself. He then sat on the couch next to her, "Jean, apart from any of these concerns, I must say I was very sorry to see you and John break up. After all those years, I find it very sad. We have all been together for so long."

Jean turned and again looked straight at him and confided, "Sev please understand, the marriage did not fail yesterday, the problems built up over years and there came a time when I'd just had had enough."

Jean stood up and faced him as a tear rolled slowly down her cheek. She whispered, "I am sad about the whole thing, but there is no turning back now, it's far too late."

Sev instinctively put his arms around her and they embraced. Feeling her body against his aroused him more than he had expected.

Once she was in his arms Sev felt that it was impossible to let her go.

Slowly he drew his lips across the tears as they continued to roll down her cheeks.

Then she turned her head until their lips met. They were soft and warm as she responded to his light kiss. They lingered for a moment both savouring the passion.

Sev broke away and said, "Jean, I have fantasied about this for as long as I can remember."

With a smile Jean replied "It may surprise you, but so have I."

They kissed again, this time with a greater passion and urgency. Before he had time to consider his actions, he unbuttoned her top and cupped her breasts in his hands as they continued kissing. With shaking hands, he then removed her top and brassiere leaving her naked from the waist up. He continued to caress her breasts while marvelling at her beauty and the softness of her flawless skin. Having now lost all sense or reasoning Sev quickly undid his belt and let his pants fall to the floor. His penis burst straight out, and Jean took it in her hand, "Oh Sev, don't stop now, please."

They made love on the couch with a depth of passion and feeling built up over the years but had remained latent. It was as if they were both trying to make up for a life of abstinence.

When their passion was spent, they sat up and before Sev could say anything Jean said, "Before you say anything Sev. You don't have to apologise, it was something that had to happen. It is a surprise that it did not happen before now. We must not spoil or degrade the moment, as we both know it will never happen again. It's our secret. You love Gloria and your children too much for it to be any other way. Let's have another drink, and then I must be away. I still have packing to do."

Finishing her drink, she said, "Thanks Sev, I think we both needed that, I will let myself out." And with that she walked out leaving him still sitting on the couch.

The following morning, Sev received a frantic phone call from John, "Sev for Christ's sake get over here and help me, Jean has been murdered. Her body was found in Croydon Park this morning.

Sev felt as if he had just been kicked in the head. He bolted out of the office, somehow got his car out of the car park and headed out to Croydon.

There was a crowd around the front of the house including several uniformed police and detectives. Sev found John and Robert in the lounge room both totally distraught to the point of hysteria.

He approached one of the police, identifying himself as the family solicitor and asked what happened.

Nobody was sure of anything at this stage except that her battered body was found in Croydon Park with what appeared to be a fatal knife wound to the chest.

Later an autopsy was held confirming that she had died from a massive haemorrhage following a wound to the chest. Other bruising to her body did not contribute to her death.

The coroner made a note that she did not appear to have been raped but there were traces of semen in her vagina. Distressingly John knew that this was not his and wondered who she had been with, and if she had been having and affair with someone else. As much as anything, this thought broke his heart.

After her body had been released, Jean was buried with a simple private ceremony attended only by her family and a few close friends.

At that stage the police did not have any clues as to who her attacker was or why. The only clue was a DNA sample from the semen, which they may never match.

Over the following weeks John never went into the office and only took calls that were absolutely necessary, preferring to spend his time pottering in the garden.

Sev called to see him regularly, always armed with a couple of bottles of beer or a bottle of scotch. On his fourth visit, Sev could sense that he had something on his mind, "Okay, John I feel you want to tell me something, what is it?"

"I have decided not to go back to work and I'm going to sell my share; do you want to buy it?"

This was not what Sev had expected, "John I am sure that between Frank and me something can be worked out, but why don't you leave it for at least a couple of months to be sure that's what you want to do?"

"If that's what you want then I'll wait, but only to give you time to work out the details. I can assure you I won't be changing my mind. Understand that it is the business that has destroyed me."

Sitting on the seat next to John's vegetable garden for quite some time neither spoke.

"What are you going to do John?"

"After I tidy up a few things here, I might rent the house out; then I'll go to Greece and spend some time tracking down my long-lost relatives."

With a sigh Sev said, "Well, whatever you do I will miss you and you know I will always be here if you ever need me."

Robert, with Barbara and son Colin, left for his overseas posting as planned, saddened that his mother was not with them.

John went to the airport to farewell them. Robert could not help but notice that his once chubby robust Dad was now thin and haggard and only a shadow of himself. For the first time he had a twinge of guilt about deserting him in his time of need. He then justified it by thinking that whatever happened he had brought it on himself.

It was an uncomfortable parting, with no one knowing what to say to each other. In the end John embraced Barbara, looked at his son and said, "I am so sorry Robert that we have not been closer. I know that it's my fault, but I only hope that one day you will understand how I am hurting. Please keep in touch; if I have moved, Sev will know where I am. Good luck, I do love you."

With that he turned and walked away.

A NEW FAMILY

CHAPTER SIX

Life for Sev continued happily. His children had grown up; his love for Gloria matured over time but never lost its intensity. Although there were times when his guilt over his night with Jean made him feel unworthy of Gloria's love.

Two lives, that at one stage could have been wasted, flourished as time went by. Sev's legal practice was now one of the largest in the city, employing twelve other solicitors as well as research assistants, office staff and secretaries.

His income from the practice, plus a bit of padding from Naxos Condiments and Catering Supplies, meant he had become moderately wealthy.

Gloria was well known and respected for her charity work, particularly working with the Sydney City Mission helping the homeless and the girls that worked on the streets. With her trim figure and smart attire, there was a regal bearing about her that never failed to impress those meeting her. In quiet moments she often thought about her early life as a girl on the streets but managed to keep this tucked away in a dark corner of her mind.

Driving home after a particularly busy day, turning from Oxford Street into Jersey Road Sev took his eyes off the road to adjust the radio.

In that split second, out of the corner of his eye he saw an old car charging out of Jersey Road heading straight at him. His last thought was, 'Shit not my new BMW,' then a screeching of rubber on bitumen followed by a piercing scream of metal against metal, and then blackness engulfed him.

In his next waking moment, he was looking through what appeared to be a smoky haze.

As his vision started to clear, he saw a white-coated man and a girl. Slowly regaining consciousness, he realised that he was in a bed with white sheets. Slowly it came to him that he must be in hospital.

The male was speaking to him, "Mr. Cockini can you hear me?" His tongue felt swollen in his mouth and with some difficulty he managed to reply, "Yes I can hear you, please can I have a drink?"

The girl reached over and held a glass with a straw up to his lips.

As things began to clear he felt a blinding headache that racked his whole body. "God, I feel awful, am I all right? Who are you?"

The man standing next to his bed announced, "I'm Doctor Spalding, and I will be looking after you. You're in Royal Prince Alfred Hospital after a nasty accident, but you're going to be alright. We will give you something for the headache and let you sleep for a while, then we'll be back to see how you're getting on."

"Thanks Doctor, has anyone told my wife?"

"Yes, we have and she will be in to see you shortly. In the meantime, try and get some rest."

As Sev drifted off to sleep, somewhere in the back of his mind he was thinking, "Doctor Spalding, that's a familiar name."

When Sev woke, he was clear headed except for the headache.

Looking around the room he felt quite alarmed at what had happened and was thankful that he appeared to be alright. Gingerly he moved his fingers, his hands and arms, and next his legs, thinking, well that's not too bad. All the bits appear to be there and working!

Then a voice interrupted his thoughts,

"Don't worry, apart from a decent bump on your head from contact with the steering wheel you are all in one piece. After we're sure that you're not concussed you can go home."

Sev looked up to see the young Doctor Spalding standing at the end of the bed checking his notes.

Suddenly like a bolt from nowhere, he realised that this doctor was most likely his son. As calmly as he could he said, "Tell me Doctor Spalding, where do you come from?"

He raised his head, smiled and said, "Why does it interest you?"

Sev countered, "Just indulge me, where do you live?"

'I have a flat close to the hospital, before that I lived in Pymble with my family."

"Is your Dad a doctor with a practice in Chatswood?"

"Yes, before he retired, why, do you know him?"

Sev had no idea how to handle this any further, and despite his gut-wrenching inner turmoil he covered himself by saying; "I did know him years ago, how is he keeping?"

"Quite well actually considering his age; he's over eighty now."

"What about your mother, Beryl?"

He replied, "Sadly, she passed away last year."

Sev said, "I am so sorry to hear that. Would you please give your Dad my regards? There is a business card in my wallet, would you please take one. Doctor, there's something very important to me that I would like to talk to you about. Would you please give me a ring after I get out of here?"

"This is all very mysterious, are you going to keep me in suspense?"

Sev hesitated for what seemed minutes, and then with more courage than he felt, said, "I am sorry, I have no choice; but please call me at my office, which may be more convenient for you."

"I see that you are a solicitor, which makes your request even more intriguing."

At that moment the door opened and Gloria, James and Vanessa, burst into the room, all talking at once,

"Dad, Dad, how are you, are you all right?"

Then they all stopped and looked at the doctor, sensing that they had interrupted something.

Gloria was looking hard at him as if she knew who he was. Gathering herself she said, "I'm so sorry doctor, we have interrupted you, I'm Mrs. Cockini, Gloria, and our children James and Vanessa."

Doctor Spalding also seemed to feel that there was something in the air, and after a moment's hesitation said, "No, not at all I was just leaving, nice to meet you all," and left.

They all stared to talk at once, then they stopped, and quietness descended on the room.

They were shocked to see their Dad quietly crying.

"Dad, what's the matter?" They all said at once.

"Nothing, I'm just so happy to see you all here, thank you."

Gloria interrupted, "enough of all this, let's just be happy that Dad is still with us and did not get seriously hurt. Pity about the BMW though. It doesn't look too good now. Now, that will really make Dad unhappy."

"Well, I may just have to buy a new one."

James leaned over and gave his Dad a hug, "Glad you're okay Dad."

Vanessa had her turn and cried all over him.

Then Gloria stepped in and said, "We must all leave so Dad can get some rest, when will they let you out Sev?"

"If my brain is alright, I should be home in a couple of days, certainly by the week end."

They all left, leaving Sev to mull over the enormity of what he had found out.

The following day they gave him the okay to go home with clear instructions to rest for a few days before returning to work and to call if he had any signs of his vision blurring or further headaches.

The following Monday Sev was back at his office feeling in good health and spirit. His only gripe was that he had to go and buy a new car.

Two weeks later Sev was sitting at his desk wondering if Dr Paul Spalding was going to ring him.

Then his long-trusted friend and secretary, Vivian Edwards knocked quietly on his door and entered.

"Excuse me Sev, there's a young man outside who would like to see you. He doesn't have an appointment. He said his name is Paul Spalding."

"Thanks Vivian, bring him in, only you could guess who he is. Please see that we are not interrupted."

"All I can say to that is that he looks remarkably like you."

"Vivian, just leave us alone for about fifteen minutes, then would you please bring us a cup of coffee, one or both of us is going to need it."

Sev stood up as Paul came in and offered his hand, and said, "Let's sit over here on the couch. Did you mention me to your Dad?"

"No, I didn't, I thought I would see what this is all about first."

"That was probably a wise move. Paul, there is quite a long story for me to tell, so I will ask your indulgence, it may take a little time."

And he started his story.

"When I was a teenager, still at secondary school, my parents left me and returned to Greece. Fortunately, I found board with an elderly widow in Glebe who took me into her care.

My school marks were good enough to get me into university and I studied law. I helped support myself by selling newspapers at Central Railway Station and Several other ventures, which were not always legal. During this period, I met a girl who had a background similar to mine. She was abandoned when she was just a child, and for some time had to live on the streets. There was an affinity between us; we understood one and other and had had similar problems.

Then towards the end of my time at university I went to a student's party in Strathfield. I remember the night so clearly.

Standing on my own, I noticed a girl standing over near the barbecue. She was beautiful, tall with long blond hair, and a flawless complexion. I introduced myself, and right from that moment I knew that one day I would marry this girl.

Her name was Elizabeth Spalding.

We went through the usual courtship period and eventually married. We never really had the blessing of her parents. They, particularly her father, thought I was just some opportunistic, devious, wog Greek.

During this time, I occasionally caught up with the other girl to see how she was going.

When I started working, I was able to give her some help financially, and eventually put a deposit on a flat for her. I also found her a real job with the local real estate agent.

My married life was on the other side of the page, so to speak, and my wife never knew about the other girl.

We were both happy and eventually Elizabeth became pregnant.

When birth time came, I took her to the Crown Street Women's

Hospital, for what should have been a normal birth. The child was born healthy, but Elizabeth died from complications."

Paul stood up, ashen faced, and was about to speak when Sev continued, "No Paul, let me finish the whole story.

Right from the start it was agreed that the Spalding's would look after the child, or at least until I was able to do so myself. Initially it was agreed that I would have open-ended access. Then Doctor Spalding decided to do a little checking through a local detective agency. They reported that I was a drug user and dealer, plus, I mixed with a known prostitute. In essence I was classified as an undesirable character.

I did trade in some pep pills, or whatever, at uni; it was the only way to pay my fees. The other girl prostituted herself for a very short time, basically so she could eat. After that she worked on the front reception desk at one of our better-known massage parlours.

With this biased information, the Spalding's denied me all access to the child. I knew there was no point in fighting it in the courts, as I could never win.

Later, I used to go to the school sports and Saturday cricket, hiding behind trees like a criminal to watch my son. I also used to write letters, which I suspect, were never handed on, as I never, ever, received a reply.

In the end I just gave up, accepting the fact that I could do no more, and the boy was probably better off without me.

Paul, no doubt you have worked out by now, you are that boy and I am your father."

After a long hesitation that seemed like hours Paul stood up and came to Sev with his arms open. They embraced in a highly-charged emotional moment.

He said, "Dad I am so sorry that we have missed so much of our lives. What do you think I should do now? Will I tell him at home?"

Sev said, "No, there is no point now, he did what he thought was best for you. He is now elderly, so let him spend the rest of his time in peace. All that I ask is that we keep in touch and see each other regularly, perhaps you might like to spend time with Gloria and your step brother and sister."

Paul replied with a smile, "Dad, for an old wog Greek you give good counsel. I agree and would love to spend time with my other family. By the way, this means that I'm half Greek too, that's one I never thought of!"

Looking at his watch Paul said, "I have to get to work, how about I give you a call tomorrow and we can arrange a visit to meet my other family?"

With that they embraced again and Paul left looking slightly bewildered.

Vivian came in and said, "Well Sev, how did it go?"

"Wonderful, I feel so happy and relieved that it's now all out in the open. It's late now, so I think I'll go home and break the news to the others."

They embraced like old friends and Vivian said, "I am so happy for you, Sev."

Currently John was still rearranging his life to extract himself from the business.

While he was waiting for Sev and Frank to come up with a proposal he had a phone call at home from Steven. It was unusual to get calls from Steven, and after a couple of polite preliminaries he said, "John, there's something I'd like to talk to you about. Could you give me a few minutes if I called around?"

John replied, "Sure, I'm not going anywhere", thinking, "what's all this about?"

"Good I'll be there in about fifteen minutes."

Shortly after, the doorbell rang, and John opened it to let Steven in. "Well this is a surprise, it's not often I have my brother call."

They sat down in the lounge and John said, "Before we get down to business or whatever is on your mind, can I get you a drink."

"I would like a Scotch if you have one thanks."

"Two Scotches, coming up."

John took a bottle with a jug of water and two glasses from the buffet and placed them on the coffee table, "Here, help yourself, you know how you like it."

They both took a swallow and John said, "I must say you've got me a little intrigued, so don't keep me in suspense, what's on your mind?"

"John, if you are going to sell your share of the business, I think we should at least keep it in the family."

"And pray, how I am going to do that, there is no one with that sort of cash."

To John's surprise Steven replied, "Sell it to me, I will pay you half the price now, and in a private deal between you and me the balance can be held over for, say, three years."

John thought for a moment then said, "I will sell it to you but no deal on delayed payment, it would have to be all now, up front or no deal."

"I didn't want to have to go too deeply into debt, but if I have to I will."

John responded with, "That's your problem, if you reckon can handle it, okay; but first we must agree on the price. You would have to pay the same price that Sev offered which is half a million dollars. If you can handle that, we have a deal. No doubt you're aware that with your existing share you would have an individual majority, but overall control would still be with Sev."

"That's fine, I'm in."

Before we go any further, I must talk to Sev about it. If he agrees, then I'll ask him to draw up a contract."

"It looks like we might have a deal. Let's shake on it and then see if we can make an impression on this bottle of Scotch.

At least Dad would be pleased if he was still with us."

"What about Robert, are you going to tell him?"

"No, I'll leave that to you guys. I haven't heard from him let alone that bitch he married. In fact, I don't really know where they are, nor do I care."

Steven sat quietly for a few moments before saying, "John, I have not said this before, but I am really sorry that you and Jean split up."

"Firstly, so am I, secondly we did not split up as you say, she left me, and I hope the business does not have the same impact on your marriage."

"Ours is a different kind of relationship and that problem is most unlikely."

With some emotion John replied, "She left me, and the obvious conspiracy with Robert, and the possibility that she was having an affair makes the whole thing even more bloody tacky. It's a pity that I didn't wake up before we formalised their share of the business; but I suppose they had that worked out some time ago.

What sort of relationship do you have with Millie, I always liked that girl, and she has a bit of spunk. Are you still a poofter or something?"

"John, whiskey does that to us, your comment does not warrant a reply. I think it's time for me to go. We will leave the next move to Sev, in the meantime if I can help you with anything please give me a ring."

They both stood up and, uncharacteristically, Steven took him in an embrace and said, "Hang in there brother, and don't forget if you ever need me, I will be there."

With that he let himself out and disappeared into the night.

Sev came around late the following week, making another good excuse for John to get the Scotch out. He had draft contracts with him for Steven's buy out.

He said, "John, I can understand you going with your brother in this deal, but I wish you had discussed it with me first. It is giving Steven a little too much control. If he happened to get Robert on his side then, between them, they would have absolute control. Anyway, it is no longer your concern; you have what you wanted, that is freedom. Anyway, let's look at the contracts."

"No, stuff it, Sev, that's your job, and you are the one person in world that I trust explicitly. I don't want to know about it. Just show me where to sign so we can settle down and have a drink. More importantly, how is Gloria and the kids?"

"They are great John, but James and Vanessa are no longer kids. I am so grateful that I have been able to give them a better start in life to what we had. I often reminisce and think how I would never have made it without your support."

"Bullshit Sev, you were always in control. The one thing I will always hang on to is that we will always be mates, no matter what course our lives take from here."

"I'll drink to that, but there are a lot of things I've done in my life that I could never be proud of that even you don't know about. So, the affluence I enjoy now is not without a little cloud of conscience. To hell with it anyway, let's have another scotch, and this is a happy bottle not a morbid one."

With the bottle well on the way to being empty, they were both wallowing in nostalgia of past times and goodwill to each other.

"Sev, do you ever wonder what happened to your parents?"

"Yes, I do, quite a lot actually. Since I have had a family of my own and they have grown up I have a little more understanding of what it must have been like for them, not being able to even speak the language in a strange country."

"When I go overseas would you like me to try and find them?"

"Thanks John, I would like you to do that for me, who knows I may be able to help them, that is if they are still alive."

With all our good luck there have been some sad things as you well know. I lost Elizabeth and my son for all those years and you have lost Jean.

So, in a way, we've paid a heavy price for what we have now."

John stood, "You're right Sev, but right now I'm pissed and am going to bed."

With that he staggered across the room and disappeared into the bedroom.

Sev let himself out thinking; he's upset and just wants to hide his emotions.

Leaving his car, he staggered down to Parramatta Road to look for a taxi to get him home.

Over the next weeks John started to feel better about himself, and for the first time in a long time, totally free.

He bought his open-ended around the world plane ticket and prepared to leave, first stop Athens.

No fanfare or farewell parties, he just said a quick goodbye to the Steven and the warehouse staff.

That evening he drove over for an emotional goodbye to Sev and Gloria.

ANOTHER GENERATION

CHAPTER SEVEN

ENGLAND YEAR 2005

Colin Naxos was tall and dark with a swarthy look inherited from his Greek parentage.

To those who did not know him he was something of an enigma with a bearing of authority and intelligence. Having been born in Australia but raised in England, he often appeared out of place in the company of his English counterparts. His father, Robert, had died from a massive heart attack when he was in his most formative years. His mother appeared to be more interested in her own social pursuits than spending time with her son. He was packed off to boarding school for his secondary education.

That was where he learned what independence meant and how to look after himself. He was an exceptional student with a retentive memory and an ability to focus on any issue. He was admitted to Oxford University and chose economics and commerce courses.

His best friend from university times was Trevor Donaldson. They both worked hard and played hard, whether it was partying or sport. They were the opening batsmen for the university first eleven and played rugby in the winter. Girls were an attraction but came second to studies and sport; they liked the ones that they didn't have to chase. With their looks that was rarely a problem.

As was their usual habit, they always met at The Cricketers Arms pub for a pint or two on Friday night and from there planned their other activities.

On this night Trevor bought the first pint of ale, and after sitting down on their stools at the bar said, "Well, what's on tonight old boy? Studies are over, so we may as well hit the town."

"I would love to, but my dear mother has been chasing me to go down to Hove to see her tomorrow, something is on. She usually doesn't bother too much about what I'm doing or where I am."

"Bugger that old boy, don't let that get in the way of a night on the town; tell her you'll come on Sunday."

"Okay, you talked me into it; I'll see if I can get her now on the mobile and tell her to expect me on Sunday." Using the automatic dialler, he rang home. As he waited for a connection, he was thinking, good she's not home, and was just about to disconnect when his mother answered. "Hello, Barbara Naxos."

"Hi Mum, it's me."

"Well it's about time you rang; I'm expecting you tomorrow, what time will you be here?"

"Actually, I won't be able to get there tomorrow, but I will definitely make it on Sunday, sorry."

"Colin that's not good enough, I've cancelled my appointments and rearranged my schedule, and there are some important family matters I must talk to you about."

Colin thought, here we go again, "Mum, I have arrangements as well as you, and I can't always change them on a moment's notice. If it's that important tell me on the phone."

Indignantly, she replied, "I will not tell you on the phone, the matter involves your relatives in Australia and it's too complicated."

Colin replied with a tone that not long ago he would have not dared use with his dictatorial mother.

"I didn't think I had any left."

"Well your father's father, your Grandfather, was still around somewhere until he apparently died a few months ago. There are some serious issues and I need to discuss them with you, so please come on Sunday."

"But mum, you realise that it will take me nearly all day to even get to Hove."

His mother was softening, and she replied, "Alright then, I'll book two rooms at the Grosvenor Kensington Hotel in Harrington Road, and meet you there on Sunday. You do know where it is, it's close to Earls Court. You can then go home on Monday morning."

Colin thought, Heavens this must be serious, and readily agreed to the meeting. Mother really likes to play the social butterfly role, all show and presence and not much substance. I shouldn't think like that about my mother, but it's true. She flits around the social scenes like the merry widow, certainly never showing any shortage of money. I wonder where it all comes from.

On Sunday he caught an early train for the journey and settled down with a book to pass the time.

He soon found that he could not concentrate and began to recall what he knew about his relatives in Australia. The only thing he had been told by his father, Robert, was that his grandfather had owned an importing business, in which in later years he had sold his share to his brother.

When his wife, Jean, had died, he disappeared, and no one knew of his whereabouts for many years.

His mother and Father Robert had moved from Australia to France and then on to England to pursue his career as an artist. His untimely death came when Colin was only fourteen.

Neither of his mother's parents was alive, nor did he recall any contact with them over the years.

Colin never thought much about having relatives in Australia. It was a subject that was never discussed in the family, particularly after his father died.

Sitting there listening to the rattle of the train on the rails, he wondered why his mother was always parsimonious with information about both sides of the family.

The closer he got to London, the more he felt that there was more to this call for a meeting than he had previously thought.

Leaving the tube, Colin took a cab for the hotel trip, arriving in time to check in and change out of his casual gear before meeting his mother for lunch.

Dressing in his best suit, with a traditional white shirt and university tie, he felt suitably attired for the occasion of dining with Mother. He thought that this was necessary for the sake of harmony, as he knew only too well what a social snob his mother was. Checking his image again in the full-length mirror, he gave his hair a last brush and left his room for the meeting.

His room was on the first floor, so ignoring the lift he walked down the richly carpeted stairway to the hotel foyer.

The area oozed luxury and refinement, an environment that Colin was quite comfortable in. He could have passed for any young executive or merchant banker of the new breed.

He found Mother in the cocktail lounge, sitting on her own, at a small table, looking as glamorous as ever in a pale green silk ensemble and fashionably cut blond hair. As he approached her, he could not help but think, "she certainly is a good looker, she appears younger every time I see her, but then she must still be only in her mid-forties."

Seeing him coming, she stood to offer herself for the obligatory cheek kissing.

"Colin, how lovely to see you, you look absolutely wonderful. Rather than running around with that friend of yours, Trevor wasn't it? You should find a nice girl and get married.

By the way, your hair is too long; you look much better with it cut short."

"Whoa, hold on mum I've only just arrived and you're trying to have me married off and have my hair cut. What about you anyway? I'm sure you would not have any trouble finding a husband."

His mother quickly replied, "Enough of that, if I ever do you will be the first to know. Now go and get me a gin and tonic in a long glass, thank you."

As he walked across to the bar Colin thought, *'that's probably why she has never married again, always bossing people around.'*

Returning to the table with her drink, and a beer for himself, Colin sat down and chided, "Well Mum, I have not heard from you for at least three months and suddenly we must have this urgent meeting. What's so important?"

"When you're sitting down so you can't fall over, I will get straight to the point.'

Colin sat down in the comfortable club lounge chair and waited for his mother to speak.

"Your Grandfather was the founder of an importing business in Sydney called, Naxos Condiments. He died several months ago in a small village somewhere north of Sydney. The scant information I have is that he was murdered. Understand that years ago he broke up the business passing a significant share to your father and a lesser portion to his brother Steven. Later your father sold his share to his brother Steven and this, with income from his paintings is what I live on today.

I believe that there was still a significant amount of money left with your Grandfather, and it appears that this has gone missing since his untimely death. This money should be our inheritance."

Colin was momentarily speechless and then said, "What can I do about that; surely there are solicitors in Sydney to handle it."

"There is a solicitor involved, Sev Cockini, an old friend of the family, who also had a share of the business. So, I would not be comfortable in having him represent us, as I am sure there would be a conflict of interest."

Colin replied, "But Mum as I said before, what do you expect me to do about it?"

"I know exactly what needs to be done, I want you to go to Australia and find out what is going on."

"You must be joking! I have never been there in my life and I don't know any of these people."

"All the better, you will have a fresh start and a clear mind to find the truth. Your university education must be worth something to you."

"That's Okay, but they never taught me how to be a detective. I need some time to think about this."

His mother took a packet out of her carry bag and handed it to him, "In here is a tape with all the information I have, plus photos of your Grandfather and his brother. If you want time to think about it you can do it over lunch. I reserved a table for one o'clock and its time now to go into the dining room."

Colin hesitated, then knowing his mother, quickly stood up and helped with her chair. With his hand respectfully on her arm, he escorted her to the dining room.

He was thinking: "She still likes a show."

Sitting down, his mother quipped, "Colin, it is quite distasteful to discuss business when trying to eat, so tell me what you have been doing during your last days at university. Have you still got that Trevor fellow hanging about? I thought he was quite crass when you brought him home that time.'

"Mum you are insulting my best friend. He is a perfect gentleman when you get to know him. He was only trying to test you out for a reaction, and you responded, predictably."

The waiter arrived to take their order, and with a flourish his mother said, "You can order Colin, something light with a nice cold bottle of Chardonnay."

While they were waiting for their meal to be served, Colin thought, "There is no way I can get out of doing this trip, but perhaps there is something I can do to ease the pain."

"Mum, I'll tell you what I will do. You pay for Trevor to go as well and you have a deal, keeping in mind that by the sound of it I may need all the help I can get."

"Colin, that sounds very expensive, but as I said, no business talk until I've finished my lunch. Are you happy with the wine? Then order another one."

After another bottle of very drinkable Australian Jacobs Creek Chardonnay they were both much more relaxed and happier with small talk, enjoying each other's company.

Coffee time came, and Colin said, "Okay Mum, I don't believe you're telling me the whole story, and unless I have all the facts then I'm not going."

"Colin, all I know is what's on that tape. After you have listened to it, you'll know as much as I do. The only thing not mentioned is that many years ago, just prior to our leaving Australia your grandmother was attacked in the local park and died from a stab wound.

The police believe she was returning home from meeting someone, but it was never established who she met.

She had not been sexually attacked, but an autopsy showed traces of semen, which did not match that of your grandfather.

The coronal inquest could not trace this to any of the people connected to the business, or for that matter your grandfather. So that's all I know, and I'm finding this conversation quite distasteful. Colin, after all, it is your inheritance as well as mine we are chasing. I suspect there could be several million pounds involved, maybe more.

If you can't do it, then I will have to hire one of those dreadful private detective agencies."

Colin replied, "Back to the question, if you agree for me to take Trevor, then I will go. That's the deal, yes or no?"

"You are being extremely difficult, and you've left me with very little choice. I agree, you can take your friend, travelling economy of course, and we must put a time limit on the trip, let's say one month. It will not be a free holiday."

"Mum you are an absolute treasure; we must find a husband for you, preferably a rich one."

"Colin you should not make fun of your mother. What would your father think?"

"Come on Mum, he's been dead for ten years."

That night Colin's mother insisted that he escort her to the theatre. to see a show.

At the interval break they stood out in the crowd, this tall, dark handsome man with a beautiful woman who obviously adored him. Colin noticed the furtive glances and felt a little like a "Toy Boy" with his rich and beautiful mistress.

Returning to the hotel they went to the lounge for a coffee and nightcap before retiring. After coffee, Colin dutifully escorted his mother back to her room, promising to meet her for breakfast.

He was in too much turmoil to even think of sleeping and decided to return to the bar for a nightcap. At a quiet table, with a window facing the street, he sat and mulled over the day's events. Engrossed in his thoughts, he became aware of a girl standing at his table, "Hello", she said, "You look lonely, do you want company?"

Uninvited she sat down. "Buy me a drink?"

Colin looked over at a quite attractive, well-dressed young woman, and thought that accent, she's not from around here.

"I wasn't looking for company, actually I'm about to retire for the night. I've had a long day, but what the hell, I'll buy you drink. It's not often that a beautiful girl picks me up, what would you like?"

She replied, "I am not picking you up, as you put it. I thought you looked lonely, or troubled. "I would just like a glass of white wine thanks; but hang on, don't stretch yourself or worry too much, I'm not a girl of the night looking for a date or anything. I was just like you, about to have a nightcap before retiring for the night."

Colin replied, "Sorry if I came over like that, just relax while I get a drink."

Returning to the table with the drinks, Colin sat down and said, "My name is Colin Naxos, what's yours?"

"Kathleen, Kathleen Morgan."

"That accent, are you an Aussie?"

"You're close; no- I'm not an Aussie. I come from New Zealand; but now I'm living in Sydney because of my work. What about Naxos, is that Greek?"

"Spot on! I was born in Australia but have lived nearly all my life here in the UK.

"Tell me Kathleen, what are you doing, wandering around the heart of London on your own?"

She replied, "I'm not wandering around London on my own as you put it. I work for one of the major department stores in Australia, and I'm on a buying trip looking for speciality kitchen items."

"How interesting, that must be quite a challenge. I thought you would be in China for that?"

"Yes, it is a challenge. Actually, I am going to Italy for a week, and then I'm off to China. The problem now is that everyone goes straight to China and arrives home with the same products. I'm spending a little time around Europe looking for some different products. What about you, what are you doing sitting here on your own?"

"Well, I live up in Oxford and I came down for lunch with my mother. Originally, she came from Sydney and she has just convinced me to go there early in the New Year to check out some long-lost relatives. It is a bit of a daunting task for me as I have never been to the Southern Hemisphere before."

Now that the ice had been broken Colin found that he was enjoying her company and was happy to sit and talk to her for the next hour about her travel experiences.

As it was getting late, and they were both weary, they retired to their respective rooms with a promise to meet tomorrow for lunch.

In bed Colin lay awake for a long time, wondering how he was going to handle this trip to Australia. He was not even sure that Trevor would go with him.

Colin woke late next morning, feeling a little jaded after his demanding day. After picking up the paper from outside his door he made himself a cup of coffee and sat out on the balcony. The paper did not interest him very much and his mind wandered back to the girl he met last night and his commitment to meet her for lunch.

Now what in the hell did I do that for? I would be better to catch the early train home. As he was thinking about how to extract himself from the date the phone rang.

It will probably be mum he thought. "Hello, Colin Naxos."

A cheery voice replied, "Hi, it's Kathleen, how are you this morning?"

"Great, considering it was a late night for me after a long day; however, after I've had my shower and another cup of coffee, I'll be back close to normal. How about you?"

"I am just great. Now what time are we meeting for lunch?"

Colin didn't have the courage to say he did not want to go, so he said, "How about twelve thirty in the foyer.

Kathleen, sounding bright and breezy, mocked, "You may not recognise me, do you want me to wear a name badge with a pink carnation?"

Colin laughed and said, "There is no way I could forget you; and if you're not there on time I will pursue you to your room, what number is it?"

"I don't let men into my room that easily, even if they are young and handsome, so I will make an effort to be there on time."

Finishing his coffee, Colin dressed, and feeling relaxed went down to the garden restaurant for breakfast with his mother.

Now that the purpose of the meeting was over, they were both relaxed and enjoyed the time together. Colin could not resist the opportunity to pester his mother over her social life, probing whether she had a male friend.

Barbara was secretly flattered by his attention but tried to remain aloof from this inquisitive banter.

"Colin I am your mother and you should not be asking me these questions. If I do have a friend, I will let you know at the appropriate time."

"I take from that that you do have a friend?"

"Enough of all this, I must go. Please take care on your trip and try to ring every couple of days to let me know how you're going."

With that they both stood and surprisingly for Colin, instead of the usual cheek kissing, she embraced him tightly and left.

Feeling in need of exercise and the need to clear his mind, Colin took a long walk before heading back to his room to have a look at the tapes, notes and photos his mother had left for him. As he didn't have a player for the tapes, the photos and notes meant little to him, He replaced them in the box.

Preparing for lunch, Colin dressed in smart casual slacks and jacket then ambled down to the foyer to meet his new friend. Deliberately, Colin thought, Kathleen arrived ten minutes late. From a distance he saw her leave the lift; look around, then cross the foyer towards him.

"Hell", he thought. "She looks great; I did not notice that last night. She is slightly older too, must be in her mid-twenties."

He stood up, and taking her hand, kissed her lightly on the cheek, then he stood back looking into her eyes. "Hello Kathleen, you look wonderful, even better than I remembered. You didn't need the pink carnation."

Fully accepting his greeting, she replied, "Thank you Colin, you are certainly the quintessential English charmer."

"Kathleen, you know how to make a man feel good, shall we go into lunch?"

Over lunch they chatted lightly about London, their travels and life Down Under. Kathleen quizzed him about his Sydney relatives, and he filled her in on the little he knew of them at that time. Suddenly, Kathleen said, "What did you say the company was?"

"Naxos Condiments, or Naxos Catering Supplies. I think they operate from a suburb near the airport, wherever that is."

"This is a huge coincidence. I know these people quite well, and our stores do quite a lot of business with them. They are by far the biggest wholesaler of condiments, cooking utensils and catering equipment in the country."

"You're joking, my mother had no idea they were now that big."

"Colin, when are you planning to go on this trip?"

"Sometime late January, Why?"

"Because I will be back in the first week of February, and if you can arrange your schedule around February then we can get together, as I'm sure that I could help you.

Apart from that I would like to see you. Here's my card and I will write my home phone number on the back; so give me a ring when you arrive. But sadly, for now I must go, as I have work to do, and you have a train to catch. Lunch is my shout, business expense!"

They parted in the foyer, this time with a hug and show of affection, both promising to meet again in Sydney.

Colin returned to Oxford in a bit of turmoil. After unpacking and changing into casual jeans and shirt, he rang Trevor. "Listen old boy get your arse over here quick, no, I will meet you down at the Pub. I know it's late, but we have some serious business to discuss, so see you in ten minutes."

Trevor was already there with two pints on the bar when he arrived and said "Right mate, what is the panic about. Have you been caught with your pants down or something?"

Colin picked up his pint, and after taking a big swallow said, "By God that's good, but they tell me it's not as good as Aussie beer."

"Since when? How would you know anyway? What's the story, what happened with your Mother?"

Colin filled him in on the story, saving the best until last.

"I still have to listen to the tape which may fill in some of the blanks, but the more I think about it the more daunting the task appears. When I get out there, this girl Kathleen may be a big help in more ways than one. I tell you mate, she is a knock-out."

Trevor remarked, "You always did have a way with the girls. Well, at least you'll have a trip, even if you don't manage to unravel all the family mysteries."

Very casually Colin announced, "Oh by the way, I forgot to mention it before, you are going too, all expenses paid." Trevor nearly fell off his stool, "You're kidding me"!

"No, this is for real, so at least you can buy me another pint. Kathleen might have a friend, but she could be too old for you."

"Go jump Colin, I'm older than you. I might even win this Kathleen away from you."

"You might too, but I doubt it. She is hooked on my English natural charm."

"Bullshit, Colin, I have seen you in action before remember."

"Down to the serious stuff, Colin replied, "Firstly I take it you want to go, and you don't have any other commitments for February."

"Yes, yes, I will go, and if I have any other dates they are cancelled as of now."

"What about that girl you've been sleeping with." Trevor asked.

"Bugger that, if she loves me, or likes my sexual charm she will be faithful and wait until I get back."

The next week they booked their tickets with British Airways and prepared for their adventure.

Colin had an inspiration and e-mailed Kathleen, giving her their arrival dates and asked if she could direct him to a suitable hotel.

There was a quick reply, originating in Milan, saying how she was looking forward to seeing him again, and suggested that he book at The Hyatt for the first few nights to get settled in. After that they could move into a serviced apartment, which would be more economical.

After the Christmas period and festivities were over, Colin and Trevor, like a couple of boys going on their first scout trip, updated their wardrobes to suit the Australian summer, bought new suitcases and a small back pack each for cabin luggage.

Colin had another meeting with his mother, to go over all the information they had and to make sure that she transferred enough funds into his account.

To Colin's surprise she went one further and arranged a Visa card for him with the account going directly to her.

By the middle of January, they were organised and ready to go. All they had to do now was to sit back and wait for departure date. This was a good time and excuse to have a constant procession of farewell parties with their university friends.

The big day came, and Colin and Trevor packed their gear and boarded a train for Heathrow Airport.

They both had a huge feeling of exuberance and exhilaration in anticipation of their big trip ahead. If they had had any idea of what was ahead, they would have stayed at home.

DOWN UNDER

CHAPTER EIGHT

The big Jumbo approached Sydney from the North East giving the passengers a marvellous panoramic view of Sydney Harbour and the famous bridge. Across the water from the bridge sat the equally famous Opera House, jutting out into the Harbour with its sail shaped structure that made it one of the world's most famous buildings.

The Harbour was a mass of ships of all shapes and sizes going about their business. The hustle and bustle of the Harbour gave it extra character.

Colin also had a view of the tall buildings which made up the central business district that ran down to the waters of the Harbour.

All the first trippers, like Colin and Trevor, were agog at the glimpses they were getting of one of world's great cities.

One returning local sitting next to Trevor, realising that this was his first trip, jokingly said, "I don't think we'll see any kangaroos in Pitt Street today, it will be too hot for them."

Trevor was quick to respond, "Well yeah mate, I suppose when it's too hot the tar sticks to their paws."

The plane landed safely after a perfect touch down at Sydney's Mascot Airport and taxied to the terminal building. Because of the city curfew, most international flights arrived after six am which also gave a faster transition through customs. One hour later they were outside the terminal waiting in a long queue for a taxi to take them to the city.

Colin had purchased a Sydney city and suburban map on his way through customs and was studying it intently when they got to the end of the queue for the next available cab.

"I would like to see this warehouse in Kent Road which appears to be on the way to the city. I'll ask the cabbie to go that way past it."

The next cab, the usual Ford, was theirs, and after dropping the luggage in the boot they clambered aboard and were ready to go.

"Where to now fellows?"

"The Hyatt please, it's at 7 Hickson Road The Rocks. Do you know where that is?"

"Listen mate, there isn't a cabbie in Sydney who would not know the Hyatt, haven't you been here before?"

"No never, this is our first trip. As it appears to be in the same direction could you go down Kent Road, I want to see a warehouse."

"What part of Kent Road mate?"

"No idea", Colin replied, "But the name of the place is Naxos Condiments."

"No problem boys, I know exactly where it is; I pick up a lot of fares from there. So, this is your first trip to Sydney eh?"

"Yes, it is actually, so we don't know our way around yet."

"No problem, you soon will. You have picked some fancy accommodation for a start. First though, I'll take you down Kent Road."

The driver took off at what seemed to them a suicidal speed and in the worldwide tradition of cabbies gave a non-stop recital on local and world affairs.

Leaving the airport, still talking non-stop, he took a fast left on an orange light, then right into a fairly major road. "This is Kent Road, the place you want is on the right-hand side down the other end, and do you want me to stop? I'll wait if you want."

Colin replied, "No, no, just slow up so I know where it is, we may have to come back tomorrow, so let's go straight to our Hotel."

Twenty minutes later they arrived at the Hyatt Hotel nestled right on the water's edge under the Harbour Bridge. After checking in they were shown to their room. Trevor opened the blinds to find they had a balcony with sweeping panoramic views across the Harbour.

"I have never seen anything like it in my life. This is going to cost a bloody fortune; does your Mother know what she is up for?" I hope she doesn't come to me later for a donation."

"She knows all right, and she has been here Several times that I know of, so don't worry about it. Let's stick to plan A and settle in for a few days until we know what we're going to do. After that we may look for a serviced apartment somewhere in the city. How about we have a quick catch-up kip and then we will go and check out the town."

Despite his outward display of confidence, Colin had a bad feeling in the pit of his stomach that they may have let themselves in for something that could be far above what was at first expected.

Seeing that Trevor was already dozing, he lay on his bed and soon fell into a troubled sleep.

Around lunchtime he woke and as Trevor was still sleeping, he took some hotel stationery and started to write a list of key contacts and an order in which to start. From the information he had, there was a fellow called Charlie Thornton who was the first to find his Grandfather. If I tackle him first, then the local police, I may then get an idea as to our next move. After that I will try the business in Mascot, then the solicitor who was involved in the business.

In case he is the one who may have pocketed the cash, I will leave his brother Steven until last. By then I may have enough background to know where I'm going with it all.

The address given for Charlie Thornton was in Ocean Parade, The Entrance, so that's a start. Tomorrow we'll hire a car and head up that way; it doesn't appear to be too far. First, I must buy a city and country directory.

"Come on Trevor, wakey, wakey, time to go, get your arse out of bed, we have things to do; but first we'll try the local cuisine for lunch."

After showering they dressed lightly for the Sydney summer and presented themselves at the dining room for lunch.

They were given a table at the window overlooking the water, the ferry terminal and on to the Opera House.

Colin mused, "I say Trevor, this is something special, maybe this is why all our lot wants to migrate out here."

"Trevor replied, 'If we can live right here count me in. I wonder what the local girls are like; I hear they are a pretty adventurous breed. When is this Kathleen going to be in touch? I am anxious to meet her friends"'!

"Now come on Trevor, get your mind above your navel, we have work to do."

After a magnificent lunch of grilled Flathead fillets and fresh salad, washed down with an excellent bottle of local wine, they were ready to check out the town.

Leaving the Hotel, they walked over to the ferry terminal, then up Pitt Street to the main shopping precinct.

Strolling down the Pitt Street Mall, Colin reminded Trevor that he was standing in the second most expensive retail strip in the world.

Trevor said, "Well, you are a fountain of knowledge, but tell me where the most expensive is?"

"I thought even you would know that; didn't you do commerce at uni? The most expensive is at home in the heart of London."

Next, they took the Sky Lift up to the top of Centrepoint Tower, the tallest building in Sydney. It was a clear day and the view over Sydney and the Harbour was awesome. "When the Olympic games where here I saw all the views of Sydney on the television, but I had no idea it was this big. That must be the Games site over there. I think we should get our detective work out of the way as quickly as possible, there must be lots to do around here."

"I would like to agree, but somehow I don't think it's going to be that easy. In fact, I would not be surprised if Mother held some of the story back. When I think about it, why would she go to all the expense to send us, when it could have been handled by local solicitors?"

Trevor old boy, I am beginning to think we might have been conned by my own mother. Anyway, it's getting late, so let's get back to the hotel and have an early night and be ready for tomorrow.

According to my trusty Gregory's map, Elizabeth Street is just up here and that's where that solicitor, Sev Cockini, who was a partner and Grandfather's friend, has his office. Let's go back that way and see where it is."

They found the office block without any trouble on the border of the CBD overlooking Hyde Park.

Colin mused, "Must be a big operation for this address." They walked into the foyer to check the tenant directory board as a lift door opened and a tall dark distinguished-looking man stepped out talking to a woman. As they walked towards them, they heard the woman say, "Good night Mr. Cockini, see you tomorrow."

Colin thought, "Hell that's Sev Cockini,' and on impulse he stepped over and said, "Excuse me, are you Mr. Cockini the solicitor?"

He stopped; looking surprised, and replied, "Yes I am, why do you ask?"

Showing confidence, he didn't feel, Colin offered his hand and said, "My name is Colin Naxos, I believe you were a friend of my late grandfather, John Naxos. This is my friend Trevor Donaldson."

He hesitated for a moment, and then said, "I most certainly was, and you would be Robert's boy then."

He warmly took Colin's hand saying, "Well how about that! We lost all contact with your father many years ago. How is he, by the way?"

Colin replied, "My Dad died nearly ten years ago."

"Well I am sorry to hear that. Are you here on holidays? Perhaps we could get together and catch up, maybe have lunch. I'm sorry but I can't stop now as I have a prior commitment. Look, here's my card, please give me a ring tomorrow and we can work something out to get together.'

"Thank you, I will do that."

With that Sev Cockini turned and walked out the door to a waiting car.

Colin and Trevor looked at one another before either spoke. Then Trevor asked, "Well, what do we make of that?"

"I'm not sure, he wasn't expecting us, that's for certain.

He did seem friendly enough though, but it was surprising that he did not know Dad died, after all he and old John were supposed to have been close.

Let's stick with plan A and go looking for this Charlie fellow first; it won't matter if we don't contact Mr. Cockini for a couple of days."

Back at the Hotel, after a couple of cold VB beers, Colin and Trevor wandered across to a Seafood restaurant situated on the waterfront in what was known as 'The Rocks' area

They splashed out on a huge seafood banquet of fish fillets, crayfish, crabs, calamari and a few oysters thrown in.

When finished, they agreed that they had never had a feed as good as that back in the old country.

Trevor, with a twinkle in his eye, raised his glass of Rosemount Chardonnay, and said, "Thanks Mum."

Colin replied, "That's alright, but I have a feeling that we are going to earn this before we're finished. For now, it's off to bed for me, are you coming or are you going to stop here."

"No, I'm coming, let's go."

The next morning Colin and Trevor were up early, and after picking up a rental car with a GPS system from the hotel they headed north for the area known as the Central Coast.

After crossing the Harbour Bridge, they found their way through the northern suburbs to pick up the M1 Northern Expressway.

An hour later they reached the Gosford exit and continued to the seaside village called "The Entrance"

It was no trouble to find Charlie Thornton's address in the small seaside village.

It was a nondescript red brick block of units in a nondescript street, but it was close to the estuary and had magnificent views across to an ocean beach.

His name was still on the tenant board in the foyer, so they took the stairs to the second floor and knocked on the door. There was an empty hollow sound to their knocking and they were not surprised that there was no answer.

They were just about to leave when the door of the neighbouring unit opened, and an elderly lady opened the door. She was short and rotund wearing an old pair of tracksuit pants with a floral shirt under a well-worn cardigan.

Her hair looked a little in need of brush, but she had nice grandmotherly face that made the boys feel comfortable.

In a croaky old smoker voice, she "Can I help you? There is no one in that unit."

Colin replied, "Thank you, we're looking for Charlie Thornton."

"Yes, you and a lot of others. As I have told everyone else, Charlie just took off and disappeared, didn't even bother to say goodbye, after all the things I did for him too. No forwarding address, or even a letter. It all looks a bit shady to me, after that mate of his was killed. There was another couple of men hanging about a while ago, all done up in suits and ties. I didn't like the look of them, so I kept out of the way."

Putting on his sincere face Colin said, "Well, I'm a relative of his, and we are out from England on a holiday and thought I'd look him up. Is there anything else you could tell me?"

"Yeah, I guessed you were a Pom, having a holiday eh? The only thing I can tell you is that his ex-wife lived down in Sydney. Come in and have a cuppa, and I'll see if I can find the address. Nobody has asked me before, so I will have to look for it."

Colin accepted the offer and they followed her inside.

Although small, it was a comfortable unit with a small balcony with some sweeping views of the estuary.

"Now you two boys just sit at the table over there and I'll get you a cuppa then see if I can find this address."

She was back in a little while with two mugs of tea and a carton of milk. Leaving them again she went off into a bedroom to reappear a short time later with an old envelope on which she had scribbled a name and phone number.

"Here you can have this, it's all I have. I remember that he gave it to me some time ago asking if I would contact her if anything ever happened to him. Her name was Hester Thornton; she never remarried, so I believe. One other thing, he told me once that he worked on the railways, as a train driver, I think.

We never talked much as he mostly kept to himself. I think he was drinker, I heard him a few times staggering up the stairs and then having trouble getting his key in the door lock.

But it's not for me to criticise, I used to enjoy a drink myself when I was younger you know.

But I never staggered about like him. The police came a few times, but they never bothered with me. He must have had a plan, because his rent was paid up and he also must have paid his phone and power accounts.

There hasn't been any mail since he left. Strange business if you ask me. Other than what was in the paper about him finding the body of his friend, that's all I know?"

Colin replied, "Thank you very much; you've been a great help. One more question, where would I find a copy of the local newspaper?"

"That's easy, just go to the local Library around the corner in the main street. I'm sure that there would be a copy there."

Colin thanked her again profusely, and they took their leave.

They found the local library and were pleased to see that they had copies of the local paper around the time that John Naxos was killed. After photocopying every article relating to the incident, Colin thought they would try their luck at the local police station.

The only statement they obtained was that the police were not looking for Charlie Thornton as he was cleared of any involvement in the death of John Naxos.

His death was the subject of a coroner's inquest, which indicated that he had been killed by persons, or a person unknown. They did not have any more information on the incident, but the case remained open.

Colin said, "I don't think there is any more we can do here so we may as well head back to the hotel."

Back in their room at the Hyatt Colin and Trevor sat out on the balcony with a cold Aussie beer to review the day's events.

Trevor, holding his Crown Larger said, "Hey John, this is so good, we don't get anything like this back home. Do I have to say thanks and do a toast to Mum every night?"

With a laugh Colin said, "No you thank me, you bloody twit!

Anyway, seriously, as I said some time ago, there is more to this than we first envisaged, and I can see it getting more and more involved. In fact, I think we should be aware that we could be stirring something up that could upset the wrong sort of people. Who knows, they may come looking for us."

Colin looked at his friend of many years thinking: he can be just a bit of a dag sometimes; then academically he was right up there with the brightest and best, but one would never know. If I ever needed someone for support, there would be none better than my slightly chubby friend Trevor.

He said, "Anyway let's enjoy ourselves while we can. You go and have a shave and smarten yourself up because I am going to ring Kathleen and invite her to dinner, so if you can make yourself look somewhere near respectable, I'll ask her to bring a friend."

A little nervously, he picked up the phone and rang the mobile number she had given him.

On the third ring she answered, "Hello Kathleen speaking."

Colin replied, "Is that the girl with the white carnation?"

"Well Hi, yes I was keeping the carnation especially for you in case you forgot me. I was wondering when I would hear from you. Where are you and how are you?"

"If you can make it into the Hyatt for dinner, I will answer all your questions. If you can bring a friend for my mate Trevor to make a foursome, I will be even more pleased. It might help to get us away on our own.

Grab a cab on my shout, you paid last time, remember."

"Colin I would love to come. I think my friend would definitely enjoy a night out too, so, see you about seven."

"Wonderful, we will wait in the foyer." Colin happily replied.

Colin managed to get Trevor spruced up and looking respectable and after changing into their best casual gear they waited in the foyer for their dates.

Kathleen came breezing in through the revolving doors first, looking fantastic, and was followed by another girl who was equally attractive. Trevor's mouth dropped about six inches in shock while Colin said, "Here are our dates. Shit mate, you owe me big time for this one, so behave yourself."

After a quick embrace Kathleen turned for the introductions with Trevor and her friend Meredith Kite.

Trevor was quick to say, "Colin you didn't tell me about this, do all the girls here look this good?"

Speaking to the girls Colin said, "I should have warned you about him. He thinks flattery will get him everywhere. Girls, if it's okay with you, we will eat here in the hotel rather than go out. First, how about we go into the lounge for a drink?"

After they settled down in the lounge and gone through the niceties of the day, Kathleen said, "Well, Colin, tell me how you are getting on with your investigative work."

"So far, So good. We had a bit of a break with John's fishing mate Charlie Thornton's neighbour. Strangely no one, including the police, had spoken to her before, and she was more than willing to tell us what she knew about Charlie; but she had no idea why he left or where he went. It appears that he just disappeared. The one thing she did was to give us his ex-wife's phone number here in Sydney, so we'll follow that one up tomorrow.

Charlie's relationship with John was purely as mates; they drank and went fishing together. There was no indication of anything deeper. He was rarely ever seen at Charlie's flat.

We checked the local papers at the library and found that the reports of my grandfather's death were pretty much the same as what my mother gave us back home. We also visited the local police station and found that they had no interest in Charlie Thornton or his whereabouts. There did not appear to be any active investigation going on into the John Naxos murder. My overall feeling is that there is certainly a bad smell about the whole thing. I am now seeing that there are three issues.

One, why was John killed? Two, where did his money go? Three, where is his friend, and why did he disappear?"

Kathleen replied, "I did a bit of research for you on the business, and as far as I can ascertain it is still run by old John's brother Steven Naxos, with two non-working partners.

One of the partners is a Frank Bennett, a real mystery man about town. It is known that he runs a chain of restaurants, and rumoured that he is or was involved in several brothels.

The other is a well-known city solicitor, Sev Cockini, who, with John Naxos, was an original founder of the business. Out in the commercial world it is a very big and respected business, supported by most of the major retailers across the country. So that's all I can help you with."

Trevor chipped in, "We've met the solicitor and can see him in the next few days, but what about this Frank Bennett, we haven't heard of him before?"

Kathleen replied, "I can't help with that one, he's not known around the retail trade. Your best hope may be to try and find him through his restaurants or even Sev Cockini."

"Thanks for all that, we certainly have some work to do. For now, maybe we should forget our problems and go and eat."

Trevor, always ready for a feed and a drink, stood up to look after his date. He had barely taken his eyes off her all evening.

After their meal the two couples split, with Trevor and Meredith, opting to retire to the cocktail lounge while Colin and Kathleen decided to take a stroll along the water front.

With his arm around her waist Colin found something enormously exciting about her. There was a sexual magnetism with an intensity he had not felt before.

There was also a sense of comfort and stability. "Hell,' he thought, "I could really fall for her."

Hopefully, but without much confidence, he suggested that they go back to his room.

Kathleen replied. "At the moment that is very tempting; however, let's just take one step at a time. It's too early for an involvement like that; sometimes it's a quick way to break up a relationship, so let's wait a while.

We will both know when we are ready for that."

Colin had no room to persist.

After a few frustratingly passionate kisses on the way back to the Hotel they parted, with Colin promising to ring her the following night with an update.

The following morning Colin woke to find Trevor already up and dressed with the phone book on his knees flipping over pages.

"Bulls eye, look at this, Thornton A, 15 Eldridge Road, Bankstown, phone 97905181, and that's the number we were given. Come on, off your bum, let's go to Bankstown, wherever that is. According to the map it's on the rail line so it shouldn't be a problem."

Sleepily Colin replied, "Cripes, who pushed your button this morning. Did good things happen to you last night?'

"You bet, I'm going to marry her and take her home."

"Have you told her that yet?"

"Well not exactly, but it sounds like a good idea at the moment."

Straight after breakfast, with the help again of the Gregory's Directory, Colin and Trevor found their way up to Wynyard station and caught a train for Bankstown in search of A. Thornton. Fearing that they would put her off, they decided not to phone ahead and take the risk that she was home.

As the address was only a couple of blocks from the Bankstown station they decided to walk.

The home was a free-standing Californian Bungalow style typical of the early 1930's. As they walked down an old brick paved pathway to the front door Colin suggested that Trevor should be the spokesperson then rang an old brass door bell, which they heard echoing through the house.

The door was opened with some gusto, and a large woman of indeterminable age bellowed,

"Look, I don't want to buy anything, and I don't want to find Jesus or anything else, so go away."

Slightly taken aback Trevor said, "No, wait it's nothing like that. My name is Trevor Donaldson, and this is my friend Colin Naxos. We have come out from England and are here to talk to your husband, Charlie Thornton, about an inheritance."

It was her turn to be taken aback, and after a long silence, "Well he's not here, and I doubt that I will be able be able to help you; tell me what it's all about."

Gaining control Trevor said, "We can't discuss it out here. May we come in?"

"I suppose so," she said opening the door, "it had better be fair dinkum or I'll be getting the police after you both."

She led Colin and Trevor down a long passageway to the dining room and indicated, not too politely, to sit at the table. Using his best English Oxford accent Trevor began with:

"We are out from England to trace a large inheritance belonging to a relative of ours. We believe he was a friend of your husband and he may be able to help us with our inquiries. If you can help us find these people then you could be in for a big reward, will you help us?"

"I might, there's a reward you say, how much?'

Trevor, taking a quick look over at Colin, said,

"If you help us to get the inheritance, then it could be several thousand dollars, if you only partly assist, then it would of course be something less. However, first things first; help us find your husband and we will give you two hundred dollars to start with. Do you know where he is?"

Mrs. Thornton replied, "Well, no, not exactly. The bastard left me years ago.

He was a drunk and got kicked off the railways before he smashed a train up or something."

Trying to be patient Trevor said, "That's very sad for you. This may be a way to even things up a bit so tell us what you know now. When was the last time you heard from him?"

"Well it was rather strange, but after not speaking to him for a long time, he rang and said he was leaving the Central Coast and going where the fishing is better. That was it. Then a few months ago he sent me a note saying, "For old time's sake'. Attached was a cheque for Five Thousand Dollars. I was very pleased to take his conscience money but if he got hold of a big amount of cash, then he ripped me off: after all the years I put up with the drunken bum. There has been no other contact."

"Do you remember what bank the cheque came from?"

She replied, "It's not often I get cheques for Five Thousand dollars, and I remember it well; it was the Commonwealth Bank in Rundle Street Adelaide.'

Trevor felt that they were getting somewhere if he could keep stirring her memory. "Has there been any other contact?"

"None. I often wondered where he was, so I phoned around The Entrance, even the Police, trying and find where he went; but he had just disappeared. I tried the Shire Council, the Power Company, even Telstra for the phone. Finally, I rang his landlord, and no one had any information as to where he went."

Colin, after sitting back listening said,

"Do you still have the letter he sent the cheque in?"

"Yes, I do still have it. Wait a sec and I'll go and get it."

She returned a moment later with a well-handled envelope and handed it to him.

The first thing Colin did was to check the post stamp and was surprised to see that it was posted in Adelaide.

"Did you know this was posted in Adelaide?"

"No' I never looked at that. If anything, I thought if he was looking for better fishing he would have gone north to Queensland. I'm sorry, that's about all I can help you with.

If you find anything, you'll send me the money, won't you?"

Trevor replied, "Maybe you have given us a couple of clues, so here's two hundred dollars for a start. If you think of anything else, or by any chance he contacts you, please give us a ring on this mobile number. We will see that you get rewarded."

They left old Hester Thornton at her front door looking much happier with the two hundred dollars clasped firmly in her arthritic hand.

On the return train trip Colin and Trevor felt quite elated that they appeared to have made some real progress. They were sitting quietly lost in their own thoughts when Trevor broke the silence,

"Hey, old chum, it looks like we have a trip to Adelaide coming up. Where is it anyway? Can we drive there in the morning?"

"You are bloody hopeless." Colin rebuked. "Didn't you learn anything at school? It would take two days to drive there."

"Well it looks like we fly, can we take the girls?"

"Good idea Trev, but I don't think so, unless you pay for them."

"Shit mate I haven't any cash, use your mother's credit card."

"No way would we get away with that, she's probably sitting home right now monitoring our spending."

Next morning, they managed to get an early direct flight to Adelaide, arriving at 10 am.

After a short cab trip to the city centre Colin and Trevor found themselves outside the Commonwealth Bank.

Colin said, "Let me handle this one, I think we will play the old relative role again."

They started by asking the girl at the service desk if they could help with the address of a Mr. C. Thornton. They were told that there is no way the bank would give out information on other people's accounts.

"Perhaps I can speak to the manager then?"

"Certainly sir, I will see when he will be free. Excuse me for a moment."

She was back in a few minutes saying that the manager could see them in half an hour, at eleven thirty.

Back out in the mall they decided it was a good time for a cup of coffee while they waited.

They returned promptly at eleven thirty and were shown into the manager's office. He stepped out from behind his desk and introduced himself; Colin in turn introduced himself and Trevor.

Colin's early idea was to lay on the story about the lost relative bit, and then he instinctively felt that that story would not wash too well and decided to tell the truth.

"As you probably guessed we are from the UK. We have come to Australia to try and find a friend of my grandfather who was recently murdered in New South Wales. There are several issues regarding his will which have to be tidied up.

His name is Charles Thornton and the last known contact we have established is that he drew a cheque on your bank for five thousand dollars in favour of his estranged wife.

This was only a few months ago. If you could in any way help with his address or whereabouts, it would be greatly appreciated."

The Manager replied, "No doubt you are aware that privacy rules do not allow me to give out any information about our clients.

Let me look on the computer to see if there is any way I can help at all. I have the details here and I will tell you this. The account was opened with a significant amount of money, shortly after most of the funds were transferred to another bank. There were only the two transactions, one of which was the cheque you mentioned. The only address recorded here was an Adelaide post office box. And that's about all I can lawfully tell you.

The only way to get full disclosure is to go to a solicitor and try for a court order, which is possible, but quite difficult.

So, gentlemen, that's about all I can do for you."

Colin replied, "Thank you very much for what you have done, it is of some help. However, one more thing before we go, could you tell me which other bank?'

"As I said before, I am not at liberty to give out any information; besides there are only two banks in this block, ours and the ANZ."

With that he rose and wished them good luck.

Out in the street, Coin and Trevor looked at one another both saying, "Let's try the ANZ."

Going through the same routine they spoke to the staff at inquiries; only this time, got an emphatic no, not even an audience with the manager. Next stop was the Post Office.

Full of bravado they went to the counter and asked for the box number for Mr. Charles Thornton.

The girl referred to her computer and said, 'What was the name again? Was it C. Thornton? The number is 1933. Here is a card if you wish to write it down. Have you anything to post?"

"No, not right now, do you have the forwarding address?" She replied, "We do have a forwarding transfer address, but I am not allowed to give that out."

Ignoring them she called, "Next please." and that was the end of the conversation.

Out in the street again they decided to plan their next move over lunch.

Trevor came up with the idea to try the Council Offices or Town Hall to see of he was listed on the Electoral role. While there they could check the local phone books.

They found that both listings were computerised which made it easy to scan all the Thornton's. To their dismay there was no Charles Thornton or C. Thornton listed on either. In case the name was wrongly spelt so they tried other variations of Thornton which produced nothing.

"Well Trevor this can mean only one thing, he does not live in Adelaide, and never intended to. I think he set all this up as a blind to put any pursuers off the track. He must have something to hide! There is nothing more we can do so we may as well see if we can get an early flight back to Sydney.

When we get to the airport, we will ring the girls, they might join us again. What do you think?"

"Colin you always come up with the good ideas. I think it would be best if I rang Meredith myself though, I don't want her thinking that I'm tied to your coat tails."

WHERE'S CHARLIE?

CHAPTER NINE

On the long flight back from Adelaide, looking out the window at the vastness of the country and empty space, Colin remarked, "Trevor, did you know that you could fit the whole of the UK into South Australia? Our man Charlie Thornton has got a big country to hide in!"

That night Kathleen and Meredith again came to the Hotel for dinner, only this time Colin sent a hire car to pick them up.

Once they were in the lounge with a drink in their hands Kathleen asked, "How are our two Sherlock Holmes doing now; have you found your man yet?"

"We have made a lot of progress and have a post office box number and a bank in Adelaide, but neither will hand out an address."

Kathleen replied, "I know someone who works in administration at the Post Office in Sydney, I wonder if she could do us a favour."

Trevor quipped, "Kathleen that's great, tell her we pay well."

Colin explained, "What Trevor means is if she wants a reward I'll pay. Talking about paying, as good as this place is, it's a bit expensive so tomorrow we should stick with our plan and find ourselves a nice serviced apartment. Tonight, can be our last splurge in the dining room, so if everybody is ready, let's go."

After another great meal with exciting company Trevor took Meredith to the cocktail lounge while Kathleen feigned tiredness and was ready to go home.

Walking out to the foyer Colin took her hand in his. Her skin shimmered under his touch. She began to trace her fingers over his in feathered strokes, so light, so inflaming.

"You excite me", she said in a low voice.

Without another word they walked to the elevators.

With the balcony doors open allowing a cooling sea breeze from across the Harbour to permeate the room, his fingers still held her hand while their eyes locked in the soft light of the bedside lamp. As they both slowly undressed Colin thought, this is one of those moments in time, complete in itself.

They lay naked on the bed feeling the sea breeze wash over them with the smell of the sea mingling with Kathleen's perfume.

Totally free of any inhibitions they moved slowly, finding each other, moulding together. Her lips soft and warm, her full breasts and erect nipples seemed to caress his chest. With his thigh between her legs Colin continued to gaze into her eyes as they momentarily drew apart, then kissing her softly he slowly entered her. They made love slowly, then urgently with a passion and excitement Colin had not experienced before.

Later, after regaining his breath, Colin spoke for the first time.

"Kathleen, I don't think I have ever felt so, complete, as I do now, I don't have the words for it. Are you stopping the night?"

Kathleen replied, "As tempting as it is, I do have a full day tomorrow. I have to catch an eight thirty flight to Brisbane, and I won't be back for two days, do you think we can be apart for that long?"

Colin smiled and chided, "It will be tough."

They both dressed with Colin pulling on a pair of jeans and polo top to take her downstairs. They quietly said their goodbyes then Kathleen got into the hire car and left.

Colin suddenly felt as if he was in a vacuum and returned to his room in a state of wonderment.

Sitting on his bed Colin felt very confused about his involvement with Kathleen and concerned about how he could finish the job he had now become intrinsically involved in. Feeling the need to clear his head he decided to go for a walk along the waterfront.

Stopping to look at the water with the lights twinkling across the Harbour he leaned on the rail drinking in the sights and sounds of the night.

For some unknown reason the hairs on the back of his neck started to bristle. He was about to turn around when a voice said, "Don't even turn around Mr. Naxos; I just want to tell you to butt out of business that does not concern you. You had best get on the next available flight back to Pommy land, and take your mate with you."

Colin turned to see two men standing on the dark side, and with more bravado than he felt, he said, "And you can just fuck off, whoever you are."

In a flash he was hit with a huge blow to the side of his face.

Colin had done a lot of boxing in the university team and was not about to keel over without a fight. Staggering from the blow he regained his balance and let go a flurry of punches at his attacker, most of which found their target.

Re-gathering himself he heard the second person say, "Hello, what have we got here, he thinks he's Mike Tyson."

Then he was hit a blinding blow across the back of the head with a rubber cycle tube filled with sand which dropped him to the footpath. Next, they both started to viciously kick him in the stomach and ribs. Trying to protect himself from more kicks he rolled into a ball and tried to get away. The larger of the two men then knelt over him and said, "This is your last and only warning, give up on your prying and go home or next time you may end up face down in the Harbour."

Colin then received another kick, this time to the side of his head. With that he blacked out.

A cabbie driving past on his way to pick up a fare at the hotel, saw him prostrate on the footpath and rang the Police. He was taken by ambulance to the Royal Prince Alfred Hospital in Camperdown and admitted with slight concussion, abrasions and two broken ribs.

The police questioned him at length and put the incident down to a random attack. They suggested that it might not be a good idea for him to be wandering around the area late at night on his own.

When Trevor returned to their room, finding Colin missing, he instinctively checked with the Police Station in The Rocks area near the hotel. They informed him that a man of that description had been found unconscious in the area and had been taken to the Royal Prince Alfred Hospital.

When Colin woke, he found Trevor sitting next to his bed.

"Christ mate, what the hell have we got ourselves into? If people will go to these lengths to stop us fossicking around there must be some serious money involved or something else, we don't know about."

"Remember I had an inkling earlier that there was more to this than we knew about, well it looks as if I was right."

Trevor said, "Well, do we keep going, or do we get the hell out of here?"

"We are not going to give into these bastards. Now we know the rules we can play a different game. While I am getting patched up go and book out of the Hotel and find a serviced apartment in the city somewhere.

Use your own credit card and I will fix you up later. Withdraw some cash and rent the apartment under another name and only use cash. I recall that Kathleen said that there were Several in Kent Street, not far from the hotel.

When you leave the hotel get the cab to take you to the Central Railway Station, and then pick another cab at random for the return trip to the apartment I don't think we need to tell the girls about this until we regroup and are settled in."

Trevor replied. "Okay boss, I have my instructions, so I will be off and get on with it. I will check in later to see how you are going and let you know where we are living."

Later a doctor, the senior registrar, called to check him over and to let him know when he could leave. Colin noticed his name badge said Dr Spalding.

Taking Colin's chart board from the end of the bed, he hesitated for a moment, 'I see your name is Naxos, that is unusual, where are you from?'

"I live in the UK, Oxford actually, why do you ask?"

"A close friend of my father was a Naxos; he owned a restaurant and catering supply business."

Colin was aware of a nervous feeling in his stomach as he replied: "This story has a familiar ring to it; but it does not fit in as the name that comes to mind that was associated with my father and Grandfather was Cockini; does that mean anything to you, I see your name is Spalding."

The Doctor slowly sat down, "My father is Sev Cockini. I use the name of his first wife or my grandparents who raised me, which is Spalding."

"Well I'll be buggered, my father who died ten years ago was Robert Naxos and his father was John Naxos who died only recently."

Doctor Paul Spalding was really taken aback at this news and said, "So, you are Robert's son, what are you doing here?"

Colin's first thought was to hide the real reason for his visit. Then the thought, this fellow may be able to help us.

"I am here on behalf of my mother to try and find out what happened to my Grandfather. As you may know he was murdered a short time ago."

The doctor was now looking quite upset and said, "Yes I am aware of all that and I am familiar with your family history. My father was a partner in the business. May I ask if your injuries and being here has anything to do with all this?"

Colin replied, "Yes it has, I did not tell the police, but my attackers told me to stop interfering and go home. If I did not, they said that next time I would be found face down in the Harbour."

"This is serious, I think we had better go and have a talk to my father. Take my card and give me a ring tomorrow morning at home. I will work out a time for us to meet.

Is that okay?"

"I have already met your father actually, and I was to ring to find out when we could get together. One thing I would like to say at this time is that we keep our chance meeting strictly between ourselves; don't even tell your father until we meet. I have had one brush with some elements of this drama and I don't want another."

"Fair enough, where are you stopping in case, I need to contact you?"

"I don't know, and if I did, I would not be telling. My friend, Trevor, who is travelling with me, is moving us out of the Hotel today. He is looking for somewhere discreet to stay until we get sorted out. I will ring you as soon as I can, but please do not even tell your father at this stage."

After a quick check on his condition, Dr Spalding said, "You're okay, so you can go when you are ready. Have you got someone to pick you up?"

"Yes thanks, Trevor will be back soon, he will look after me."

"Please ring me early tomorrow at home."

After he left, a nurse came in, helped him to get dressed and gave him a cup of tea and a biscuit.

While he sat there waiting for Trevor he thought;

"Hell, what a night, first there was the absolute beauty of Kathleen, then some bastards try to kill me. If it wasn't for Kathleen, I think I would do what Trevor suggested and get the hell out of here and go home. Who needs this."

A little while later Trevor arrived and helped him down to the foyer and into a cab.

"Thanks mate, where are we living?"

Trevor replied, "Well it's not like our previous digs at the Hyatt. I found a small two-bed apartment in Sussex Street and leased it under the name of Coleman, so remember that."

Colin found that Trevor had unpacked and put all his clothes away for him, noticing also that he had taken the best bedroom for himself.

"Thanks for all that, but how come you get the best room."

Trevor merrily replied, "When I bring Meredith home, I think it only appropriate that she is entertained in the best room."

"Come on, what happens if I brought Kathleen here?"

"We swap, rooms I mean, not girls."

That evening Trevor went down to China Town and brought back some takeaway.

"Here, this is the best I can do for you now. I know it is not Hyatt standard, however it is a change."

After a disturbed night's sleep worrying about the recent events and how far they were prepared to take it, Colin rose early then waited until eight thirty before ringing Paul Spalding.

He had already left for the day and had left a message on his answering machine to be at Cockini Legal in Elizabeth Street at eleven o'clock.

Colin and Trevor arrived at Cockini Legal Offices a little after eleven and after a short wait were ushered into Sev Cockini's office. To their surprise the found Paul waiting beside Sevs desk. The office was plush and large, with a huge uncluttered desk at one end and another smaller desk set up with computers and communication equipment. A complete lounge suite and a round conference table completed the furnishings.

After re-introductions Sev suggested that they sit at the conference table.

"I am sorry we could not have met prior to this under much better circumstances. However, just before you arrived, I had a phone call from my son Paul: he asked for your understanding in breaking your confidence. I was quite shocked after he briefly filled me in on the situation that seems to engulf us all. Before we go any further, I should explain my situation or involvement with the Naxos operation.

I have been, since its inception, a financial partner in the business. In the early days when your grandfather was starting the business, I used to take an active role in the day by day operation of the business. Nowadays John's brother, Steven, who has the controlling interest, runs the business. My only involvement is occasionally giving legal advice, purely on a commercial basis, and attending the Annual General Meetings.

Colin, your grandfather and I were very close friends, going right back to our teenage years. We went to school together, grew up together and went into business together.

He was my best mate nearly all my life, and I still mourn his passing. I find it impossible to believe that the attack on you has anything to do with the Naxos business."

Colin was quick to jump in, "Sev, let's wait right there, I never ever said or indicated that it did, so I do not know why you are jumping in to defend John Naxos when he has not even been mentioned. We came here for one simple reason. My mother, Robert's wife, asked me to come out and try to find out what happened to what she believes could be a significant amount of money. Our investigations so far have purely been trying to track down John's friend, Charlie Thornton."

Sev thought, "*I think I might have underestimated these boys.*"

Colin continued, "So frankly, at this stage we are not interested in your Naxos Empire, unless it has something to do with the attack on me or the search for Charlie Thornton and the missing money. We know that he had accumulated a significant amount of money from earnings and the sale of his share of the business, plus the money from the sale of the Concord home. There may also have been an insurance payout on his wife Jean's unfortunate death. Sev, could you enlighten us on the whereabouts of the missing money or Charlie Thornton? The other question I have is, why was my maternal grandmother murdered, and who was the mysterious man she was with the night she died?"

For a long time, Sev appeared to be slightly rattled by Colin's questions and directness.

"Colin, firstly the police conducted a huge investigation into Jean's murder and they never found out who her attacker was. It was never established why she was killed or if there was any connection with the business or John. From my knowledge I don't think that John had anywhere near the money it was thought he had. There were some who believe that he disappeared to hide from something or somebody. If he did, he certainly never told me.

As far as this Charlie Thornton is concerned, he was nothing more than a railway worker who was sacked because of alcoholism. It was reported by the police that they used to go fishing together. The police report said that he received an invalid pension and was an alcoholic. I find it hard to see how he could get hold of John's money."

Colin was well steamed up by this time listening to all this vague information. It appeared that nobody had tried too hard to find answers to any of it.

"Tell me then, why did he leave his flat at The Entrance; paying all his bills and back rent before he left, then creating a false address in Adelaide and opening a Bank account there with significant funds, which, after a short period, he transferred to another bank. He used a private mailbox at the Adelaide Post Office without a forwarding address. After that he left for God knows where, taking the money with him. Trevor and I found all this out in a few days, and then someone tries hard to warn me off by bashing the shit out of me. So, what the hell is going on?"

Sev replied, "Now Colin, it looks as if you have come to the wrong person. I am just a city solicitor going about my work. I know nothing about all this, and I have never tried to find answers to the questions you have raised, as it is the responsibility of the police. I think you should take your story to them."

Colin replied, "We may do that, but before we go, where does this Frank Bennett fit into all this?"

Sev was again surprised at the information Colin and Trevor had unearthed in a short period,

Many years ago, Frank invested money in the business when it badly needed capital, and over the years he has held a cash interest in the Naxos business. Other than that, I know nothing about him."

Colin thought; what the hell, I might as well go all the way; this fellow might get really rattled if I play dirty. It was hardly Boy Scout stuff for me nearly getting kicked to death.

Remembering the information, he had on the tape his mother had given him he said; "I believe that he also runs a chain of brothels, doesn't he?"

Sev replied, "I know nothing about Frank Bennett's other business."

"That's strange, I thought that you acted as his solicitor in private and business matters."

Sev was now enraged and, standing on his feet, was about to speak when Colin said, "Your wife also worked for him, and yet you do not know him"!

At that Sev lunged across the table at him and had to be restrained by his son Paul who up to now had remained silent.

"Get out." Sev screamed, "Don't you dare come in here making all sorts of wild comments. Make one false move and you are in court."

"Time to go", Colin said to Trevor. On his way out the door he turned back to Sev saying, "Well I suppose court would be easier than getting kicked in the ribs."

Back out in the street Trevor said, "Shit mate, you know how to play rough. I have never seen this side of you before, I'm glad I'm on your side."

"A lot of things change when two thugs kick the shit out of you while you're lying down. I think we need lunch and a mid-day beer to settle us down, lets' go."

They had only just reached the corner when Paul Spalding caught up with them.

"Colin, I am sorry the way that turned out. Despite what you may think he really is a good man and would have done anything to protect his friend. Not only because he is my real father, but I believe that he's as straight as they come."

Colin replied, "I will reserve my judgement on that until we find out what really happened."

"Fair enough, but in future it may be a good idea if we worked together, or at least communicated. Do you have a mobile phone?"

"No, I don't." he said.

Paul replied, "Well take this one and use it to keep in touch. It has recharge cards, so you don't have to worry about an account. The number is, 0418 4291 1965, I'll write it on one of my business cards which has my home and office number as well. I will not even ask where you are staying, but please keep in touch; there may be an occasion where you need help from someone you can trust."

With that he turned and disappeared into the lunch time crowd.

Over lunch Trevor asked, "What did you make of that?"

"My feeling is that the doctor is okay. I think we could trust him if it is not too close to his Dad. He may come in handy one day."

"Fair enough, what's our next step?"

"I think we should go back and see Hester Thornton." Colin replied, "Do you have something in mind?"

"Yes, I have, how about we ask her to write to Charlie, asking for financial help for a hip replacement or something. While writing she could also feed out a little information that people were looking for him.

She could address the letter through the bank asking them to forward it on. If he replies we may get a postage area stamp or a new bank branch, what do you think?"

Let's go now; we can compose a letter for her while we sit in the train."

Knocking on her door Colin and Trevor were again thankful that she was home. "Oh hello boys, come in, I'll put the kettle on."

Sitting down at the kitchen table they found her much friendlier than their first visit. Colin thought the money might have something to do with that.

Trevor, playing Mr. Smooth again, said, "Do you mind if I call you Hester?"

"No not at all darling. Have you found where Charlie is yet?'

"No not yet, we have made some progress though.

We have an idea that may work, and we need your help. How about you send him a letter through his bank telling him you are not well and need some help. With a bit of luck he may answer, and then we have a chance to trace his letter."

"That's all right, do I get paid again?"

If he answers we will give you another two hundred."

Colin interrupted, "Hester, we have a writing pad and I'll help you compose your letter, how about it?"

Hester replied, "Alright you tell me what to write."

> *Dear Charlie*
>
> *It is a long time since we parted, and we are both now getting old.*
>
> *Maybe it's time for us to get together again, or at least you should let me know where you are in case something happens to one of us. If I was to die then this is still your house, remember. The old place is badly in need of some repairs to the roof and I do not have the money to do it on my pension. The money you gave me last time was just enough to paint*

the kitchen. *The bathroom needs re-tiling or something as the water leaks into the wall and is rotting the floorboards.*

In case you forgot I had my 70th birthday last month and the old heart is starting to slow up. The doctors tell me I have some blockages, which could become a problem.

My problem now is that my hip has collapsed, and the doctor said I must have an operation, as I cannot even walk down to the shops any more. Could you please write and let me know where you are and if you can afford it help me with some money, at least enough to get my hip fixed. I will send the letter to the bank manager enclosing this letter asking him to forward it on.

Love Hester

Dear Manager

I have been apart from my husband Mr. Charles Thornton for many years and sadly do not even know where he is. We do not have any children and I am now over seventy and live on my own. If I was to die there is no way anybody can contact Charlie.

I know that he had an account with your bank, so I assume that you must have his address.

Would you be kind enough to forward the enclosed letter to him for me?

Mrs. Hester Thornton
15 Eldridge Road Bankstown 2200

Colin said, "Hester if you are happy with that, we will post them off and see if he replies. If by any chance he rings, make sure he tells you where he is, and write it down.

We have a mobile phone so give us a ring straight away if you hear anything. The number is 0148 4291 1965."

With the letters signed they made copies at the local post office and sent them off to the Adelaide bank.

With nothing left to do they returned to the apartment for Colin to rest his wounds and plan the next move.

The next day they decided it was time to see Grandfather John's brother, Steven Naxos, who they believed was still running the business.

To safeguard where they were now stopping, they walked up to George Street and caught a passing cab for the trip out to Mascot. The cab let them off at the front office door of Naxos Condiments and they boldly went straight into the front foyer to the reception desk.

The girl at the desk gave her best customer smile and said,

"Good morning gentlemen, how can I help you?"

Pulling himself up to his full six-foot two height, Colin in a businesslike manner said, "Yes thank you. We are here to see Mr. Steven Naxos."

She replied, "I am not sure that he is free, may I say who is calling?"

"Yes, just says its Colin from the UK, he'll know who it is."

She returned a minute later and said, "Please come this way gentlemen."

They were shown into an expansive, but business-like office. A large man, looking like he enjoyed the good life too much, came from behind the desk with his arm extended to shake hands.

"Well, if you are who I think you are I must be your great uncle. Your Grandfather was my older brother; your father was his son. I'm Steven Naxos. You must be Colin."

Colin replied, "You're correct on all counts, and this my friend Trevor Donaldson."

"I have not heard from your parents for years.

We used to exchange Xmas cards once, but we somehow drifted apart. How is your father and mother, Barbara?"

Colin thought; I will complete the formalities, and replied, "Dad died ten years ago, but mother is very much alive and well. I thought you would have known that, considering you inherited his share of the business."

"No, no, I bought Robert's share many years before then. Well what brings you here is it business or holidays?"

Colin thought: here we go again; this prick knows exactly why I am here.

"Steven, I thought you had a call from Sev Cockini to let you know we were about and may turn up."

Steven replied with a fixed stare, "No I did not. What does it have to do with him anyway?"

"Well I will get straight to the point, my mother asked me to come out to find out what happened to my grandfather's assets after he was murdered. Our understanding is that they may have ended up with Charlie Thornton, his fishing mate. Nobody seems to know, or if they do, they won't tell where he is. He has disappeared.

If by any chance John legally willed his assets to Charlie, why didn't he use Sev Cockini as his solicitor, when he was supposed to be his life-long friend? If he did, why won't Cockini tell? The other Issue is that I was attacked outside our hotel and told to stop my inquiries, or else I would end up face down in the Harbour. This is serious stuff.

We were hoping you might be able to help us with our search for this Charlie Thornton."

Steven replied, "I know nothing of any of this, John sold out of the business not long after he lost his wife Jean, and initially he went overseas for quite some time. I saw him a couple of times after he returned, then he just disappeared. We did not know where he was until the police contacted us about his death.

So, you probably know more about it than me."

"Steven, you were all family, and you spent all those years together, firstly in the old Naxos restaurant, then building up this business together, didn't that mean anything?"

Not to be riled like Sev was yesterday Steven said,

"You have obviously done your family homework; however, you must understand that before and after Jeans death John was severely depressed and his choice was to get out of the business and just go and retire. He did not want to have anything more to do with the business. It seemed that the effort of building up the business was too much for him. He had lost or was losing his wife by then.

I believe that she was going to leave him and go overseas with your father and mother, Robert and Barbara. That of course never happened because of her untimely death.

After that I often went across to the old home in Croydon, and once found him unconscious on the floor, with an empty whisky bottle next to him. He was at the time banned from the local pub because of his excessive drinking.

Around the time he first disappeared I often wondered if he ended up in some sort of sanatorium for rehabilitation, but that is a guess. It was all very sad, as right back to the time before our parents died, and for years after, John was the backbone of the family.

He had a lovely wife who, in the early times, loved him dearly; but as I said, the business engulfed him, and he neglected his family. In the end Jean tired of it all and his drinking so she decided to leave him.

As you well know, she was killed before she left. There was even one line of thought that the police pursued that it was John himself who killed her.

That is the story of your family and ancestors, and I can't help any further. If you find Charlie Thornton let me know. How can I contact you, are you still at the Hyatt?' Without even blinking Colin said, "We have a mobile phone, the number is 0418 4291 1965.'

They all stood and shook hands, with Colin saying, "We may see you again before we return home."

Outside waiting for a cab, Trevor yelled, "Fucking Hell, did you hear that? How did he know we were at the Hyatt?"

Colin said, "I think we will go straight back to the apartment and check out again and look for new digs. We had better become a moving target."

Arriving back in Sussex Street, the cab stopped on the corner away from the apartments. They got out and started to walk along the footpath; suddenly Colin said, "Don't look sideways now, just keep walking there are a couple of gorillas sitting in a car over there who look suspicious. You walk ahead of me and we'll meet around the back at the service entrance."

The rear service dock door was open, so they went in and took the service lift to their floor. In their room, without even talking, they quickly packed and were ready to go.

Trevor then called, "Hang on a minute; we need a change of plans. Let's only take our backpacks and what we can fit in them. Ditch everything else including the cases, and we'll become just another couple of Pommy back packers."

"Great idea Trevor, let's do it."

They had just finished repacking and were about to leave when the door burst open with a load crash. They both stood there looking at the two gorillas they had seen down in the street.

The bigger one snarled, "Thought you would give us the slip eh."

Before he could even draw breath, Colin hit with a straight right, flush on the chin. From the corner of his eye he saw the other one flying at him from his left.

Before he could react, Trevor hit him over the head with a brass bedside lamp sending him down like a bag of potatoes. He was not going to move.

The big fellow was mobile again and with an animal roar he rushed at Colin with both arms swinging. Colin managed to dodge the first couple of punches then the next hit him with a sickening thud above his eye.

He reeled back with blood spraying from a large gash above his eye.

With his vision blurred, and he was just about to go to the floor to dodge another punch, when Trevor took the big man in a classic rugby tackle. They rolled over and over on the floor smashing furniture as they went. Trevor was first up and grabbed the bedside lamp again and swung it hitting him flush on the side of the head. His assailant's knees buckled, and he collapsed in a heap amongst the broken furniture.

Trevor stood over him with the lamp in his hand,

"Hey, this thing is a good weapon mate. These guys will think again before mixing it with a couple of old uni pub brawlers. Are you alright? Let's get out of here quick in case they have reserves."

They grabbed their packs and bolted down the fire escape stairs, taking at least three steps at a time.

Out in the street they headed down Sussex Street, past King and Market Streets and then over the footbridge to the Darling Harbour complex.

Finding a public toilet block they washed Colin's face with toilet paper and water and tried to stem the flow of blood with a Band-Aid from Colin's bathroom pack.

Looking at the gash Trevor said, we had better find a doctor. That is going to require at least three stitches. Do you think we can trust Paul Spalding?"

Colin said, "I think so, let's put him to the test, ring him at his office on the mobile."

Trevor rang the number and handed the phone to Colin.

A girl answered, and Colin said, "May I speak to Doctor Spalding please?"

"I am sorry the Doctor has a patient with him, if you leave your number, I will ask him to call you as soon as he is free."

Colin replied, "No, just interrupt him and say it's Colin and I need him urgently."

About ten seconds later Paul was on the phone. "Colin, what's the problem?"

We've been attacked by a couple of gorillas again and I need a couple of stitches. I don't want anyone to know about it, nor where we are, can you help?"

"Come straight over to my rooms and I'll have a look at it. The address is suite 10, 205 Missenden Road, Camperdown. Can you get a taxi?"

"I think so; we'll be there in about fifteen minutes."

The cabbie took them straight there and they were shown directly into the doctor's surgery. Fortunately, there was no one left in the waiting room.

Paul took him into the surgery and sat him on a stool. "Firstly, let's have a look at the damage; hell what did he hit you with?"

"I think it was a looping right cross, but he is out for the count now, thanks to my old brawling mate here."

Well you're right; it will need stitches. Can you stand the pain without a local anaesthetic?"

Trevor answered for him, "Sure he can Doc, go for it."

Stitching it up Paul said, "It is not as bad as it looks; it's just that anything around that area bleeds profusely. All done, now just try and keep it covered and clean for a few days. Perhaps you can tell me now what the hell is going on with you two."

Colin stammered, "Well someone very much wants us out of the way. We went to see Steven Naxos out at the warehouse this morning and when we returned to our, "secret" apartment these two gorillas were waiting for us.

They were the same two that jumped me down at The Rocks; but this time I had my own gorilla, Trevor, with me, and we left them unconscious on the apartment floor.

This was only one lucky punch they got in."

Paul said, "Well where are you going to go now? No, hold it, I don't want to know. Appreciate that I can't get involved.

I will help you wherever I can, but you never, I repeat never mention me. Anyway, keep in touch and let me know how you're going."

"Thanks very much Paul, you are a great comfort. By the way, can you do any pro bono work?"

"Why do you ask?"

"Well we have this little old pensioner lady who needs a new hip or something, I will pay part of the costs, to say five hundred dollars if you can help her."

With a grin Paul replied, "Okay I'll see what I can do, ask her to ring me, what is her name?"

With a straight face Colin said, "Her name is Hester Thornton."

"You bugger, you got me, and I should have known there was a catch somewhere."

He laughed and said, "If we go ahead, like I said before, keep it to yourself. I have to go now to do my ward rounds but keep in touch."

Back out in the street Colin said", Where do all the back-packers go?

I have heard that Bondi Beach is the popular spot, why don't we grab a cab and ask him to take us there."

"Fine with me, let's go, here's a cab now."

The cabbie, continuing with tradition, talked non-stop all the way to Bondi giving his comments on tourism, particularly the Japanese, and politics.

"Hell mate, half of all New Zealanders live around Bondi.

"Here we are, where can I drop you off?" he asked.

Not really knowing, Trevor said, "Right over there at the shops will be fine thanks."

After getting a cup of coffee in a paper cup and a doughnut they walked across the road and sat on a seat overlooking the beach.

Through a mouthful of iced doughnut Trevor said, "Now that's what I call a beach. I read somewhere once that this is where all the Pommy tourists come on New Year's Eve. Apparently, they really carve it up and they need the army to control them. They usually drown a couple who try to swim with a belly full of local beer and wine."

Colin wasn't really listening to Trevor's great wisdom and was intently studying his map.

"In this town where would you look for a couple of Pommy backpackers, Bondi of course." Why don't we catch a bus and go further down the coast to Coogee."?

"You are the brains of this outfit, let's go."

"No, let's split, you go first, and I'll follow in fifteen minutes."

About half and hour later in Coogee Colin found Trevor sitting on the sea wall watching the girls on the beach.

An expanse of clean white sand with a backdrop of rolling green waves was nothing like Colin had ever seen before. Board riders were out on the water challenging the waves and each other. Colin thought to himself, "I would really like to try that."

Across the road was a huge complex called the Coogee Beach Hotel which was a gathering place for backpackers from around the world.

Two blocks back from the beach they found Several backpacker guest houses that looked good enough to hide in. Picking one at random they asked for accommodation. "No problem." said the man at the desk whom they thought was the cleaner.

"Can I see your passports?"

Colin mumbled, "We don't have them with us, we heard there was a lot of robberies around here, so we had them and our travellers' cheques locked in a safety deposit box in the city. If you really must have them, we can drop them in the next couple of days.

"No problem", he said, "Just put you names and address in the registration book."

They found their own way to their beds in a long dormitory.

Trevor remarked, "This is a long way from the Hyatt; but it's cheap I suppose. Another thought old boy, how are we going to bring the girls here?"

"You don't, you will have to take Meredith down the beach and sit on the sand."

With mock horror Trevor replied, "No way, have you ever got the old fellow caught in the sand?"

"It's obvious that I don't have the same problem as you. Anyway, what's our next move?"

"I think we should dig in here for a week or more for some R&R while we wait to see if we get a reply from Hester Thornton."

"Good idea; as a bit of extra insurance why don't we split and go our separate ways? If anybody is looking, they would be after a couple of Poms together. Not someone on his own."

They spent the next couple of weeks doing their own thing, playing the tourist role, swimming, sitting on the beach, and checking out the local sights.

Trevor spent his nights drinking beer and playing Pool at the pub with another couple of backpackers he had met in the bar.

Feeling a bit lonely, Colin decided to ring Kathleen.

"Well hello, where have you been, I thought we had lost you."

"Believe me, I have desperately wanted to see you, but we had to go into hiding. In fact, I am not even going to tell you where we are. We have these thugs looking for us, and I have already had one trip to hospital to get patched up from a beating, plus another split eye, so we are being very careful."

"Where can we meet?"

"Could you find your way to my place?"

"No, it could be too dangerous; I don't want to drag you into this."

Kathleen said, "Well if we have to be clandestine, I will book a motel room. There's a motel on the Pacific Highway at Artarmon called the North Shore Inn. Meet me there after eight."

After studying his map Colin elected to take a bus to the city then a train to Artarmon. The motel appeared to be only a short walk from the station.

Arriving at Seven thirty, feeling a little paranoid, he hid in a shop doorway on the opposite side of the road to see if any suspicious characters were loitering about.

Apart from the constant stream of traffic on the highway, all was quiet.

Just to be sure he walked the perimeter of the motel complex looking for anything unusual and an escape route in case he needed it. Returning to the shop doorway he waited another ten minutes before he saw a Honda sedan pull up then enter the car park. He saw Kathleen get out and walk to the front entrance. With gathering excitement, he crossed the road and walked into the foyer. There was a man at the desk clicking away on a computer who did not seem very interested in him.

Colin asked, "Excuse me my wife just booked in, what room is she in?' Without looking up or questioning him he replied, "Room 301."

Colin knocked lightly on the door, which was opened immediately. A radiant, smiling Kathleen stood there.

With an appreciative look at her, he said, "Do you have a pink carnation, if not I may have the wrong room."

"Wrong room or not you are not getting away", she purred slamming the door behind him.

Looking into her eyes Colin momentarily noticed that her pupils were dilated, then in the excitement of the moment forgot about it.

Taking a bottle of champagne from the fridge she handed it to Colin, "Open this to celebrate and you can tell me what's been happening."

Pulling the cork Colin replied, "Do you want to talk then go to bed or go to bed then talk."

Putting on a sultry look Kathleen whispered, "One drink then I will allow you one kiss, but I am not saying how long it is."

After one sip Colin said, "To hell with this I can't wait."

Kathleen stood with the glass of champagne in her hand and an inviting smile on her lips while Colin started to slowly remove her clothes. When she was naked, still with the champagne and smile, Colin ran his hands ever so softly over her body. Her flawless, creamy skin felt like silk to his touch. Without any haste he led her to the bed and gently laid her down. They made love again that even surpassed their experience at the Hotel.

"Now where is that champagne?"

They sat on the bed with feet and legs entwined while they drank.

"And don't drink too much champagne, I may want you again.

But first tell me all about what you've been doing."

Kathleen was shocked when Colin told her all that had happened since they parted that night at the Hyatt Hotel.

"What on earth are you going to do; you can't hide or run around waiting for someone to kill you?"

Well Trevor and I are keeping apart. Actually, it's good to have a break from each other's company. We are both in a secure spot where we will stay for a couple of weeks until we hear from Hester Thornton. Hopefully we'll get enough information from her to continue our search for Charlie.

He is the key to the whole thing. As I see it, nobody else knows where he is either.

Strangely it all seems a hell of a drama for what could be a moderate amount of money.

One thing for sure, we are too far involved now to pack up and run home."

Kathleen said, "I picked up a bit of gossip about Steven Naxos. Apparently, he is extremely wealthy. He is still married to his American wife and they never ever had any children. Some say the marriage is one of convenience.

He is involved in Several other businesses including, you will be interested in this, a security company."

Colin sat bolt upright, "That's it; I recall that one of those gorillas had some sort of insignia on his shirt, I could see the outline of it through his jumper. Christ! How far can this go?"

Much later in the night, when they were both sated and exhausted from love making, Colin thought it would be wise to let Kathleen go home and he return to his Coogee accommodation. They said their goodbyes and parted, with Colin promising to ring her every night.

Sitting in the train on the way back to the city he was thinking, "What am I going to do about this girl when it is time to return home? I can feel myself getting drawn in further each time we are together. It is not just the sex; it's her totally."

Over the next two weeks they managed to get together a couple of times using the same Motel.

Colin spent his time swimming and relaxing on the beach managing to put on a bit of weight and tan up his English paleness. The only time he saw Trevor was when he fell out of bed in the mornings.

One morning Colin said, "I think it's time we paid Hester Thornton a visit. How about we make our own way to Central Station and meet up there to catch the train to Bankstown, in case there are people looking for a couple of backpackers.

We could take a new look and dress up in suits."

"Great idea, but who's going to press them after being screwed up in bottom of our packs."

"You iron the shirts and I'll take our suits down to the dry cleaners, I'm sure they'll do them while I wait."

Looking more like young executives, they met at Central and with great hope headed for a meeting with dear old Hester Thornton.

When they knocked on the front door Hester was absolutely ecstatic to see them. She hugged them both and took them to the kitchen for a much-needed cuppa.

"Thank you so much, that nice doctor rang and asked me to go and see him, he is arranging a hip replacement for me."

Colin said, "Well there is a Santa Clause after all."

"The next news is I have had a letter from Charlie and he sent me some money. He has not given me his address only that he is living at Hervey Bay. He said I was not to tell anyone. I am sure he won't mind though if I tell you, because you would never hurt him, would you?"

Trying to hide their excitement, in unison they both said, "definitely not, we promise."

Hester was quietly crying saying, "I know you are nice boys, and you have helped me, so here's his letter."

Feeling a little emotional himself, Colin took the letter and read Charlie's scratchy writing.

Dear Hester

I know I was a very poor husband to you and all our troubles were my fault mainly because of my drinking.

I will not try to explain now, but I was fortunate to come into a little bit of money, which I should have shared with you. I came about it honestly, but there are still people looking for me who would take it off me. It was a nasty business, one day I will explain. You will be surprised to hear that I no longer drink in fact I have not had a drop for six months. I am living in Hervey Bay and spend my time helping at the Senior Citizens Club and going fishing.

I do feel bad about the way I treated you and I agree we should get together again for whatever years we may have left.

I need to sort a few things out first and when I am finished, I will come and see you. In the meantime, I have put some money in to help you along.

Try not to think too badly about me.

Love Charlie

Both Colin and Trevor had lumps in their throats when they read the letter. Trevor took over and said, "Hester that's wonderful, we are so pleased for you. He has not given us an actual address, but the post mark is Hervey Bay in Queensland. Do you know where that is?"

"No, but I have a map, I'll get it for you."

They spread the map out on the kitchen table and were not surprised to find that the town was on the Queensland north coast, approximately 330 kilometres north of Brisbane.

"We will go and see him in a couple of days and maybe we can help him get sorted out. The first thing is to ring the airlines and find out how we can get there."

While Trevor went off out to the hallway to use the mobile phone, Colin sat down with Hester.

We will look after him. What is most important is that if anybody arrives on your doorstep looking for him, you know nothing.

We wish we could explain more, all we can say is there are some evil people out there."

Trevor opened the mobile phone and luckily was able to book a Qantas flight to Brisbane with a connecting regional flight direct to Hervey Bay for the next day.

When he returned to the kitchen Colin muttered, "I have another idea. We know that there are some people out there with an agenda we don't even understand. This must be much bigger than our quest to find out about the so-called inheritance and Charlie's involvement. If we can find Hester, then we would have to believe that the other people could as well.

How about we take Hester away from here and move her in with Kathleen at least until we get the whole thing sorted out."

"Hester, for your own safety would you go and live with a friend of ours for a couple of weeks?"

"You boys have me really worried now; I don't even know what this is all about."

"We don't either, but we're sure as hell going to find out. You have to trust us to look after you."

"Is she a nice person? Will she look after me?"

Surprising himself Colin said, "She is a lovely girl and I love her dearly, I would leave my own mother in her care, what more can I say."

"All right then, if you say so, I will go. Will I pack now?"

"Yes, that would be a good idea; you won't need much for a few days."

As Hester could not walk far, they rang for a cab to take them back to the city.

After leaving Trevor and Hester in a coffee shop Colin rang to break the news to Kathleen. He was not surprised when she enthusiastically agreed and offered to get away from work in the next hour to meet them at her apartment.

Arriving at her Lane Cove apartment block they found that Kathleen was already there and was busy making up a bed in her spare room.

After showing Hester around and how to work the television and make a cup of tea they left her on her own. Hester's only comment was, "This is nice, much better than my old house."

Kathleen went back to her office and Trevor and Colin returned to their Coogee refuge to plan and pack for their trip to Hervey Bay.

Trevor said, "By the look of the map this place is on the other end of the world, and it will be hot."

"Believe me it will be; shorts and sandals will be the go.

I'll see if I can catch up with Mum to let her know what's going on and tell her to put some money in my account, so we don't have to resort to using the credit cards. We certainly do not want to run out of cash."

There were more serious concerns festering in Colin's mind, the major one being that if anything happened to them there would be no record of the events that led them to being in Australia. With this in mind, he went down to the local electronics store and purchased a mini tape recorder which was compatible with the cassettes his mother had given him.

The next move was to record everything that had transpired since they'd left home.

Sitting down on the Coogee beach in the bright sun of the Australian summer he began his documentary of the happenings since his meeting with his mother. Several hours later when he was happy that he had covered everything, he pondered as to what he would do with the tapes. If I keep them with me, they could still get lost, but who would I give them to?

He found the answer and went back to the electronics store and had three copies taken of his original. Next, he had another three copies made of his mother's tapes and had them spliced together.

Keeping one copy he posted a second copy home to his mother. The third copy, with some reluctance, he posted to Dr Paul Spalding with an accompanying note.

> *Dear Paul*
>
> *Firstly, many thanks for the support you have given Trevor and me.*
>
> *No doubt you have a good understanding what a dramatic and frightening experience it has been for us. Following the call from my mother to help her track down her family I had no idea what I was getting myself into. If I had I most definitely would have stayed home. After arriving, if it was not for the company and support of Trevor, I would have given up. Any way, we are too far down the track and involved now to even consider quitting.*
>
> *Without going into all the details as to how, we have the address of Charlie Thornton who we suspect has the key to the whole story. We have booked an interstate flight for Friday to finally meet this elusive man and hopefully find out what it is all about.*
>
> *I have serious concerns that there is something very sinister about what has been going on that far outweighs just a simple and small inheritance left by my grandfather.*
>
> *There is little doubt that Steven Naxos is somehow involved, and I cannot understand why your father either did not draw up my grandfathers will, or if he did, why is he hiding the fact? However, despite our altercation a couple of weeks ago I see him as an honourable man and would like to have another talk to him when we return.*
>
> *I am justifiably worried about our safety and in case something does happen to us, I have recorded all we know on the enclosed tapes and have entrusted them into your care. If the worst does happen, I am sure that you will take them to the police. However, in the meantime I would appreciate*

your absolute confidence; perhaps you could carefully lock them in your office safe.

I am very sorry to burden you with this, but frankly, I have no one else that I feel I could trust.

I will contact you as soon as we return.

Many Thanks
Kind Regards
Colin

HEADING NORTH

CHAPTER TEN

James Cockini was also a lawyer and was now the senior partner in his father's practice. At forty-eight he was one of most respected corporate lawyers in Sydney. Although his father was now in his Seventies he still came into the office on most days, but only in an advisory capacity, helping the junior members of their staff. Also, in an honorary capacity, he held meetings and classes for other young lawyers who were fresh out of university and starting to make their way in the world of law. His desire to help others grew from his own childhood where he had no help or guidance. He was effectively orphaned at sixteen and worked his own way through school and university. He carried deep emotional scars from those times that he would not even admit to himself.

There were many fledging lawyers who were fortunate to have had the respected Sev Cockini beside them for support on their first day in court. His counsel to other, sometimes struggling lawyers was legendary.

James' passage through life was much different from his father's.

Educated at the exclusive Sydney Grammar School and later at the prestigious University of New South Wales, he could not have had a better start in life.

His father was a stern disciplinarian and closely monitored James every move in school and play. His mother, Gloria, gave balance to the family, wiping away the tears, comforting him through troubled times and being a good listener.

Once, after James had suffered a tirade from his Dad over what he saw as a poor school examination result, it was Gloria who later sat with him and explained why his Dad was so obsessed with seeing him succeed.

When he was in his teens she felt he was old enough to understand the reasons behind his father's mania.

She explained how his parents had returned to Greece leaving him at sixteen years old with only one hundred pounds in his pocket to fend for himself. His involvement with the Naxos family was explained and how he and John Naxos had a deep friendship starting when they were together in primary school. "It was your father and John who started the Naxos business, which grew from humble beginnings with the restaurant at Newtown."

As the years went by James grew to understand and respect his father more and more. But it was his mother for whom he had a huge amount of love and affection.

Her life began in even more difficult circumstances than his father, which was never totally explained.

He was aware that there was nothing in the home indicating where she came from or about her family.

Once he asked her where she had lived, what school she went to, and why she did not have any old photos.

His questions upset her, and with big tears sliding down her cheeks she said, "One day when you are older I will tell you, but not yet."

She was now a sprightly Seventy-five-year-old and never missed an opportunity to be with her children and grandchildren. Occasionally James asked her to tell him about the years before she married his father, but the answer was always the same, "One day we will talk about it."

James' sister Vanessa, in the family tradition, was also a lawyer working in the practice.

The third child was Brendan, seen as the rebel of the family. The last James knew he was working on a prawn trawler up in the Gulf of Carpentaria.

In the tradition of the old country, as he referred to their native Greece, Sev looked to the eldest for support and to look after the extended family.

Even now he was not past giving James a verbal blast over some issue that they disagreed on.

In later years, to save upsetting his father James would generally agree with him and let him have his say unchallenged, then go his own way.

James was aware that there were some dramas with the Naxos Business around the time that his father sold his share to John's brother Steven. There was also something about an old friend Frank Bennett, who was not talked about.

Nowadays he knew better than to even ask.

He thought: one day it will all come out, but right now I don't care.

A lot of this was about to change when he received a phone call from his close friend and stepbrother Paul Spalding.

"Hello James, how are you?" James only had time for a brief reply when Paul said, "James, something important has come up that I need to discuss with you can we meet for lunch today'?

"Sure Paul. Where?"

"How about the City Tattersalls Club at one o'clock, and Paul, in the meantime do not mention our meeting to anyone, including Dad."

"That's fine; I suppose this has got something to do with our long-lost relative from England?"

"Yes, it has but please don't mention this until after we have talked."

Paul, looking quite apprehensive, was waiting in the lounge when James arrived.

He stood and said, 'Hello James, thanks for coming at such short notice, will we go straight into the dining room?" He picked up a small satchel, which James noticed that he did not usually carry, and headed for the dining room.

Without any preamble Paul said, "James, I am going to break a confidence here, so I have to rely on you to keep what I am about to tell you between us. He picked up his satchel and removed an envelope containing three audio cassette tapes and handed them to James.

"These were sent to me by Colin Naxos and they carry some quite startling information.

I will briefly fill you in now as to their contents then you can take them home and listen to them in detail.

Colin's mother, Barbara Naxos (nee White) had recorded on tape information concerning the Naxos and Cockini families which her husband had gathered over many years. Included in the tapes is detailed information about the Naxos Condiment business.

Much of this is about the period prior to the Jean Naxos' murder and John's state of mind following the tragedy, and his later supposed alcoholism.

When it became known that John was murdered up in The Entrance, she wrote to Steven asking for details, and never received a reply.

As a result of that she wrote to our father asking for details of his death and if he left a will. He answered the letter giving her the same scant information that she had read in the Sydney papers.

His letter, according to her, said that he did not prepare a will for John and did not know who did, so he could not help her. It was at this point that she decided to send her son Colin with his friend Trevor to see what was going on.

Her motivation for this was that she believed that there was some huge inheritance that had gone missing.

The information gathered by the boys in a short space of time is quite alarming and indicates that there is much more to the story than we know about.

They have tracked down John's friend, Charlie Thornton, who they believe ended up with John's money. They are going to see him on Friday.

Colin has already been attacked and warned off by someone they believe is connected to a security company.

If their suspicions are correct, the security gorillas, as they referred to them, came from a company owned by Steven Naxos. Considering the information, we now have, it is not unreasonable to believe that they both could be in grave danger."

A little shaken James said, "Why don't you take all the information to the police and let them handle it."

Paul hesitated then took a long look at his stepbrother.

"For one very good reason. You will understand when you listen to the tapes. They have suggested that somehow Dad is or has been involved.

The claim is that he was peddling drugs way back in university days to pay his fees.

His source was Frank Bennett, who as you know was a partner in Naxos Condiments, a client and a friend."

They both sat silently lost in their own thoughts while the waitress served their meal, which neither had much appetite for.

James was the first to break the silence; "Do you know where they are going?"

"No, but they may tell me if I rang and asked."

"Then ask, they have your mobile so ring now."

Paul took his phone out of his satchel and rang the familiar number. It was answered immediately with a short "Hello." Without any introduction or preamble Paul said, "If you guys want my help you need to tell me where you are going for this meeting. If something happens to you, I would not even know where to begin looking, so tell me now."

"I will give it to you, don't write it down, and just memorise it.

Paul listened for a moment then the connection was abruptly cut.

Paul turned to James and said, Charlie is in Hervey Bay and the boys have found his actual address through the Post Office. The address is, 136 Old Marlborough Road Hervey Bay QLD."

"That's one hurdle, the next is I think we should find some good private investigators to tail them. If someone is after them they need all the protection they can get. I don't think we would want it on our conscience if we did nothing and something happened to them.

I know two girls in the police force who have handled private jobs for me before, and they are the very best in the business, so leave it to me."

"James, I have to get back to the surgery for appointments, can we meet again tomorrow after you've listened to the tapes?"

"Yes, I think we should, will here do?"

It was two very worried men who left the club and headed back to their offices.

The following day, using separate bookings and seats, Colin and Trevor with scruffy old backpacks and untidy clothes, boarded a Qantas Jetstar plane for Brisbane with a connecting flight to Hervey Bay.

The airport at Hervey Bay was, at best, very basic catering for few locals and tourists.

After clearing the baggage collection, they left the confines of the air-conditioned airport and went out into the hot humid air of north Queensland. Taking separate taxis, they asked the cabbie to take them to a backpackers' hostel in the main tourist shopping district.

With a couple of hotels and an endless variety of restaurants along the strip they felt that could obtain a fair degree of anonymity.

The following morning while Trevor went for a swim in the resort pool Colin took the opportunity to ring Kathleen. He gave her a brief run down on developments since they last met and where they were to meet Charlie. He strongly emphasised the need not to mention this to anyone.

As she would be in Brisbane in a few days' time they tentatively arranged to rendezvous at her Hotel the following week.

Later, feeling quite stressed and lethargic from lack of exercise Colin took a long walk along the beach. The beach bore no resemblance to the golden sand and clean water of the Sydney beaches. A strip of near mud running to calm murky water was, to Colin, quiet disappointing. The reason being was that the narrow strip of ocean was protected by the world-famous Great Barrier Reef further out to sea.

Soon he came to a long pier that ran for nearly a mile straight out to sea, presumably to clear the shallow waters of the beach. He thought, "this is interesting", and turned to walk out on the pier.

It was then that he noticed a man wearing a green shirt loitering behind him who he had also seen back near the shops.

Pretending not to notice, Colin took the long walk out to the end of the pier and sat for about half an hour watching the fisherman and letting the fresh salty air wash over him. Returning to the beach he was not surprised to see the fellow still there. Trying to appear that he had not noticed him Colin strolled nonchalantly back along the beach and across the road to a Hotel, where he sat and nursed a beer. Looking across the road towards the beach-side caravan park he saw his follower sitting under a tree.

That evening Colin unobtrusively passed a note to Trevor in the passageway.

> *Trevor.*
>
> *We may be being followed. Look for a skinny little guy in tan shorts and a green top; he has popped up a few times. If you see him look at the eyes, they are shifty. (I read that in a detective magazine) Why don't you look your natural self and find a girl to hang on your arm? As in the classics, burn this letter. I will meet you at the barbecue area in the park at 10 o'clock. I don't think we will look up Charlie yet.*
>
> *Colin*

———— ❀ ————

Meanwhile, back in Sydney, James and Paul met again for lunch. Paul thought James looks a bit ragged, as if he had not slept too well last night. Sitting down at their table, Paul said, "Rough night eh."

"Yes, it was a bit hard getting to sleep after listening to the tapes. The whole thing has enormous implications. Assuming of course it is anywhere near factual."

Paul's comment was "There doesn't seem to be any reason why it's not all true."

James ruminated, "Maybe you are right, but I cannot come to terms about Dads involvement. I think I know him better than you and it does not fit him at all. He is so kind and thoughtful to his children and grandchildren and he absolutely dotes on Gloria. He is always helping someone, even the time he donates to help the young lawyers leaving uni and trying to establish themselves.

The personality does not fit that of a drug-running shyster. In fact, the more I think about it the more I am convinced that he is not and was never involved.

Paul sighed, "Spoken like a supporting son; however, I am inclined to agree with you. Although I do recall that when I was young living with my grandparents, they had some quite disparaging comments about my natural father.

Grandmother Spalding once told me that he was not a nice person and he was having affairs while my mother was pregnant.

There was also some story that the Doc had some private investigators check him out and the result of that was why they raised me, not him. Anyway, let's not speculate any more, it's only important now that we find the truth."

James, looking even paler, replied, "Paul you are absolutely frightening the shit out of me. Let's can it, at least until we see what eventuates. It is totally wrong for us to jump to conclusions at this point."

"Have you heard from your girls up there yet?"

"Yes, she rang this morning. All she had to report was that they had separated again and were both wandering around like Pommy backpackers; having a swim and doing the usual touristy things. They have made no move to contact Charlie yet.

I spoke to the leader, her name is Senior Constable Joan Sterling, and her partner is Constable Maureen Stewart. They are both very attractive girls.

The boys have been frequenting one of the local pubs and I suggested that they see if they would go for a pick up.

"It is quite likely that this may work. Trevor seems to think he is a bit of a lady's man."

"Time to go back to work, how about we skip tomorrow and meet on Friday?"

"That's fine with me. Give me a ring if anything develops."

That night Trevor was down at pub having a beer and playing pool with the locals.

"Christ" he thought, "they're a rough lot, but good fun with a typical

Aussie sense of humour. Slagging seemed to a natural pastime, especially when it came to be taking the piss out of Pommy backpackers."

While this was going on two attractive girls dressed for the hot Queensland climate walked in. They walked straight to the bar and ordered two Bourbon and Cokes.

All conversation stopped, and the bar became strangely quiet. Then one of Trevor's adversaries in sledging and pool said, "I bet you fifty bucks you can't muscle in on those two within five minutes. They would want someone manlier than you, and cleaner."

Trevor responded with. "You are on, this is easy cash.

Here's my fifty, put yours on the table."

With that, Trevor walked across to the girls and said, "Hi my name is Trevor, can I buy you another drink?"

The taller one of the two looked him up and down and with an expression of distaste said, "No thanks, we're not anybody's pick up."

"Girls I can see that, you are too classy for the likes of me, so I will tell you the story. That rough looking character over there who needs a wash and a haircut bet me fifty dollars I could not get you to sit with me. So, if you allow me, I will collect his money and buy your drinks with it, then I will leave you alone. Now you can't get a better deal than that, can you?"

The girls looked at one another and laughed.

"That is the best line I've heard in a long time and it would be hard to knock back, you can go and buy our drinks."

Trevor spent half an hour sitting with the girls buying their drinks chatting away about his, mostly fictitious travels, then got up and went over to the pool table to collect his bet.

The big Aussie drawled, "Okay you win, but bullshit is all you Poms have got, you can't even play cricket, that's for sure."

As Trevor walked away with the money in his hand he chortled, "I whipped you at pool though."

The reply was, "Aw fuck, where did he come from."

Later in the night Trevor, slightly the worse for wear left the girls promising to meet them the next night in another more up market establishment.

It was still only ten o'clock and he was on time to meet Colin. They both agreed that as there had been no further sign of anybody tailing them, they would loosen up a bit. If all was quiet over the weekend, they would tackle Charlie on Sunday night.

Trevor mischievously added, "Now down to the real business, I have these two absolutely smashing girls for a date tomorrow night, like one each. You have the taller one and I have the other. Now, they've insisted that we get cleaned up, so you'd better get out your best gear. I'm going into town tomorrow to buy myself a new pair of shorts to show off my lily-white legs. I have a clean shirt, but I'll probably lash out on a pair of sandals as well. Showering and shaving will be mandatory."

Colin looking rather bemused at this behaviour from Trevor replied, "Bloody hell Trevor, these birds must be really special.

You can count me in as long as you don't mention them to Kathleen, as I just might take her home with me."

"God, you are a heart breaker, I bet you will leave her crying at the airport."

Colin's reply was, "By the way, what happened with your other love, Meredith?"

"Unfortunately, I found that she had a husband, and we have enough troubles now without being chased by an angry spouse."

After another uneventful day they cleaned up, dressed in their new shorts and sandals, and headed for the nightspot.

Colin remarked, "Well Trevor old boy, if there is anyone out there looking for us, they will never recognise us in this gear."

They rolled into the bar lounge area with Trevor, full of confidence. He headed straight for Joan and Maureen who were on sitting on their own at a small table. Colin was gob smacked, thinking, "How in the hell did he get these two beauties?"

They were tall girls with similar short hair styles, one was very dark and the other a honey coloured blond hair. Both were shapely and looked as if they spent a lot of time in a gym.

As the night rolled on there was much frivolity and good humour.

Trevor of course gave them a much expanded and exaggerated tale of their life back home in Oxford.

Late in the night Colin asked what Joan and Maureen did for a living. He nearly fell off the chair when Joan said; "We are in the Police Force and are just taking two weeks leave away from the city life."

Colin said, "You're joking; you would be the most unlikely and best-looking police women I have ever seen."

Joan responded with, "You guys are a little out of touch with today's world. We work in special operations, mostly on corporate fraud, and occasionally missing persons. We don't really go out in the street having fist fights with the baddies."

Poor Trevor was nearly choking on his beer.

Colin was being a bit more calculating, thinking, we may be able to use them later.

After the shock, the night passed quickly. Bumping around the small dance floor they both tried hard, but unsuccessfully, to get the girls back to their rooms for the night.

On the way back to the hostel they agreed that as there appeared to be no threat to the purpose of being in Harvey Bay they decided to stick with their plan. They would meet the girls again tomorrow night and take them to a nice restaurant for dinner. With a bit of luck this may soften them up enough to get into their rooms at the Hotel.

Trevor was optimistic, but Colin did not share his confidence.

"Christ Trevor, if you try anything, she would probably twist your arm up your back; now that would be really embarrassing."

Distracted by alcohol and the fun of the night they failed to notice two shadows under a tree as they walked through the park. Simultaneously they stepped out behind the tree and Colin and Trevor suddenly both felt an arm with a grip of steel around their necks.

Trevor was just about to execute a Judo manoeuvre, dropping down low enough to throw his assailant over his head, when he felt cold steel like the tip of a knife against his neck and a voice said, "Don't even think about it."

Out of the corner of his eye he saw that Colin was in the same predicament.

"Now boys all we want is information and then we leave you alone and you won't get hurt.

Otherwise you are going to lose a lot of blood."

With his arm tightening even more he said, "Just tell us where Charlie Thornton is and we'll let you go, no trouble. You can do it the easy way or the hard way."

Colin and Trevor were both contemplating their future, if any, when a voice called, "Police, freeze. Now don't do anything silly, just let them go or I blow your stupid heads off."

Slowly they were released and turned to see the girls about five meters away. Both stood in the classic shooting position, legs apart, arms straight out, holding what looked like Glock pistols. "Right you two, now up against the tree, arms around the trunk. Maureen, secure them both."

After their arms were securely tied around a tree with plastic cable ties, they put their pistols away in carry bags.

Joan said, "You won't learn will you. Why walk across the park in the dark? These people are not playing party games. As far as we know these boys are not alone and you had better get out of here, fast. Besides you would not like to see how we treat these two."

Colin responded. "Just hold on a moment, before we go anywhere or do anything, I want to know who sent you to baby sit us."

"We have been sent to look after you, so do as you're told and follow instructions. You will find out later who your minders are."

Colin and Trevor looked at one another and both came to the same conclusion. They had better follow directions. Maureen led them across the road to a white Toyota Land Cruiser.

"Here are the keys; the tank's full and there's a map on the seat showing you exactly where to go. There is also a mobile phone in the glove box. I want you to collect your gear from the hostel, pick up Charlie Thornton and get the hell out of here as fast as you can.

We want you to go inland, and then head back to Sydney. If you take the coastal route down the Pacific highway you are sure to be intercepted along the way.'

Colin jumped in behind the wheel and kicked over the big V8. Both were too shocked to argue or even talk until they pulled up in front of the

Hostel. Colin said, "You go and grab our gear, so we can get the hell out of here."

Trevor returned in no less than two minutes carrying their packs and a plastic bag of things that he could not quickly fit in. "While our innocent little dates look after those two, let's go and pick up Charlie."

Five minutes later they were knocking on the door of a tidy little cottage with a neatly tended garden and freshly cut lawn.

A sleepy voice said, "Who's there?"

Colin yelled through the door, 'My name is Colin Naxos, we are friends of Hester's; could you open the door please?"

A slight man with a tanned, weather-beaten face opened the door and said, "I have been expecting you blokes." "Charlie, we haven't got time to beat around the bush. There are a few people in town looking for you and it could become very dangerous for us to stop here."

Charlie replied, "I have been expecting this for a long time, what do you want me to do."

"Grab a few clothes, lock up the house, and come with us."

THE OUTBACK

CHAPTER ELEVEN

Once they were loaded, with old Charlie settled in the back, Colin said, "Trevor I'll drive, and you grab that map and tell us where we're going."

From the back-seat Charlie chipped in, "I know the area, give the map to me. Someone has highlighted a route; it looks like we're going north. Turn left at the next intersection, then left again through the roundabout, and head for the Bruce Highway about thirty kilometres up the road. Next stop Rockhampton, 320 kilometres away.

How much juice does this bus hold?"

"Great Charlie, you are now the official navigator. The tank is full, and I think it would hold 120 litres."

Two hours later they had a comfort stop and changed drivers.

"Well that feels better." Charlie said as he climbed back in the car. "Perhaps you guys can now tell me what the hell is going on."

With Trevor now driving, Colin filled Charlie in on what had happened since they'd arrived in Australia. Charlie did not interrupt until he finished with the girls rescuing them in Harvey Bay.

"Well I am surprised; you have done well for a couple of Poms. But fancy having a couple of girls rescue you. That would never have happened in my day."

This seemed to amuse Charlie no end.

Colin retorted, "Okay Charlie you've had your fun; perhaps you can tell us what it's all about."

"It would take too long now, so let's leave it for tomorrow. Right now, I'm going to get some sleep and I suggest you do the same."

The big four-wheel drive hummed along smoothly, and Colin was just about asleep when the phone in the glove box beeped.

Colin pushed the call button and was not surprised to hear Joann's voice, "Hello, are you boys all right, where are you?"

"We are about a hundred kilometres out of Rockhampton. But tell me what the hell is going on back there?"

"You don't need to know, but you're in good hands, so just do as we tell you. Don't go off on any hair-brained scheme, next time help may not be available for you. Have you got Charlie with you, is he alright?"

"Yes, he's fine- typical Aussie, a bit of a cheeky old bugger."

"Colin it is absolutely paramount that you follow instructions. When you get to Rockhampton go left and head for a town called Emerald. I will ring you at lunchtime tomorrow."

Colin replied, "But wait a moment, we would like to know what's going on. Who are you? Are you really in the Police Force and if so how did you get involved?"

"We are Police officers, but for this job we're on leave. When it is appropriate you will be told."

Without giving Colin a chance to reply she disconnected.

Colin filled Trevor in on the conversation and said, "God, you know how to pick up the right girls." As dawn broke they pulled into an all-night McDonald's in Rockhampton for breakfast and a cup of coffee.

Later, with their hunger quelled and feeling refreshed, they returned to the Toyota and decided to have a brief look around the town. They found it an attractive prosperous town with considerable architectural charm set on the Fitzroy River. Many of the original buildings remain, set off by flowering Bauhinia and brilliant Bougainvillea.

Charlie helped by explaining that 'Rocky' was considered the beef capital of Australia and had the two largest meat processing and exporting facilities in the country. Colin reminded them they were not there for an outback tour of Queensland and they needed to get back on the road for their next destination, Emerald.

They covered the 263 kilometres in just over three hours, arriving in time for lunch and to find somewhere to bed down for the night.

At the meeting of the Capricorn and Gregory Highways, Emerald is the hub of the Central Highlands. Trevor and Colin found the countryside fascinating; just so far removed from home. Apart from the huge distances, the mostly barren countryside seemed to be devoid of life.

They found a respectable looking Motel in the centre of town called the Country Comfort. After dropping their bags in their rooms, they went to the dining room for lunch.

They had just sat down when the 'Bat Phone,' as Trevor was calling it, beeped. Colin picked it up, "Hello."

As anticipated Joan answered and said, "You have made it to Emerald I see, is everything okay?"

Colin replied, "Yes, just fine, no problems, but how did you know we are at Emerald."

"We have a satellite tracker on your car, that's why."

"You appear to think of everything, but please tell me what the hell we are doing out here in the middle of nowhere doing a Cook's tour of the Australian outback."

"Well it would have been very difficult to get you on a plane or down the coast road undetected. So just follow our instruction on a day by day basis. Charlie is vital to our ongoing investigations and we cannot afford to lose him. Have you got any information out of him yet?"

Rather testily Colin answered, "There will be no more on that until you tell me who you are working for or who is paying you."

"I cannot divulge that yet, but I can assure you that they are on your side. The other thing I must impress on you is if you receive any calls, including from your girlfriend, on your other phone do not answer it. Nowadays it is a simple matter to trace the call. In fact it would be safer if you turn it off right now."

After lunch, complimented with a couple of much needed cold beers, Colin said, "Well Charlie, talk time. If we are to save our skins as well as yours, and Hester's, we need to have the full story on your association with John Naxos. And we don't leave here until we have it. I have a mini recorder here and I will be recording what you tell us, so make sure you get the story right."

Colin then switched the recorder on and spoke into it.

"Charles Thornton, of his own free will, will speak for this recording on the 5th day of March 2005."

Charlie, now looking every bit of his 77 years, sighed and said, "Well I have not had a drink for a long time, but I will have one now before I start.

Hester and I were married in 1953, in the old Methodist Church in Bankstown. It was a great wedding with all the relatives and friends there for the celebration. Typical of that time there was no grog at the reception and the meal was pretty basic, as no one had a lot of money.

We had a short honeymoon up in Katoomba, which was the place to go in those times. We were both virgins and our first night was a bit confusing for us both.

Over the following years, as hard as we tried, we were never able to have children, which was a huge disappointment for Hester. She would have made a wonderful mother. I often thought later that if we had been fortunate enough to have children it may have put some direction in my own life.

Not long after our marriage I got a job on the railways, and three years later I became a train driver. The dormant hurt of not being able to have children came to the front of my life several years later.

Early one morning I picked up my train from the old Eveleigh depot and took the early run to Penrith. On the return trip, as usual, I slowed down coming into Strathfield station to pick up the city office workers and kids going to various schools.

I was not really paying attention as I did the final braking, then I noticed two boys skylarking on the edge of the platform. I put my hand up to pull the cord for the horn when to my horror they both fell under the train.

By the time I activated the emergency brakes we were another fifty metres down the track. When they were pulled from under the train's wheels, they were both dead.

Somehow, I related the boys to the ones I never had.

Over the following years I got into the habit of having a tipple to get up the courage to drive the trains. As the years went by drinking became more and more compulsive and I rarely went home sober. Hester used to plead with me to slow up or get help, but the more she hassled me the more I drank.

The years went by and we had little marriage left. Fortunately, in the early times we had managed to put a deposit on a nice home in Bankstown.

Hester went back to work at the local Bank and we used her wages to pay off the mortgage.

Finally, the railways decided that I was a problem and a liability, so they gave me a severance pay and took my job away. When I went home and told Hester that I had lost my job she gave me an ultimatum, give up the booze or leave.

I left.

You may wonder why I am telling you boys all this, but it may help you understand my relationship with John and why I did not come forward with the truth about the time of his murder. After that I left Sydney and rented a unit up in The Entrance, away from all the city problems.

Every night I used to take my rods and go fishing along the channel entrance. Sometimes I went for the Black Fish, and in the season, I fished for Whiting.

One evening, a fellow around my age, came and sat next to me and proceeded to try to catch a fish.

He was bloody hopeless and had no idea what he was doing. After Several nights of this, when I would usually at least have a feed, this fellow would go home with nothing.

I could not stand it anymore and went over to him and said, "Look mate you are going about it in the wrong way. Let me get you sorted out, so you have a chance. Christ all you are doing is feeding them; they probably line up every night for their 'free meal'. So, I taught John how to fish.

After that we would meet every night and later, we took it in turns to bring a few cans of beer.

Sometimes if the mood took us, instead of going home we would head for the Bridge View Hotel and wipe ourselves out.

I had an old Ford Falcon that I used to get around in; it was rough, so much so that I never even bothered to lock it. I saw that John drove a Mercedes, which looked pretty new to me. Even if he was pissed, he was always very careful with his car. As time went by we became good mates and were rarely apart. He had a unit around the corner from me in Denning Street; however, it was rare for us to visit each other's homes.

One night early in the piece, when I was totally pissed, I had blurted out my life story to John; but it took a long time for him to confide his past to me.

Little by little he told me about his parents' restaurant in Newtown and the business he built up in catering supplies after his parents died.

Such was the detail of his stories that I became to feel like one of his family. I heard about his friend, Sev Cockini, his brother Steven, that other bloke Frank Bennett, and all the people who were part of the business. He told me about his wife Jean, how much he loved her and how he never connected with his son Robert.

As the business grew John found it more and more difficult to control an operation of that size. In the later times, by his own admission, he left more and more to other people and had no real idea what was going on. He started spending all his spare time at the office and less and less at home with his wife and son.

One night he was in the warehouse alone and was about to lock up when he saw some boxes stacked apart from others. Casually he looked at the labels and saw they contained olives from Greece, these look will be good he thought, I will take a couple of tins home to have with my beer.

At home he found a note from Jean saying she had gone out to play bridge with some friends. "Bugger" he thought, "I may as well get myself a beer.

I might try the olives as well." After pouring his beer he opened the olives to find there were no olives in it.

Strange he thought, and up-ended the can to find it contained Several clear plastic bags of white powder. At that time Jean walked in and said, "What have you got here?"

Realising what she was facing she screamed at John saying, "What are you doing, are you mad. How long has this been going on? I am going to the police."

She did not go to the police, instead she told him she was finished with him and was going to leave. There was no way John could convince her that he had nothing to do with it. Next he fronted Steven about it who claimed he knew nothing about it. He convinced John not to go to the police as it would bring the whole business down. He gave John assurances that he would get to the bottom of it internally.

In the following weeks John withdrew from the business and tried to reconcile with his wife. Her response was that it was too late and that she was going overseas with their son Robert.

Shortly after that Jean's mutilated body was found in the local park.

John believed that she must have told someone about the drugs and threatened to go to the police. Whoever she told must have been responsible for her death.

At this time his drinking became excessive and he became totally dependent on alcohol to survive. It was believed that he sold his remaining share of the business to Steven and left for an extended trip to Europe. He never ever saw his son again.

When he returned, he started to receive threatening phone calls saying that if he ever mentioned the drugs he would end up under a bus. That was when he went into hiding and joined me bumming around The Entrance.

We know now that eventually they, whoever "they" are, found him. He was attacked in the car park just across from where we fished and whoever it was belted the shit out of him and left him for dead. I found him some minutes later. He died in my arms from that terrible attack. Before he passed out he told me where to find his keys and security numbers for his bank accounts. His last words to me were to go to his safety deposit box in the Bank of New South Wales and take all the contents, cash, bonds and share scripts.

A detailed will to that effect was in the box which I have put away for safe keeping.

Finally, all John's assets were legally willed to me, and frankly it was not a huge amount of money, which may surprise you. As I see it now, the danger for me is not about a small inheritance but my knowledge of a pretty big drug importing and distribution operation. If I am found I could go the same way as John, and possibly his wife Jean."

At this point Colin said, "Who made out the will, was it Sev Cockini?"

"No, he did it himself; but I have had it checked out and it is perfectly legal."

"What about Sev Cockini, did he ever say if he was involved?"

"No, he only said that he was his best friend going back to primary school days."

"Did he ever tell you who was really behind the drug operation?"

"No, but he did say that it was an ideal set up because no one would ever suspect such a long-established, respected business like that of importing drugs. The operation must be enormous, as there must be a huge overseas network to supply and package the drugs. In addition, someone must control the shipping. The only way the operation could be exposed was through an informer."

Trevor spluttered, "Holy shit, where do we go from here? Let's catch the first plane home."

Charlie then commented, "Look fellows, all I want is to finish with all this and get on with what is left of my life. I want to be able to sell the Bankstown house, take Hester up to The Entrance and settle into a nice unit overlooking the beach. I really gave her a bad time over the years and I would like to make some amends for that in the time we have left.

At my age we don't need this fuckin drama. I wish I had never seen the bloody money, or John, as it has turned out."

Colin replied, "Charlie I can understand that, but we have no choice but to see it through. We will sit and wait to hear what our two girls come up with. In the meantime, I will ring Hester and let her know all is well."

"And no doubt say hello to Kathleen while you're there." joked Trevor.

While Charlie took Trevor for a walk around the town Colin went in search of an electronics shop to get the tape copied. When he was finished, he placed a copy in a small Jiffy Mailing Bag with a short note and sent it by registered post to Dr Paul Spalding.

That evening, the "Bat Phone" rang and Joan, all cheery this time, asked how they were and if there had been any trouble.

Colin said that all was quiet, but they had a tape of Charlie's story.

"About time," she replied, "What have you done with it?"

"I have posted it down to Sydney, and I am not saying where until you tell me who you're working for."

"I cannot divulge that without consulting with them. I will see if I can fill you in tomorrow or at the worst the following day. In the meantime, don't worry; you have nothing to be concerned about on that score. We are as confident as we can be that nobody else knows where you are, so we would like you to work your way south with care.

Tomorrow you can have a full day playing tourist. Then follow this on your map. Take the Gregory Highway out of Emerald to a place called Banana. Stop for lunch then pick up the Leichhardt Highway to Goondiwindi. Find yourself a nice hotel and stay there until we contact you again. I didn't tell you this before, but if you look just under the steering wheel you will find a red panic button. If you have any trouble at all, press it and an alarm will be activated on our phones."

After a troubled night's sleep Colin was up early rousing the others to get ready to leave. They devoured a hearty country breakfast, and then threw their bags in the back. After refuelling they were on the road for Goondiwindi.

The longest drive Colin and Trevor had ever experienced before was from London to Liverpool. The distances here to them were so immense that they felt as if they were on another planet. They passed barren open plains with grazing sheep and cattle, and into vast cotton and wheat fields that would have swallowed up half of England.

If it were not for the circumstances of being there, it would have been the experience of a lifetime.

With Colin driving they had just passed a small roadside truck stop at Rolleston when he became aware of a white Ford Fairlane sedan that had been hanging behind them for some time. Charlie was asleep in the back and Colin said to Trevor, "Have a look at the car behind us; it's been there for the last half hour or more. I don't like it, there appears to be two men in the front. We won't out pace them so we'll slow right down and see if they pass us." Colin slowed down to forty, and his gut turned over when the Fairlane did the same. "Shit mate, I think we're in trouble again.

We haven't even got anything to defend ourselves with. Remembering the panic button under the dash he reached under and hit it. They were maintaining the low speed with their obvious pursuers keeping the same distance behind them when the "Bat Phone" rang

Trevor grabbed it and before he had time speak Joan answered, "What is the problem?"

A very nervous Trevor literally screamed into the phone. "We have a bloody car on our tail; he's been behind us for nearly an hour."

Joan replied, "Are you sure he is following you."

"I am fucking sure. When we go fast, he sticks behind us; when we slow right down, he does the same, and there are two goons in the front."

Joan reply was hesitant, "Just try to remain calm and I'll get help to you as fast as I can. In the meantime, you can out-run them if you take to the scrub. Their car won't handle off-road. At the first chance, get off the road and take to the open country. Your Toyota will handle just about anything."

Trevor relayed this to Colin as they entered an open stretch of road through what seemed an endless landscape of barren country side. Separating the road from the open land was a simple wire fence. Without any hesitation He wrenched the wheel to the right, bounced over a shallow culvert and straight at the wire fence. The momentum of the vehicle smashed through the fence, the only awareness of the impact was screech as the fence wire met with the metal of the Toyota. Trevor yelled, 'We are free as the Toyota burst through the fence.

The big 4WD bucked and bounced and threatened to roll over when it hit a big drainage ditch and a pile of small rocks as it crashed through some low scrub then into some open ground.

While Trevor and Colin hung on with their seat belts tight across their chests in the front seats, Charlie was violently woken as he was thrown off the back seat onto the floor.

"What the fuck is going on? Are you Pommy idiots trying to kill me?"

Colin yelled over the noise of flying rocks hitting the vehicle, "Just shut up and buckle your seat belt; we're in for a rough ride"."

At a suicidal pace they flew across the now open country with Colin desperately trying to keep the Toyota upright.

Just when they thought they were in the clear Colin glanced in the rear vision mirror to see the pursuing car leave the road and two men get out with what appeared to be rifles.

"Everybody down on the floor, quick", he yelled. Next, they felt a thud then the crack of a rifle when a bullet hit the rear door and whined away into the distance. Then another thud as a bullet hit the rear window. It flew through the interior of the wagon and out the front windscreen leaving only a small hole in the toughened laminated glass.

The big Toyota careered on over the rough terrain with Colin desperately trying to keep control as, yet another bullet smashed through the roof.

Just when they thought they would never survive, they bounced over a small rise into a dry creek bed and out of sight from their attackers. Colin slowed down, and without hesitation, turned and followed the creek bed, which ran away from the road keeping them out of vision.

After about five hundred metres he stopped and jumped out saying, "Let's check for damage and see if they managed to follow."

Charlie was speechless and would not get out.

While Colin walked around the wagon Trevor grabbed a pair of binoculars out of the glove box and climbed up the creek bank. Careful not to be seen, he lay in the dirt and raised the glasses to his eyes.

To his great relief Trevor saw the car back on the road travelling towards Rolleston at high speed. Clambering back down the creek bank he called to Colin, "They have gone."

"Thank God for that, but let's just wait here for a while to make sure they have really gone."

They sat in dry creek bed with the sun relentlessly beating down on them for about half an hour before deciding it was safe enough to move on. While Trevor continued to scan the countryside through the binoculars looking for signs of their pursuers, Colin picked up the "Bat Phone" and pushed the button for direct access to Joan.

She answered on the first ring, "What's happened, Is everybody alright?"

"We are lucky that they can't shoot straight, but we are a bit shaken up, but okay. We took to the scrub as you suggested, and apart from a few bullet holes in your Toyota, we are all safe. Our pursuers have given up and have headed back towards Rolleston. We are now sitting in this dry creek bed in the middle of nowhere wondering what the hell to do next. Do you have any ideas?"

Joan replied, "You have a compass mounted on the dashboard. Keep driving across the open plains in an easterly direction. After about 30ks you will run into an unsurfaced road called, The Fitzroy Devil Road. Turn right on this and it will take you to a small town called Taroom. Do not attempt to get back onto the main road before this.

You will then be on the Leichhardt Highway, which takes you to another town called Miles. We will have you on the satellite tracker so don't worry about getting lost. I have contacted the police at Moura, Rolleston and Emerald, and between them they should pick up the two who were hell bent on wiping you out. At the worst they can hold them for a while on firearms charges.

When you reach Miles stop the night there, but don't leave the Toyota out the front of the motel. Park it in a back street somewhere out of the way.

As soon as you get a chance buy a roll of adhesive tape and cover up the bullet holes, at least so they don't look too obvious.'

With Colin driving they ricocheted across the open plain at a frightening speed, dodging boulders and small gnarled trees.

Suddenly Trevor screamed, "Colin, for Christ's sake slow down, or you'll kill us all. There is no one chasing us out here."

Gathering himself, Colin came back to reality and slowed down to a more manageable speed just as a herd of kangaroos appeared from the scrub and bolted across their path.

He said, "Did you see that, the big ones must be two metres tall."

They had forgotten Charlie until he spoke from the back seat, "Don't worry, they are only the babies; start worrying if their Daddy comes along and takes an exception to our being here."

Worrying about the kangaroos, Colin nearly missed seeing a wire fence stretched across in front of them.

"Hell, what do we do now?"

Charlie chipped in again. "You bloody Poms are hopeless; just follow it, and somewhere we'll find a gate."

They headed south east along the fence and sure enough, after about two kilometres they came across a farm gate.

Colin stopped while Trevor got out to open the wire gate with Charlie yelling in background, "Make sure you close it."

After that, travelling became easier, with the landscape improving and showing signs of habitation. They crested a small rise to see some low, rolling countryside that was tinged with green. Then in the distance they saw a motor bike travelling fast in a cloud of dust on an angle that would intercept them. Having no other choice Colin kept going for a while before slowing down then stopping as the bike caught up.

The man on the bike was tall and lean, dressed in jeans and a denim shirt with a country style broad-brimmed hat. There was no welcoming smile on his tanned craggy face as he looked them over with a steely stare.

Colin immediately became alarmed when, without getting off the bike, he took what looked to be a lever action 30/30 Winchester from a scabbard on the bike. Laying it across his knees he drawled, "Now what the hell do you blokes think you're doing?"

Taking the initiative Trevor, replied in his strongest Pommy accent, "We were travelling on the highway when we were attacked and shot at, so we took to the bush to escape. Look at the bullet holes in our car. Now we're lost. Can you tell us how the hell we can get out of here and back to the road?"

Still on the bike, the man said, "Don't get out, just sit in the car until I check this out."

He then rode his bike around the Toyota looking at the damage and bullet holes.

Taking what looked like a satellite phone from a basket on the front handlebars the rider keyed in a number and waited for a reply.

"Constable Baker please,

After for a moment he said, "Hello Peter, it's Bob out on Bald Hill Station, I've just pulled up three men in a Land Cruiser roaring across the back paddock. They reckon they were shot at down on the highway and took to the bush. Do you know anything about it?' The rego number is NSW BKS5089. Yes, I will hold for a moment."

He listened for quite some time, then still on the bike, he switched off the phone and said, "There is something strange about this; the local police know you are about and suggested that you get off my property and back on the highway as fast as you can. This vehicle is registered with the NSW Police. It's not my business and I don't want to know, I just want you off my land. Follow me and I'll take you back to the road."

He returned the rifle to the scabbard and roared off across the paddock.

Trevor managed to keep him in sight, mainly from his trail of dust, until about half an hour later when they stopped at an unmade dirt road. They presumed it was the Fitzroy Devil Road. The farmer levered himself off his bike and sauntered over to the Toyota, this time without his rifle, and said. "Follow this road and it will take you into town. Have you got plenty of fuel and water?"

Colin replied, "Yeah, sure, we're okay. By the way, what is the rifle for?"

"Mainly wild pigs and foxes, and sometimes trespassers", was the drawled reply. "So, on your way boys"!

Colin did not require any further encouragement and drove off over the dusty corrugated road.

After what seemed an eternity, they came to a major sealed road, which led them into a small town called Taroom. Estimating that they still had two hours of daylight left they decided to push on to Miles, as was their original plan.

Arriving in Miles totally exhausted they took two rooms in a local pub. After a couple of cold pies washed down with a can of beer, they all collapsed into bed.

As Colin turned the light out Trevor said, "Hey Colin, is there any truth in the rumour that you wet your pants out there before we got to the creek bed?"

"Get stuffed"! Was the reply.

Early next morning, after refuelling at the local BP service station, they were back on the road heading for Goondiwindi. Without any further drama they covered the 250 kilometres in just over three hours.

Still feeling exhausted and in need of a serious rest Colin booked them rooms at the "Early Settlers Motel."

This time they had a room each and after a shower and change of clothes they met in the bar for a much-needed beer and lunch.

Charlie declined Colin's offer of a beer, saying, "A Coke will do me, and I've had my beer for the year"!

Later, Colin used a public phone to check in with Kathleen and allowed Charlie a moment to speak to Hester. He was obviously a little nervous and mumbled, "How you going love? It's been a long time, are you okay?" They did not hear Hester's reply, and Charlie then rambled, "Well love, that's great, with a new hip there will be no stopping you. Did you say the boys here are paying for this operation? That's a lot of money." There was another silence, then with some outward show of emotion Charlie sputtered,

"When we get all this mess sorted we'll have a talk, and maybe you'll come up the coast with me."

After composing himself he uttered, "Thanks boys." then walked back to his room. A little later, looking more relaxed he returned to join them for dinner.

The long day on the road had been tiring and as there was no further communication from the girls or Sydney, they took a leisurely stroll around the town before returning to the motel. Back in their rooms Colin was surprised that there were still no further calls from the girls. They had little choice but to sit and wait for a message.

For a couple of Poms who had never been far from home, let alone to the great outback of Australia, Goondiwindi was another interesting experience. For a time, they forgot the reason they were there.

While they considered themselves physically fit from their sporting activities back home, they were not prepared for the harshness of the Australian outback. The heat and humidity sapped whatever energy they had.

This modern country town, built on the banks of the Macintyre River at the NSW and Queensland border, had a bustling economy based on cotton, wheat, beef and wool.

Colin pondered as to how much of these primary products found their way back home.

The day went by without any calls on the "Bat Phone", so they decided to try the beer and food at the local RSL club.

The beer was good, and the steaks they ordered were better and bigger than anything they had ever seen.

There was a Disco going in the auditorium and Trevor was all for seeing if they could make a strike with the local girls.

Colin could only laugh at the suggestion. "Shit mate, you never give up. The last time you tried you turned up with the local Police Force. For me I'm going back to the motel for an early night."

"Your problem is that you are infatuated with Kathleen. I have a much more relaxed and open mind."

"Yes, and it's all below your navel."

Next morning, they were up early, refuelled the Toyota and drove out of town to see a bit of the district.

They were about thirty kilometres out of town when the "Bat Phone" rang. Colin picked it up, and through a bit of static, he heard it was Joan, "Colin we have just been told that four men, who are known to the police, have been seen boarding a regional flight for Goondiwindi. It may not mean anything, but we are not taking any chances; Charlie must have his day in court.

We want you out of there within the hour and on your way to Coonabarabran, you should reach it by sunset. The same rules apply no phone calls. Not even one, okay! There appears to be a leak and we don't know where it is coming from."

Colin was quite shocked; "Does this also mean that you have heard the tapes?"

"Yes, we have."

"Well, that answers my next question."

"Colin if the leaks came from there, I wouldn't have a copy of the tapes. I can tell you, Paul Spalding is solidly on your side. He is your strongest ally."

It took just over an hour to get back to the motel, pack and be on the road again. Trevor and Charlie both sat in the back saying, "This is like the Queensland Country Derby, now I know how the Japanese tourists feel. See Australia in five days."

They covered the 340 kilometres in an easy five hours, arriving in Coonabarabran in late afternoon.

For a change they booked rooms in a local pub. After unpacking and a quick shower they went downstairs and propped in the bar to escape the heat. The bar smelt of stale beer with cigarette smoke and looked as if it had not changed since the nineteen thirties; which it probably hadn't. However, there was an intimate friendliness about it that can only be found in a country pub. A couple of local looking blokes huddled over the bar with their schooners and packets of fags in front of them. Apart from them the place was deserted which would most likely change towards the end of the day.

Colin and Trevor now understood to ask for schooners not the English pint of ale. As they sat nursing their beers Charlie was content with his coke, promising to keep an eye on them.

"You are both becoming a couple of piss-pots." He told them.

Trevor laughed and replied with, "Why don't you piss off and go to bed, you old wowser."

Charlie replied with gusto "I am not welcome here so I may as well." With that he left stomped out of the bar.

Now that he had the number he went out to the public phone in the foyer and rang Hester for a chat.

Later they ordered hamburgers from the kitchen and took them up to their room.

Next morning Colin was up early and while Trevor and Charlie had breakfast, he drove the Toyota down the main street to refuel. As he left the service station to return to their hotel the "Bat Phone" rang.

There was terse comment that someone was on their tail and they were to go straight to Dubbo and wait there for a flight to Sydney.

Accommodation had been booked for them at the Settlers Motel. There they would meet a man called Jim, who would watch over them.

They were to follow his instructions explicitly.

After a much easier and relaxed trip on a good road they arrived in Dubbo and found their motel on the main road through town. The motel was much more upmarket than most of their previous accommodation which was welcomed by all. As the rooms and parking area could not be seen from the street, they left the Toyota outside their unit door.

With time to spare before dinner Colin and Trevor walked into town to check out the local shops, leaving Charlie in his room to rest. They were impressed with the local country style shops and decided to buy some new clothes to replace what had been either left behind or discarded because they needed washing.

They were quite surprised at the size of the town and the shopping centre. A lot of the men's clothing was strictly "country and western" which suited them fine. Trevor remarked, "If we ever get home, we can really impress with this Aussie Country gear."

Back at the motel they found Joan s friend Jim waiting for them in the motel lounge, He was a big burly fellow smartly dressed in grey slacks, blue shirt, tie and dark jacket, looking a business type very much. After curt introductions his next words were, "Understand fellows that is the last time you go anywhere without me, no exceptions."

That night during dinner in the motel dining room their newly acquired friend sat on his own at another table reading a newspaper. He looked like another city salesman doing his country trip.

Colin felt that he should ring Kathleen and at least let her know where there were. He went out into the foyer to the public phone and started to dial the number. On the fifth digit a large hand came over the top, took the receiver and slammed it back in the cradle.

Their keeper said, "No phone calls was the instruction." Colin absolutely bristled, "Hang on, who the hell do you think you are, now piss off."

"You have choices mate, either do as you're told, or we will leave you to your own fate; or walk with me around to the local police station and put the burden of your safety on them. Neither are very attractive options. So, it's up to you, are you with me or not?"

Colin did not like the sound of that and whispered, "Okay let's just leave it, but don't think you can come pushing me around." He then stalked off to his room.

After another night of disturbed sleep Doctor Spalding arrived early in his surgery with an hour to spare before his first appointment. His secretary came in with his usual cup of coffee and the day's mail. His eyes went straight to the padded postbag, addressed by hand to him. Intuitively he knew what is was. His stomach fluttered alarmingly as he picked it up and saw the Emerald post office stamp.

Taking a small cassette recorder from his desk drawer he told his secretary that he did not wish to be disturbed for a while.

With a shaking hand he put the tape in the cassette and pressed play.

The tape went for thirty minutes, and the story that unfolded left him totally shocked. Regaining some sense of composure, he rang James and spoke forcibly, "James I think I had better see you right away, I have just received a tape spoken by Charlie Thornton. Colin posted it yesterday in Emerald. I'll meet you at the club."

James arrived twenty minutes later and after a brief exchange and ordering coffee he took the cassette from his brief case and placed it on the table. With a shaking hand he turned it on. Neither spoke until it the tape had finished, then James whispered, "There is good and bad in that. Dad has not been implicated nor has he been exonerated. Where do we go now?"

"How about the police?"

"Not until we are reasonably sure that Dad has not been involved. Firstly, let me use your phone to call the girls and get their take on the situation. What must be paramount is the safety of the three of them. Then I think we should see Dad and ask for his side of the story."

Paul put the phone on the speaker, punched in the numbers and greeted Joan with, "Do you know where they are?" Joan briefly filled him in and said that according to the satellite tracker they left Coonabarabran and are heading for Dubbo. She was confident that they had not been followed or traced. They have been told not to use their phone and that any leak could only come from either of you."

James stated emphatically, "There is no chance of that. I think we should get them back to Sydney under guard as soon as possible, then consider at what point we report to the police. We have Charlie's taped story and it could be hugely damaging to a lot of people."

"James, I agree, nevertheless we should give Dad a chance to have his say first."

Joan interrupted, "We will bring them back close to Sydney and ask them to wait. Before they arrive, we will set up a safe house for them, complete with guards, somewhere in the inner suburbs. As a further precaution we could meet them in Dubbo.

There is a regular air service from there and it may be wise to fly them back to Sydney, even if we must hire a private plane. Do you both agree with that? Okay then, let's get on with it."

The phone was switched off and they both sat for a moment without speaking.

James broke the silence, "Apart from the boys and Charlie I am worried about Dad. Neither of us want him vilified when he has done nothing wrong. We must support him unless or until we find some reason why we should not. How about, we arrange to meet him in his office tonight around six. We will play the tapes and his response will dictate when we go to the police and with what.

Frankly I would be surprised if Joan and her partner have not already compiled a report for when they return from their so-called leave."

At 6 o'clock that evening two very nervous and worried men arrived at Sevs office.

In his usual authoritative manner Sev stood behind his desk and uttered, "This must be something serious to have me back here when I should be home with Gloria, she is not well at the moment. I hope it's got nothing to do with those two troublemakers who were here the other day

James being the closest to him said, "Hang on Dad, yes, it is serious, very serious. We have some recorded tape here that we would like you to listen to."

"If this comes from that wet behind the ears Colin Naxos, it should have come to me first. I do not like this conspiracy at all and if you are involved in working against me you can both get out, now"! He bellowed.

James stood his ground, "The tape comes from John's friend Charlie Thornton."

Paul stood up, went over to him and touched his arm, "Dad we both love you dearly, and that's why we are here.

We want to sort this matter out before it goes any further.

Will you please just sit down and listen to the tapes?"

Sev looking totally distressed sat down, "Alright then, let's get it over with."

Paul switched on the cassette player, adjusted the volume and they all sat down.

Without speaking they listened through the early part recorded by Barbara Naxos to the part put together by Colin and finally Charlie Thornton's story with a closing comment by Colin.

James and Paul watched their Dad sitting in his chair; eyes clouded with tears streaming down his face.

He looked up, "My boys, I have done nothing wrong and nothing to deserve this inquisition. Why can't I be left alone with Gloria to enjoy my retirement?

James you know where the whisky is, please get a bottle and three glasses. This is going to take quite some time. First I must ring Gloria to tell her I will be here a while."

After taking a big swallow of scotch Sev began his story.

"Most of what is in the tape is correct; however, it does not tell the whole story. John and I were schoolboy friends, both from Greek parents and to some extent shunned by the locals.

We needed each other for the support we never got at home, or anywhere else. Through primary and secondary school, we were not blessed with brilliant intellects. We achieved results because we worked harder than others. My parents were worse than John's; they never learnt to speak English and never fitted into life in Australia. I got into trouble a couple of times, usual boy stuff, and took many a horrific belting from my father. It was as if he tried to exorcise himself through me.

When I was sixteen, my father and mother returned to the old country, leaving me to fend for myself. Without the friendship of John Naxos, I would not have survived.

A stroke of luck came my way when an elderly widow took me in as a boarder. With money earned from selling papers down at Central Station and the hundred pounds Dad left me, I survived secondary school and gained university entrance.

I still had a huge problem because I did not have the money to pay my board, let alone university fees.

Through a contact from selling papers I drifted up to Kings Cross and soon found I could earn good money pimping and selling pep pills to my fellow university colleagues. So that's how I managed to pay my board and university fees.

My landlady, Gladys McMurray, was the sweetest most caring person you would ever meet. As the years went by she really became my surrogate mother. She cared for me, pushed me through my studies, and if it was not for her God knows where I would have ended up. I called her Nanna.

Sadly, in 1960 Gladys died suddenly. As she had no family, she left what money she had and her house in Glebe to me. At this time, I had just turned 20.

This may hurt but I feel compelled now to tell all. How you will take it, I don't know, particularly you James. Paul knows part of what I'm about to tell you.

During my time wandering around the Cross I met a girl whose background was similar to mine. She was orphaned at fifteen, and like me, had to fend for herself.

She sold her body and then managed to get a front desk job in one of the brothels owned by Frank Bennett. We understood one another and gave each other comfort when it was needed most. I didn't understand it at the time but way back then we built up an enduring love for each other.

James, I see you're looking a bit pale, have another scotch. Get me one too. No doubt you've guessed by now, the girl's name was Gloria.

Around this time, I met and fell in love with a beautiful girl whom I married. Her name was Elizabeth Spalding. She died in childbirth with Paul.

I had never lost contact with Gloria and quietly helped her to get out of the business and find work with a local Real Estate agency. When Elizabeth died, I tried to take Paul and raise him. Elizabeth's parents found out about Gloria's background and they denied me access.

Later I married Gloria and got on with my life. We had three children and have lived very happily together.

I tell you both now that there is no better, more compassionate woman anywhere than her. I would die for her right now if I had to.

After university days I was never ever involved in drugs again. The only contact I had was with Frank Bennett who owned a string of restaurants and several brothels. I did a lot of legal work for him and he was instrumental in helping me set up in this office. There was never any discussion about it, although I became aware that he was my principal supplier in university days. While this was going on and I was getting established I became a financial partner with John in setting up Naxos Condiments. You know most of the story after that.

At one stage we badly needed a cash injection to expand the business and Frank came on board becoming the third partner. Both he and I were executive directors and never had any involvement in the day by day running of the business.

Later when John's brother, Steven Naxos returned from overseas we took him on board as Marketing Manager, with share options as part of his remuneration package. Much later he bought John out and effectively took over the business.

The tapes refer to John's wife, Jean. She was a lovely person and in my own way I had loved her since we first met when John was helping his mother and father run the restaurant. The tapes also refer to a mysterious man she was with before she was brutally murdered.

That man was me; she came to me asking me to make up her will before leaving for overseas. Our ties and closeness, over, at that time 20 years, led to an emotional farewell. This was my only ever infidelity to Gloria in thirty years.

Much to my concern at the time she willed her share of the business to her son Robert. Later this share was sold to Steven and I can recall now wondering where he got the money.

I never found out or had any idea of who murdered Jean. Now it appears that she may have threatened to expose somebody over drug dealing.

From that point on John became totally depressed and alcohol dependant. He could no longer cope with the business. Hearing the tapes now and his discovery of drugs I can understand why. I only attended monthly board meetings, and with Steven in control nothing was like the good old days when John and I started out.

I did not want to be involved anymore and also sold my share to Steven. Frank remained on board, but I had little to do with them. Never at any time did I know about the drug importation. If Frank was involved, he never told me.

I can only promise you both that this is the total truth and I would give my life defending it."

Emotion then overtook him, and he just sat and cried.

Gathering himself he looked up and said, "Well boys, where do we go from here?"

They stood up and embraced their father; words could not be found or spoken through the flood of emotion that engulfed them all.

Paul was the first to speak, "I think we should stick with the original plan and get the boys and Charlie back here. Then we take them and the tapes to the police.

Where are they now?"

"Last I heard they were in Dubbo waiting for instructions."

Sev spoke for the first time, "The important thing is, are they safe?"

James replied to the question, "They should be, we have sent a security guard up there to watch them and our police lady friend is on her way. When she arrives, they are on the first available flight to Sydney then they will be taken to a secure house with 24-hour guards. We can't do any more now, so we had better get home to our wives. Joan will contact me first, so I'll keep you both informed of developments."

In Dubbo, for the first time Colin, Trevor and Charlie were all sharing the same room which nobody was happy about.

Jim had an adjoining room with a connecting door.

"All for your security", he explained.

In the early hours of the morning Colin was partly awake worrying about what would confront them next. Then he saw a crack of light as their door slowly opened; the hair on the back of his neck stood up as a figure entered the room. He sat bolt upright and was about to yell when the light came on momentarily blinding him.

Then Trevor stirred mumbling, "Christ, what time is it?"

Colin was paralysed with fear when he saw that the intruder held what looked like a sawn-off shotgun.

He screamed, "Which one of you is Charlie?"

Charlie, unable to speak, just nodded vigorously.

"Okay, then, you're coming with me, so move now"!

Suddenly, the other door burst open and Jim stood there holding a large pistol in a shaking hand. The intruder turned his gun and fired.

The blast was deafening, and Jim was hit full in the chest.

In that mini second, which seemed to be in slow motion, they saw a spray of blood and body parts splatter the wall behind him. The killer turned and screamed again, "Nobody move."

Next, out of the corner of his eye Colin saw Charlie take a pistol from under his pillow and in one movement swing it towards their attacker. He fired three times from point blank range.

The first two shots missed, but the third hit him in the chest. He was thrown backwards by the impact then crumpled to the floor with blood gushing from his chest. They watched in horror as blood spurted out with the last beats of his heart. Suddenly it was quiet with the only sound coming from the rasping of the last breaths of the attacker.

Through the smoke haze and the smell of cordite Colin screamed, "Christ Charlie, where did you get that? You have killed him."

In an obvious state of shock himself, Charlie mumbled,

"I found it in John's flat and thought I had better keep it in case I needed it."

Trevor was first to react and pull everyone together. Picking up some clothes and his pack, he yelled "Grab your gear and let's get out of here, fast."

Still in their pyjamas they threw their clothes and packs into the Toyota outside the door and with a scream of tyres ripping on bitumen, they bolted down the street in the direction of Bathurst and Sydney.

Colin remembered the panic button and reached under the dash and hit it hard. As they cleared the built-up area they could hear sirens screaming in the distance.

Old Charlie was sitting in the back, shaking and looking as if he was about to have a heart attack.

Colin yelled to Trevor, "Get over in the back and see if you can help him."

"First you slow down before you kill us all, Shit, you are doing a hundred and thirty. Charlie does not look good his pulse is racing and erratic."

"There is some aspirin in my pack, break up about six and put them in that bottle of water and make him drink it. It will thin his blood and maybe stave off any clotting."

Colin slowed just as the bat phone ran. It was Joan, "What the hell is going on?"

Colin shouted back, "I will tell you what's going on, some gorilla just shot Jim, and Charlie shot him. They are both very dead."

Calm as could be she replied, "Are you all, alright?"

"Charlie looked like he was about to have a heart attack, but he is coming around now. We're okay."

Joan came back on the line, "I will see if we can slow the local police down; in the meantime, you just keep heading for Bathurst. We have your vehicle on the tracker and can see exactly where you are. Maureen and I are close to Bathurst, so we will meet you there in front of the local Post Office. It's five am now so we should see you about Seven.

Take your time, do not speed, just sit on the speed limit at one hundred and ten."

After a period of silence, with Colin concentrating on his driving, Trevor called, "He is looking better and breathing more normally. His pulse has slowed, thank Christ! He's a tough old bugger."

"Why didn't you tell us about the pistol before? You must have been carrying it right from the start."

Charlie replied, "So what, I don't have to tell you pricks everything, and I probably saved your lives."

"Great Charlie, no doubt the police will be able to trace it. I think you threw it on the floor, fingerprints and all. The big question is how did those people know where to find us?"

In the early morning, with the sun over the distant ranges, and virtually no traffic on the country road, they found time to relax a little and take in some of the surrounding countryside. Under a clear blue sky, the gently rolling plains were patched with clusters of trees; in the distance they could see mountain ranges that were strangely tinted blue. The trees were a dull green, nothing like the vivid greens back home, and yet they carried their own beauty and character.

The fields were dry, and the raw but sweet smell of the dry grass, laid bare by the relentless sun over a long period without rain, invaded the car. On other areas they could see large flocks of sheep meandering about in an aimless search for food. Colin could not but wonder how, less than one hundred and fifty years ago, the early pioneers settled these vast lands.

Right on schedule, they arrived in Bathurst which they found to be one of the larger country towns. Many of the buildings had an architectural resemblance to back home; some dwellings were even clustered together in terraces. Colin wondered why, when there must have been unlimited space in the early settlement days.

Joan and Maureen were waiting for them at the local Post Office standing next to a nondescript blue Ford Falcon sedan. Colin pulled up next to them. It was a tired and dejected pair that stepped out of the big Toyota. Joan came straight over and said, "You made it okay? How is Charlie? Let me have a look at him."

A feeble voice came from the back seat, "I'm alright, and I don't need any bloody girl copper fussing over me."

Joan looked in his eyes, "Forget the copper bit, and just think I am someone else." She took his pulse, "Eighty, that looks better."

Never one to lay down Charlie replied, "Hey you look pretty good for a copper, I think you could put my pulse up any time."

The tension was broken a bit and Trevor had to say,

"Hey Joan, I would not stop in there too long if I were you."

"We cannot stand here exchanging pleasantries, half the country police force is looking for you lot. Throw your gear in the Falcon, we will take the Toyota, because that is the vehicle they will be looking for and all they will find is a couple of off duty police officers. Look for a McDonald's on the way out of town, you can stop there for breakfast then head for Sydney. The tank is full. There's a road map in the glove box marked with an address in Glebe. It is a safe house and the people there will look after you. The trip is two hundred kilometres and should take you about three and half hours. There is no rush, so don't speed. We don't want you picked up by the local police just yet.

We'll have our meeting when we all get to Glebe.

Good luck."

After forty-five minutes of travelling through open country side they started the long twisting climb up the mountain range called the Blue Mountains. The landscape changed to heavy bush and with it the temperature dropped dramatically. At the top of the climb up they came to a small village aptly named Mount Victoria

An old weather-beaten timber hotel with rusting wrought iron encrusted balconies from an earlier era, dominated the village. There was a notice board out on the front on the footpath saying, "Take a break-Bistro now open." It sounded like a good idea, so they stopped for a badly needed coffee.

Sitting at a scarred old table, that no doubt would have its own tales to tell, they relaxed somewhat, although they could not erase memories of the violence back at Dubbo.

The journey over the mountains took them through Several small villages all of which had links to early settlers and explorers looking for a way over the mountains to the rich countryside to the west. Finally, they began the long descent to the flat plains of the eastern coastal area and then on to Sydney.

Navigating like a couple of London cabbies, Colin and Trevor found their way through the Sydney suburbs to the address given on the map, Toxteth Road Glebe.

The house was a charming substantial old two storied building that looked more English than what they expected. Colin parked the Ford a short distance down the street, then with some apprehension approached the house and rang the doorbell. Before the door was opened Colin felt a jolt of fear as he noticed the dark shape of a man lurking in the front garden.

The door was quickly opened by a fresh-faced lady and before they could speak, she said, "You must be Colin, please come in. My name is Pat." Turning to a burly middle-aged man behind her, "This is my husband Robert."

They immediately felt comfortable as they were ushered down a long hallway to a large comfortably furnished lounge.

Robert spoke for the first time suggesting that they give him the car keys and he would bring their luggage in and park the car in the rear garage while Pat showed them to their rooms.

"Now, you may like to have a shower and get changed while I cook up something to eat."

A doctor arrived shortly after to check on Charlie. His blood pressure and pulse were normal, so he left after telling him to have a full medical check-up as soon as possible.

After they had eaten, Pat suggested that they all lie down and have a good rest, and not to worry as there were full-time guards watching the house.

"You can relax to prepare for the meeting in the morning at seven."

Colin, Trevor and particularly Charlie were thankful to be able to climb into comfortable beds with nice crisp white sheets without the fear they had experienced driving down from Queensland.

At Seven o'clock next morning they were all ushered into the front dining room, which was set up for a conference, complete with a white board, a large flat TV screen, computers and projector. Already sitting around the table were Paul Spalding, Sev Cockini, James Cockini, Senior Constable Joan Cummings and Constable Maureen Stewart.

Paul thanked the boys and Charlie for their persistence in helping to bring the matter to this stage. "Your courage has been amazing."

With a smile, he looked over at Charlie, "We have checked and one good thing to come out of this mess is that Charlie is legally entitled to John's estate."

Sev commented. "Our first legal and moral responsibility is to take all the information we have to the police as soon as possible. As citizens it is not our role to take it any further."

They all agreed on that point; however, Joan had some further facts that they were not aware of. She explained that their big area of concern was who was leaking information as to their whereabouts. The communication amongst them had been extremely tight, which indicated that it came from inside the group.

She turned to Colin and said, "Did you at any time ring Kathleen Morgan, despite instruction to the contrary?"

"Yes, I did, firstly because I trust her explicitly. Secondly, we have Charlie's wife Hester staying with her and he was understandably anxious about her well-being."

"You what?" exploded Joan, "Why in the hell didn't you tell us? You may have put her in danger."

Colin responded with, "From what'?

Joan turned to Maureen and exploded, "That confirms our thinking; the way this is going I think we should pick her up now. Ring for a back-up car and go and bring her back here as quickly as you can."

After Maureen left, Joan turned to Colin again, "We're not out of the woods yet, why in hell didn't you tell us about her?"

"Because I trusted Kathleen and Hester was alone and vulnerable."

"I'd better show you this." She stood and turned on the computer, which lit up the big screen.

Quickly some data appeared.

Laura Watt, alias Kathleen Morgan
Aged 32
Last known address
Unit 8 / 21-24 Mowbray Road Lane Cove.
Known drug user, Convictions 1998 and 2000
Drug trafficking Convictions 2001 and 2003
Felony convictions, stealing from parked car 1997.
Mixing with known felons 1999
Assisting in break and enter 1996.
Various other convictions, going back over ten years.

"That's not all, have a look at this. These photos were taken over the last three weeks showing Kathleen Morgan visiting Steven Naxos after hours at his office, and his home in Rose Bay. There's little doubt that she is heavily involved in this drug trafficking operation with Steven Naxos; most likely to help feed her own habit.

It was she who was able to pass on information as to the whereabouts of Colin and Trevor. They were desperate to get to Charlie before the police did, as he was the only one outside of the group who knew of the drug operation."

Listening to this Colin was absolutely sickened by the revelations and was having difficulty in believing it. Realising that the girl he had gone to bed with, fell in love with, had been deceiving him to arrange a murder, left him feeling ill. He made a dash for the bathroom and vomited violently.

"My god, *what have I got myself into?*"

Returning to the table Joan looked across and saw his shaking hands and his pale face. "Colin you may be finding this hard to believe, but I assure you that unfortunately it's all very true. We have known Laura Watt, or Kathleen Morgan, for a long time.

Moving on, we have some pressing problems over three separate issues. The bashing of two men in a unit in Sussex Street; two men left tied to a tree in Cairns and the death of two men in Dubbo. It's become important that we formally bring the whole matter before the police as soon as possible, although they have been kept up to date on the situation over the last few days."

Just then Joan's phone rang.

She listened for a moment, and then said, "Ring area command and report it in as a kidnapping."

By now Trevor and Colin had both turned a sickly shade of grey.

Without fuss, Joan explained the situation, "Kathleen and Hester aren't at the Lane Cove unit; there's good enough reason to believe that Kathleen has cracked under the pressure and fled, taking Hester with her. The positive aspect is that she's in her own car and we should be able to pick her up fairly quickly."

Colin cut in, "What next! Do you think Hester is in any danger?"

"Frankly, we have no way of telling. If Kathleen can get herself topped up on whatever drugs she's taking, then she may act rationally; if not, according to her history, she could lose touch with reality at any time."

Colin said, "Can I help? I think she'd listen to me. We became very close."

Joan replied, "No I don't think so. When we find them and need your help we'll come and get you. Apart from that you've been in enough drama already. We want you locked up here until the police have been briefed and they have started on the warrants. You will be kept informed; that is, providing we don't get pulled off the case and disciplined for our involvement while technically on leave."

James stood up. "This is about as far as we can go for now, so if you all agree, Joan and I will set up a meeting with the District Police Superintendent for tomorrow."

Joan explained again, "In the meantime nothing can go outside this room until the Special Operations Squad move in with arrest warrants. And, contact the airport to get a stop on her passport in case she tries to get back to New Zealand. She may have New Zealand passport under her real name, Laura Watt, as well as an Australian one under Kathleen Morgan.

Colin and Trevor were left without any alternative except to retire to their rooms, and hopefully get some rest. Colin was about to fall asleep when his mobile phone rang. Having forgotten that he still had the phone in his pack he made a dive for it before it alerted up the entire household. After fumbling with the buttons, he managed to get a connection. A very distressed voice said, "Colin, this is Kathleen, I just want to say how sorry I am. I never intended for things to get out of hand. I have this problem that you were not aware of, and it controls my life. Before I fold completely, I want to say, I genuinely love you and I'm so sorry things could not have turned out differently."

There was then some uncontrolled sobbing.

Colin screamed into the phone, "Kathleen I love you too, but nothing will ever work now. You can make some amends which will help you later. Just let Hester go, drop her on the next street corner. Please do this for me."

"No no, she's my insurance." With that her phone was turned off. *"Shit"*, Colin thought, *"What do I do now?"*

A couple of moments later the mobile rang again. "I've just dropped Hester off at the BP Service Station in Old South Head Road. Good bye Colin."

Looking for somewhere to stay she drove over to Artarmon and booked a room in the motel where she and Colin had their trysts.

By that evening Kathleen was in a highly distressed state.

The urgent need for drugs was overpowering. Her withdrawal symptoms were compounded by her conscience over her role in the attacks on Colin and the deaths in Dubbo.

Her most urgent problem was to get a "fix" so she could think clearly and plan what to do next. Her only thought was to book a seat on the next flight to New Zealand and loose herself there. She rang Qantas and to her relief got a booking leaving at 9.00 tomorrow. "That's good" she thought. "I will just hole up here for the night, drive to airport in the morning and dump the car in the car-park. First, I will go to the bank in Artarmon and transfer everything I can back to my old bank in Auckland. As the ANZ Bank had offices in both countries there was no difficulty. Her only concern was that she was leaving a trail as to where she went.

Next, ring Steven for some supplies to take with me.

Stephen answered on the third ring. "Hello Kathleen."

She quickly interrupted. "We have some big problems. Meet me in your office about six o'clock, leave the back door open for me."

"That's okay everybody will have gone by then."

Promptly at six Kathleen drove into the rear car park noticing Steven's silver BMW near the door. Without even bothering to shut and lock her car door, she sprinted to the open rear door of the warehouse. Hurriedly she walked through the familiar warehouse and straight into Steven's office.

Without any preliminaries Kathleen said, "Get me a scotch and a tin of your famous olives. I need a fix."

Steven ignored her then walked over and closed and locked the office door. Turning back to her he said. "Sure babe, whatever turns you on."

Kathleen said, "Cut the crap. It's too late for your bullshit, just get my drink."

After Kathleen had a whisky in her shaking hand, she took a couple of big gulps then related the events of the last few days up to dropping Hester off at the BP Service Station.

Steven looked decidedly worried before saying, "There is no way anyone can trace this to us, so just relax.

Reaching into the bottom drawer of his desk he took out two large cans branded Naxos Olives and said, "Here's a couple of cans to keep you going, no charge either."

The thought of getting a "Fix" to bring her system back to a high, or near normal, put tremors through her body.

"That's not enough I want a whole carton."

"Stephen replied, "What, are you going to do, start dealing again?"

"No, right now all I need is a fix then tomorrow I'm on the first available flight to New Zealand."

As Kathleen reached for a can, he withdrew it and placed it on the desk behind him. "How about a little reward first, I haven't seen you for a while."

She was now at a point where only one thing mattered. "Sure,' she replied, "Whatever turns you on."

Steven moved around the desk close to Kathleen, then reached over and ripped open her shirt exposing her breasts.

"Now my dear, you just take off your jeans and those fancy panties and sit on the desk with your legs apart." She did as directed while he lowered his pants.

In an obviously excited state he tried to kiss her before slobbering over her breasts. Kathleen felt totally revolted as he carried on like an over excited child.

At that vulnerable time when he was focused only on his own desires Kathleen felt a large brass desk lamp next to her right hand.

Without thinking, in one motion she picked up the lamp and swung it with all her strength at his head. With a sickening thud it connected just above his ear, knocking him to the floor. Still conscious, he started to get up and screamed, "You fucking bitch, you want to play rough."

Kathleen swung the lamp again yelling,

"That was for me. This is for all the others whose lives you have fucked up."

Blood and splintered bone splashed across the room, as he fell to the floor. Kathleen stood over him gasping when to her horror the body started to shake and tremble in the last throes of life. His brain was exposed, and she could see it pulsating to the last beats of his heart.

Stepping over him she picked up her carry bag and went to the desk looking for the olive tins. In the bottom drawer she found four more tins and a bottle of brandy. After putting the tins in her carry bag, Kathleen picked up the bottle of brandy and began to pour the spirit over the still-twitching body.

With her mind screaming to the point where she had little control over what she was doing, she took out her Zippo lighter and ignited the brandy. The flames were slow to get started, so she scooped up all the papers from the desk and threw them onto the flickering flames. Still without any thought or idea of the consequences of what she was doing, Kathleen began ripping down the curtains and anything else she could find that would burn.

Soon the fire was burning strongly and began to spread across the carpet.

After putting her jeans and torn shirt back on Kathleen grabbed her bag with the precious tins and ran to the door.

"God almighty", she screamed, "The door's locked, where's the fucking key? He must have it in his pocket." Running back across the room she found that his clothes and the surrounding carpet were well alight.

Franticly, she thrust her hand into his pockets to find the key.

Her shirt started to burn, and her skin blistered from the heat. Ignoring the pain, coughing and gasping for air, she located the key then made a desperate attempt to reach the window; fumbling with the catch she opened window hoping to escape that way, but it was too late.

The open window only fuelled the fire further and with the room filling with smoke she groped her way towards the door and managed to get the key in the lock. As she swung the door open there was a huge blast of hot air as the room erupted in a ball of fire throwing Kathleen to the outer passage way floor.

Her survival instincts kicked in and after picking herself up she staggered down the stairs.

At this moment a passing taxi saw the smoke and radioed the fire brigade.

Thankfully she had left her car open with the keys still in the ignition.

Ignoring the pain, she managed to control herself enough to get in the car and drive out onto Kent Road and headed towards the city and then over the bridge and on to her motel in Artarmon.

As she left, she could hear the wail of sirens getting louder and louder as they approached the warehouse.

Fortunately, there was nobody on the reception desk at the motel, so she managed to get back to her room without being seen.

Kathleen's first move was to open an olive tin then to find a syringe. She found a well-used one in the pocket of her suit case. Using a spoon and a cigarette lighter she prepared to dose herself up with her magic powder. As she slipped the needle under the skin in her thigh and push the plunger down, she felt a surge of energy through her body. She sat for a moment marvelling at the transformation in her body. After a moment she had the strength to undress and check her wounds.

Now thinking clearly, to her relief she found her arm although covered in blisters they were shallow and there did not appear to be any serious burns. Feeling much more alive she thought, "Where to now?"

"A long-sleeved shirt and I will still be aboard that flight to New Zealand tomorrow."

Next morning, after a good night's sleep, fortified by another drug injection, Kathleen opened her lap top computer and transferred everything in her Sydney bank account to her ANZ account in New Zealand.

She wisely thought that there was no way she could return to her Lane Cove unit, so she packed what clothes she had in a small overnight bag together with the contents of the olive tins, ordered a room service breakfast and was ready to leave. Without bothering to pay her account Kathleen stowed her meagre belongings in her car and drove off to the Sydney International airport for her journey to New Zealand.

Feeling buoyed at her good fortune to date she confidently

walked straight to the Qantas check in desk. The ever-friendly staff processed her ticketing and accepted he bag as luggage. No problem she thought, "I off."

Feeling totally relaxed Kathleen, after picking a copy of the Sydney

Morning Herald, she breezily wandered over to the food hall and ordered a cup of coffee.

Sitting at the table browsing through the paper she was caught by surprise when a voice said, "Ms Watt, would you please come with us?" She looked up to see two uniformed men standing next to the table.

"What for she exclaimed."

"You are under arrest for drug possession."

Kathleen stood up then fainted, falling to the floor.

The officers rang for medical assistance. After establishing that she was alright to leave she was escorted to a waiting police car.

The Naxos office area was completely destroyed, and with it the computers holding records of overseas transactions and shipping. The main warehouse building, plant, equipment and stock were left intact.

The body of Steven Naxos was removed and held for an autopsy as to the cause of death.

When it was discovered that he was bashed to death the police swung into action to try and find the assailant.

The drug dealing side of the Naxos business was yet unknown to the local police as were the links to Kathleen Morgan, and the first assumption at that time was that it was all part of a botched-up burglary.

The burnt olive tins containing the drugs were not discovered and were eventually taken to the tip and dumped.

Hester, although a little distressed, was picked up and brought to the safe house where she was reunited with Charlie.

The years of being apart evaporated and he took her into his arms.

"From here on love, we start a new life."

When Colin heard the news of the fire he felt as if he had been kicked in the guts yet again. "How many more people are to die?"

Despite Kathleen's deceit and breach of his trust he still felt for her.

Somehow, he understood that the road she had taken was not the one she had wanted.

When the drug dealing became known the police moved quickly, with forensic and investigative teams pouring over the remains of the Naxos Condiments offices.

A check on the tinned and packaged imported products revealed a serial numbering system that separated the normal products from those containing contraband drugs.

The company General Manager and the office accountant were interviewed and subsequently charged over their involvement in the scheme.

As the fire had not touched the warehouse side of the building and packaging plant, its operation could continue under the control of warehouse manager, Gerald Patterson.

The manager and staff of Steven's Security Company were also interviewed, and several were charged with various serious offences. The security business was shut down immediately and its license revoked.

Millie had returned to her native America some months previously where she died from a drug overdose.

Another senior police team interviewed former Naxos directors Sev Cockini and Frank Bennett. Sev Cockini was completely exonerated of any knowledge of the drug scheme.

Frank Bennett was not charged with any offence but remained as "A person of interest." This was, in part, because of his long association with the Naxos Empire, having his own chain of restaurants, and owning three brothels.

He died from a massive heart attack at the age of 83 before any further investigations took place.

Information on the overseas links was handed over to the Greek and Italian Police. Vigorous investigations revealed a huge international drug operation with tentacles around the world including New York, which was thought to have been run by Millie Naxos.

Colin and Trevor were cleared to return home with a commitment to be available for court appearance if required.

HOMEWARD BOUND

CHAPTER TWELVE

With Colin and Trevor aboard, the big Qantas Australian Airways jumbo touched down at Heathrow Airport; two months after they'd left in such high spirits and a sense of adventure. As the crowd spewed through customs and out to the terminal it was two much subdued and gaunt-looking boys that greeted Barbara Naxos.

"Why've they done to you? Have you been sick?" she exclaimed.

"You could say that", replied Colin, "Let's go and find somewhere to have a coffee."

When they were seated Barbara exuded excitement and anticipation, "Well Colin, don't hold back, did you sort out our inheritance?"

"Mother you never had an inheritance; you lost it when you and Dad left our grandfather when he needed you most.

If you had taken some interest and care, a lot of things may have been different. I am sorry mother, but you pay now for your self-centred ways. Families have responsibilities and you failed to exercise yours."

Barbara Naxos was shocked and angered by her son's words and spluttered, "How dare you speak to me like that, I am your mother, and besides, what do you know about your fathers and my life, and how cruelly his father treated us."

Colin looked sadly at his mother saying, "We may discuss this another time, right now I'm tired and am going home. Here's a set of tapes that cover the whole sorry story. Perhaps you can ring me after you've listened to them."

With that, a saddened and much wiser Colin walked away, down the terminal towards the rail link.

Trevor followed, "Hey big brother, wait for me."

After returning to their respective homes in Oxford, life slowly returned to normal for Colin and Trevor.

Neither was ready to go job hunting, so they decided to take some time off and maybe even do a little travelling; but not to Australia where memories of their last trip was still fresh in their minds.

After a particularly boisterous night at the Cricketer's Arms Hotel, Colin rose late with an urgent need for a drink of water and a cup of coffee. Sipping his coffee, he was thinking, "It's that bloody Trevor, I would have come home early if it was not for him. He was certainly in full party mode last night."

Colin started to laugh to himself when he recalled Trevor's party show, holding everybody spellbound with his greatly exaggerated stories about their Australian sortie.

A knock on the door brought him out of his reverie. Stepping down the passage he saw a card that had been pushed under the door. He thought, "Hello what's this?" The card was advising him that there was registered mail for him at the local Post Office. Suddenly he had a premonition that there was trouble ahead.

Later that day he collected an envelope with Australian postmarks and the sender noted as Cockini Legal Services, Sydney Australia.

Without waiting to get home he sat on a bus stop seat, and with a trembling hand, tore open the envelope.

Inside he found a letter from James Cockini.

> *Dear Colin,*
>
> *I trust that you had an uneventful trip home and have settled back into normality, if there is such a thing.*
>
> *The Naxos dramas are finally off the front pages and have been, in part, dispatched to history. The business is still operating successfully under the control of the warehouse*

manager, Gerald Patterson. I hear that he is doing a good job of steering the company in the right direction.

We, Cockini Legal, have been charged to establish who actually owns the business.

Stevens wife, who may have had a claim to it, as you are aware died in New York some time ago. Although American by birth, she grew up in Israel and the Middle East. We have made searches in both Israel and the USA and it appears that she has no living relatives.

As there were no children, the nearest relative is your mother, Barbara Naxos, and in turn, yourself. So, it is our judgement that your mother could claim the business.

I have taken the liberty of advising you of this first, giving you an opportunity to relate the situation to her personally.

As I see it, although the business is operating well in the trusteeship of Gerald Patterson handling the day by day operation, it is going to require a permanent management structure put in place as soon as possible.

You have several choices, either sell the business as a going concern or appoint a management team to run it.

The other option, which you may consider, is to manage the business yourself.

Could you please discuss the situation with your mother and let me know which direction you would consider taking? Either way it will be necessary for you to make the trip to Sydney to tidy up all the legal aspects.

There is also another matter that requires attention. It appears that Steven Naxos did not leave a will and has left a considerable amount of money in a Bank account. Again, our judgement is that you, as the nearest relative, could claim this. As he was never convicted of a crime, the courts have no claim on it. Please let me know how you would like to handle these matters.

Kind regards,
James Cockini.

Colin's first reaction was one of absolute shock. He sat at the bus stop trembling with a mixture of despair, excitement, joy, and concern, all at once. He thought; "what is mother going to think of this? I have not spoken to her since that day at the Airport when I left her in a very unhappy state."

With his mind racing, he slowly made his way home, trying to decide how he was going to handle the unexpected turn of events. The first obvious decision was that he would tell his mother.

With a cup of strong coffee, he sat down and picked up the phone. As he dialled, he thought, she probably thinks I'm ringing to apologise and ask for reconciliation.

The phone was answered on the second ring; she knew who it was by the sender message on her display dial.

"Well hello, I was just wondering last night when you were going to call me."

Before you say anything, I'm not looking for apologies or anything else; I just want the whole Australian episode forgotten. Now when are you coming to see me?"

Colin was surprised at the reconciliatory tone and replied, "That's Okay Mum, but we're not over the saga yet.

We have to meet again; would you book two rooms at the Grosvenor Kensington again? Make it for Thursday and I will see you there for lunch."

"Colin, tell me what is happening, what's this all about? I listened to the tapes. I thought we were finished with the whole nasty business."

"No Mother we haven't, but it is not all bad. It is too complicated to tell you on the phone so let's leave it for Thursday."

With her still protesting Colin said, "I will see you on Thursday, Goodbye Mother."

Later, he rang Trevor, "Some urgent business has come up and I may need your counsel. Can you meet me down at the Pub about six; I might even buy you a feed."

Trevor replied, "I don't like the sound of this. The last time you rang me with a story like that, you nearly had me killed. Curiosity has got the better of me, so I'll be there."

Trevor arrived a bit before six to find Colin sitting on his usual stool hunched over a tankard of ale.

"Well old boy, it can't be that bad, can it? Where's my beer anyway?"

Colin turned and said, "the beers on the way. Before we go any further, I must ask you, how would you like another trip Down Under?"

"You must be kidding me, what's this all about?"

"Let's order a snack first, and then I'll tell you the story."

Soon they had a generous serving of cottage pie and veggies in front of them with a fresh beer.

Colin then related the latest developments in the Naxos saga.

"After I see Mum on Thursday, I'll no doubt be booking another flight to Sydney. If I can work it, do you want to come with me? I'll need you as a talent scout for the girls!

At least we won't have to worry about someone trying to push us under a bus this time."

Trevor replied, "I'll make the big sacrifice and cancel all my social engagements, so I can come and look after you. Count me in. Hey, we might pick up with our two police lady friends. Would we be game enough for that?"

After catching an early train, Colin checked into the hotel in time for a rest before facing his mother.

In contrast to the early meeting where Colin felt like a boy receiving his instructions, he felt confident and in control for this next encounter.

Dressing casually, he went down to the lounge for a cup of coffee and to wait, his mother was always tactically late for important meetings.

To his surprise, he found Barbara already there, drinking tea instead of her usual wine. She stood as he approached, and he could not fail to notice, in contrast to his expectation, a very reticent woman. Gone was the abrasive gusto of the past which always rankled him.

Offering her cheek for a kiss she said, "Hello Colin, it's so nice to see you again. Let's sit down for a while.

Before you tell me the reason for your call, we should not need a reason should we; I want to say how sorry I am that things turned out the way they did. I have listened to the tapes and they did deeply disturb me. Since then, I've spent a lot of time thinking about the past, your father, grandfather, and the rest of the family and friends we left behind when we left Australia so many years ago. I can see now that we were wrong and selfish, even with the time we gave to you.

Please understand also, that in the later years your grandfather, John Naxos, was not the easiest person to get along with. He gave your father a hell of a time.

He had an obsession about schooling, the business, and family that became impossible to live with. I suppose this trait came from his parents, and his own difficult childhood.

If you'll give me the chance, I'd like to start again and build a new relationship with you. Who knows, one day soon you may marry and have children, and I'd hate to miss out on being part of my grand children's lives. We do not want another generation to take the same direction as the past two."

Colin was quite touched by his mother's words and he felt a rush of emotion towards her. He stood and went to her, holding her tightly in his arms as she quietly sobbed.

Barbara sat down again and after regaining some composure, with a smile said, "Now, look what I've done to my make up."

Looking at this youthful woman, Colin said "From here on we start again. I'm sure we can become really close, as we should be. For a start you will be Barbara, not Mother. You look too young to be my mum. Now I must tell you the good news."

Colin took the solicitor's letter from his pocket and handed it to her.

After reading the letter twice she turned to Colin,

"Without even thinking about it, I can tell you now that I want no part of it. That business has caused more than enough distress and unhappiness. I'm comfortable and can live quite well without it, so I think we should sell it, and you can have the proceeds."

Colin paused for a moment before saying. "Whatever we do, we need to get on with it straight away. I'm sure that we cannot leave the business running under control of the warehouse foreman.

This looks like another trip down under; I suppose you'll want to take your friend with you."

Colin replied, "why don't we both go?"

"Thanks for the thought, maybe one day I'd like to see the place, right now I couldn't think of anything worse.

If that's all settled, we can now go to lunch."

Escorting her to the dining room Colin had the distinct feeling that people were viewing them as a couple, not mother and son.

For the first time he felt comfortable and proud to be with her.

Over lunch they chatted happily, with Barbara telling Colin of her social life and activities in her home town of Hove.

To his surprise he found that she still played tennis in a mid-week ladies' competition, was an active member of a Bridge Club and contributed at least one day a week to a local charity. Colin was getting a different picture of his mother; she wasn't just the social butterfly he imagined.

Colin was shocked when she told him what her friends had given her for her forty-fifth birthday. A parachute jump from a small plane. And she was going to do it.

Colin exuberantly responded, "If you are really going to do it then I will be there to watch. Do you have any male friends, Like a regular boyfriend?"

Barbara coyly replied, "Well I do actually; perhaps you can meet him if you come to my birthday party."

With a surprised look Colin said, "Well, you have been keeping secrets from me."

She looked directly at him saying, "No, not at all, it is just that for a time there was a distance between us, which is all going to change."

Later in the day they parted with a rush of emotion, promising to keep in touch regularly. Colin and Barbara were both very aware that the first challenge was to clear up their involvement with Naxos Condiments in Sydney.

On his return home Colin booked two business class tickets to Sydney with Qantas.

Two weeks later, with Trevor in tow, they were on a flight back to the place where so much had happened, which could change their lives forever.

THE INHERITANCE

CHAPTER THIRTEEN

It was a much more relaxed and comfortable trip on the long haul to Sydney than their first trip some months before. The more spacious and comfortable seats in business class even allowed some opportunity for sleep.

When the plane reached Sydney, it took its customary sweep over the great city and Harbour below. Looking out the window Colin felt a strong sense of homecoming.

He was never totally comfortable flying, particularly when landing, and this was no exception. His knuckles were white from gripping the arm rests when the engines slowed as they hit the tarmac. Then the engines screamed in protest as they went into reverse thrust to slow the monster down. The cabin shook and rattled then went quiet as they came to halt near the end of the runway. Colin started to relax and release his iron like grip on the armrest when the plane slowly taxied towards the airport terminal.

Next to him Trevor was relaxed and comfortable and continued to read his book.

Looking over at Colin he said, "What's the matter old boy, did you want me to hold your hand?"

The only reply he got was, "Get stuffed."

Despite their outward frivolities it was a much more mature and wiser Colin Naxos who stepped out of the plane to make his way to customs at Sydney Airport. He was feeling the weight of the responsibilities with the control of the business about to descend upon him. On one side he was frightened, on the other he felt stimulated and challenged.

He was intelligent, had a university education in commerce and carried the ancestral genes of the past generations of the Naxos men.

After a quick passage through customs Colin and Trevor took a cab, and as on their first trip, asked the driver to take them to the Hyatt. Colin's first impulse was to stop off at the Naxos warehouse before he realised that it was only seven am, and the place would still be closed.

Checking in at the Hotel he said to Trevor, "Same deal as last time, two nights only for a treat, then we'll look for a serviced apartment somewhere in the city."

Trevor's response was, "That's great, but we won't have any company this time."

"Yes, we will, I'm going to ring our police friends, and ask them to join us for dinner. We can catch up on what happened after we left."

After they were settled into their Harbour-side room, Colin rang the mobile number Joan had given him on their previous trip

It was answered immediately, "Joan Sterling."

"Hello Joan, its Colin Naxos."

"Well this is a surprise, where are you?"

"Trevor and I have just arrived, we're at the Hyatt."

"Hey, that's great, what brings you back so soon? Not just to see me surely."

"Why don't we talk about it over dinner tonight?"

"I'm free, and I would love to, where do we meet?"

"We may as well eat here at the Hyatt; can I pick you up? Trevor is too shy to ask himself! Can you ring Maureen to see if she's free?"

"First question, no problem, I can find my own way, second question, yes I will ring Maureen, she's on the same roster as me, so I'm sure she'd love to come. Will around Seven suit?"

"That's great; I'm looking forward to seeing you."

Colin could not help but make a comparison with the very strong police officers from their previous adventurous trip to the two very feminine and attractive girls they met in the foyer. They seemed like different people.

After embraces and kisses all round, at Colin's suggestion, they made their way to the cocktail lounge.

Forever the leader, Joan said, "Now tell me what brings you two adventures back here so soon."

"We came all this way just to see you," Trevor quickly replied."

"Maureen chipped in, "Well now you're here, what are you going to do about it?"

"Firstly, buy you a drink then a candle-lit dinner."

"Sounds good."

After the waiter came and took their drink orders, Colin thought he should briefly tell them why they were here.

"Several weeks back I had a letter from James Cockini advising that my mother Barbara Naxos, as the only living relative, was the rightful heir to the Naxos business. My job is to now decide what we're going to do with it.

Another issue is that Steven Naxos left a significant amount of cash in a bank account which has not been claimed. The solicitors believe that I can rightly claim it.'

"Well, lucky you, congratulations. As far as I know the business is still trading well. All the staff were kept on, and the bad publicity over Steven Naxos didn't seem to have any adverse effect. As police investigations have been completed, I haven't been back there for a while, so I don't know what's going on at the moment. But if there's any way I can help, let me know."

They spent an hour reminiscing about their previous trip, and how lucky they were to escape without any injuries.

Colin and Trevor were both interested to hear the details of how James Cockini and Paul Spalding had taken it upon themselves to look after them, and personally hired Joan and Maureen to follow their every move.

A little nervously Colin could wait any longer to ask Joan if she knew what happened to Kathleen.

With understanding of Colin's early involvement Joan replied, "She was picked up at the airport attempting to board a flight to New Zealand. She is still in custody awaiting trial on drug charges which will come up later this month. The charges only relate to carrying a commercial quantity of heroin, so it is likely that any sentence may be relatively light. Apparently, she was not involved in the fire at Naxos Condiments. Or if she did, it is not known to the police.

Colin proclaimed, "Enough office talk, we're here to have a good time. Finish your drinks and we'll go to the dining room."

In the dining room they appeared to be just four young people having dinner together and enjoying themselves.

Although she was a couple of years older than Colin, the more time he spent with Joan the better she looked. By the end of the night she had gone from being attractive to very desirable, and he was thinking how he could take the relationship further. However, instinct told him not to rush it; any move tonight would certainly result in a rebuff.

After coffee in the lounge, they said good night, promising to keep in touch and ring if they needed any help.

The next morning, still feeling a little jet lagged, Colin and Trevor rose late and enjoyed a leisurely room service breakfast out on the balcony. Fresh fruit, bacon and eggs, followed by coffee was just what they needed.

Colin's thoughts drifted back to Joan Sterling. "It would have been nice if she had stayed the night and was now sharing breakfast with me."

Relaxing in their easy chairs on the balcony, drinking their second cups of coffee, Colin and Trevor could not but continue to be enthralled by the panorama of the Sydney Harbour.

Colin's first move was to ring James Cockini and make an appointment to see him in the afternoon.

Trevor went off on his own to find a suitable serviced apartment somewhere in the city. He made a note not to return to the one in Sussex Street that they had previously left in a mess, with two unconscious bodies on the floor.

Stepping out of the Hotel foyer into a bright warm summer day with the temperature in the high twenties, Colin could not but compare it with the drab winter's day he had left behind in the UK.

As it was not far, Colin decided that he would walk to the city for his appointment.

Walking along the waterfront, past the International Passenger Terminal, Colin stopped for a moment to watch the ferries bustling in and out of the docks disgorging their passengers.

Standing there in the brilliant sunshine leaning on the old iron railing he could not help but think; there is something almost human about ferries, they seem to have a character all of their own. What a delightful way to get to work every day.

Making his way up Pitt Street, past Martin Place and the historic Post Office, on through the main retail shopping Mall, Colin felt completely at home in this vibrant city.

He saw the Australian people of today as very different from the English, and yet it was his ancestors who founded this great country only two hundred years ago. Turning left into Bathurst Street then into Elizabeth Street, he was thinking, "Even the names are English. Yes, I could live here."

At Cockini Legal offices Colin asked the receptionist if Mr. Cockini senior was in. After an internal call the girl told Colin that he could see him, "Do you know the way?" To which Colin replied, "Yes thank you, I have been before."

Taking the lift to the next level he thought of the very different circumstances now to his first visit not so long ago.

Sev welcomed him at the door with open arms for a quite emotional greeting. He reminded Colin that because of his long friendship with his grandfather he considered him as family.

After they sat down with a cup of coffee, Colin filled him in on life back in England since their return. Surprising himself, he confided in Sev telling him of his reconciliation with his mother.

Sev explained that because of the circumstances at the time, he'd never had an opportunity to get to know Barbara well at all. He took great pains to tell Colin of the need for family bonds and unity. "Otherwise what was life for." he exclaimed.

"Tonight, I'd like you to come home and have dinner with Gloria and me. Bring your friend; there will just be the four of us."

Colin eagerly accepted and was pleased that he would get the opportunity to meet Gloria.

As he made his way down the corridor for his meeting with James, he felt quite elated from the warmth of his meeting with Sev. As with his father, James greeted him warmly as one of the family.

Ever the lawyer, James carefully explained where they were at with the Naxos business and the cash inheritance left by Steven Naxos. He told him that he could now legally claim ownership of both the business and the cash.

A decision regarding the future of the business was needed as soon as possible.

"Before you make any decision, I suggest that you should firstly go and talk to the acting manager, Gerald Patterson, and meet the staff. Next, from whatever information is available, try to get a handle on the future viability of the business. You may feel confident to handle this yourself, however, if not, I can recommend a good accountant to assist. Any legal problems you can bring them to me."

"I think we can handle, at least the initial investigations ourselves. If we feel the need for outside help later, we will look at it then. Also, I have a backup in Trevor. We are both university graduates, well qualified to handle this but Trevor has had more hands-on experience. He's spent the last two years contracted part time to one of the largest accounting firms in London while completing his honours degree. He's smarter than me, but I won't tell him that.

It might be appropriate if you could ring the manager on my behalf and tell him we will be there first thing tomorrow.

No, I'll give him a chance to get his day started, tell him 10 o'clock."

At this moment there was a quiet knock on the door, James said, "Excuse me for a moment, that will be my daughter."

He then called out, "Come in."

A strikingly good-looking dark-haired girl walked in, "Hello Dad, I just dropped in to see if you were free for a coffee. I'm sorry I didn't know you were busy."

James replied, "No, no, not at all, you will be interested to meet this man, Maria, meet Colin Naxos."

Maria stepped over to shake hands saying, "Well, we finally meet; I feel I know you already. You have been the topic of conversation in our house for some time."

Colin took her hand and felt that he was being drawn into her large dark eyes. "Nice to meet you Maria, I hope I was not given too bad a report in all that household discussion."

"Quite the contrary, Dad is actually a fan of yours; he looks upon you as family. You can let go of my hand now!"

Colin stammered, "I'm sorry, you have confused me. I didn't realise that you would be so grown up and beautiful."

Maria replied, "Well, I don't know about the beautiful bit, but yes I am grown up, actually I think I am as old as you."

Watching the exchange James could sense a mutual attraction between them and was amused by Colin's nervousness. "Okay you two, I have work to do. Colin why don't you take Maria to the coffee shop downstairs and you can chat down there?"

Maria replied, "Love too, but I'm on my way to uni and I am already late, maybe next time."

With a lingering look straight at Colin she said, "I must go, see you tonight Dad," and with a seductive swing of her hips, turned and left.

Colin felt that he had just been bowled over.

Collecting his thoughts, he said, "James, Thanks for your time, I must go too. I'll give you a call and let you know how we get on at the warehouse."

As he was leaving, Colin turned and said, "If I ever loose faith in humanity, for whatever reason, I will remind myself to think of you. I could never find the words to express my gratitude for how you have helped me."

"Thanks Colin, we only did what had to be done. You know, without anything to substantiate my thoughts, I would like to see you stop here and run the business yourself. It would be like keeping it in the family, something that your grandfather, and to some extent my father, worked so hard for and made so many sacrifices for over the years.

Old John wore himself out trying to establish something that would ensure that the next generation could have a better life than he did. It would be a shame to see it now just disappear."

"James, that would be a big ask, particularly as my mother and my life has always been in the UK. But who knows which way the wind will blow?"

With that he left to return to the Hotel for a rest and change before heading out to dinner with Sev and Gloria Cockini.

Back in their room he found Trevor with a cup of coffee studying the Sydney Morning Herald.

As Colin walked in, Trevor looked up and said, "We now have accommodation in the Park Regis Tower in Park Street for the moderate cost of Seven hundred dollars a week. The building has full time security, so nobody can bother us."

"Trevor old boy, our days of fighting the bad people are over, you can relax in my care now. Tonight, we are dining out with Sev and Gloria; you must be on your best behaviour; no slurping your soup or eating off your knife.

Tomorrow we visit the Naxos warehouse, and you will have to put your business accounting hat on."

Colin and Trevor, appropriately attired, arrived at the Eastern Suburbs home of one of Sydney's best-known and respected lawyers, Sev Cockini. Sev greeted them at the door enthusiastically, "Come in, come in, first, meet my wife Gloria."

Standing behind Sev was a tall elegant lady in a full length flowing floral satin dress, obviously an expensive item. She carried herself with confidence and an unmistakable regal bearing. Colin felt drawn to her thinking this is a very special lady.

Offering her hand and cheek for a kiss, she enthused, "I am so glad Sev asked you both to come. I have been so much a part of all your dramas, hearing all the details over dinner every night. I have been looking forward to meeting you. Now come and sit in the lounge while I get you a drink. What would you like? Sev will be having his usual scotch."

Colin replied, "I'd love a glass of white wine thanks."

Trevor followed, "Same for me, thanks Gloria."

Mischievously he followed with, "Colin gave me a lecture on behaving tonight, so if I dribble, start to eat off my knife or do anything outrageous you will let me know, won't you!"

Gloria gave a tinkling laugh; "Trevor I don't think you would know how to misbehave."

Over drinks in the lounge they found Sev quietly taking a back seat while Gloria entertained the boys with her wit and sharp mind. She was genuinely interested in them and their lives back home. Inquiring about Colin's mother she expressed disappointment that she never had the opportunity to get to know her well before she and Robert went overseas.

Gloria was comfortable talking to the boys about old times and her loving marriage with Sev. To them this was quite remarkable considering she understood they knew about her past life through the Naxos tapes.

Looking at her and listening to her speaking, Colin found it hard to believe that she was a prostitute when Sev first met her fifty years ago. She was a picture of elegance and intelligence.

After a period of light chit chat, getting to know each other they all adjoined to the dining room. Gloria handled the seating while Sev went off in search of some of his favourite wines.

The very pleasant evening concluded rather late and Sev offered to drive them back to their Hotel.

Trevor refused the offer saying, "No way, you would probably get pinched for DUI. We will ring for a cab."

Back at the Hotel Colin and Trevor took time to sit in the lounge for a nightcap and discuss how they were going to handle the trip to Naxos Condiments. Trevor listened and started to formulate a plan as to the best way to go about it.

Next morning, they quickly packed, checked out, and moved into their apartment. By nine thirty they were on their way to the Naxos warehouse.

An obviously nervous Gerald Patterson greeted them.

Settling into his rather austere office with a mug of coffee, he apologised for the lack of space and facilities, explaining that there had been no move to replace the office section which was gutted by the fire. The only work that he had done was to clear the site of rubbish for health and safety reasons.

Colin went to great lengths to explain the situation regarding ownership, and that no decision had been made regarding the future direction. What they needed now was access to whatever records were available to help them come to a decision. However, the first move would be to address the staff and fill them in as much as they could.

Gerald arranged for all the staff to be called together for a meeting after their lunch break.

Colin left this role to Trevor. Gone was the flippant playboy, the other Trevor spoke clearly and on a level that they all understood and could relate to.

Bravely, (thought Colin) he asked for questions and was hit by a barrage of concerns mostly about employment security and entitlements should they lose their jobs. After a nod from Colin he assured them that in the case of any dismissals emanating from a change of direction, all entitlements would be protected. He closed the meeting by reassuring them that the business would go on, the only question was under what management structure and this would be resolved within the next two weeks.

Back in the office, Trevor suggested that they had done enough for the day and they return early tomorrow to begin the task of reviewing the financial viability of the business.

Sitting in the taxi on the way back to the city Trevor turned to Colin, "Now, do you want me to take the lead in this project? I've had more experience than you and can get through it quicker." Colin, not always used to taking the back seat, was only too pleased for him to tackle the first line appraisal.

"Yes I'm more than happy to have you do it; I'll basically take a back seat and accept instruction from you."

"Now that's settled, and we know what direction we're taking, we need to go shopping. Find me a computer shop. I need to get a good Laptop and a couple of calculators.

Tomorrow I'd like you to start preparing for a stocktake while I wrestle with what information we can get out of the office and bank statements."

Colin replied, "Okay chief, it will be done", while thinking; this is the other Trevor, I'm not sure that I even know him myself.

Two weeks later Trevor presented Colin with a detailed assessment of the business, with a summary showing that the business was sound and profitable. It was encouraging to note that, apart from a small drop in sales immediately after the fire, the business had continued to run at expected levels. This spoke well of the strength of the structure, loyalty of staff and the client base.

The important aspect was that, in Trevor's view, there were significant opportunities for future development, particularly in importing foodstuffs.

That night, sitting alone in his apartment, Colin felt that he was increasingly being drawn into life in Australia and the Naxos Business. His heritage was here in Sydney with the business started by his Grandfather nearly fifty years before.

He was starting to feel that he had a duty to see that Naxos Condiments continued in the family and was beginning to feel a buzz of excitement at the prospect of taking the helm.

Without any further hesitation he rang Barbara and told her that he was going to take over running of the business. To his relief and joy, she was as excited as he was, and gave her unequivocal blessing.

Over breakfast next morning he looked at Trevor and told him of his decision. "What I'll need is a good financial director; do you know anybody who could work with me?"

Trevor replied, "Well you don't have to look far, I'm your man, someone has to keep an eye on you. How much are you paying?"

"Frankly I have no idea; you will have to trust me."

They shook hands on the deal, with Colin enthusing how he was looking forward to the challenges ahead together.

"I now have a financial director, a solicitor, and don't forget a doctor so that's a good start."

A partnership was forged, not unlike when the business started with John Naxos and Sev Cockini two generations earlier. After another meeting at the warehouse, and a further briefing with James Cockini, they were ready to return home to Oxford.

On the return flight Colin's thoughts on the challenge ahead were continually interrupted by visions of Maria Cockini. Her vibrancy, physicality and sexual allure was overwhelming.

Finally, back home again, Barbara met them at Heathrow Airport and was anxious to hear how they had got on.

The warm greeting, returned by Colin, was in stark contrast to their airport meeting not so long ago.

In the following weeks, after some legal work to transfer ownership of Naxos Condiments and associated companies from Barbara to Colin, it was time to say goodbye to home and friends.

Within a month Colin and Trevor were back in Sydney.

THE OASIS RESTAURANT

CHAPTER FOURTEEN

The long flight from London to Sydney on the Qantas Kangaroo Hop route was for Colin Naxos and his friend Trevor Donaldson, boringly slow and uncomfortable. The aircraft seats were no more designed for Colin's six foot two, ninety kilo frame, than for Trevor's shorter but much heavier body. They were pleased to finally arrive in Sydney to a glorious spring day, eager to begin their new lives. They were now wise in the ways of negotiating Sydney airport and were quickly through customs and out in spring sunshine fighting for a cab with other business types anxious to get home to their families.

This trip as they were spending their own money, they went straight to the Park Regis in Park Street and booked a two-bed room apartment.

The challenge of taking over the business of Naxos Condiments excited them both and their spirits were high.

Ever since they had left Sydney, Colin had dreamed of meeting James Cockini's daughter, Maria, again. On their second day Colin, rang her mobile.

She answered promptly with, "Hello Maria speaking."

Colin, feeling uncharacteristically nervous, spluttered, "Hello Maria, its Colin."

"Colin who?" she replied.

"Colin Naxos."

"Oh, I'm sorry Colin; I didn't even know you were in town. Dad did mention that you were coming but he didn't say when. Did you want to speak to him?"

"No, no, it's you I wanted to speak to; actually, I rang to ask if you would have dinner with me tonight."

To his delight she replied, "Yes, I'd like to, where are you taking me?"

Much encouraged and feeling more comfortable Colin said, "There's a nice restaurant at the Hilton, which is just around the corner from here, will that do?"

Maria replied, "Good choice. Rather than you coming all the way here and I will take a Taxi, you can take me home."

"It's a deal; I'll wait in the foyer for you."

Maria arrived a little after Seven, looking stunning, even better than he remembered. There was a freshness and vitality about her that turned heads as she strode across the foyer. Her slim but rounded figure was accentuated by a red silk dress that seemed to follow her every movement. From her Greek heritage she had clear olive skin, deep brown eyes, and black hair cut in a short stylish fashion. She was exciting just to watch.

There was a cheeky sparkle in her eyes as she took his hand and said, "Well this is a nice surprise, last time you only offered me a cup of coffee."

In the spirit of the conversation, Colin replied, "But that time I was not going to ask you to marry me."

She laughed and said, "Of course I will marry you, but not yet. Are you going to take me to the lounge for a drink or do we stand here all night?"

After a couple of aperitifs, they went to the dining room and devoured a huge seafood platter, complimented with a bottle of Hunter Chardonnay.

Colin could never remember any time when he had enjoyed a girl's company so much; Maria had such a relaxed casual manner that was totally infectious. After the meal and a coffee in the lounge Colin took her home in a cab and reluctantly said goodnight at the door, promising to call her in a couple of days.

Colin and Trevor had previously agreed that they would not mix their private lives with business and the first job was to find suitable separate accommodation. Trevor found an apartment near the beach in Coogee.

Colin rented a larger and more convenient flat in Woollahra closer to the business.

With both being totally absorbed in making a success of the business the next months went by very quickly.

Colin saw as much of Maria as he could and was soon hopelessly in love with her. He rarely thought of how Trevor was filling in his leisure time. Feeling a little guilty, he asked if he would like a night out, maybe they would just go to a local pub, for a beer and a meal.

To Colin's surprise Trevor replied, "Sorry mate, but I'm taking Maureen to dinner and a show tonight."

Colin asked, "Do you have a regular thing going with Maureen?"

"Yes, I have, I might marry the girl one day. I have asked her to move in with me next week."

"You lucky bugger! Why have you been hiding all this from me?"

Trevor replied, "I haven't, you've been too busy to notice or ask."

The following month Colin convinced Maria that they should also live together. Her father, James, was not impressed, but in the end had to bow to the inevitable. The fact that they had a very good relationship and that Colin promised to marry her, made acceptance much easier.

The phone call came just as Colin was about to leave the office. The office staff had left for the day, so the main phone switchboard was closed. Colin could not ignore the insistent ringing of his office phone. Without any premonition as to what was coming, he picked it up. "Hello, Colin Naxos."

A muffled, heavily accented voice replied. "We have some unfinished business Mr. Naxos, like half a million dollars not paid for the last shipment, the syndicate want their money."

Colin felt that he'd just been kicked in the stomach and fell back in his chair. Gathering himself he replied, "Look I don't know who you are, but let me tell you this, if it is the drug business, that all finished a long time ago and has nothing to do with me or the Naxos business now."

Before he could say any more his caller interrupted. 'Your name is Naxos and you run the business, correct? So just shut up and listen, the business is still there making money, so you pay your debts, and don't even think about talking to the police. If you do, you won't live long. Get the cash together, you have Seven days."

The call was disconnected.

Colin dropped the phone and sat there trembling all over; he could feel his heart racing and for some time felt as if he was having a heart attack. Slowly he got to his feet and stepped over to a cupboard where he had a small bar. Taking out a bottle of scotch he poured himself a liberal drink and downed half of it in one gulp.

Gathering his wits, he tried to concentrate his thoughts on what to do. After some hesitation he picked up the phone and rang his friend and police officer, Joan Sterling.

Joan identified the caller on her mobile before she answered. "Well hello, this is a surprise call, I haven't heard from you for a while."

Without any preamble Colin said, "Joan I'm in trouble, can we meet privately?"

"Sure, where would like?"

"If you are free now, could you meet me in the coffee shop in the arcade behind the Town Hall Station? Let's say, it's six thirty now, we could make it by Seven."

Joan sensed that something was seriously wrong, and without asking why, agreed to meet.

Colin was about to take his BMW out of the office car park, when he thought; no, someone may know this car. Returning to his office he picked up the keys for an office Ford. Feeling a little paranoid, he drove out quietly and took a varied route for the journey from Mascot to the city. All the time with one eye in the rear mirror looking to see if he was being followed.

Parking in the Hoyt's Theatre car park, Colin walked the short distance to the Town Hall Arcade coffee shop and took a table in the back corner, so he could have an uninterrupted view across the arcade. He then sat and nervously waited for his friend.

A few moments later Colin saw Joan walking down the arcade towards him. Even in his distressed state he could not help but notice how good she looked. Smartly dressed in civvies and with a new short haircut, she could have been a top model rather than a senior officer with the NSW Police.

There was robustness about her as well as a purpose in her stride.

Colin stood up when Joan reached the table and held her hand while giving her a light kiss on the cheek.

"Hello Colin, despite what bothers you, I'm pleased to see that you have not lost any of your English charm. What's the problem?"

Inwardly she noticed that the soft youthful look had gone and she was looking at a much more mature man than the one she first met all that time ago in Cairns.

"Firstly, let me order coffees. If my memory is still okay, yours is black, correct?"

After ordering, trying to control his emotions he took a big breath and then proceeded to tell Joan about the phone call.

"Heavens Colin, I thought we were well and truly finished with all this."

Colin stammered, "The point now is how do we handle it?"

Joan pondered for a moment before continuing,

"I think we should officially record the incident but keep it in the hush file, at least until we establish that it's what is claimed. It could be some local who knew about the previous situation and is using that knowledge to blackmail you. On the other hand, it could be some Mafia group from the past who are still in business. First thing tomorrow I'll get a tap on all your phones, and then we can trace any incoming calls. The important thing is that you do not respond to their demands. If you do, they will think they have a cash cow just waiting to be milked. Also, it is now nearly twelve months since you took over the business, so why did they wait all this time? If we ignore the request, we may just flush them out into the open. In the meantime, I suggest that you hire private security guards to protect the warehouse.

If it does turn out to be a local trying to blackmail for quick cash, then we would have a good chance of picking him up quickly. Drugs locally and internationally are a huge issue. My greatest fear at this point is that the call is from someone connected to the original overseas syndicate. If this is the case, then the problem will be far greater. Following the episode with Steven Naxos, arrests were made here and overseas. At the time we felt that we had broken up the original syndicate, or at least curtailed their activities. However, so huge is the international drug business that we could never be sure of anything."

Colin sat quietly attentively listening to what his friend was suggesting.

He was a quiet, sometimes emotional man but underneath there was a steely determination that was not at first apparent.

Looking straight at Joan he said, "Joan, I will make it very clear, after all our previous experiences I will not roll over to these bastards. Thanks, yet again, for your help. If anything develops, I'll ring you."

Colin arrived home at about 8 o'clock to be greeted by Maria at the door. "Colin you're late, why didn't you ring me, I've been worried."

"Sorry love let's get a drink and sit down then I'll tell you."

"Colin you look quite distressed, what is going on?"

Just then the phone rang, and with a sinking feeling Colin stepped over to the coffee table and picked up the remote household phone.

The same voice was there, "Listen arsehole, you're not following instructions, your little meeting with that policewoman was noticed. You have one more chance, shut up and pay up or your pretty little girl will be the first to pay dearly, after that it'll be you." Before Colin could reply, the phone went dead. Ashen-faced and trembling he slumped into a chair.

She rushed to him, "My god, what's the matter?"

After Colin composed himself, he told her of the events of the evening.

It was now Maria's turn to go into shock. With a quavering voice she said, "What are we going to do?"

"The first thing will be to get you out of here to somewhere that you will be safe."

"But, Colin, I can't just walk out of here, I have commitments at the office, Dad is relying on me to tidy up several matters that are due in court next week."

"The studio apartment above the office in the city is unoccupied; you can go there, at least temporally until we sort this out. There are full time guards in the building as well, so you'll be safe there. I doubt that anybody would be likely to break into the largest Law Office in Sydney."

Maria replied, "That's fine, but what about you?"

"I will have to trust Joan. I will arrange another meeting with her for tomorrow. In the meantime, you could pack some clothes and be ready to move into the unit first thing in the morning." Fear showed on Maria's face and with tears glistening in her eyes she went to the bedroom to pack.

After taking Maria to the unit early the following morning Colin took a few moments to tell James what was going on.

He was aghast and concerned that the problems of the previous year had resurfaced. After some discussion he agreed with Colin that he had to work through the Police, with Joan Sterling as their contact.

Using James office phone Colin rang and told Joan of the latest developments. She replied with growing concern that the situation was much more serious than they first thought. They could well be the remnants of the overseas group. Her view was that they should now use all the resources of the NSW and Federal Police to apprehend these people before the situation got totally out of control, or even more dangerous than it was now.

Joan emphasised that, "We could not in any way handle this on our own. I think we should arrange a meeting here at Police Headquarters for late this afternoon. Let's make it at four o'clock, and ask James to come, but travel individually."

Colin hung up and relayed the message to James.

Without any attempt to conceal his movements, Colin drove the Ford to the office taking his usual route along Botany Road. After getting himself a cup of coffee, he called Trevor into his office and explained the situation.

After listening to what Colin had to say Trevor said. "Colin, as you know, life has changed since we first came to Australia and were chased around the country. I now have responsibilities I didn't have before. Maureen is pregnant, and my first thoughts are, above all, for her safety. We have been friends for a long time and I would not ever want to leave you, but sometimes things become bigger than we can handle. From what you've told me we could quite well be involved in some huge International drug cartel. If that's in any way a possibility, I want out, and as soon as possible. Listen old mate, this is all too much for us, why don't you just put the business on the market and leave someone else to worry about it. The company that expressed interest when we first took over may still be interested."

Looking at is old friend whom he had spent all his teenage years with Colin felt a sadness engulf him. With a tremor in his voice he gave a very subdued reply, "Thanks for being so frank, I do understand your feelings, and if you really want out, then I suggest that we make the split as quickly and cleanly as possible. The broader problem is that even if I sold the business and retired, they could still come after me for the money. I may have to see this through to the bitter end. You manage the finances and know we can meet all your entitlements any time; however, it may take some time to settle on your option shares. How about we give it a month to see if the problems can be sorted out.

If they are, then we can stay as we are; if not, the business is on the market and we're both out of it. While this is going on, take a month's leave, you and Maureen can go away. Take her up to the Gold Coast or somewhere you can relax and just sit in the sun."

Trevor replied, "I think that's a good deal; but let's hope we don't have to go down that road. The real worry is that internationally, the law enforcement agencies seem to have lost control over the drug barons. Colin, I'm sure you understand that I just want to lead my life and bring up my children without any involvement in the shady side of life."

Later in day Colin left the office and drove over to the airport carrying his brief case and an overnight carry bag. He parked the office Ford in the long-term car park and walked over to the Qantas check-in counter. After appearing to check in he made his way to the Frequent Flyer Lounge. He sat down with his newspaper nursing a glass of wine. After a short time, he got up and went to the rest rooms, taking his carry bag and brief case with him. In the bathroom he quickly changed his suit coat for a light reefer-type jacket, put on a pair of dark glasses and left, going straight to the arrivals area.

From there Colin mingled with a group of interstate passengers who appeared to be in a hurry to get to wherever they were going. Next, he hurried out to the taxi rank and joined the cue for a cab. When his turn came Colin asked to be taken to the police headquarters in College Street, Darlinghurst.

Joan chaired the meeting, which was attended by high-ranking officers and senior detectives. All were explicit in their views and confident that they would quickly track down the fellow or people behind the extortion demands. A lot of information regarding the original group was still held in the police computer system and an officer would be detailed to check the whereabouts of anybody suspected of being involved in any way with the original group. They admitted that they had no idea about where the demands came from and had no fresh leads to follow up. The main strategy appeared to be to wait and see if the extortionists could be flushed out into the open.

Colin left the meeting without sharing their optimism, in fact he was feeling utterly terrified about where the situation might take him.

With a troubled mind Colin decided to risk walking the relatively short distance back to the city and the Cockini Legal Offices to update James. He might also ask him to prepare contracts for sale of the business to have them ready should he decide to go down that path.

As he walked through Hyde Park, lost in his thoughts, a dirty scruffy looking individual carrying a brown paper bag with what looked like a wine bottle in it crossed his path. Colin took little notice, but to sub consciously register the scene, until he started walking alongside him.

Quietly the man spoke, "Have you got the money ready? We are not prepared to wait; you have only two more days." With that he turned and fled across the park in the direction of the war memorial.

Colin thought of chasing him until he realised that it was unlikely that he would catch him, also that it could be dangerous. He continued his way to see James with one thought on his mind. The world of criminals and drugs was not where he wanted to be and the quicker, he distanced himself from it the better.

Back in the opulent offices of Cockini Legal, Colin brought James up to date with the latest developments then walked down the corridor to

Maria's office. After convincing her to put her work aside, using the private lift, they went up to the apartment. At Colin's suggestion, they agreed that he should stop in the unit for the night rather than go home.

Later after changing into comfortable casual clothes they walked to a city restaurant and tried to relax over a nice meal and a good bottle of Hunter red wine. The restaurant, downstairs in the bottom end of Castlereagh Street, was known more for the quality of the food than the décor.

Trying hard to relax Colin nervously looked across the room wondering if one of the other diners was following them.

Later, as they lay in bed, Colin felt the pressure of the last days begin to overwhelm him. Maria, sensing his distress, put her arm around his neck and slowly caressed him while fleetingly kissing his face until she felt his muscles loosen and his body relax. He slowly turned to her and after softly kissing her lips, drew away and said, "Maria I love you so much, when I get out of all this mess, I will sell the business and we will go away together and leave it all behind."

Next morning, they felt a stronger than ever bond towards each other.

Over breakfast Maria had a glow about her that Colin could only assume came from their love for each other.

He was still nursing his coffee when Maria went to the bathroom to shower and dress for work.

Later, they were both silent for a moment, when Maria giggled and said, "Colin Naxos you are absolutely mad."

"Only about you. Tell me, why didn't a girl like you have a boyfriend when I first rang?"

"I did."

"What happened?"

"I dropped him for you. Now we both must get to work."

After kissing Maria goodbye at the door on her way downstairs to the offices, Colin went back inside to dress for work.

He had just completed knotting his tie when the phone rang. Thinking it would be his office to see if he would be there for a nine thirty appointment, he picked up the receiver. As in previous calls, before he could speak the now familiar voice said. "Time to pay up is getting close; do you have the money ready?"

This time Colin exploded, "Listen you fuckwit, your claims over my dead uncle have nothing to do with me, I did not even know the man, besides I could not raise ten thousand dollars let alone five hundred thousand. So, for the last time, fuck off, and leave me alone. And listen to this, if I catch up with you, I'll rip your balls out and stuff them in your big loud mouth."

The quick reply was, "It is the business that owes the money, so get a loan, if you don't, it is you, or your pretty girl friend might find a bomb right up her arse. Tomorrow I will let you know where to deliver."

Colin quickly dialled Joan Sterling's direct number and impatiently waited for her to answer, "Hello Colin, are there any developments?"

"Yes, I've just had another call, this time at the city apartment, how do they get all our numbers?"

Joan replied, "We don't know but we have a tap on all of them, so I'll see where this one originated from and give you a call in about half an hour."

"I'm on my way to the warehouse in Alexandra, so ring me there."

Colin again took a cab. During the short trip he thought, bloody hell, the police haven't a clue who these people are or where they're from.

I don't want to reform the whole fucking world, I want out of here; I will put the business on the market today. With a feeling of despair, he realised that nobody would buy the business while this was going on.

At the warehouse Colin went straight to Trevor's office to catch up before he left on his holiday. As he eased himself into the spare office chair Colin was a little overwhelmed with emotion. He and Trevor had been through a lot since they first left home so long ago full of excitement and adventurous spirit.

Trevor looked at his best friend noticing how tired and drawn out he looked. Feeling a little guilty about leaving him at this time he said,

"Everything is up to date; there's nothing the girls in the office can't handle over the next few weeks. If you really need me I will be on the next plane back. We've been mates for a long time and you know that I'll be there if you need me. I'll have my mobile so keep in touch and let me know how things are going."

Since arriving in Sydney, Trevor had put on more weight and was now decidedly chubby. Colin could not help but notice that there was a serenity about him, no doubt brought about by his relationship with Maureen and imminent fatherhood.

With some emotion Colin replied, "Yes, we've been through a lot together. Let me assure you that when all this is over, I want you back at work, but more importantly, I treasure your friendship. Partly in case something happens to me, I've instructed James to review my will and set up a framework to put the business into a private company structure.

I'll take 30%, you will own 20%, Gerald Patterson 15% and the remaining 35% will go to the staff, distributed on a years-of-service basis.

Safeguards will be in place to stop shareholders voting in a block to gain overall control. In effect the scheme will be for profit-sharing, rather than an opportunity to gain control over management. When you are free, set up a meeting with Cockini Legal to tidy up the detail. In the meantime, go and enjoy yourself in sunny Queensland, just give me a ring occasionally so I can keep you up to date."

Trevor said, "Colin I'm overwhelmed by your generosity, not only to me but also to the staff. Thank you."

Shortly after Trevor left, Joan rang. "Bad news, as with all the others this call was made from a public phone box in the city, so we're no further advanced."

Rather testily Colin replied, "The fact is then, that the police don't have a bloody clue as to what is going on or who these people are. Do you think they are local or from overseas as claimed?"

Joan replied. "The strongest belief is that they're from an overseas drug syndicate which makes it even more difficult."

Colin said, "Well I tend to think there's only one fellow involved, and he's a local. Have you done a check on, or interviewed the Naxos employees, particularly any that were there at the time of the fire and have left since?

"Yes, we have done all that and came up blank."

Persisting, Colin followed up with. "What about that now defunct security company that was run by Steven Naxos. Someone who was working there may have known enough about the business and the people to try and pull a stunt like this. The whole lot of them were a bunch of crooks."

This suggestion struck a chord with Joan and, after a moment's silence she said, "Colin, you're right, but we've already checked that out as well and could not even find anybody who was even remotely connected with the security company."

Fractiously, Colin responded. "Joan, I don't think your people are doing enough and at this stage I am tempted to just walk away from the whole bloody business and return to England."

"Yes, Colin you could, but what about all those people relying on the business to earn their living? We must clear this up first, then you can do as you please."

With a disturbing sense of finality, Colin accepted that he was locked in until the perpetrators of the extortion were found. His thoughts then came back to Maria, "How can I keep her safe?"

With his mind in turmoil he attended to a few pressing matters that had been on his desk for days and prepared to leave. What was frustrating Colin was that business was thriving and he could see many more opportunities to expand particularly in importing more packaged foodstuffs from both Europe and Asia. Free trade agreements that had come into force over recent years opened markets that were previously closed.

Walking through the car park; he decided that there was no longer any point in trying to hide; they obviously knew all his movements, so what's the point?

His next thought was that his best chance to flush them out into the open was to refuse to cooperate in any way, even at risk to his own safety.

Firstly, I must convince Maria to get out of Sydney and go into hiding. Perhaps I could put her in a unit up in the Central Coast area and hide her up there as old Charlie Thornton did. Now, that's an idea, Charlie and Hester live up there somewhere. She could board with them, they would love to see her. Hopefully it may only be for a couple of weeks.

Later, back at the Naxos Warehouse Colin rang Maria's office and left a message that he would come to the city apartment at around six thirty. Taking his own car, Colin went directly to his Woollahra apartment for a change of clothes and to empty the mailbox. Opening the door, he could hear the phone ringing and hurried down the hallway to answer it. With more confidence than he felt, Colin picked it up, only to hear the familiar voice.

"Get a pen and write down this number, then repeat it back to me. It's for an international bank account where you're to deposit the money."

Colin bellowed. "Get fucked, you will get nothing out of me," and hung up.

Now that he'd decided on a direction to take, he felt much better, and even stronger. Looking forward to being with Maria, he quickly changed out of his business suit and drove to the city.

Taking the private lift to the apartment Colin pushed the buzzer rather than use his key, just to see if Maria would open the door without checking first. He saw an eye at the security peep-hole and a voice said, "All right I'll let you in if you promise to take me to a nice restaurant for dinner."

"Now you're blackmailing me, but you win, so open the door."

After a hug and quick kiss Colin elected to get them a drink, scotch for himself and a white wine for Maria. Settled comfortably on the couch, he filled her in on the day's developments and that he wanted her to go and stay with Charlie and Hester for a few days.

Maria was quiet for a moment then said, "I'm quite safe here, and I am not going anywhere and don't ask again. We are in this together and that is the way we continue. Now where are you taking me for dinner tonight?"

Mischievously she added, "Make it somewhere nice and I will let you sleep here again, do you think you could handle it?"

Colin could not but marvel at how beautiful she was and that she was his. With a croak in his voice he said. "Yes, I think I could handle it, what do you think?"

Out the front in Elizabeth Street Colin hailed a passing taxi and directed the driver to take them to a restaurant in Oxford Street called "The Oasis."

The eatery was unimpressive from the street and Maria was wondering why Colin had chosen it for their night out. Lace curtains behind the etched glass front shielded the diners inside from gawking people passing by. Opening the door, they stepped inside and were immediately greeted by the elderly maitre d" in a smart, conservatively cut dark suit. "Welcome Mr. Naxos, my name is Jeanette; we have your table ready, unless you wish to have a drink in the cocktail lounge first."

"No thanks, Jeanette, we will go straight to our table."

When they were settled at their table Jeanette was keen to chat about some old times. "Mr. Naxos, that's an unusual name. Years ago we had a Mr. John Naxos as a regular customer; he and a solicitor, Mr. Cockini dined regularly with the owner, Mr. Bennett. Would he be a relative of yours?"

"Yes, he was my grandfather and Mr. Cockini was his business partner, but that was a long time ago now."

Jeanette replied, "I've been here for many years and I recall their lunches when they hosted many important people. I read once where Mr. Naxos died and Mr. Bennett has also passed away, but I believe that Mr. Cockini is still alive.

Maria joined the conversation, "Yes he was still very much alive when I saw him this afternoon, he's my grandfather."

Jeanette was becoming quite animated, "Well that is quite amazing, a special welcome to you both. The restaurant has changed little over the years, there is an old photo of the three of them still on the back wall."

Colin had never seen a photo of his grandfather and stepped over to have a look. "Well I'll be dammed" he said. The photo showed two good-looking young men with an older man who he assumed to be the infamous Frank Bennett. For a moment Colin felt a rush of emotion looking at the grandfather he'd never met, but now knew so much of his life.

Maria came over to have a look and after a moment remarked, "Colin, he looks just like you, there's certainly a very strong resemblance."

Enthusiastically, Colin asked, "Jeanette, if I called in tomorrow would you allow me to borrow the photo? I would very much like to get it copied."

"You certainly can Mr. Naxos, there's a lot of history there."

Colin and Maria went back to their table and sat down ready to study the menu.

There was something eerie about the place for Colin, he couldn't help but think how his grandfather and Sev Cockini probably sat at this same table many times, all those years ago.

Jeanette explained how the décor had never changed over the years as their clients were comfortable as it was. The rich red carpet, heavily embossed wall paper, starched white table cloths set with heavy silver cutlery and the traditional Waterford crystal water jug gave the restaurant its character. With emotions running through him Colin still felt strangely comfortable in the surroundings.

Much later, after they had finished their meal, of baked snapper and salad washed down with an excellent Hunter Chardonnay, Jeanette returned to inquire if they had enjoyed their meal, to which they both replied, "Lovely, thank you."

Colin then added, "Jeanette, you were here in those early times, I wonder if you could give me some of your time tomorrow. I'd very much like to hear your memories of when my grandfather was a regular customer."

"Yes, I'd be happy to have a chat about those times of which I carry such fond memories. Come at ten o'clock so we'll have some uninterrupted time before we open for lunch.

Colin knocked on the door at ten o'clock sharp next morning and was enthusiastically greeted by Jeanette. "Come in Mr. Naxos, I have a coffee ready for us." Colin gained some confidence by seeing her happy open face and did not detect any signs that would make him distrust or doubt her.

After they'd settled down Colin told her of the happenings over the later years, right down to his current problem with the extortionist.

She was already aware of most of what he told her except the extortion attempts. With gathering confidence, he thought, *I might as well get straight to the point,* and asked,

"Jeanette were you ever aware of any drug dealing going on through Frank Bennett's businesses?"

"There were always rumours, mostly about his brothels, but I can honestly say that they were never ever substantiated and in all my years looking after his restaurants, I never ever saw, or even suspected that there were drugs about.

Although Mr. Bennett sometimes came over as being a bit glib, I only saw him as a gentleman. All the staff had the greatest respect for him. The fact that he ran those dreadful brothels, as well as the restaurants, people assumed that he was some sort of crook. I knew him well for forty years, and apart from a little nonsense when he was young, he was nothing but an astute business man. Have a talk to his friend Sev Cockini, and I'm sure that he would support my views."

Colin replied, "I have spoken to him and he claimed to have no knowledge of Frank's business outside Naxos Condiments. Not that I ever doubted his word. I'm looking for another angle, outside the old group, which may give me a lead on where the extortion attempts are coming from."

Jeanette added, "The only gossip I ever heard was that Steven Naxos was involved in importing drugs and distribution. Most of this came to light after the warehouse was partly burnt down and he was killed. There were stories about a girl called Kathleen who was well known user and dealer around parts of town. My guess is that you would have to look overseas to find who Steven Naxos's associates were. That's about all I know. If I remember or hear anything, I will certainly let you know."

Colin stood and sighed, "Well, thanks Jeanette, what you've told me confirms my thinking. Let's just hope that whoever these people are, they just give up, and go away. Anyway, before I go, can I borrow the photo?"

"Of course, you can, I'll get it for you. Please come back and have another meal with us soon."

With the framed photo under his arm Colin returned to his office thinking, how will I ever get to the bottom of this?

The police don't appear to have any idea. Maybe Jeanette is right in that you would have to look overseas to find where the drugs originated.

Sitting at his desk he studied the photo again and marvelled at the likeness of his grandfather to himself. Turning the frame over Colin noticed an inscription on the back;

Taken by Steven's friend Mario Leotta from Milan
August 1995.

Colin was staggered that what could be an enormous lead to finding his adversaries, was staring at him. He was not so naive that he thought that this could be the total answer; however, it certainly could be a serious lead to finding where the threats were coming from.

Apart from going to Milan himself, or employing a private investigator, he felt that his best option was to talk to Joan before he did anything. Then another thought, I may be able to get the Milan phone directory up on the internet and see if I can find a Mario Leotta.

With eager anticipation, he scrolled through Several internet sites, and to his delight came up with the local Milan Directory.

His scant knowledge of the Italian language hindered him for a while, then, "Bingo", he found three Mario Leotta's listed. Two were nondescript; the third looked more interesting, giving a business listing as "Importer/exporter".

Next, he rang Sev Cockini, and after explaining how he obtained the photo, asked Sev if he remembered the lunch and the Mario Leotta.

Sev replied. "Well that is a long time ago, but I vaguely remember the occasion and Frank's friend. Do you have a photo of him as well or just the three of us? As he was an overseas visitor, it's likely that there were many photos taken that day. Frank always enjoyed being in the limelight and I would not be surprised if he sent pictures off to the Herald for insertion in the social pages. Get the police to follow up on that and find out also where his personal belongings ended up, as there may be other photos."

"Thanks, Sev, I knew you would point me in the right direction."

Sitting at his desk Colin turned the photo frame over and noticed that the tape holding the back on was peeling off. He slowly pulled it right off and took out the cardboard backing. To his amazement he found two other photos inside. One showed Steven Naxos with a swarthy looking man around the same age.

On the back was pencilled, Steven and Mario.

The other photo was of Mario with a girl; on the back was pencilled, Mario and Millie Naxos who was of course Steven's American wife.

With a growing sense of excitement, he promptly rang Joan Sterling on her direct mobile number and nervously waited for her to answer. "Hello Colin, what's the problem?"

"Joan I think we both would now agree that the extortionist is probably connected to an overseas drug cartel. Most likely with connections to the original mob that Steven Naxos was involved with. I have a name and photos which may open a door for us if you can put an agent onto it in Milan." He then went on to explain how he got the name from the back of the old photos, and Sev's suggestion to search for other photos in Frank's personal effects.

Joan responded. "This could be a huge breakthrough, are you in your office? I'll be there in fifteen minutes."

On schedule Joan arrived accompanied by another detective, John Blake. Colin had the photos spread out on his desk, and after introductions they studied them at great length.

"Here it is, but I'm only assuming it is the same bloke."

Detective Blake turned to Joan. "We can get these copied and emailed to Milan and Interpol and see what they come up with. The quicker, the better."

VIOLENCE ERUPTS

CHAPTER FIFTEEN

As was her normal practice Maria had left her BMW in the office car park under the building, wisely electing to take a taxi to make any business calls. The car park was typical of those under city buildings, narrow in and out ramps, attendants' box and emergency exit stairs in the far corner. The dull grey concrete of the construction was lit by flickering florescent lights.

On this day when Colin and Maria were upstairs in the studio apartment preparing for the day ahead a car park attendant decided that as Maria's car was not being used, he would move it to a spot down the back out of the way. He always relished the opportunity to drive a BMW, or sometimes just to sit in the car dreaming that one day he might have a car like this.

With a spare key from the office he opened the door and sat in the plush leather upholstery. Boy, he thought as he sat for a moment before turning the key, how I would love one of these. That was his last thought as he turned the key.

All he saw was a blinding red flash and a roar as the car erupted into a fireball and a twisted metal wreck. Then there was silence except for the crackle of flames burning the interior of what was left of the car.

The sprinkler system came on but was having little effect on the inferno. Two other cars nearby caught alight and there was an immediate danger of the fire spreading into the building itself.

The Sydney City fire station was just around the corner in Castlereagh Street and when the automatic alarms sounded, the response was swift. The Fire Trucks were at the scene in minutes and the men managed to quickly contain the fire before it got out of control.

Colin and Maria were dressed ready to leave when they heard the explosion and felt a tremor vibrate through the building. Colin reacted immediately and grabbing Maria's hand together they bolted for the lift. "No", he said. "We must use the fire escape."

They reached the ground floor as pandemonium was breaking out, with people screaming and running in all directions. James was there trying hard to put the building's rehearsed fire drill into action; but because it was an explosion rather than a fire, everyone was trying to just look after themselves. Everybody was thinking it was some sort of terrorist attack.

As the fire trucks and police arrived Colin and Maria sprinted across the road and sat on the sand stone wall of the park opposite.

Using his mobile, Colin rang Joan Sterling and said. "You had better get around here fast; it looks as though someone has tried to blow up the building."

Maria was shaking uncontrollably with the realisation that the bomb, or whatever it was, could have been meant for her or Colin. Taking off his jacket Colin wrapped it around her as he said. "Now everything is okay, we're still here together, just take some deep breaths. We will be away from here as soon as Joan arrives."

Colin saw Joan sprinting across the road towards them just as his mobile phone rang. His first impulse was to ignore it, then he took it off his belt and hit the connect button.

"You were warned, now you have one more chance, do an electronic funds transfer to the account number you were given and there will be no more trouble."

Joan arrived and knew immediately who was on the phone and whispered. "Keep him on the line." Grabbing her own phone, she yelled into it, "Get a trace on 04180653421 now, quickly, ring me straight back".

Colin held the phone to his ear wondering what to say. Then he responded with, "I can't, I threw the number away."

"Well I will give it to you again, write this down."

"Wait, I haven't got a pen or paper."

"Well arsehole, get one."

"Okay, Okay, hang on."

Colin dropped the phone loudly on the brickwork, so he could hear it, and called out, "Quick, has anybody got a pen?"

Another police car pulled up with its siren screaming, drowning out further conversation.

Colin let it go as long as he dared without losing contact, and then picked up the phone again, "Hello, are you still there?"

He pretended not to hear the reply and kept repeating the call, then said, "I can hear you now what is the number again?"

"This is your last chance so listen, 'The number is, 0011/0018/41.22. 692 3347 1089. Don't stuff it up."

Colin replied, "I've got the number, but I will have to see our bank tomorrow, so the money could take a couple of days."

"I will give you two days to do the transfer, after that you are dead if you fuck me around anymore." The call was disconnected.

Joan was immediately on her phone to headquarters. "Did you get it?" She clipped the phone on to her belt and yelled. "We've got him, he called from a mobile phone in the Museum Station just down the street; he could have used a mobile to set the bomb off. Let's go."

With Joan ringing for back-up, they bolted towards the station. As they ran down the entry ramp, they saw a short stocky man wearing a black shirt with a woollen beanie and dark glasses hurriedly moving away from the vicinity of the station entrance. Taking a punt Joan drew her pistol and called, "Hey you, stop right there."

He had seen them coming and ran into the crowd, not giving Joan any chance to use her pistol. They gave chase only to be losing ground on him as they battled to get through the crowd. Then Colin briefly saw him again running up the ramp to platform two. Gasping for air and with his heart thumping Colin followed, leaving Joan behind fighting her way through the onlookers. The last glimpse Colin had was seeing him jump off the end of the platform and disappear into the underground train tunnel.

Joan was immediately on her radio yelling instructions to seal off the city underground tunnel network.

Without even considering the danger, or his own safety, Colin kept running to where he last saw him. Jumping off the platform into the darkness of the tunnel he stumbled after him. It was now pitch black and he was becoming disorientated, then he tripped, falling face down on the crushed rock on the railway track.

Colin lay still for a moment accessing the certain damage to his face. Running his hand across his cheek he felt warm sticky blood oozing out of a cut on his forehead. Colin looked up and in light filtering down a ventilation shaft he saw a man standing against the wall, looking in his direction. Without getting up Colin threw a rock over to the other side of the tunnel.

He watched in horror as a silhouette of the man came into view. He raised his arm and fired two shots at where he threw the rock. The bullets hit the wall and whined away down the tunnel.

"Shit now I'm in trouble," Colin thought. He slowly stood up and two paces to his left he found a small recess in the tunnel wall which would offer some protection.

His attacker heard his feet crunch on the gravel floor of the railway tracks and fired two more shots in Colin's direction which again whined harmlessly down the tunnel.

He heard it coming before he saw the lights of a train swing around a bend not far ahead, slowing down for the station. Pressed hard up against the wall in his little recess, he felt the whoosh of wind as the train passed him in a deafening roar. Taking a punt that his adversary would have taken the opportunity to flee further along the tunnel, Colin again moved forward, stopping every few minutes to listen; hearing nothing he continued until he saw light from the tunnel entrance across from the park next to Central station.

With his head pounding and his heart racing he ran out into bright sunshine which momentarily blinded him. He stood for a moment getting his breathing under control and allowing his eyes to refocus and get his bearings. Realising that he was still bleeding from the gash on his head he unsuccessfully tried to stem the flow of blood with his handkerchief.

Staggering erratically across the park lawn, Colin reached a garden tap where he wet his handkerchief and attempted to wash the blood off his face. Bending over the tap splashing cold water on his face, he felt his heart slowing and his vision clearing. Absorbed in his own problems he was slow to notice the man in the black shirt and beanie standing under a tree less than thirty metres away. Fearing that he would be still armed, Colin moved away slowly not to attract attention in a direction that would bring him up behind him.

With fear churning in his stomach; Colin stepped around the tree and rugby tackled the man.

Although Colin had a size and weight advantage, he was not prepared for the quick reaction and strength of the other man. Before he could think, he received a smashing karate blow across his neck followed by an attempt to knee him in the groin. Instinctively Colin retaliated by freeing one arm and elbowing him in the mouth, feeling teeth smashing under the blow. To regain control Colin attempted to lock his arms to his body but was forced to ease his grip when his assailant clamped his teeth on his ear.

Colin screamed in pain, which was choked off as he was then head-butted across the bridge of his nose, sending a spray of blood over them both.

Still dizzy with pain Colin delivered a couple of short right jabs to his face and then managed to hold on until his size and weight started to take over. He was then able to partly roll him over and to get his arms under his shoulders and linked across the back of his head, effectively gaining control despite his frantic attempt to lean back and head-but him again. Colin was wondering how long he could hold on and started screaming for help

People passing by on their way to the station stopped to see what the fuss was about as Colin asked for someone to call the police. Nobody seemed particularly interested until a youth walked up saying, "What's the problem mate, do you want a hand?" Colin quickly replied, "Please just call the police."

Taking his mobile phone off his belt he replied with a frustratingly slow drawl, "Sure mate, no problem."

Even in his dire situation, with his adversary wildly kicking in an attempt to free himself, Colin had to laugh to himself over the youth's casual attitude. He stood closer and took a left foot kick at Colin's adversary, connecting around the kidney area. "That should slow him down a bit."

His adversary screamed in pain and drew himself into a foetal position. Colin got up and stood over him in case he tried to get up again.

His youthful helper said, "That fixed him, see ya mate." and walked off in the direction of the station.

Colin heard police sirens screaming close by, then looked up to see Joan Sterling sprinting across the park followed by two uniformed police. "Thank god for that," he thought.

The two constables quickly handcuffed Colin's adversary as Joan said, "Get him over to the wagon and lock him in. Take him down to Central and book him under anti-terrorists' laws."

Turning to Colin she snapped, "Are you all right? For god's sake, next time leave the heroics to the police."

"I caught him didn't I, where were you lot?" he taunted.

Ignoring his taunt Joan commanded," Firstly let's get back to the offices to see what is going on and where Maria is; then, by the look of you we had better get you to hospital. Colin, get in the car, quick, come on let's go!" With a squeal of tires and the siren blaring they sped back to the scene of the bombing.

Elizabeth Street was closed to traffic with police cars and fire trucks blocking the road. Television crews, with outside broadcast units, were stationed around the edge of the no-go zones with camera operators and reporters jostling for position. Stepping across a tangled mass of fire hoses and cables, Joan and Colin made it to the front of the building to find an ashen-faced James and his father talking to the senior fire officer. Without any preamble, Joan interrupted: "What's the situation officer?"

"Well as far as we can see there is no structural damage to the building only Several wrecked cars and smoke damage. After the police scientific and forensic people have finished, and the wrecked cars removed, it should be accessible for use again."

Colin broke into the conversation, "James, where is Maria?"

"Apart from being a bit shaken up she's fine. I've sent her up to the unit. You had better go up and see if she is alright."

Not needing any encouragement Colin sprinted across the foyer to the stairs. Taking three steps at a time, he reached the top floor unit out of breath with his head spinning and pulse racing. He found Maria sitting at the table shaking uncontrollably. It was obvious to Colin that she had been crying, and the shock from realising that the bomb had been meant for her showed heavily in her face and shaking hands.

She stood and they embraced, holding each other tightly without speaking until Maria saw his blood splattered face. "My god what have they done to you?"

At that moment Joan appeared at the door. 'Come on we'd better get you to hospital; you need a bit of work on that face by the look of it."

Maria again held him in her arms. When he did not immediately reply she realised that he was crying.

Controlling himself he said. "All I care about is you. But I will get those bastards no matter what it takes. We caught the fellow who set the bomb off and they should be able to get out of him who he was working for. I am now convinced that he is part of the Italian syndicate who were supplying Steven Naxos, and we are about to find out who.

You wait here until I get back. I think we should stop here tonight and try to recover. Before I go, I think we all need a drink to get settled down."

Colin poured a scotch for himself and a brandy for Maria and they just sat for a moment wondering what might have been and how lucky they were. Both their thoughts were also for the boy in the car park who lost his life.

Joan drove Colin to Saint Vincent's hospital. After a couple of stitches in his ear, a HIV test and tetanus injections he could leave.

At Police headquarters Detective Inspector Joan Sterling and two other senior detectives sat at a bare table with the bomber across the other side. The small interrogation room was bare of any other furnishings and sound-proofed.

"Okay now, listen carefully, we want you to answer some questions without any fuss or you will be in even greater trouble than you already are. Firstly, we want your name, address, and where you come from. Do you have any identification, passport perhaps?"

He continued to look down at the table without replying. The older of the two detectives suddenly reached across the table and gave him a huge open-handed smash across his face. "Now answer the questions."

With blood and spittle running from the corner of his mouth he looked straight at Joan. "Get fucked, I'm not saying anything."

With that he fell off the chair and rolled himself into a ball on the floor.

Joan left the room not feeling comfortable about how the man might be treated.

Returning an hour later she was concerned and frustrated to find that the only information they got out of the man was his address, which he gave as the Hotel Central in Parramatta Road Leichhardt.

"Okay let's go and have a look at his room."

Joan and an accompanying constable, Andy Harper, took an unmarked car from the pool for the short drive along Parramatta Road to the Hotel Central.

The pub was old and still decorated with cream tiles embossed with adverts for Reschs Pilsner from another era. The surrounding areas had multiple coats of brown paint which was peeling off, revealing cracked and rotting woodwork. The pub had seen better times and no doubt relied on their local bar trade and poker machines to make a profit. They both wondered what sort of lonely souls would find solace in spending their time in a smelly dump like this.

Finding the entrance foyer deserted, Joan and her partner went into the bar looking for the licensee.

The bar was dark and smoke-filled, but with a surprising large number of customers, some sitting on stools at the bar with their schooners of beer and cigarettes in front of them watching the race results on a flickering television screen above the bar; others were bent over an ancient pool table, engrossed in their game.

Amidst catcalls from the back of the bar, Joan approached the barman and asked for the licensee.

"Yeah mate, that's me, what can I do for you?"

"We would like to see the room of one of your lodgers;

we don't know his name, but he is a dark swarthy type, thick set, about 171 centre metres."

"That's not hard, we only have one room let, there are two blokes in it, I think they are brothers. They arrived about two months ago for an unspecified time. Here's the key, the room is upstairs, at the end of the corridor."

The stairway carpet was old and stained, with bare patches where the pile had worn off from years of use. There was a pungent smell made up of stale beer and tobacco smoke mixed with an over use of deodorants. The door to the room was scratched and had seen too many coats of brown paint.

Joan drew her pistol and stood to one side while Constable Harper turned the key in the lock and carefully opened the door.

To their relief the room was unoccupied. Two single beds with a small three drawer locker supporting an ancient lamp, an old-fashioned wardrobe with a few shirts and pants hanging on rusty wire coat hangers were the only furnishings and sign of habitation. Joan emptied the contents of the drawers onto the bed and found only some underwear, a toothbrush and a couple of disposable razors. Next, they searched through all the clothes and found that all the labels had been removed. There was no identification anywhere as to who they might be, or where they came from. The room had a suffocating smell of body odour, stale beer and cigarettes. Joan covered her mouth and nose with a handkerchief trying to block out the stench. Their spirits lifted when they discovered a plastic bag taped under the wardrobe with several thousand dollars in Australian and US currency. "With this stash they must have intended to return to wherever they came from." Joan said "Let's get out of here. We will leave everything as we found it and go back to the station. Someone can return and stake out the building, it's a fair bet that the second one will come back for the cash."

After asking the publican to forget they were there, they walked around the corner to their unmarked car.

Turning back into Parramatta Road they failed to notice a tall dark man sitting on the bus stop seat reading the Daily Telegraph, appearing to be waiting for the bus. When the car was out of sight he casually walked across the road and slipped unnoticed into the Hotel foyer then up the stairs to the room. Standing on the bed he retrieved a plastic bag containing passports and airline tickets from behind the grill of an old air conditioning unit.

He stuffed his clothes into a rucksack and carefully tucked the cash from under the wardrobe and the passports into a front zip pocket. Being careful not to be seen he left using the fire escape exit at the back of the building.

So as not to be identified later, he walked three blocks along Parramatta Road before boarding a bus for the city.

He alighted at the Town Hall Station and walked unobtrusively through the arcade. Finding a menswear shop he purchased a casual jacket and shirt which he changed into in the toilet block. Looking a bit more respectable he casually walked out into George Street and hailed a passing Taxi asking to be taken to the International Airport.

On arrival he sauntered across to the departure board to find the earliest flight out of Sydney. To his relief he found a Singapore Airlines flight to Singapore, with a spare first-class seat, leaving in two hours. He paid in cash using his American dollars, checking his rucksack in as normal luggage. He then made his way to the VIP lounge to wait for his flight. His passport, showing him as an Italian residing in Milan was legitimate and his passage through customs was unimpeded.

From a public phone in the departure hall he stopped and made a call to a number he had committed to memory. After depositing the coins, he waited for an answer.

In the city apartment Colin sat with Maria holding a scotch, trying to gather himself after the day's ordeal when his mobile phone rang.

"That will be Joan." he thought.

Before he could speak a heavily accented voice said. "That was your first and last warning, now you pay up or you are dead." The call was disconnected.

A week later as there had been no further threats, Colin returned to work.

Sitting in his office listening to the constant drone of voices and packing machinery from the warehouse, he tried to shut the problem out of his mind and to think about the future. He had found that his manager had everything under control and it was business as usual. As the weeks passed, he started to feel more hopeful that maybe it was all over.

Trevor came back to work and they agreed that they would allow another six months to be sure that there were no more problems and then decide whether they would sell up or keep going. Joan Sterling had rung to let him know that the Milan Police had picked up Mario Leotta but had to release him because of a lack of any evidence of criminal activity.

The concerning aspect was that the police were sure that he was part of a much larger organisation. A check with customs at Sydney airport revealed that he had recently spent a month in Australia, departing on a Singapore airline flight the day after the bombing.

This news gave Colin some comfort in that that maybe his troubles were over.

A NEW START

CHAPTER SIXTEEN

At the end of the day, Colin went home with a feeling of elation and happiness that he had not felt for some time.

Maria greeted him at the door looking radiant with a big smile and her dark eyes flashing. Immediately she hugged him.

"Hello, hello, what brings this on, have we won the lottery?"

Pulling him down the passageway to the lounge she announced, "Well we have in a way, I can't hold it back any longer, we're going to have a baby."

Colin was too dumbfounded to reply and just stood there with his mouth open.

"Don't just stand there, say something, are you happy? It does happen you know, particularly when I have a sex-crazed partner like you."

"Maria, I am thrilled. I don't know what to say, when did you find out, how far are you? Have you told your parents?"

"No, I would not tell anybody before you. Are we going to celebrate? Tonight, could be my last drink for eight months. Then tomorrow I will tell the others. You will have to ring your mother and tell her that she will soon be a grandmother."

With some emotion, Colin replied. "This is one of the happiest moments of my life; the only one that surpasses it is when I first met you. Let's open a bottle of champagne, and then I will take you to dinner at the Oasis."

Maria surprised Colin by dressing in the same body-hugging red silk dress that she wore on their first date at the Hilton Hotel. Standing in a provocative pose she said, "Well I'm ready, what do think?"

Colin thought that he had never seen anyone so alarming beautiful.

At the Oasis Colin and Maria were greeted warmly by Jeanette and shown to their favourite table. "You look a happy couple tonight; do you have something special to celebrate?"

Impulsively, Colin blurted out, "Yes of course, we have just found out that we are having a baby."

Maria protested, "Colin it's still a secret, we haven't even told our parents yet."

"Sorry about that, I got carried away, Jeanette, you are the first to know."

'Well I am privileged, and I will keep your secret. Firstly, I will bring you a complimentary bottle of our best champagne. Next, I recommend that you have the rack of lamb tonight, it's delicious."

Colin replied, "Thank you Jeanette we will take your advice. After we demolish this very good champagne, would you please bring us bottle of your best red wine?"

During the evening Colin talked non-stop, drinking much more than he normally would.

"It is definitely a boy," he extolled, "The Naxos dynasty lives on."

They made plans to buy a new house, where to send him to school and any other issue Colin could think of, all much to Maria's amusement.

When it was time to go, Colin was quite unsteady and out the front in the fresh air he was rocking slightly on his feet with Maria holding his arm while waiting for their taxi.

Turning to Maria he slurred, "I may have celebrated too hard, I think I am pissed."

Maria chided, "Well tonight I will excuse you of anything, but don't forget you will be a Dad soon.

Do you think you will be okay when we get to bed, or will you fall to sleep on me?"

—————— ❀ ——————

The next two months were the happiest of Colin and Maria's lives. An ultrasound confirmed that they were having a boy which really made Colin puff his chest out and he never gave up a chance to brag about it.

They sold the unit and purchased a home on the North Shore suburb of Pymble and prepared to settle down to a family life.

Ironically their new home was in the street where Sev Cockini's first wife, Elizabeth, grew up. Colin often walked past the house and pondered on what history was there for Paul and the Spalding family.

As the city apartment was under the office lease it was retained which was hugely convenient for overnight stopovers.

Naxos Condiments and Catering Supplies were trading well, again under the financial control of Trevor.

Now that he had a son on the way, Colin called on Father-in-law James to adjust his will, mindful of the possibility that one day there could be a third generation Naxos in the business. The new family situation also dispelled any thought he had of selling the business.

In the middle of the year it was decided that Colin should accompany their manager on the annual overseas trip to the Milan Kitchen and Catering Fair. His plan was to leave a week early, taking the opportunity to visit his mother in London prior to meeting the manager in Milan.

On a sunny Sydney day, Maria drove him out to Sydney International Airport, and after an emotional farewell Colin went through the now familiar ticketing routine.

Checking in his one suit case and carrying his brief case as cabin luggage he made his way through customs.

Once inside he again had that feeling of being cut off from the world outside. He took the long walk past all the Duty Free and Souvenir shops down to his departure gate.

The Jumbo touched down at Heathrow on schedule at nine am local time,

While waiting to disembark Colin thought about his mother and how they had parted on such amiable terms when he left all those months ago.

Remembering also those times not so long ago when Barbara met him at the Airport under less than pleasant circumstances.

He cleared customs in record time and made his way down to baggage collection. Happily, Colin found that his case was one of the first out on the carousel.

Picking it up he eagerly looked around for Barbara; not seeing her, he felt a pang of disappointment; maybe she's in the arrivals area he thought.

Struggling with his loaded trolley, Colin stood in the main concourse area looking at the sea of faces. He was contemplating what he should do when he felt a tap on the shoulder.

Without a word Barbara fell into his arms for what was an emotional reunion.

He then held her at arm's length looking at this alluring woman. "You look absolutely wonderful, what is your secret?"

"He's right behind you."

Colin turned to see a heavy set jovial looking man with flaming red hair.

Barbara put her arm through his saying, "Colin meet my friend, Andrew."

He put his hand out saying, "Hello Colin, Andrew Shackleton."

Colin acknowledged the greeting and turned back to Barbara.

"You know how to pull surprises and confuse me. Dare I ask if Andrew is the mystery man you mentioned once before?"

"He certainly is, but before we go any further let's go and get a coffee and I will explain."

Battling their way through the never-ending crush of people, they found their way to the food area and were lucky to find an empty table. Andrew volunteered to get the coffees leaving Colin alone with his mother. "Come on, don't hold back, what's the story?"

"Andrew and I became engaged last week, and we thought we would wait until you were here to tell you personally rather than by phone. So, there you are, your mother is going to be married again and we are both very happy."

Andrew returned with the coffees, and after setting them down on the table stood back with a grin on his face,

"Well did you tell him?"

Colin stood up to shake his hand, "Congratulations I wish you both every happiness. Now when is the big day?"

Barbara replied, "We will be having a quiet registry office wedding in two weeks, then we thought we would come out to Sydney and spend some time with you and Maria. Andrew has never been before, so we are both looking forward to it. For now, Andrew has his car, so we can drive you into London. Where are you staying?"

'At the Grosvenor Kensington, which you introduced me to quite some time ago. Where else?"

"Great, we anticipated that and have booked in for a couple of days ourselves. When you have settled in and recovered from your jet lag, we can catch up on what you have been doing."

Colin felt relaxed and comfortable back home in London and took the opportunity to do some shopping and a couple of trips to the theatre with Barbara and Andrew.

Returning to his room on his last night before leaving for Milan, Colin noticed the message light flashing on his phone. He rang reception to find he had a message to ring Joan Sterling. This smells like trouble he thought. Ignoring the ten-hour time gap, after he had settled into his room, he nervously rang Joan on her mobile.

A sleepy voice answered, "Hello."

"Joan, it's Colin, you rang, what's the problem?"

As usual Joan was straight to the point dispensing with any frivolous chatter.

"Colin there may not be a problem, but we picked up a bit of talk from Milan that it would not be wise for you to go there. Remember we never ever established conclusively that the two brothers we apprehended were not part of a wider organisation. What we do know for certain is that they both lived in Milan. I can't tell you not to go, but I do suggest that you take every care and don't go out alone. Perhaps you could even hire a bodyguard. Kidnappings and murders are much more prevalent there than in Sydney. We would be very naive to think that the original drug cartel has totally disbanded, and they may still think they are owed some money. So, it's up to you as to what you do, all I can suggest is that you take extreme care when away from your hotel."

"Thanks for your concern Joan. I think it's too late to cancel all our appointments and besides we still have a business to run. We can't just run and hide, so I will heed your advice and take extra care. Later in the week I will also have our manager with me, which may be of some help."

Joan replied, "Well fair enough, but please keep in touch, even to ringing me every day in case I hear something more."

Colin hung up the phone with a sense of anguish, wondering when he could be free of all this and feel that Maria and their soon to be born child would be safe to go about their lives. 'How far do to the tentacles of these international drug syndicates go?'

The more he thought about it the more concerned and depressed he became.

To bolster his spirits, he rang Maria to see if all was okay. Adding further to his anguish he learnt that there had been Several phone calls inquiring about his whereabouts, specifically asking what hotel he was staying at in Milan. The caller refused to identify himself. There were also other calls to his office inquiring about his whereabouts.

Two days later after the usual grind of battling with the masses of travellers at Heathrow Airport, Colin boarded an Air Alitalia flight for Italy and Milan.

After booking into the Milan Hilton he rang Maria and Trevor to let them know where he was staying, making a point that they were not to tell anyone.

After a restless night, the next morning he was roused by the incessant ringing of his doorbell.

Leaving the security chain on he opened the door to find a housemaid with his breakfast. Without any embarrassment about his near nakedness he dreamily opened the door and allowed the maid to bring the trolley in. After palming her a few Lira as a tip, not being sure what he had actually given her, he closed the door and re-attached the security chain.

The smell of bacon, mingling with the aroma of freshly brewed coffee, stimulated his appetite and sitting at the small table next to the window with views over the city, he enthusiastically attacked his breakfast.

Returning his plate to the trolley he noticed a hotel envelope with his name hand-written on the front. Thinking that it would be his booking confirmation or deposit receipt, Colin Idly opened the envelope with his breakfast knife. As his mind drifted towards his schedule for the day, he unfolded the single sheet of paper. His breath caught, and he felt a sickening flutter deep in his stomach as he read the note, just three words,

REMEMBER OUR BROTHERS

In a state of rage mingled with fear, Colin hurriedly pulled on a pair of jeans and shirt, ran out of the room into the lift and down to the reception area.

Ignoring other guests checking in or out, he bellowed at the clerk, 'Where is the manager?'

A portly man in a grey suit stepped from behind the desk, 'Sir, I am the duty manager, how can I help you?'

'Somebody left this note on my breakfast trolley and I want to know who and how anybody knew I was staying here, and my room number.'

'Sir, this is a big hotel with many staff, many of who could have access to our records and catering services. However, I will investigate and see what I can find out for you. Is it that important?'

'Your bet your bloody life it is. You find out, I will be back later with the police for your report.'

Without waiting for a further reply Colin stormed back to his room to dress and collect his briefcase. Briefly he considered changing his room but thought that there was little purpose as they could still find him anyway.

After a frustrating day visiting suppliers where his mind was not on the job, Colin returned to his hotel to find that the morning's duty manager had left for the day. The afternoon duty manager knew nothing of his request. After checking his computer, he politely informed Colin that there were no messages for him in the system.

Returning to his room Colin tidied up his paper work from the day's activity and prepared to e-mail a report back home to Trevor.

Against his better judgement, thinking that no harm would come to him in the middle of one of the biggest and busiest cities in Europe, he decided that rather than have his evening meal in the hotel, he would find a nice small local restaurant in a nearby street. Picking up his jacket he left the room and took the lift down to the foyer. From the front of the hotel he turned left past the designer label clothing shops and others extolling the virtues of Italian handmade leather shoes.

The street was awash with traffic; every car seemed to have its horn permanently blaring, adding more noise to the incessant scream of the thousands of motor scooters dodging around the sometimes-stalled cars.

Lost in his thoughts, Colin was about to pass a narrow alleyway when he was suddenly dragged by his jacket into the dark space between the buildings. Before he could react to defend himself, a vicious blow to his head knocked him to the cobblestone pathway. With his head ringing from the blow, through a haze he saw a burly man standing over him.

As Colin tried to get up, his attacker put him in a head lock with his arms pinned behind his back, effectively demobilising his upper body. As his head started to clear Colin knew he was fighting for his life and started wildly thrashing about with his legs. Then an excruciating pain, as his assailant released him, swung him around and kicked him in the groin. The pain was of such intensity that he could not take a breath. He gasped then vomited over his assailant's shoes.

At this moment Colin lost any ability he may have had to defend himself. Then he felt a searing pain in his side as he was stabbed with a long-bladed knife.

A heavily accented voice filtered into his confused brain. 'That was for not paying your bills, this is for my brother.'

This time the pain was in his chest.

Colin's attacker released him and let him fall to the cobbled stones of the lane-way. With his arms now free Colin put a hand on his chest. As he lay prostrate on the cold cobblestones, to his horror, he felt warm blood pulsating between his fingers with the weakening beat of his heart.

He then started to perspire heavily and felt dizzy as his blood pressure dropped from massive blood loss.

At that time Colin was vaguely aware of a man and woman standing over him, 'I think he's been hurt, we had better call an ambulance.'

Time meant nothing anymore; he could not focus or organise his thoughts, but at one stage he thought he heard the distant wail of sirens, which then seemed to be getting louder.

His rapidly fading thoughts were of Maria and his unborn child.

MILAN

CHAPTER SEVENTEEN

Colin was barely conscious when he felt strong arms roll him onto a stretcher and then into a waiting ambulance.

He was aware of people talking but could not fully understand. He was trying to concentrate but the only words he heard were Italian and he had no idea what they were saying.

Weak and perspiring heavily, in his befuddled brain Colin knew he was in trouble. He was hearing people talking and the scream of a siren, it all seemed so far away, like at the end of a great tunnel but he could not separate one from the other.

Above the pain in his chest he felt the jab of a needle as medics hurriedly rammed an intravenous drip into his arm.

Early the next day Colin's head started to clear, and he slowly became aware of his surroundings. He was on a single bed with crisp white sheets in a small room festooned with medical equipment. A shunt in his left arm held in place with a large strip of sticking plaster put a steady drip of fluids into his ravaged body. Through a small plastic tube inserted in his nostril, oxygen was being pumped into his lungs. Slowly Colin became aware of white coated man with a stethoscope draped around his neck and a young girl, he presumed to be a nurse, standing next to his bed.

"Well, we have patched you up and you look much better; we'll just take your blood pressure. If it's okay and you feel up to it, we will let the police in as they are anxious to talk to you. You were very lucky; the knife missed your heart and vital organs; however, it will be some time before you can move about as there are a lot of stitches in there.

Colin was not outwardly an emotional man but at this time he could not control the rush of tears and emotion as he came to understand how close he came to death. Then he felt an overwhelming rage engulf him. The bastards, it's now payback time, I am not going to sit back and cop this, I'm going to become the aggressor. I will go to any lengths to protect myself and family.

'Thank you doctor." He mumbled.

'Don't thank me, thank the ambulance medics, they were the ones that held you together.'

Colin slowly realised that the doctor he was talking to was an Aussie. 'Where are you from Doctor, you don't sound Italian?'

'Well I'm not; I grew up in Sydney and did my training there. I am here on secondment for a year. My name is Jim Cooper, why do you ask?'

'I live in Sydney and am here on a business trip. Where did you train?' Colin asked

'Royal Prince Alfred Hospital.'

'Well you may know a friend of mine, Doctor Paul Spalding; he would be about your age.'

Looking rather bewildered Dr Cooper replied, 'Of course, I know him well. Anyway, enough of all this you need to rest. The police will be here in another hour or so. By the way, does any of this have anything to do with your business trip?'

On impulse Colin replied, 'No, it must have been an attempted robbery. Doctor, would you do me a small favour?'

'If I can, what is it?'

Picking up his wallet from the bedside locker Colin said, 'See if you can find an old friend of my grandfather and ask him to ring me here, if not, at my hotel, The Milan Hilton.

Colin took a battered old business card from his wallet and handed it to Dr Cooper. 'His name is Sergio Capaldi. He was still at that address here in Milan a couple of years ago.'

The doctor nodded and said, 'That shouldn't be too hard, I will do my best for you. In the meantime, I suggest that you get some rest.'

The next morning after a drug induced sleep Colin felt stronger and agreed to talk to the local Police. With their lack of English and his limited

Italian they soon lost interest and appeared happy to record the incident as a random attack by local thugs looking for cash to feed a drug habit.

Later in the afternoon, a nurse roused Colin out of a light sleep. In quite clear English she called, 'Mr. Naxos, you have a visitor.'

A tall distinguished elderly man stepped into his room.

'Hello Colin. I am Sergio Capaldi. You look very much like your grandfather and my great friend. I was very distressed to hear of his death. Over the years we became good friends and I always took an interest in the Naxos business.'

'Hello Sergio, it's nice to meet you. Your name always seemed to pop up back in the Sydney office. Please take a seat.'

Colin immediately felt comfortable with this friend of his grandfather, guessing that they would have been about the same age. They spent the next hour chatting about the early days of the business with Sergio filling a lot of blanks that Colin had never been aware of. Somehow it made Colin feel much more a part of the Naxos family.

Sitting up a little straighter in the chair Sergio brought them back to the present. 'Now tell me Colin, how did you end up here with holes in your chest?'

Starting with his first involvement back in Sydney, Colin filled him in on all that had transpired since.

'This is not going to go away so I am going to take the initiative myself. Instead of being hunted I am going to become the hunter. I am not asking you to be involved.

I only want help with three things. Firstly, find the address of this thug that attacked me. His name is Mario Leotta. He was listed in the local phone book. Secondly, I need another passport, maybe two, preferably English. I intend to leave Italy on my passport and re-enter using the fake. Within a couple of days, I will return to the UK then on to Australia using my own. Finally, could you find an unregistered pistol for me, preferably a twelve shot Glock or something similar?'

Sergio, looking quite alarmed at Colin's request, hesitated before speaking. 'I have my own agenda with Mr Leotta, so I will help you. I don't want to know what you intend to do, but my friend you are dealing with dangerous people who would have no qualms about killing you.'

'They have already tried, and I am still alive, and what about the bombing and violence in Sydney? I don't think they will let up on me. Early police inquiries indicated that there is just one family involved rather than a large Mafia type organisation. There are two brothers, one is safely locked away for a long time in an Australian jail, the older one who tried to kill me is here in Milan and no doubt once he hears that I am still alive he will come after me again. I will stay at the Hilton until I hear from you.

Without any further conversation Sergio stood and said, 'I'll help you, but we must not be seen together.

I will contact you. Have five thousand US dollars in cash available. Please don't try to contact me again.' Sergio embraced Colin in the continental way and said, 'Good luck my friend.'

Colin lay back in bed, his stomach churning, staring at the unadorned white walls thinking of what he was going to do and the huge risks involved. His resolve to end the madness wavered. Then he thought again of his options if he was going to protect his friends and Maria back home, there was none. The bastards are turning me into a criminal.

Five days later Colin was discharged from the hospital and after settling his account took a cab through the mayhem of the Milan traffic back to the Hilton Hotel.

The first thing he did was to cancel all his appointments and reschedule them for the Sydney manager who was scheduled to arrive the next week. Over the next few days he concentrated on resting and letting his wounds heal.

Sitting on his small balcony basking in the morning sun, he heard a light knock on the door. Opening the door, he found Sergio complete with turned up collar and dark wrap around glasses holding a small parcel. Colin quickly took him into the room and closed the door.

'Colin, I do not wish to be seen, so if you have the money I will go.'

Colin retrieved a plastic bag from the room safe and handed it to him. 'Do you want to count it?'

'No, my friend, I trust you, so I will wish you well and leave.'

After he closed the door Colin, with shaking hands nervously opened the box. Wrapped an oiled cloth he found a twelve shot Glock pistol and a box of fifty bullets.

In the bottom of the box he found a plastic bag containing a British passport in the name of Andrew Carter and another in the name of William Trainer. Also, importantly, there was a scribbled note with the address of Mario Leotta.

Colin felt physically sick thinking about what he was about to embark on.

Sitting at his small desk he carefully inspected the passport and was quite amazed at the quality of it. His careful inspection showed no faults or indications that it was anything but original. It will get me through customs, he thought.

Colin's plan was to leave Italy on his own passport, return to London and in a few days book a return flight to Sydney for two weeks later. In the meantime, he would return to Italy using his Andrew Carter passport.

'I have unfinished business with Mr. Leotta.' he thought

As there was no way he could take the pistol through customs Colin rebooked his room at the Hilton and left most of luggage behind, hiding the pistol the best he could in a shoe bag.

At Heathrow there was no one there to greet him so he hired a taxi for the trip to London.

Using his own passport Colin booked himself into the Grosvenor Kensington Hotel making a fuss about a reservation he did not have. He wanted to be sure they would remember the booking if ever asked. Up in his room Colin unpacked, took a shower, and ordered a room service meal.

Waiting for his meal he took a bottle of whiskey out of the bar and poured himself a liberal dose.

Settling back in the comfortable lounge chair his mind drifted back to his carefree days before the Naxos Australian business came into his life.

"Everything was so simple, all he had to do was a bit of study for his university course, which he found quite easy, play cricket and flirt with the

girls. One lingering sadness was that he never really understood or knew his father. Mother was always there for him in his early days at boarding school, but he never felt a lot of warmth or emotion with her. But then, he preferred the company of his boarding school buddies and later, when older, there was more fun to be had around the university social scene. So, I guess I was probably seen as a bit of a problem child. In contrast some of my wilder friends saw me as a bit of goody boy.

Trevor was my only close friend and there were many times that I had to extradite him out of trouble.

How in hell did I ever end up in this situation where I'm about to commit murder? Love does strange things to you.

I am about to kill someone to protect the girl I love. If I waver, I will think of what would happen to Maria and our baby if I can't protect them".

His meal arrived which he quickly devoured, then washed it down with more whiskey which did little to lift his spirits. Looking across the expensively furnished room Colin could not help but look at his image in the mirror and was shocked to see how haggard and drawn he had become.

After yet another big gulp of whiskey he became quite maudlin and emotion took over as tears began sliding down his cheeks.

'Get yourself together,' he screamed at his image in the wall mirror.

Feeling totally out of control Colin dropped his glass, letting the remains of the whiskey splash across the carpet. With a couple of shaky steps, he found the bed and fell across it unconscious.

Hours later he woke to the whirring sound of a vacuum cleaner in the hallway. Gingerly picking himself up off the bed, Colin undressed and made his way to the shower and turned the cold on full blast.

Somewhat refreshed he felt the need for exercise and remembering that he had his favourite old joggers in his case Colin dressed casually and took the lift down to the hotel gymnasium.

He thought that in view of the what could be a punishing time in front of him he needed to be in the best physical condition possible. "I should book in for at least another week or more."

Colin then began a punishing exercise program to build up his fitness level. Feeling a need to punish himself he worked hard twice a day before deciding that he had had enough. Two weeks later, back in his room in his room after a vigorous workout Colin showered, then dressed formally in a dark suit and tie and made his way to the hotel bistro. After a solid breakfast, washed down with two cups of coffee Colin started to feel somewhere near normal again. He felt that he had somehow exorcised his fears and was ready to face his problems.

Later that day he reserved his return flight to Milan using his new passport.

Back at Heathrow with a small overnight bag he had purchased for the trip he sailed through Customs looking every bit the young executive.

Not that he really thought it would help, Colin purchased a hat and a pair of dark glasses in hope that it would make him at least less identifiable.

Travelling first class helped him to quickly get through Airport Customs. Outside the airport, Colin stood at the rank waiting for a taxi he found that he was sweating profusely from nervousness.

'How I would love a drink,' he thought.

Then told himself, 'Get over it; no alcohol until I am safely on the Qantas flight for home.'

Back at the Milan Hilton, trying not to be noticed, Colin went straight to his pre-booked room. After a freshen up he changed into casual clothes, and again unobtrusively left the hotel.

With his spare time on the plane Colin had gone over and over his plans. Somewhere he realised that his weak link was the Hilton Hotel.

Striding down the narrow streets, within two blocks Colin found a small nondescript Backpackers Hostel. Taking the only private room available he paid cash for a week in advance.

Returning to the Hilton, he quickly packed making sure his pistol was safely hidden, settled his account, and returned to Backpackers Hostel.

His room was small and smelly, a product of many unwashed bodies and poor housekeeping. The mattress was thin and lumpy, not the sort of bedding Colin was used to. Blocking this out of his mind he tried to concentrate on job in front of him.

In the bathroom mirror Colin was again shocked to see a face he felt he did not know. His skin looked grey his eyes were bloodshot with heavy bags.

I can't go through with this he told the stranger in the mirror; then his stomach heaved, and the remains of his last meal burst out splashing across the basin and floor. Gasping for breath, his head throbbing, Colin fought to get control of himself. Discarding his clothes, he stepped into the shower and turned on the cold tap and just stood there letting the sharp cold needles massage his body.

Refreshed and with a clearer mind he vigorously dried himself, took a clean pair of shorts from his case and fell exhausted on the bed.

Drifting off to sleep his last thought was; I must do this for my family otherwise there is no future.

Next morning after a troubled night's sleep, Colin was up early and breakfasted at a street café that was packed with early starters. The fact that it was so busy gave Colin some comfort as to the quality of the food. After some wonderful Italian coffee, it was time to go looking for a rental car.

A Car Rental Agency across the road from the Milan Railway Station with a line-up of tired looking Fiats seemed like a place that would not ask too many questions. In his limited Italian Colin asked the price for three-day hire.

'You bring the car back here?'

'Yes, three days.'

'Our special price for you today is 60000 lire. You American?'

Colin was quick to remember his British passport, 'No British. You want my passport?'

'Fill out this form with your details.'

The formalities over Colin nervously drove off down the street in the usual chaotic Milan traffic.

In case he was recognised by someone from the Leotta clan Colin took an indirect route to the Backpackers Hostel, but the fact that he had some difficulty finding his way back was of some concern.

Walking across the foyer the desk clerk called, 'uno momento Mr Carter, I have a letter for you.'

At first the name 'Carter' did not register, then it hit him like a kick in the stomach, 'That's me!'

He turned and faced the clerk who handed him a plain envelope with, A Carter,' hand written on the face.

In a daze Colin accepted the envelope and after handing the clerk a few Lira walked across to the foyer to the stairs.

In his room, with violently shaking hands he ripped the envelope open and took out a folded single sheet of paper. In a mixture of Italian and English was a short message;

Colin. I hear that people have been to the Hilton inquiring on your whereabouts. There is no need to move but keep your eyes and ears open. Suggest you get the job done and get out of the country as soon as possible.

Colin's initial shock was tempered by the thought.
'My friend is still keeping an eye on me. I'm glad someone is.'
Then another thought, *'If Sergio can find me then others can.'*

Leaving most of his clothes Colin packed his overnight bag with bare necessities along with his travel documents and the pistol.

Using the fire escape, he made his way to the rear car park unlocked the Fiat and quietly drove around to the front of the building. After parking a short distance down the street where he may not be noticed Colin sat and waited.

An hour later as he was fighting to stay awake, he heard the roar of a large car coming down the street. Instinctively Colin became wide awake and drew himself lower into the seat.

He watched in horror as a large swarthy man got out of the car, walked across the footpath and disappeared into the hostel.

'Christ almighty it's him. Mario Leotta.'

Steeling himself, Colin took the pistol from his bag, inserted a twelve-shot clip, turned the safety catch to the off position and pushed it into his trouser belt. Getting out of car on the offside he walked further down the street where he crossed the road in relative darkness. Slowly making his way door by door he concealed himself close to the Hostel entrance to wait. After what seemed an eternity he watched as Sergio Leotta looked up and down the street then stepped out onto the footpath.

At that moment Colin stepped out of the shadows and rammed the pistol into his back.

'Don't turn around or make a sound just keep walking.'

The realisation then came to Colin that this is not how he planned it, he could not bring himself to shoot a man cold bloodedly in the back. Entering the darker area, he said, 'Mario, slowly now, turn around.'

At that precise moment with surprising agility the big man threw himself sideways towards the ground at the same time drawing a pistol from an under-arm holster.

Before he could react, Colin heard the deafening thud of two shots and then the whine of bullets screaming away into the distance. Fortunately for Colin, Leotta had shot too early before he got his balance.

Trembling with fear, holding the pistol in both sweating hands, Colin pulled the trigger only to realise that he had shot nowhere near his target. With a grin on his face Sergio Leotta levelled his pistol straight at Colin's chest. He was paralysed with fear and in that split second waited for certain death. Then he saw blood spurt from Leotta's chest as a shot rang out from another direction. He was thrown backwards as if by a giant hand.

His rescuer was then next to him screaming, "Let's go, into the car quick."

Colin still had enough awareness to respond, "What about my bag?'

"We already have it. Run damn it."

In what seemed an eternity, but was only seconds, Colin found himself in the back of a strange car.

With the tires screaming on the bitumen they roared down the street at a breakneck speed.

Around the corner after they had slowed down the driver turned and said, "We will drop you off in the city, have a coffee then take a cab to the airport."

A very traumatised Colin opened the car door and said, "Please pass on my thanks to Sergio. He is God to me."

Colin nervously walked another four blocks before he found a small coffee shop. Stepping inside he took a table where he could not be seen from the street. An elderly waiter appeared, "Bon journo amigo."

So as not to give away his accent Colin just nodded as he picked up the menu and indicated a coffee. Trying to look unobtrusive he pretended to read a newspaper left by a previous diner. Just as the waiter returned with his 'strong black' Colin heard the faint beep of his mobile phone indicating a text message.

Scrolling down he found a short message: -

"Do not go to airport take a train." Sergio.

Colin suddenly conjured up visages of police or Mafia types waiting for him at the airport.

Leaving a Five Hundred Lira note to more than cover his coffee he left the café and walked a short distance then hailed a taxi and asked to be taken to the Milan Railway Station.

Entering the cavernous interior of the station Colin went straight to the ticket office and using his other passport, with the name of William Trainer he booked a first-class ticket to Paris.

From his time at the nearby Hilton Hotel he remembered a Pizza restaurant in the street next to the station. Having an hour to wait before his train left, he splurged on a large Pizza washed down with a cold local beer. Feeling better Colin returned to the station to sit and wait for his train.

The train left on time and as Colin settled into his seat, he felt totally exhausted from the dramas of the last few days and it was not long before the regular clatter of the wheels lulled him into a restful sleep.

Paris was as he remembered it from his student days, so vibrant and full of life. Artists sat on the banks of the Seine, lovers walked hand in hand, occasionally stopping to embrace. The coffee shops were packed with the trendies chatting over their 'café latte'.

The ambience of the surroundings failed to lift Colin from his depression. As he had neither the time or desire to do the 'tourist thing' he booked into the Hotel de Grandees Ecole in the Latin Quarter. After a simple meal in the hotel dining room he retired to his room and hopefully a good night's sleep without the nightmares of the last days.

Next morning Colin booked on the Paris-London Eurostar and after a comfortable two-hour fifteen-minute train journey he arrived unnoticed back in London and finally the Grosvenor Kensington Hotel.

Nonchalantly Colin strolled across the foyer to collect what European newspapers were available, making a point to greet the staff at the reception desk.

After taking a scotch from the bar fridge Colin opened the Italian newspaper. On page three bold headlines screamed.

DRUG TRAFFICKER SLAIN

Mario Leotta a well-known identity with links to the drug trade has been fatally shot in a gang like execution outside a suburban backpacker's hostel. Police are trying to locate a man, believed to be English, aged in the mid-twenties who checked into the hotel the day before the shooting and disappeared at the time of the shooting without checking out. Details are scarce and a sweep of the airports, rail stations and hire car companies has failed to trace the man or unearth any clues. It is believed that he was travelling on a British Passport. His name and details were not available at the hostel, however the desk clerk remembered him as Mr Carter. Enquiries are continuing.

Feeling a little unnerved Colin read the report a second time and recounted his journey across Europe and back to London. He began to feel a little more confident that he had covered his movements well enough travelling on the three different passports.

His immediate problem was to get rid of them along with the European newspapers. He certainly did not want to get caught with them or leave the newspapers in his room which may trigger some suspicion.

After cutting the passports into small pieces he stuffed them in his pocket, picked up the papers and took a walk down the street until he found a commercial sized rubbish bin. After scattering the passport pieces and newspapers in the dump bin he returned to the Grosvenor Kingston Hotel for what was to be his last night in London for some time.

Next morning Colin woke to an un-typical sunny winter's day, after breakfasting he packed and left for Heathrow Airport to catch a Qantas flight for home.

WINDING UP

CHAPTER EIGHTEEN

On his long flight home to Sydney Colin had plenty of time to reflect on his life and the direction fate had taken him since his grandfather's death. He treasured memories of his school and university days and of all his friends, however Colin pondered about where he would be now if fate had not intervened. Probably working in some dull Bank or Financial Institution he mused. His new-found relationship with his mother brought a rush of emotion which was fuelled further when he thought of the very little time he had spent with his late father.

His new life in Australia was now going to be exciting and full of promise. The drug syndicate who had threatened not only his future but life itself, hopefully, was now a thing of the past. Colin vowed that his whole focus in life would now be on Maria and their unborn child.

Sitting in the comfort of business class travel he thought of his involvement in the death of Mario Leotta. A shudder went through his body and his stomach churned when he thought of how close he had come to killing another human being. Then Colin thought of the Sydney bombings; the others who had been killed, and the attempts on his life, all wrapped around the drug business. The life of his wife Maria and unborn child had been threatened. The guilt he felt slowly evaporated.

After landing at the now familiar Sydney Airport and with a speedy passage through customs Colin was overwhelmed to see Maria running down the concourse to greet him. Arms outstretched, crying and laughing she ran towards him then they hugged and cried before moving towards the baggage carousel. Colin whispered in her ear, "Have you been looking after my baby?"

Finally, back home in their Woollahra apartment he was saddened to hear that Gloria Cockini had died peacefully in her sleep. Sev had taken her death badly and had aged dramatically. Apart from an occasion consult he retired and spent his time sitting in his favourite chair reading his much-loved law books and reviews.

His law firm continued to flourish under the care and direction of his son, James.

Paul Cockini continued with his medical practice becoming one of the country's most revered surgeons.

The Naxos business was split into two divisions, Foodstuffs and Catering Equipment. Partly out of a sense of loyalty to his ancestors Colin managed the Foodstuffs and gave responsibility for the Kitchen and Catering Equipment to his great friend Trevor Donaldson in thanks for his loyalty and friendship over those early difficult times.

As the business grew another share distribution was made to long standing and loyal employees.

Several offers were made by large multinational companies to take over the business, which were rejected. Colin felt a responsibility to his grandfather, who had toiled so hard and sacrificed so much to develop the business in those early years.

Four years later the company moved into the Hotel and Tourism industry purchasing one of Sydney's major hotels and a struggling Travel Agency

Colin and Trevor kept in touch with their aging old friends Charlie and Hester Thornton, who were a link to the past, particularly his grandfather, John Naxos.

Maria gave birth to a healthy son who Colin looked upon as his heir and destined to one day take over the ever-expanding business empire.

However, he was very mindful of how his grandfather wrongly tried to push his father into the business many years ago.

Colin's mother, with her new husband, Andrew Shackleton, visited the following year and decided to make Australia their home.

In later years Andrew joined the expanding conglomerate and was to manage the new Hotel and Tourism division.

Importantly Colin maintained contact with, now Police Superintendent, Joan Sterling, as there was always that niggling fear that one day his adversaries may re-appear. The "family" was not likely to forgive and forget.

Sitting his now opulent office Colin was shaken out of his musing by the incessant ringing of his private phone.

Who could this be he thought? He nonchalantly picked up the phone saying, "Hello, Colin Naxos,"

For a moment there was no reply and he was about to hang up when a quiet timid voice said,

"Hello Colin, Its Kathleen."

Colin was left speechless, the last time they had spoken was during the drama when she had Hester in her car before dropping her off at the BP service station.

"Kathleen! Where are you, I thought you were still in goal."

"No, I was released yesterday and I'm at the Airport.

I'm going home to New Zealand, hopefully to start my life afresh. I would really love to see you before I go, could you come over to the airport, perhaps we could have a cup of coffee and talk.

Colin without hesitation replied, "Kathleen I would love to see you, I will come straight over. I will be there in about fifteen minutes. I will look for you in the departure lounge."

Scanning the crowd Colin at first did not see her, then he saw a solitary figure sitting at a table in the food area.

With a thumping heart he quickly made his way through the crowds of travellers, stopping beside her table,

"Hello Kathleen."

Kathleen jumped to her feet to emotionally embrace him. They then stood apart still holding hands and Colin was surprised at how well she looked, maybe a little heavier but the beauty was still there. Her eyes held his and he could not but notice how clear and bright they were.

Kathleen broke the silence, the words tumbling out, "Colin you look great, is life good to now all those dreadful times of violence are over. I hear that you are now married and have a baby boy. Congratulations."

Colin replied with some emotion, "Yes to all that, how are you going, are you now clear of your addictions, you look great. Yes, I fell in love and married Maria and we are extremely happy.

Kathleen, I want you to know that I really loved you during all those early times we had together. I was so sad when everything fell in a heap, but life must go on.

They then spent some time chatting over their lives during those troubled times.

"By the way you did kill him, didn't you." Colin said.

"Yes, I did, I hit him on the head with a brass desk lamp. But I was so out of my mind with the drugs, or lack of them, I had no control over what I was doing. At least goal gave me the opportunity to come clean and get my life back in order. So now I'm going home to New Zealand to start my life afresh. I can't dwell on what could have been and what ever happened I brought upon myself. But I really loved you then, and I still do."

At that moment the PA system announced that flight QF 163 to Auckland was ready for boarding.

Breaking the moment, they both stood and embraced.

With a tear in his eye Colin said, "Good luck Kathleen, I hope life is good to you from now on, I will never forget you or those times we had together."

In a flood of tears Kathleen could not speak coherently and just mumbled, "I love you Colin," picked up her hand luggage and walked away towards the departure gates. She did not look back and kept walking until swallowed by the departing crowd.

Printed in the United States
By Bookmasters